The Silent War

DAVID FIDDIMORE was born in 1944 in Yorkshire and is married with two children. He worked for five years at the Royal Veterinary College before joining HM Customs and Excise, where his work included postings to the investigation and intelligence divisions. *The Silent War* is the fifth novel in the Charlie Bassett series following *Tuesday's War*, *Charlie's War*, *The Forgotten War* and *The Hidden War*.

DAVID FIDDIMORE

The Silent War

PAN BOOKS

First published 2010 by Pan Books
an imprint of Pan Macmillan, a division of Macmillan Publishers Limited
Pan Macmillan, 20 New Wharf Road, London N1 9RR
Basingstoke and Oxford
Associated companies throughout the world
www.panmacmillan.com

ISBN 978-0-330-50582-6

Copyright © David Fiddimore 2010

The right of David Fiddimore to be identified as the
author of this work has been asserted by him in accordance
with the Copyright, Designs and Patents Act 1988.

1 3 5 7 9 8 6 4 2

A CIP catalogue record for this book is available from
the British Library.

Typeset by SetSystems Ltd, Saffron Walden, Essex
Printed and bound in Great Britain by
CPI Mackays, Chatham ME5 8TD

Visit **www.panmacmillan.com** to read more about all our books
and to buy them. You will also find features, author interviews and
news of any author events, and you can sign up for e-newsletters
so that you're always first to hear about our new releases.

For the National Service veterans of Suez

. . . and of Korea, Malaya, Kenya, Aden and Cyprus,
and all those other dirty little wars they were led into by
ungrateful governments that should have known better.
God bless you boys.

PART ONE

This Is Not a War

Chapter One

Straighten up and fly right

David Watson had been a squadron leader and a drunk the last time I had seen him in 1947. Now it looked as if someone had cleaned him up again, and the silver bars doing the 'Beer barrel polka' on his shoulders said that the silly buggers upstairs had made him a wing commander. Bollocks. I was in a scruffy office in a seedy part of North London, and he was asking me, 'Are you now, or have you ever been, a member of the Communist Party?'

I probably sniffed: I had a cold. 'Would it matter if I was . . . or had been?'

'Yes. You couldn't come back to the Service.'

'I don't want to come back to the Service. All that bullshit's behind me now.'

'No it isn't. You are still in the Reserve even if you haven't attended any of your obligatory annual parades, so you're liable to be called up at times of national emergency.'

'In that case *yes* I was, and am. Can I go home now?'

'Can you prove it?'

'Yes. I've got a CP membership card somewhere – it was an accident by the way, but lucky for me. You can't have me back.'

He leaned back in his chair and said, 'Yes I can, because we happen to want men with your old-fashioned skills at the

3

moment. I forgive you for being a Communist. Welcome back to the RAF, Charlie, and start calling me *sir*, there's a good fellow. Care for a snifter?'

I've said it before, and I'll say it again: bollocks.

The last national emergency I'd danced in had been the Berlin Airlift. It didn't like me one bit, and tried to kill me in a Dakota smash. I didn't like it back, and consequently didn't return to the Fatherland. To be strictly honest I had little choice in the matter: the War Office banned me. It's a long story, and one that might amuse you one day. For once the Germans and the Brits had agreed about something: neither wanted me to set foot in Germany again. I never imagined that the RAF would want me back after that.

Watson had been my last proper RAF senior officer, although the word *proper* is probably on a shoogly peg, because at the time he was heading up a radio station in a halfway house between the old Empire Code and Cipher School, and the GCHQ it later became. In those days he was all tweed jackets, leather elbow patches and pipes. It had been meant to be a cushy number for my last few months in blue, but hadn't turned out that way. Four years later he called me up, and told me to report to an office over Woolworths on Kentish Town High Street . . . and here I was, feeling like a snake which has been picked up by the tail. I wanted to lash out and bite someone. The bastards couldn't do this to me again. He picked up a green telephone hand set and told it, 'The bottle and two glasses please, Daisy. You'll remember Mr Bassett. He's coming out to play with us again.' As he replaced the receiver he asked me, 'You do remember Daisy? I had her at Cheltenham.'

'If she's still with you she's even madder than you are.'

'*Sir*. Madder than you are, sir.'

'Do I have to?'

'Yes you bloody *do*, Charlie. Bloody done and bloody dusted . . . so not so much of the bloody lip from now on.'

Daisy walked in with a nice bottle of Dimple and two cut-glass tumblers on a silver tray. My favourite kind of woman is the type I see walking towards me carrying my drink. She'd even remembered that I watered my whisky, and had brought a small glass jug of the stuff. It was the first time I'd seen her in uniform, and uniforms do something for a woman.

She smiled. 'Welcome back, Mr Bassett; we've all missed you.'

It did occur to me to wonder who *we* were. Watson poured, I watered and we clinked glasses – I thought I might as well get a drink out of him, because I'd already worked out that this could only be a bad dream. He said, 'We can relax now, Charlie . . .'

Even although the word curdled in my mouth I called him *sir*.

'I've already got a job, sir, running a cuddly little airline down on the South Coast. It's where you phoned me. I'm sure that my boss will argue it's in the national interest to leave me exactly where I am.'

'Your cuddly little airline is in the same state as all of the other cuddly little airlines, Charlie: practically skint. The government is handing out precious few contracts these days, and the big outfits are hoovering up the freight work before you even have time to offer. Hard times are upon us, Charlie: that was a book title once, wasn't it?'

'Dickens. Unreadable.' What did *I* know? 'What are you trying to tell me?'

'Your Mr Halton has already been spoken to. He'll be glad for us to take you off his hands for a few months, as long as we pay your salary . . . and don't take it personally; there are dozens of bods all over the country sitting exactly where you're sitting, getting the same bad news. I have three more of you to do today.'

'What about my job?'

'It will be kept open for you . . . they have to do that by law. I understand that your secretary is going to be promoted to company secretary, and sit in your chair until you get back. All's well that ends well.' I remembered how someone often used to say that in 1947. It irritated me then as well . . . and Elaine must have known the score before I set off, but didn't tell me. I'd have to watch her. That was interesting.

'Where exactly is this national emergency you're packing me off to, sir?'

'Egypt I expect: the wogs are getting uppity again. Time to get your knees brown, Charlie, and sand in your shoes.'

'What's my alternative?'

'Jankers for failure to report. Maybe even with the Brown Jobs at Aldershot. They're a bad lot, I understand.' For the uninformed among you – Brown Jobs are soldiers: the guys with guns, and khaki suits, who *walk* everywhere. They have a penal colony at Aldershot.

'And that's it?'

'. . . or you could always get married instead. We're only taking single men.' He raised his glass again, and an eyebrow. 'Cheerio.'

Ah.

I suddenly felt Old Man Halton's hand jerking my chain. I'd proposed to his ward in 1948, grown less keen on her with every passing minute, and had been putting off the evil day. Halton hadn't said anything but I sensed he was taking a dim view of it. The bastards had me now, hadn't they? Get married, or get chased round the pyramids by a bunch of wogs armed with goolie knives.

I raised my glass back at him. 'That's it then; back to bloody war I suppose. Cheers. Where do I get measured for a tropical rig?'

'Sir . . .'

'. . . sir.'

'We'll take care of all that. After you've had a couple of refreshers I expect . . . and this is not a *war* by the way.'

'What is it then?'

I expected his nagging little *sir* again, but he just shook his head. 'It's a police action.'

'What does that mean when it's at home?'

'That they don't have to pay your dependants a decent pension when you cop it.'

I swirled my drink in the glass, and watched the circles it made. 'They think of everything, don't they, sir?'

'Apparently; but in your case, Charlie, I suspect they will live to regret it. Now all you have to do is sort out your bloody father.'

'The old man? What's it got to do with him?'

'He was arrested three days ago at the Cenotaph. He disrupted the Remembrance service. Didn't anyone tell you?'

Charing Cross nick. I suspect that by the time I was in my twenties I was more familiar with the inside of police stations than your average Joe. It hadn't always been my fault, and the only advantage I can see is that I could generally get up the front steps and through the door without my apprehensions on parade. In the 1950s, having got that far you usually found yourself facing a front desk behind which, if you were lucky, was a desk sergeant.

After I introduced myself this one introduced himself back as Sergeant Pry . . . and then paused as if his name should mean something to me. Maybe he had won the George Cross when my back was turned. He continued, 'So, you're Albert Bassett's son?'

'Yes, Sergeant. What's happened to him?'

'Less than he deserved. He was up in front of the magistrate yesterday and was admonished.'

'What for?'

Pry had a kindly face. 'Shouldn't you ask him yourself, son?'

'I will, when I catch up with him. I didn't even know he was in town. He lives just outside Glasgow.'

'He made a mockery of the service at the Cenotaph, and was eventually charged with being drunk and disorderly, being a public nuisance and resisting arrest. He's a bit of a tough old bird, your old man.'

'He was one of the Old Contemptibles, and served all the way through to 1919 . . . I can never remember him being anything else except tough.'

That wasn't true. He had wept openly at the funerals of my mother and sister.

'The magistrate is an old soldier as well; he threw out the drunk and resisting charges, and only admonished on the public nuisance. I don't know why we even bothered.'

'What exactly did he do?'

'He sang.'

'That's what we usually do at the Remembrance parade isn't it? March up and down, shout silly orders at each other, and sing hymns? Hitler used to do that sort of thing as well.'

He frowned, but ignored that last bit. 'He managed to wriggle his way near the front, and bawl out some of the old soldiers' songs, but with very disrespectful lyrics – disrespectful to the Top Brass in attendance that is. I understand that the Duke of Gloucester smiled, and even Her uncrowned Majesty's lips gave a little twitch.'

'Good old Dad. I must find him and buy him a pint. Where did he go to?'

'He gave the Union Jack Club as his London address, but I don't know if he's still there.' Then he added, 'You don't seem all that respectful yourself.'

'They just called me up again,' I explained.

'Do you good I expect. Teach you some manners.'

I had a phrase waiting for him, but didn't use it. I didn't want to be the second person in my family to be arrested inside a week. As I turned away I saw a framed theatre bill on the wall. It advertised a show called the *Great Tay Kin* – *a Japanese Mystery*, but its star billing was reserved for one Paul Pry. I turned back, and asked the Sergeant,

'That your father?'

'No.' He grinned. 'It was Granddad. It dates from 1885, and Toole's Theatre stood on this very spot. The old guy was on the halls there.'

'What happened to him?'

'A Zep got him and Grandma in 1916. Jerry bastards.'

'Bastards.' We could agree about something anyway. Suddenly he reached into a trouser pocket, and from it handed me a half-crown.

'Buy your old man that pint from me. Tell him it was bloody funny.'

I gave him a little salute, then turned and got out of there while I was still ahead.

I crossed the Thames on the walkway running alongside Hunger-ford Bridge, and got caught in a November squall halfway across. My old American raincoat no longer kept out the rain the way it did years ago, so it was a damp Charlie who dropped anchor alongside his father in a dirty little pub on the corner of Stamford

Street. The receptionist at the club had taken pity on me, and told me where to find him.

The old man didn't even look round when I took the stool alongside him. He said, '*You* took your time.'

'I'm not bloody psychic, Dad. You could have told me you were in trouble.'

'I wasn't in trouble, son. I was exactly where I wanted to be, doing exactly what I wanted to do.'

'That's what I was afraid of. Why don't you tell me what's going on?'

'Only after you've set up the beer. You're so bloody slow to put your hand in your pocket I sometimes think you were fathered by a Yorkshireman.'

'Maybe I just take after you.'

After a couple of rounds he said, 'I just didn't want to embarrass you.'

'Don't ever worry about that. I embarrass myself far more than you ever could.' The words didn't come out in exactly the right order, but he understood me.

'You know I ain't scared of doing my bit, Charlie?'

'Yes?' Doing his bit had included soldiering through the First War from start to finish as a Pioneer, and then joining up again in 1945 to help the British Army dig holes all over Holland and Germany.

'I got fed up with it, that's all.'

'Fed up with Glasgow?'

'No, don't be daft. Why should anyone get fed up with Glasgow? – it has the best boozers in the world.' I didn't know if he meant the pubs or the people in them, so I kept shtum, and let him finish what he'd started. 'I got fed up with the war.'

'Which one?'

'All of them. Malaya, Korea and now bloody Kenya . . . it's

never-bloody-ending. We can't be at war for ever: it's got to stop somewhere. My war was supposed to be *the war to end wars*, remember?'

'What brought this on?'

'Mrs Johnson did.'

'Mrs Johnson?'

'She's a nice widow who lives underneath me.' He had a red-brick tenement flat. But that was interesting: I hadn't heard him mention her before. 'They called her son up last month. He's only seventeen, and he already knows he's off to Kenya after his *basic*: fucking Kenya is *not* worth fighting for – it was the last straw.'

'What about all the coffee?'

'What's wrong with a bottle of old Camp coffee? . . . Anyway I thought that someone had got to do something about it, so I decided to go down to the Cenotaph and tell the bastards a few home truths about fighting and dying for your country. I thought I might get in the papers.' What was wrong with Camp coffee was that it wasn't coffee at all, but I wasn't prepared to contradict him.

'Did it work?'

'No. Everyone ignored me, so I started to sing.'

'What?'

'I sang "They'll never believe me", and a couple of others. We had some soldiers' verses for them in my day. That's when the cops got nasty.'

'The desk sergeant at Agar Street gave me half a crown to buy you a pint. He said it was bloody funny.'

'The magistrate said, "Even if I was to sympathize with you, Mr Bassett, I could not condone your disrespect to our young sovereign. You are to consider yourself formally admonished." What do you think he meant by that?'

'He agreed with you, of course, but he wasn't going to say so. So did the copper; that's why he asked me to buy you a pint. You might have started something after all.'

'Do you think so?' He brightened up a bit. 'What are you doing here anyway?'

'They called me up again, Dad. They want me to go to Egypt.'

'Bollocks!'

At least my father and I had reached a stage where we had a vocabulary in common.

We got drunk. Until his dying day my father was a better drinker than me. We slept back to back on his bed at the Club, like a married couple who were no longer talking.

The next day I went back to Lympne-sur-mer, which is where the airline I worked for was based.

My secretary Elaine said, 'I'm sorry, Charlie,' as soon as I walked in. I just gave her the look, went through to my office and shut the door. Firmly. One of the few things I'd learned about the women who liked me is that they could stand anything except being denied access. They needed to see my face, as if from that they could work out what was going on upstairs. Elaine had a son who was three now, and I was his godfather. It was only by the grace of God that I hadn't become the real thing. She had had no more children, and her figure and looks had come back with a bang – forgive the pun. I still fancied her like mad, but the only times we had touched since her boy was born was when she handed me a mug of char. Anyway, I'd met her old man and liked him, so that complicated things.

I gave her ten minutes before she'd try again. She came in after just seven, after knocking on my office door. That was interesting. To my recollection she'd never knocked before either.

'You bloody should be!' I told her. 'You're a treacherous little git, and I don't love you any more.' That made her smile; but it was a sad little smile, not a come-on.

'They made me promise not to tell anyone.'

'Who did?'

'Mr Halton and the man in Army uniform.'

'You're not in the Army, Elaine. You didn't have to pay them any attention.'

'He said I could go to prison if I told anyone before it was out. They didn't want people to know we were mobilizing . . .' She let drop a couple of tears; though I'm sure they were deliberate. How do women manage that?

'When was that?'

'Three weeks ago.'

'Bloody hell!' Then I told her. 'I've been called up, and they told my secretary three weeks before they told me . . . I have a rotten hangover because I was stupid enough to go drinking with my dad . . . and I'm so mad I've dreamed about nothing else on the way down in the train except bending you over the desk, and giving you the sort of thrashing my old schoolmaster gave me . . . smacking your backside until you yelled.'

Her eyes widened slightly, and the grin she shot me was almost like old times. 'You could still do that.'

She'd yorked me with five words, hadn't she? A middle-stumper . . . because her grin made me smile as well, and the storm was over. But I shook my head and confessed, 'I don't think my heart could stand it.'

She was still laughing. 'If you were ill they couldn't call you up. You'd have to stay at home.'

I gave her enough of a look for her to know I was semi-serious, then glanced away. Shyness between old lovers is really sad.

'Go away and leave me with the maintenance lists. I'll come

out in an hour in a better temper, and you can tell me all about it.'

'Cup of tea?'

'Mm, thanks.' But the truth was I was already thinking about something else.

Watson had told me that I could expect at least three weeks before I got the brown envelope with OHMS on it. *This is the new RAF* he explained to me, *and nothing happens very quickly.* I tapped a pencil against my teeth – trying to remember an Air Force officer I once met who used to do that – and considered haring off around the country for a few months, never staying anywhere long enough for the call-up letter to catch up with me. What do you do with three weeks? Carry on like normal, and pretend it isn't happening? Spend time with the kids? – I had two who stayed in a pub at Bosham with a couple of good friends – the best really. Go out and roll as many willing ladies on their backs as my wallet and constitution could stand? The truth was more prosaic: I was suddenly and overwhelmingly apprehensive in a way I had never been before. I wanted to dig a large hole, get down into it and never come out. Something odd had happened to the bold old Charlie I once knew and loved – he'd scarpered.

My telephone rang and when I lifted it Elaine said, 'It's Frieda. Shall I tell her you're out?'

Frieda was the woman I'd proposed to . . . which wouldn't have been a problem if she hadn't taken me seriously. It had been great at first; she had the body of a Hindu temple goddess, and we'd been wonderfully handy in bed. Her guardian was my employer, Lord God Almighty Halton, who, although he hadn't exactly smiled upon the impending union, hadn't scowled upon it either. Now, to be honest, I almost couldn't stand the sight of her – she was an arrogant, stuck-up, German ogress – and our relationship had declined to a weekly meet in a hotel up in Town, with supper and a desperate fuck. So you might even say that the romance had gone out of it. I didn't know who to tell first; Frieda herself or Old Man Halton, and if I played it with my usual skill I'd probably end up losing my fiancée and my job at the same time. It was time to show some pluck for a change.

'Yes, tell her I'm out,' I replied.

I waited until Elaine had left the outer office to go to where most women seem to go about seventy times a day, and then dialled the number of a girl in Town who I knew. Dolly worked as a driver for a department that dared not speak its own name in the War Office. We hadn't spoken for a year. She sounded pleased to hear me, but you never know, do you?

After the usual ping-pong she asked me, 'Did you get married?'

'No. I would have invited you.'

'Are you still engaged?'

'Yes . . . but I'm in the process of becoming unengaged. What about you?'

Pause. That old Glenn Miller eight beat intro . . .

'I'm getting married next week, Charlie.' She said it flatly, like someone trumping you in a game of whist. Then she put the phone down.

I looked out of the window for a minute before I opened my desk diary, with the company's name on the cover, and wrote an entry which read, *This is the week I didn't have much luck.* Then I put my passport into a pocket in my old flying jacket, pulled it on, and climbed inside the first of our aircraft leaving the damned place. Even Elaine looked worried.

Bozey Borland drove out to meet me in the jeep he'd won in a crap game. You might have said that he was one of our overseas station officers. In fact he was our *only* one, and he stayed in Berlin because he would have been arrested by Customs if he set foot back in the UK. So far they'd shown little appetite for following him to Germany.

I had flown there in the company's scarlet-painted Avro York, as a passenger with a pilot I hardly knew. It was a jittery flight, and he flew in a jittery way: that was because I was unable to convince him that I wasn't on board to check him out. I felt bilious as I came down the short step from the door under her great red wing.

Bozey enquired, 'Are you supposed to be here, boss? Has the War Office lifted your banning notice?'

'I don't fucking care, Bozey. I wanted to see Germany again for some unaccountable reason . . . the bastards have called me up, and I may not get another chance. I just wanted another look at the last country that was really worth bombing.'

'You're not having a good day, are you?'

'No, I'm not.'

He drove me out through the military entrance to avoid the civilian authorities. His three-legged dog Spartacus was in the rear footwell. Because Spartacus lacked a back leg, when he wagged his tail his whole rear end wagged with it, like a clipper ship rounding Cape Horn in a blow. When he got excited he pissed at the same time. It could get messy.

'He's pissing in your car,' I told Bozey.

'I expect he's pleased to see you. It's a good job jeeps have no carpets.'

'It stinks.'

'He probably thinks that about us, boss. I think I should take you somewhere for a few drinks before I give you the news.'

The flight had been so bad that I had forgotten my hangover.

'I knew I was right to take you on, Bozey.' But I also wondered what his news was.

He took me to the Leihhaus – that's a Jerry word that means pawnshop. But it wasn't a pawnshop; it was a nightclub that stayed open most of the day as well. It was called the Leihhaus because in the early days after the war there wasn't anything you couldn't buy or sell there. I remembered it well.

'I'm surprised it's still here,' I told him. 'Is this still the neutral zone?'

The neutral zone had been a triangular scrape of land where the American, British and Russian zones of postwar Berlin all kissed . . . only whoever had drawn the maps had made sure that they didn't quite join up, so there was a couple of acres that fell under nobody's jurisdiction. An American and a Russian I'd known had opened a nightclub on it. If you want to know more about that you'll have to read another book.

'No, they redrew the lines after we all made up. It's ours now.' *Ours.*

'So you don't get the Russians in here any more?'

'No, we get a load of French instead . . . though on the whole I preferred the Reds. The Yanks still come, but their service cops are a problem they never used to be.'

I smiled. In my day nothing seemed to be a problem at the Leihhaus.

'I'm sure the club copes with that.'

'Yes,' Bozey said. 'We does.' Never mind the tense; the second possessive was interesting, wasn't it?

We sat at what I could almost call my old table: a round scarred affair around which you could get six chairs at a squeeze. It was the only furniture I recognized. A newish hard-wearing brown carpet could only have come from the PX, and the other chairs and tables were lightweight chrome and steel things. It was late afternoon and the decent drinkers hadn't begun to show yet. There was a small new dance floor with a parquet surface, and a bandstand for a sextet. In a corner a Negro pianist in a royal blue jacket played a blues tune, and crooned to himself.

I went over to him. I put the couple of dollars I'd hit Bozey for on the piano top, and asked, 'You know "Blues for Jimmy Noone"? It means something for me.'

'Sho boy; but you ken take them back.' He moved effortlessly into the opening bars of 'Blues for Jimmy', but nodded at the banknotes. 'You already pay me well enough, boss.'

'Do I?'

'Sho do, boss.' He was milking the Uncle Tom for all it was worth. He was taking the mickey out of me, but I'd never be able to pin it on him. I took the money back to Bozey and sat down.

'Why don't you tell me what's going on?'

That old pause exactly as long as the 'String of pearls' intro again . . . I still love it. Bozey held his hand out over the table for a shake. I took it not knowing quite what was going on.

He said, 'Congratulations. You have a third share in the Leihhaus. I used that money you left behind. We had to do something with it after Tommo and the Red screwed up.' Screwed up as in *died*.

There was something missing. 'Who owns the rest?'

'I have a third as well.'

There was still something missing. 'Who has the rest?'

It was the first time I had ever seen him thrown slightly off line. He looked away, and then back at me. 'Halton Air. I did a deal with the American military for cheap fuel, and used the difference in here. I needed some extra cash to restyle the place, and to get the girls in.'

At that precise moment I didn't want to know about the girls. I asked him, 'Does the Old Man know about this?'

This time it was a pause you could have run a hundred yards in.

'No, boss. I thought maybe you could be the one to tell him.'

Bollocks.

Chapter Two

Lady be good

He took me upstairs and showed me one of the rooms. It was fine. It looked like an expensive hotel room from the 1930s. The furniture was light wood but had those wonderful bold curves that still look modern sixty years later. It even had its own bathroom attached, with an Edwardian hip bath and a shower. The bed cover was turned back and the sheets were clean. There were even clean towels.

I asked him, 'How much do we get a night for this?'

'We don't, boss: it's not a hotel. This is your room for whenever you're visiting. It won't be used when you're not here.'

'What about you?'

'Don't worry about me. I have a flat around the corner, with Irma.'

'Did you win her in a game as well?'

He had that slightly uncomfortable look again.

'No. She came round looking for someone, and we took a shine to each other. She says she knows you.' I ran *Irma* through the memory bank, and came out not guilty. I was still shaking my head as I opened the door on another room. It was also furnished with loot, the same as mine. It looked a bit more lived-in though, with a skirt and stockings draped over the back of a

19

small dressing-table chair. It was also furnished with a woman in the bed.

She peeked over the sheets – just her head mind you – as I looked in, yawned, smiled and said, 'Hello, Joe. What time is it?' She had tousled dark hair. I could smell last night's perfume.

'Nearly half past five after noon, and I'm not Joe, I'm Charlie.'

That seemed to register. She said, 'Oh, hello, boss,' stuck out a long pale arm and waved. Then she disappeared back under the covers again. It was a nice arm, and she had a nice smile, and I was happy we'd met, so it was all right with me. You know the song, don't you? It came out just about then. I hope I smiled back. I said, 'Wrong room. Sorry,' and closed the door gently. Outside I asked Bozey the poser, 'She called me *boss.*'

'Yes, boss. She's one of our workers here. I thought I mentioned the girls – there are four of them.'

'Yes. And I thought that if I didn't pay any attention to it, then maybe it would go away.'

'That's Reimey. She's French – from Paris. She's a nice kid.'

'Is this a brothel now, Bozey?'

He looked uncomfortable again. That was interesting. 'Only partly,' he said.

'Is it legal?'

'Only partly.'

'And you want me to explain to the Old Man that he now has a third share in a Berlin cat-house, and a nightclub. Christ, Bozey, what have you got us into?'

'A lot of dosh, actually. I can afford to buy you out soon if you're unhappy about it.'

It was one of those moments. I leaned my arm on the wall of the corridor, bent and rested my head against it, and began to laugh. And laugh.

*

Later I met Marthe again. I had slept in her place before the Berlin Airlift. The hug she gave me might have been more encouraging if her husband wasn't pumping my hand up and down at the same time. There was a girl of ten or so dressed in school clothes standing shyly behind them. I pulled her forward.

'Lottie?'

'Yes, Uncle Charlie . . .' I hugged her too.

'You've grown so; shot up. It's so *good* to see you all.'

Then I turned to her parents and asked them, 'But what are you doing here?'

'Marthe runs the kitchen,' Bozey explained, '. . . and Otto runs the floor.'

'Who runs upstairs?'

'I do.' At least he hadn't ducked the issue. 'Lottie comes round after school. Sometimes she helps the girls clean upstairs.'

'Not any more. This isn't a place for her. Find her a chair and table somewhere out of the way: she can do her homework in a corner, but that's it.' Nobody liked my change of tone. Lottie looked suddenly hurt; they probably needed the money. 'Do you want to be my Berlin secretary, Lottie? You can keep a diary that tells everyone where I am . . .' Then I put on a thoughtful face, and added, 'But of course we'd have to put you on the pay roll then. Would that be OK?' She nodded, so I told her, 'Ask your dad first; get his permission.' Later, if I had the chance, I'd tell the others what I thought about them letting a child that age work upstairs in a cat-house.

I needn't have bothered with the thought. Marthe gave me a kiss and said, 'You're a hypocrite, Charlie Bassett.' *Heuchler* was the word she actually used: at least my German was coming back.

'How? Why?'

'Because you would use a place like this yourself without a backward glance, but you don't like my little Lottie in here . . .'

It was interesting that she'd formed that opinion of me, because I had never overnighted with a proper whore in my life. Not that I want you to think I'm coming all wings and halo on you: the truth was all my girlfriends so far had been like car accidents that I'd walked away from.

'I'll take your word for it, but if I'm the boss around here, then little Lottie doesn't go upstairs, *capisce?*'

They're all the bloody same, aren't they? Marthe couldn't resist the last word. 'You're in Germany, Charlie, not Italy. Stop showing off.'

I couldn't work out why Bozey and Otto were grinning. Then I realized what I'd said: I'd said *I'm the boss around here*, which is what they'd all been waiting to bloody well hear.

I knew that I wasn't going to hang around for long, and that I was unlikely to return for a year at least, so I did what you always do – I revisited old haunts to get them stuck in my head. I went to the Rattlesnake Bar first, the Klapperschlange. It had also been owned by my pal Tommo, a Yank who had died in an air crash in 1949. I hadn't realized it when he was alive, but he had always been my best pal. I still deal with problems sixty years later by asking myself what Tommo would have done. If I had asked him about pulling my RAF blues back on, and going out to the Canal Zone for Queen and Country he would have said, 'Bollocks to that', and handed me a first-class air ticket to Rio.

From the outside the bar hadn't changed much: a small door at the end of a steep cobbled alley, with a big pink neon rattlesnake above it, blinking in the drizzle. It always seemed to rain in that street. The big man on the door had probably been a stormtrooper in another life.

He spotted me for an Anglo immediately and snarled, 'Members only.' Then he had second thoughts, and repeated himself in German, *'Nur für Mitglieder.'*

I couldn't be arsed to struggle with another language, so I kept it natural.

'That's me chum: Charlie Bassett – founder member. I even met the rattlesnake herself; I bet you didn't.'

'*Bitte?*'

'That's exactly what I'm feeling: very bitter. The buggers want to send me back to war, so I want a drink at my old bar.' I forgot that I wasn't supposed to mention the war. This was 1952: the war hadn't happened, there were no such things as Nazis, and we hadn't bombed the fuck out of them for trying.

Fritz breathed in, and expanded to about twice the size. He towered above me like Hercules. But he looked confused, and spat, 'I do not understand.'

'I do,' the woman said. 'This is Mr Bassett, and he is a very bad man. You should never let him in.' But she was smiling, and pushed past him to hug and kiss me. She must have come through the bead curtain behind the door to see what was happening. Things were looking up. So was I because she was nearly a foot taller than me. I remembered her long straight dark hair, and her perfect heart-shaped face. The last time I'd seen her she'd been Tommo's girl, and I'd stayed with them in a little country hideaway which had been two railway carriages in a forest sitting on top of half a dozen Teller mines. You really don't want to know what *they* were. But I couldn't remember her name.

I asked, 'Can I come in from the rain now?'

'*Ja*, sure. Let him in, Pauli.' This last had been addressed to the man mountain who had been clenching and unclenching his fists. I think he'd been looking forward to thumping me. He moved slowly – just to make a point.

Inside she told me, 'He gets jealous. I think I'll have to let him go.' That was the first time I'd heard the particular phrase used about a job; maybe that's what Old Man Halton was thinking about me. On the only occasion I'd met her before we hadn't exchanged five words. I thought then that either she was thick, or couldn't speak God's language. Now I realized that her English was flawless; probably better than mine.

'You run this place?' I asked her.

'Yes. I own it, too.'

'Useful.'

'I thought so too. David put it in my name for tax reasons I think. When he died it was mine: like a going-away present.'

'Miss him?'

'Not so much now. It's been three years.'

'*I* do.'

'That's because you are a man.' Birds have been trumping me in conversations like that for years. I hate it. But I didn't hate her, because she next said, 'Let's get drunk and talk about him all night; it's good to see you, Charlie.'

'It's good to see you too . . .' and then I paused because of the name thing. 'The silly thing is I don't think I ever learned your name.'

'It's Irma.'

'*Ah.*' Bozey's bird. Who used to be Tommo's bird. You'll have heard all the crap that's being talked about recycling these days, well we were far better at it in the 1940s and '50s: the war had taught us how to recycle living people.

I got drunk with Irma, and then she took me somewhere and put me to bed. When I awoke in the morning a radio from another room was belting out 'Lady be good' as if it was a bounce – good old Benny Goodman. I followed the noise, and found Bozey tucking into bacon sandwiches.

He said, 'You'd better get some of these inside you; there'll be precious few where you're going – they're all Muslims over there, so they don't eat pig.'

'What *do* they do with it?'

24

'In the war there was an athletic belly dancer in one of the Cairo nightclubs; she had a very interesting act with a pig.'

'Ow!' I said, because my head hurt when I moved it. 'Why don't women get men to do that sort thing to entertain *them*?'

'Because they're too grown-up already, but I suspect they'll get round to it eventually. Good morning, boss. Headache?'

'Yes. Your woman's a mean drinker. How much did I get through last night?'

'Less than her. She's still sleeping it off. I'll get you some-thing . . .' He pulled a bottle of PX marked Coca-Cola from their fat refrigerator, popped its cap, dropped in four aspirins and shook it up. When he finally poured it into a tumbler it looked and tasted just like Coke should. It took about five minutes to do the job, and then I began to feel exceptionally happy – as if I could party all night.

'How did you know I was going to Egypt?' I asked him. 'Did I tell you yesterday?'

'You may have, but Mr Halton called the office after you had gone. He told me; he's worried about you.'

'He bloody should be. He's sold me back to the RAF.'

'Only for a while, he said.'

'How long is a *while*? A long while or a short while?'

'Don't know, boss. I'm not that much in his confidence – you are.'

'Fat lot of good it's done me.' I looked around for the first time. We were in a nice new kitchen, in a decent-sized apart-ment. I found myself smiling at a portrait photograph of David 'Tommo' Thomsett staring back at me from the kitchen dresser. Just at that moment Benny came on from the radio station again with a slow number, 'Someone to watch over me'. Just one of God's little messages.

I observed, 'Irma was Tommo's girl. I met her in the Black Forest or somewhere.'

'I didn't know if you'd mind.'

I nodded. I wasn't going to tell him that if I minded it was because I'd rather fancied her myself.

'Life goes on, Bozey; even if sometimes we don't want it to. Tommo wouldn't mind.'

'Halton does. I think he'd rather have you back where he can see you, until you ship out.'

'I know. I was just running away from it for a couple of days. I'll get the next flight out.'

That was that really. I jumped a BOAC York into the new airport at Heathrow. I can't say I liked the place; it hadn't the style of Croydon. There was something about the new terminal building that reminded me of a refurbished toilet in a three-star hotel. I've flown out of there hundreds of times since and never changed my mind.

Old Man Halton had a new office at the Cargo Side so I sidled over there for a showdown. The door of the office was the same colour as our aircraft – red. I reckoned he was angling to get the mail contracts away from BOAC and BEA. The receptionist behind the small counter in the front office was a redhead. She was wearing a red suit, but was about two sizes too big for it . . . which was interesting. The smile on her face was upside down. I reckoned she'd look quite interesting upside down, but I didn't have a chance – the Old Man came out from his own place as soon as he heard my voice. He smiled as he pulled me through, and said, 'Don't bother to ask her out, Charlie. She's already quit.'

'So would I, sir, if you dressed me up like a carrot.'

He laughed, and began to cough a cough that had started in the trenches at Loos, and had held out for thirty-six years so far. He poured us a couple of fingers of Dimple each – it wasn't his favourite tipple, but there seemed to be a fair bit of it around –

and waved me to a seat across the desk from him. His slow cough rumbled all that time, like thunder in the distance, and whenever he finished it left him breathless.

'You should see a doctor about that,' I told him.

'I do: all the time. Frieda nags me about it.'

I noticed how quickly he'd brought her name into it, but ignored that.

'What do they say?'

'That I died several years ago, but no one noticed. Cheers.'

He'd told me the joke before. I raised my glass, wondering if it was the last drink he'd pour me before I was sacked.

'Cheers. I'm sorry I ran off to Berlin, boss; I needed a couple of days to think. Getting called up was a bit of a shock. Nothing happened while I was away.'

'I know.'

'Did I cause a problem?'

'The War Office became a little agitated. The woman who phoned me seemed to think that you weren't above setting off another little war, if you were sufficiently browned off.' That made me smile. I wondered if she had been Dolly, but then remembered Dolly was off getting married somewhere.

'What did you say?'

'That if you wanted to start a war I wouldn't dream of stopping you, and since they hadn't a chance of catching you, they should just cross their fingers and wait for you to come back . . .'

'And?'

'And she put the phone down on me. Best thing all week.' He engaged in a bout of explosive coughing again, and I played advantage by not giving him a chance. As soon as he finished I said, 'I'm sorry, but I can't marry Frieda. We don't like each other enough. I don't want to hurt you or Mrs Halton, but that's just how it is.'

Halton went into displacement activity. He got us another couple of drinks: bigger ones this time. Then he sighed, and almost mumbled, 'I always knew you'd stand aside as soon as you found out Charlie . . . always knew you'd do the right thing. Thank you.'

I didn't know what the hell he was talking about, so I tried to look intelligent and hoped for the best. 'That's all right, boss.'

'How long have you known about Robert?'

I hadn't known about Robert at all, but, whoever the bastard was, he'd appeared at the right time to give me a way out. I hope that I now lied smoothly. When you lie to people you like it's important to do it well.

'Since it started, probably. Are they serious?'

'She says she loves him.' He sounded like a caring guardian, but undid the sentence with a shrug.

'Maybe my going a couple of thousand miles away isn't a bad idea at the moment.' I told him. 'She can go out without worrying that I'm around the next corner.'

'Do you think that would concern her?'

'It's what another woman I knew once told me, and I trusted her judgement – still do, but don't know where she is.'

I could see the conversation was in danger of becoming maudlin, so I switched the points on him and we talked about the airline business and, as it turned out, the road haulage and coach travel businesses, because the Old Man was branching out. He'd bought five big Fodens and a couple of Duple coaches, and based them at Watford – not too far from where we sat. Halton Air was now just an arm of Halton Transport, although I hoped that it was still where his heart lay. It was inevitable that we'd eventually talk about my impending departure, and I was still half inclined to think he'd sack me.

He didn't apologize for keeping me in the dark, but asked, 'Where are they sending you?'

'Egypt, I expect. I haven't heard anything good about it, except a story about a belly dancer and an imaginative pig in a Cairo nightclub.'

He ignored the last part. 'What do they want you to do?'

'Dunno. Radios I expect. It's the only thing I'm any good at.'

'How much are they paying you?'

'Dunno, boss: not as much as you. Most of the men I knew in the war lost rank after it, and the turds from the officer schools all floated back up to the top again.' He ignored that as well. 'It wouldn't surprise me to find that I'm a sergeant again.'

'I'll make up the difference.'

'Thanks, but why? I mean, why would you do that?'

'Because I don't want to lose you, of course. Halton Air was making a loss until you began to manage it for me.'

'That was a fluke. The Airlift came along just at the right time for us. Anyway, I thought we were dropping down the league again.'

He gave me the three-minute cough before observing, 'In six months' time, when we've linked up our own road haulage units and coaches with the aircraft, the work will come rolling in again. You'll see. We'll have the only integrated transport company in the country.' He was always ahead of the game, Old Man Halton. When he finished coughing there were specks of blood on the white lawn handkerchief. So, the Old Man didn't want to lose me. I could have said, *You could have fooled me*, but you don't look a gift horse in the mouth, do you?

Later he asked me if I wanted to go on leave until I got the brown envelope.

I told him, 'No. I don't think so. I'll hang about for a while to make sure Elaine has got the hang of things, and I'll also spend some time with my boys.'

'I told you to bring them along some time, didn't I? Boys like aeroplanes and lorries.'

'I'll remember that, sir.'

He laughed and then he coughed. He laughed because I'd just told him to mind his own business, and we both knew it. I just kept my work and private life apart. That was my way.

Just before I left him I told him that he had a third share in one of the most notorious nightspots in Berlin. It stopped him coughing for all of a couple of minutes.

The girl in the outer office said her name was June. *Flaming June*, I thought.

Sometimes it happens just like that: the dice roll for you. Less than a minute into a conversation with her I said, 'I'm only up here for a night. Can you come out with me?'

'You're Mr Bassett, aren't you?'

'Yes, Charlie . . .'

What I'd had in mind was an evening in a pub and then chancing my arm, but she replied, 'There's a lovely new restaurant in Hounslow.'

'OK then?'

'OK, Charlie.'

I had my hour in a pub after all, waiting for her to get off work. The owner was a burly man in his fifties, who stood the other side of the bar, polished the glasses and made conversation until my date came along. Just before June arrived the radio above the bar launched into a jaunty old Tommy Dorsey number. I recognized it, but couldn't place it. It was playing when she walked in.

'What's that called?' I asked him, but it was June who answered,

'It's "Satan takes a holiday".'

Yeah. The next number was 'What is this thing called love?' I've told you before; God's sending out His little signals all the time, but we're usually on the wrong frequency for decent reception.

We were the last to leave the restaurant and when it was empty they let us dance a couple to the radio. The last song was 'I'll be seeing you'. I think it was that guy Sinatra.

Her bedsit, in a suburban house in a suburban avenue, was a comfy little room. There was a heavy crocheted cover on the bed, and a gas fire. We made love as if we had known each other for years.

I'd meant what I'd said. I went down to Lympne the next day and threw myself into the books and forms. Elaine looked subdued when I walked in. I wondered why, but thought I'd let her come out with it in her own good time. She couldn't even conjure up a quick grin when I offered to make her coffee, so I loaded up two mugs with black Camp and topped off each with an inch of Five Bells — that's export-strength rum. She took one hefty swig, and then spluttered.

'Strewth, Charlie, what did you put in this?'

'Navy neaters. OK?'

'Are you trying to get me drunk?'

'I've done worse.'

I had, actually . . . or rather *we* had. Once upon a time. But that was three years past, and she'd had a son since then and, as I told you, I'd met her husband and rather liked him. It's always best to quit when you're ahead, but, thinking about it, it was she who'd done the quitting, not me. So I asked, 'What's up?'

'My Terry.' Husband. He flogged long-distance lorries up and down the Great North Road. It had meant that before the kid came along she might have had too much time on her hands. I know that sounds unkind, but that was the way we looked at things then. Learn to put up with it: I have.

31

'What's the matter with him?'

'Nothing. He wants to change jobs and drive for Mr Halton; that's all.'

'You'll see more of him if he's based at Watford.'

'I know. That's the problem. I like it just fine with him only home at weekends, and now I realize that I feel guilty about that: I'm being selfish. I ought to be a better wife.'

I waited for an intro and the first few bars before leaning over, and dabbing the end of her nose lightly with my forefinger. I said, 'Maybe someone should tell you that it's sometimes OK to be selfish. It's allowed; and what's more it's probably good for you.'

I had leaned towards her. Now I straightened, and began to turn away. She had smiled and blushed. Momentarily the Elaine I had known had shown herself. I also knew that if I had reached towards her she wouldn't have pulled back. But I didn't. I did the right thing for once. I've told you before: the women in my life are like buses. I wait weeks for one, and then a small convoy arrives all at the same time.

She said, 'I don't want you to go away, Charlie.'

'That makes two of us; neither do I. But I don't think I can get out of it.' I made a joke of it. 'I'll send you something from Egypt. What can you get out there?'

'One of my uncles brought me a beautiful photograph album from Alex once: it had a black leather cover with Egyptian hieroglyphs painted on it. It's almost full now. You could bring me another: I'd like that.' She rummaged in her handbag for a handkerchief, and dabbed at her eyes – her make-up was running. What had I said now to upset her? Nothing apparently, because she asked, 'What would you like me to do for you?'

That was asking for it, wasn't it? But I made a reply that surprised even me.

'Why don't you write to me? No one else will: letters from home to keep my morale up.'

She waited for ages before she replied; as if I had asked her for something far more important. Then she made up her mind and said, 'OK.' Then, 'Panic over; now you can give me a hug.'

'Before you go home,' I promised, and fled.

I sipped my coffee slowly in my own office, took the conversation apart, and put it back together again. Then I understood something about myself. I understood that I had a difficulty with people liking me or loving me, and wondered if that was why my girlfriends never stuck around for long.

It was time to go home and ask Maggs about it: she always knew what to do.

I've probably told you about Maggs before. She's the person who was bringing my two boys up when I was away. Which was all too often. I had a nerve regarding them as *my boys*, if I come to think about it. I'd found Dieter on a battlefield in Germany in '45, and Carlo dropped into my life in Bremen about a week later – the son of an ex-girlfriend who was heading east. It's a long story, but I'll tell you sometime if I haven't already.

When I was away they lived with Mrs Maggs and my old major above a pub in Bosham – that's a small port near Chichester – and they lived with me in the prefab next door when I was home. I'd signed DP papers for them a couple of years ago, but now the local authority was getting iffy, and we were making a proper adoption of it. What that meant was that I had to behave myself until everyone said *yes*, and gave me the forms to prove it. I'd had two interviews with an old biddy in the Council Offices already. I thought she was against me until she came up with a woman from the local WRI to sponsor my claim . . . the only problem was that both made it plain they'd prefer me to be married, or at least engaged. Now that Frieda was out of the picture I had a problem, didn't I? I thought I'd better go down for a couple of days and see how the land lay.

Before I walked away from Elaine she hit me with a limpet of a kiss out of the blue; I hadn't seen one like that from her for a couple of years – not even at Christmas. I pushed her gently off with a laugh, and said something like, 'Go away and stay married.'

'I will, but sometimes it's not quite enough.' Another girl had told me that another time, and I'd got into trouble with her too. As she turned away I put my hand on her bum. Round as a football. I have been known to weaken.

The year hadn't yet made its mind up about seasons, so I drove down in bright sunshine, with the roof of my old Singer roadster open, and bloody near froze to death. One day I'll thank God for the man who designed the flying jacket I wore over my clothes. I dropped over the Downs and into Chichester in time to pick up Carly from his primary school at three, and we played hopscotch outside Dieter's school gate until the elder showed himself, weighed down by a tattered RAF small pack full of homework and gym kit. Ice cream, Tizer and then home. We played with their Dinky army lorries on the floor in front of the fire, and then Ludo until it was time for them to go to bed. Boys can be easy to please sometimes.

Later I helped James and Maggs to repel the Friday rush, from behind the bar. On Fridays all the yachties came down to pretend to be sailors. I'm showing my prejudice, of course; some of them were quite keen, and two of the old wooden ladies in the basin had been to Dunkirk and back a few times in 1940. When I walked back to the prefab, frosted gravel crackling beneath my shoes, the boys were no longer in their beds. They were on either side of the kitchen table with mugs of Ovaltine that Dieter had obviously made.

I feigned horror, which made them laugh, and then asked, 'What's going on? Couldn't you sleep?'

'We were talking about you, Dad.' Dieter said. He often spoke for the both of them.

'Yeah?'

'We heard the Major tell Mrs Maggs that you were going to Egypt. There's a war on there.' We all called James the Major, unless we addressed him directly.

'You shouldn't listen in to other people's conversations, but as it happens, you're right. I do have to go to Egypt.'

'Do you want to go?'

'No, but I'm being called up. I don't have a choice.'

'You can write *Bollocks* on the call-up letter, and send it back. Martin's eldest brother did that.' I knew Martin. Dieter and he fished together on the Arun. That made me smile.

'That's maybe not a bad idea, but they'll send the police after him. Try not to swear, son; not 'til you're older.'

There was more to this round-the-table conference than met the eye. I got myself a whisky from the cupboard, and as I sat down Carlo suddenly burst out with, 'We don't want you to go. You'll get killed.'

I hugged him, and ruffled his hair. 'No I won't. I'll be very careful . . . and they're only sending reservists like me out for six months. That's twenty-four weeks: it will pass in a flash.' I didn't actually know that: no one had told me.

'Peter Harding's dad was killed,' Dieter explained. 'He didn't even get as far as the Middle East. The Gyppoes killed him in Cyprus.'

'Don't call them *Gyppoes*,' I cautioned him. 'They're Egyptians. Peter Harding's dad must have been unlucky. Is Peter in your class?'

'No: 3b. They cut him up with cheese wire, and sent the pieces back in a parcel.'

Why do boys always manage to recall the gorier details?

'Don't worry about me. I will be working with a radio in a fortified camp; somewhere very safe . . . and I'll have time to write you letters, and maybe I'll even be able to call you up on the Major's telephone.' Then I suddenly stopped talking because I realized that all over the country similar conversations were going on, and we couldn't all be right, could we? Whenever Britannia flexes her muscles there is a blood tax to be paid.

Carly was fishing about in the bottom of his drink with a spoon: they were almost done. But Dieter was never one to let you away safe once he'd pinned you to a chair. He asked, 'You're *not* going to marry Miss Frieda are you, Dad?'

'No, I'm not. We thought we would, for a time, but now we realize we argue too much. Does that upset you?'

'No. We didn't like her very much. She used to scold Carly.'

'We call her *the scary girlfriend*,' Carly chipped in.

'Then I won't marry her. I'll only marry someone you like.'

'Have you got a girlfriend at all at the moment, Dad?' That was Dieter again. He was always trying to marry me off.

'I had one last week. I could call her up and ask.'

'What's she like?'

'Her name is June. She has bright red hair, and very white skin . . . and a big smile. She laughs very loud when she's happy, but I think she probably has a bit of a temper as well.'

'Like Mrs Maggs?'

'A bit. Why?'

'Maybe you could bring her down here to meet us.'

'I'll think about it,' I promised them. Then I packed them off to bed again, hoping that it would stick this time.

Saying goodbye to Maggs, James and the kids was harder than it ever had been before.

36

Chapter Three

Doctor Jazz

I didn't like the way that Elaine looked at me. It was as if she was watching all the time; sizing me up for something, although I'd only been back in the office ten minutes.

'There were only two personal calls when you were away, and I decided to bother you with neither of them.'

'Good.'

'One was from a Wing Commander Watson. He left a telephone number, asked if you had received any letters yet, and said he had notice of your overseas medical. He asked you to call him.'

'What did you say?'

'I told him he should be ashamed of himself, and put the phone down.'

That made me snort.

'What about the other one?'

'A woman named June wanted to speak to you. She left a telephone number, as well.'

'What did you say to her?'

'The same. I thought she sounded much too young for you, so I told her she should be ashamed of herself, and put the telephone down on her too.'

'I've only been away three days and you've already destroyed my next military career, and ruined my love life.'

'I know. I did rather well, didn't I? Now neither of them will want you.'

It was a nice try, but I smiled, probably a little sadly. 'Life doesn't work out like that, does it?'

Then I noticed that she was wearing her white shirt with more buttons popped open than usual, and that the view out over the foothills was still very interesting. She noticed me noticing, and didn't seem to mind. That was interesting too; maybe Terry had been away from home too long again. Oddly enough I felt a little shy once more. I hoped that was nothing to do with growing up, for if it was I wanted nothing to do with it.

She asked, 'What were you thinking about?'

'When?'

'When you looked at me just then.'

Tell the truth, Charlie. 'You . . . and old times.'

'Good. I've also been thinking a lot about old times recently. I'll make you a decent cup of char, and switch on *Workers Playtime*. Then we can think about them again.' I just then began to get that feeling I was sailing back into troubled waters.

I was subjected to my medical in a dingy shed of a place in Croydon, just up the road from the Fairfield Halls. There was a plant producing domestic gas somewhere in the vicinity: all of the buildings seemed stained by soot, and a smell of sulphur hung in the air. Old Man Halton would have felt at home here because he'd been gassed in the trenches in the First World War. Maybe you already knew that. This part of South London smelled like a school locker room after a spinach lunch. No wonder they moved the bleeding airport – it wasn't a smell with which to welcome visitors to the Capital of Empire.

There were twelve of us in a small waiting room lined with

wooden benches . . . and three of my co-defendants were taken before me: two As and another B. We were a mixture of reservists and national servicemen, and I'd already been told that the medical the former got was a makeweight – not so much a matter of 'fit for service' as 'not unfit for service': there's a subtle difference. The other B in the room was named Babcock, and I guess he'd had a bad time before, because his hands never stopped shaking, and his head gave the occasional twitch. He also looked decidedly jaundiced.

A RAF corporal checked our names off on a clipboard, called us 'gentlemen' and seated us in alphabetical order. When I stood up and crossed the room ten minutes later, because I was fed up with the sun shining in my eyes, he almost had a fit.

'Mr Bassett is it, sir?'

'Yes, Corporal.'

'Then sit where you're fucking well told, sir.'

'No, Corporal.'

'What did you say, sir?'

'I said "No, Corporal" . . . and wash your fucking ears out if you didn't hear me the first time.'

He swelled like a party balloon receiving the benefit of a particularly decent pair of lungs. And he turned red. Sweat broke along his hairline in his attempt to keep a lid on his temper. If he'd been subject to a medical himself just then, he would never have passed. He literally stamped a foot – I'd not seen that before – before he shouted, 'We'll bloody well see about that,' and banged out through a flimsy door which warped in his grasp.

'You forgot to say *sir*,' I called after him helpfully.

Someone – an L, I think – said, 'Blimey, now you're for it.'

The twitcher's head was now permanently to either one side or the other, ticking like a metronome. I wouldn't have minded being 'for it' if it would get me out of this madhouse.

A huge head, about eight feet above the ground, looked

around the door through which the corporal had bolted. It roared, 'Fucking *Bassett* – I mighta guessed.'

I said, 'Yes, WO,' meekly. Then I grinned, and said, 'Hello, Alex.'

Watson had told me years ago that the new postwar RAF was so small that you kept on bumping into people you knew. He had been right. Alex was a service policeman, a giant and a sort of recurring nightmare.

He grinned back, 'Wotcha, Charlie. Heard you were coming back. Thought I'd surprise you.'

'You did. You sent an idiot in here to look after us.'

'The corporal is not an idiot. He is your perfectly average corporal.'

'I see your point,' I told him, '. . . and it saddens me. If I'm too rude for the RAF can I go home now?'

'Not a chance. You're all A1 medical passes – bound for glory the lot of you.' He glanced around the room, and smiled. Tigers smile like that. When Alex was in a room he dominated it by size alone. He didn't have to do anything else: in that small waiting room it was like being in the presence of a fairy-tale ogre. I didn't like to ask how he knew our results even before the medical exams had been completed.

'That thing can't be A1.' I indicated Babcock. His tongue was lolling out now. It was a peculiarly large tongue, and a funny colour. A small waterfall of saliva dribbled from his mouth to the lapel of his expensive camel-coloured coat.

Alex said, 'We'll give him to the Army then. They'll make him one of their B1s and call him an LC: that's all we'll need from you lot anyway.' LC was *Lines of Communication*, a medical grading that kept half-dead soldiers away from the front line, but enabled the mad sods in charge to deploy them just about anywhere else. It meant they still got you, and was no bar to being sent abroad. 'Now just you lot behave yourselves, and I'll send in the char wallah — but don't go for a piss afterwards, you'll need it later.' *Ah*, the romance of serving the Crown.

We did what waiting rooms are designed for. We waited. Babcock's eyes closed. At times I didn't know if he was asleep or dead. His twitch became slow, but more pronounced. He was probably still alive. The damp patch on his lapel grew larger. His name was called from behind the door three times before he responded.

He came back into the waiting room half an hour later, alert but miserable. He no longer twitched, and the damp stain was drying nicely.

'*A* fucking *one. Fucking* bastards,' he snarled at us, and slammed the outside door almost off its hinges as he left. Then it was me.

Two doctors: one female and one male. The female looked as friendly as Irma Grese on leave from Auschwitz. The man could have done with a clean white coat. He looked tired.

He told me, 'I do the pricks and backsides, just to save the real doctor's blushes. She does the rest; you'll find she's very good.'

'Am I a prick or a backside?' I asked him.

'A bit of both I expect. The Warrant Officer told me you were the troublemaker.'

'What was the matter with the man who just left, sir?'

Irma actually smiled. It changed her completely. If I had hung around long enough I might have fallen in love.

She said, 'Nothing. Nothing but having drunk half a gallon of lemon Cremola Foam stirred up with about eight Alka-Seltzers. It makes you look very strange for a short time, but the effects wear off quickly. You've no idea what some men will do to avoid conscription.'

'I have. I don't suppose it would help if I started falling off my chair?'

'Not in the slightest.' She gave me the smile again. I would have told jokes all day to be rewarded with smiles like that. 'You're perfectly A1 – I can tell it just by looking at you . . . but we'll go through the motions just in case. If you go behind the curtain and drop your trousers, Dr Crippen will be with you in a moment.'

It could only happen to me, I thought.

Both medics took less than fifteen minutes between them. I finished in front of Irma. She said, 'You'll do, Mr Bassett, although you drink too much. You'll have a beer gut by the time you're forty unless you ease up and take some exercise.'

'I'll remember that, Doctor.'

'Good. Now bend over that chair back please, and drop your trousers again.' For a moment she sounded like my old head-master: when you walked into his study he invariably had a glint in his eye, and a cane in his hand.

'I thought you didn't do backsides, Doctor.'

'I don't, but I do give the inoculations, and you have a bucketful coming up, according to your RAF forms. Try to relax: I'll re-sharpen the needle after the first ten.'

They always like to finish with a laugh, the doctors – have you noticed? After she'd finished with my bum and my upper thigh I felt as if I would never sit down again. Bloody sadist. The last thing she said was, 'We always tell people not to drink alcohol for at least twenty-four hours after this course of injections.'

'I'll remember that too, Doctor.' I hate people telling me what not to do.

Alex always brings out the Jerry in me: you know – *orders will be obeyed at all times without question*. He told me to get lost afterwards, but not so lost that I couldn't meet him back near the medical centre for opening time. He thought we could get drunk together, and get up to date. I don't know where he got the idea I'd enjoy going to a pub; after all, the doctor had just banned me.

I walked around Croydon to kill time. It was, and is, a terrible place. Grey people, living in grey houses, driving grey Hillmans, working in grey offices and grey factories. For the first time in my life it occurred to me that God was inordinately fond of grey, and in Croydon had created His masterpiece. After that I was ready to get drunk, and from the number of people already in the pub by half past five, I reckoned that most of Croydon agreed with me.

A few hours later, the woman doctor came pushing through the crowd with her medical bag. She nodded to me, but moved on up to a small raised stage. I wondered if she moonlighted as a stripper, but wasn't all that disappointed when she was joined by a small jazz band, put the silver cornet she'd pulled from her bag to her lips, and began to blow like an angel. She caught my eye halfway through the set, smiled that smile again, and began to drop the spectacular notes of 'Doctor Jazz' in front of us. That was when I realized that Croydon had always been one of my favourite places on the planet.

I remembered what it was like in the war – having joined up in the RAF then, I was sent back home again with a silly little silver badge to stick on my jacket, and told to wait my turn. The badge was to prove to strangers you were doing your bit. I had been impatient as hell to get into uniform. This time it wasn't like that. Not at all. I simply didn't want to go, and a moany little voice at the back of my brain was wheedling away with *You've done your bloody bit; why can't they pick on somebody else?*

The weeks before I had been called up to my basic training unit in the 1940s had been full of purpose and vigour . . . principally trying it on with girls I might never get a chance with again, and eventually losing my virginity with a generous neighbour. This time I prevaricated, did nothing, avoided decisions and wasted time. I slept with Elaine again – more for the form of it than anything else, both of us working off guilts we didn't understand – and afterwards I felt even more fed up than before.

When the brown envelope eventually arrived it was smaller than I remembered, but almost a relief. Elaine was watching me in my cramped office when I opened it – she had taken to standing close to me all the time, which crowded me. I didn't like that, but we'd been skin-to-skin like old times the night before, so it wouldn't have been right to tell her to back off. And before you get the idea that I was demonstrating some of my finer feelings by that decision, I wasn't. I simply didn't know when I'd want her again, and wasn't going to cut off my nose to spite my face.

She asked, 'This is it, isn't it?'

'Yes, love; I'm afraid it is. This time I really have to pack my bag.'

'Well then? *Where?*'

I had been afraid she'd ask that. *The Canal Zone, Malaya, Cyprus or Kenya?* What romantic destination was suitable for a brave British serviceman these days?

'Dungeness.'

'What?'

'You heard me. Fucking Dungeness. Just up the road.'

'I wish you wouldn't swear.'

'You'd swear if you'd been posted to Dungeness.'

'You'll still be able to see me if you get any time off.'

'I'm sure that was exactly what was in the RAF Board's mind when they decided!' I shouldn't have snapped. It hurt her. She looked down.

'I thought you didn't *want* to go to Egypt?'

'I didn't, but that's not the point. I didn't want to go to Dungeness either. Even less, in fact. Have you ever been to Dungeness?'

'Once; one night with Terry. I bruised my bum on the pebbles.'

That lifted it: my black mood, I mean. I grabbed her around the waist, swung her and gave her a hefty kiss. She threw a Force Nine right back at me. We went down to the small hut I bunked in, even although it was the middle of the morning, and when we came out again it was as if we had settled something rather good. She followed me into my office and grabbed me for another kiss, saying something like, 'I don't ever want to be without you for good, Charlie.'

'I can cope with that, sweetheart.' Why are the good ones always married? 'I'm mad about your belly,' I told her, '. . . and your legs, and . . .' Sometimes I say the right thing.

She smiled. 'That will do for now, Charlie.'

The way I saw it bloody Dungeness was as bad as a living bloody death sentence. Devil's Island without even the Devil for company. But Dungeness was only going to be a stepping stone to somewhere nastier, of course: the station designation number of its location had a large black **T** behind it so I was in for some more bleeding training in something or other.

Then they would probably stuff me in an aircraft again.

I don't know if you've ever been to Dungeness. If you haven't then you made a good decision. It's a fat thumb of a few trillion pebbles sticking out into the English Channel, battered by wind and wave, with the French looking on from the other side. It's the least hospitable place, after Bergen, in the whole world . . . and has more flies than an Egyptian karzi. Believe me; I know.

There was a lighthouse on it in my time, but that may have fallen down since the bastards built a nuclear power station next door in the Sixties. That should tell you something: they only

45

put nuclear piles where no sensible people go. I suspect that the lighthouse was in fact surplus to requirements – any sea captain who had experienced the dubious attractions of Dungeness before would hug the French coast twenty miles away, just to stay away from it.

You can take it from that little outburst that I was not enamoured of the place. At that time, as well as the lighthouse, it had a large, damp, concrete bomb-proof box: especially for me. And rain of course, and the bloody wind never stopped blowing. I still hadn't had a uniform issue, so I reported in my old RAF battledress blues which had long since lost their proper buttons. The black ones I'd sewn on looked much better anyway. Three shirts, one spare set of thins, five pairs of socks and my washing kit . . . and I also had a small pistol a mate had once given me, tucked into my flying jacket's pocket. Charlie Bassett, gent, reporting for duty, sir. Able, but far from bloody willing.

By 1952 we hadn't quite got round to taking down all the barbed wire we'd strung along the South Coast. That was probably something to do with still not trusting the French not to invade us while our back was turned: you know what they're like. In 1377 the bastards sailed right up to Rye, a neighbouring port, burned it to the ground and stole the church bells. As far as Rye, Sussex and Kent are concerned a state of war still exists between them and the Frogs, and will until we get those bells back. As far as *I'm* concerned we should have left the barbed wire up – we're going to need it one day. They had even overlooked a landmine or two, so no summer went by without news of a family being blown to kingdom come making sandcastles on a beach. I suppose Dungeness had some sort of excuse for the rusty wire . . . there were still live firing ranges just round the corner at Camber: still are, come to that.

At least they'd taken the gate away, so the road along the spit started at a gap in a barbed-wire fence left there to discourage the holidaymakers. And also a corporal in RAF uniform. He was unhappy-looking and definitely familiar. The little bastard from the Croydon medical unit. I stopped my old Singer alongside him.

'Mr Bassett is it, sir?' He hadn't a clipboard of names this time, so I guessed that I was the only one expected.

'Of course it is. We met a few weeks ago.'

'So we did, sir.'

'What are you doing here?'

'Posted, sir; same as you.'

'No, I mean what are you doing here at the end of the road?'

'I'm to drive the car, sir.'

'I don't need a driver.'

'Begging your pardon, sir, but you do. I'm to do the driving and you're to do the walking. CO's orders, sir. Everyone walks up to the station the first time. She says it's good for us.'

'She?'

'Yes, sir; the CO's a Wren officer. If you don't mind my saying, sir . . . it does seem odd to begin with, but you soon gets used to it.'

'It's a training station, right?'

'No, sir. It's an OLP, but there's always a couple of people like you around going through the refresher.'

'I'm not sure about *OLP*.'

'Operational Listening Post, sir. We got them all up the East Coast now, and along the Channel. Some up in Scotland too. We listen to the Commies as they sail past.' Then he shivered and said, 'Would you mind getting out of the car an' swappin' over, sir? It's bleedin' perishin' out here.' It was too.

'Sure you can drive it, Corporal . . . ?'

'Baxter, sir . . . and yes, I can drive it. Drove three-tonners in the war.' That was hardly reassuring, but you never know when you'll need someone on your side, so I said, 'Baxter and

Bassett. Sounds like a couple of sand dancers, doesn't it? We'd better watch out for each other.'

I thought for a moment he was going to laugh, but he said, 'I'll think about that, sir,' and put my little car into gear. I stood there and watched him dwindle into nothing as he drove away towards the shadowy buildings in the mist at the end of the causeway. They looked miles away.

They were, and it started to rain before I was halfway there. My last RAF posting had been to a listening station like this one, and I'd had a few mad moments of mad passion with a mad Wren there, so you can see that my interest was engaged by the time I walked through the gate of a proper barbed-wire enclosure.

The guard didn't salute because I wasn't properly dressed – *Salute the uniform, son, not the man*: I can still hear my first drill sergeant barking that in my face. This guy had the face of a twelve-year-old; I guessed he only shaved weekly – and, oh yeah, he had a Stirling sub-machine gun looped casually over his shoulder like a girl's handbag. He probably scared the Russians half to death.

The concrete block was enormous: much bigger than I had imagined. Three storeys and the only windows I could see were long narrow slits near the top: it wasn't a building designed for beauty. The discipline there was my sort of discipline – casual – or so it seemed at first. People saying *hello*, smiling and shaking your hand. I didn't get to meet the CO immediately: she was away at a meeting in the WD bunker at Hythe. When we collided in the afternoon her sailor suit looked familiar – a Wren – but that's where hope died: I'd never met her before. She was small; smaller than me. Very smart and with short black hair. I reckoned she was about forty.

It's funny how your values change: in those days I thought a woman in her forties was old. Now I look at a woman of fifty and think she's just approaching her prime – a perspective of age you see. What I mean is that I didn't fancy her. I know you don't like it, but that's what I was like in my twenties: the first good look I had at a woman was generally an estimate of her sexual potential. It got the decision to chance my arm out of the way. Just get used to it, and accept that most men are like that, even if we don't admit it all that often.

She probably knew this because she didn't ask me to sit. She had a metal desk and metal furniture inside a concrete office. It looked just like a place that people could run wars from. I hated it instantly. The atmosphere had the romantic charm of a pub's outside urinal. An educated voice: 'Welcome,' but not to where, or to whom. Then, 'I'll be your CO for two or three weeks – until we come to a decision about you. Call it an assessment if you like, or a judgement.'

'What kind of judgement, ma'am?' She smiled at the *ma'am*. Maybe I'd got it right first time for a change.

'Whether you're any good as you are, need retraining, or are no damned good at all.' She had a tight little smile that meant precisely nothing. It irritated me.

'. . . And if I'm no damned good at all, ma'am?'

'Back to Civvy Street as sharp as you like.'

'. . . Then can't you send me back right away, ma'am? I'll be no damned good at all – I promise you, ma'am.'

She leaned back in her state-of-the art CO's chair, smiled at me and fiddled with a pencil.

'Too many *ma'ams*, Bassett.' A week ago I had managed an airline; now I was back to being just bloody *Bassett* again. 'You're trying too hard. I spoke to a warrant officer in the RAF Police about you last week. He called you a comedian who couldn't keep his hands off women, and had an interesting but fatal disregard for Queen's Regs. He said that your next permanent address will probably be a prison somewhere.' Bloody Alex.

'There you are, then. Get rid of me while you can.'

She smiled again. Maybe I'd been shipped in to provide the entertainment. She said, 'You'll work four-hour shifts, one on three off, with a regular operator on your elbow all the time. Your first shift starts in' – she consulted a man's wristwatch that looked as if it had been liberated a few years ago – 'about three quarters of an hour. Just time for you to stow your gear. By the way, what happened to your uniform?'

'Not issued, ma'am. Maybe they are waiting for the results of my assessment.'

'We'll see about that.' I was sure she would. 'We're a Joint Services establishment here – you probably realized that – and there are a few civvies around as well, so we lack some of the service formality you're used to. Keep your paws off the ladies, though, do your job and we'll all get on.'

I didn't ask what would happen if I didn't; it was written all over her face. My first more or less normal CO in eight years was the Angel of Death, and she scared the wits out of me.

'Do I get any time off?' I asked her. 'I still have things to take care of.'

'Ask me next week; I'll think about it. That's all for now.' She put her head down and began to find a file on her desk of obsessive interest. Dismissed. She hadn't even told me her bloody name. As I about turned she said, still looking down at her papers, 'Mr Baxter will have told you a woman naval officer was in command here. You expected someone else, didn't you?'

I stopped in the doorway and turned to face her.

'How did you know that?'

'She warned me to look out for you. She's a friend of mine; out of the Service now – she has a couple of sprogs.'

I said the first thing that came into my mind – never a good thing. 'Neither of them is mine.'

'I know that too.'

'She never wanted children either; she told me that.'

She took pity on me, smiled her little smile — but it was as if it was intended for someone else — and said, 'Never believe a woman who says that, Pilot Officer; they're only testing you.'

'How is she?'

'. . . a bit heavier than when you last saw her.' *Fat*, she meant. Women are cruel about each other's looks.

'I didn't mean that. Is she well? Happy?'

This little woman had eyes that could be as black as coal; or the muzzles of gun barrels. This time her stage directions obviously read *softly*, and *with feeling*.

'I'm glad you asked that. If you hadn't I would have given you the hardest time here you've ever had anywhere in your life . . . and then made sure they sent you to the Arctic Circle for three years!' I made no response. Dumb insolence had always been my speciality. She added, 'From what she's told me I'd say she was as well as could be expected, having experienced you. I would also say that it was none of your damned business.' Frozen moment in time. I waited for the music but it never came, and she said, 'You can go now.'

I didn't trust myself to say anything, nodded, turned and left as smartly as I could. Stuffed. I felt as if I'd had the biggest roasting of my service career, and she'd done it all without raising her voice, or swearing directly at me.

Six hours later I lay on a flock mattress on a concrete shelf in the four-bedded bunk room I'd been allocated, trying to get some sleep. It stank of farts and sweat, and a dull warehouse light, without a switch to extinguish it, glowed on the ceiling. The guy beneath me was snoring, and a civvy technician on the opposite bunk had his nose buried in a Mickey Spillane book. The woman my new CO had spoken of earlier had been named Gloria, and I'd loved her more than I ever let on. I was always falling in love with the wrong types, but I suppose that I began to look at Gloria in a new light that evening. I'd thought of her

as a hard-hearted bitch who'd nearly wrecked my mind; it hadn't
occurred to me before that maybe I'd hurt her as well. I was still
hoping that I hadn't when I fell asleep. How stupid was that?

The work wasn't difficult. We just listened to the vibes in the air
until we heard a bandit, and then listened more closely. I was
surprised to see we were still using some of the kit I'd been
brought up on. In a curtained alcove, at one side of the concrete
box we worked in, was a set of radios straight out of a Lancaster
or a Hallibag, back to back with the smaller sets out of a B-17.
I'd worked with both, and could still dismantle most of their
vitals and reassemble them in my sleep. That's what one of my
Army trainers made me do to begin with; I spent a day stripping
them down, and putting them back together. He followed my
every move and made copious notes in a notebook, but he said
nothing. How can you know how you're doing if the buggers
won't speak to you? I did two four-hour stints with him back to
back, and when I finished with the Yankee job and tested it he
said, 'I've always wanted to know how to do that.'

'What?'

'Strip the American set. I've never done it.'

'Now you know then. Anyway, I thought you were supposed
to be teaching me.'

'Where'd you get that idea? Lucy?'

'Lucy?'

'The CO. It's what the girls call her, and they can be a bit
nasty. Juicy Lucy or sometimes "Mother". She's worse than a
mother hen. I'm a tankie, by the way – Royal Armoured Corps.
Call me Rob. You?'

'Charlie. RAF. Seems a long time ago, though. What next?'

'I thought we'd get in your wee car and go and find a pub.
Lucy said you could have a night off once you'd fixed the spare
radios. They haven't worked for weeks.'

'What kind of show is this?'

'A very poor one at times, but refreshingly informal.'

'That's what the CO said.'

'She can get some things right, can't she? You get yourself a wash, while I round up a couple of the girls.'

'Which girls?'

'We have a few mysterious civvies from the electronics factories. Philips Electrical I think, or Mallards. They're likely to be a bit stir-crazy, so watch yourself.'

I even polished my shoes. Rob sat in the back with one of the girls, his arm quickly looped around her shoulders. It was dark back there. I heard her giggle and say *Stop it; it's too early for that!* The girl alongside me had a starched white blouse, below-the-knee-length dark, wide skirt, and white socks above her dancing pumps. She had short dark hair, a nice smile and a sad sigh. I asked her name.

'Ivy.' Nice voice. Sutton or Epsom. Somewhere round there. Grammar-school voice.

'What's the matter? . . . I heard you sigh.' The car was in gear, and moving forward now. So were we.

'I miss my boyfriend. He only gets down once a month.' I wouldn't have minded getting down a bit myself. My old mate Tommo once told me that some girls liked it.

'What are you down here for, then?'

'The money; what else? We're saving to get married.'

'Don't worry,' I told her – feeling as old as her father. She was probably as old as I was on my first night visit to Germany in the war. '. . . you've plenty of time yet.'

Minutes later we pulled up after Rob shouted, 'Stop: we're here!' by a funny-shaped building with a sign saying The Pilot Inn above one of its doors. It looked a bit ramshackle, but if you'd had to withstand what the Dungeness weather threw at you for a hundred years you'd look a bit ramshackle too.

Before we got out I asked, 'What is this place?'

'Originally it was a fairly big wooden ship,' Ivy replied. 'The landlord says it was a smuggling ship, but nobody really knows. When it got stuck on the Ness the locals dismantled it and built a house out of her. The house became a pub.'

'When was that?'

'Seventeen something I expect.'

Rob said, 'I like hearing you two getting to know each other, but can you get a bleeding move on? We're freezin' to bleedin' death back here.' It was the way the old Singer was built – only two doors, so we had to lean the front seat backs forward to let the rear passengers out.

'I thought you'd never ask,' I told him. 'Mine's a bitter, and Ivy's a . . .' I glanced at her and grinned.

She smiled back and said, 'A port and lemon. A large one if you can afford it.' She'd clearly said that before.

There was a public telephone in the small wood-lined passage before the saloon bar. I looked at my watch, but it was already too late to call Elaine, so I didn't feel bad about it.

Two port and lemons and two pints later I asked Ivy, 'What do you do, Ivy . . . I mean, what do you do really well?'

She smiled. It was a nice smile, but a bit goofy and lopsided. Her reply was slow coming. It wasn't what I'd meant, but it would do.

'Cling,' she told me, then reached out and touched the rough cloth of my old blue battledress blouse.

Maybe I could put up with Dungeness for a fortnight.

Chapter Four

One o'clock jump

Lucy was someone you could never please entirely. I suppose that was what cut her out to be a member of the boss class in the first place. It's people like her who turn the rest of us into raving socialists. I was a better bloody operator than most of the layabouts on the station, could transmit and receive Morse faster, and at times seemed to be the only one on duty capable of chasing a signal if it leapt from band to band. The Reds were getting quite good at that sort of thing; Rob thought they were so sharp that the switch must be operating mechanically, and independently of the signaller. The only problem he couldn't solve was how they coordinated the jump for both receiving and transmitting stations at the same time, in order not to lose part of the signal. He spent all of his time at a small ill-lit bench in the corner, fiddling with a couple of oscillators, some tuners and a couple of new-fangled electric clocks from the Mallards factory. He swore imaginatively each time the device gave him a shock.

Lucy used to look over my shoulder, place a manicured finger on one of my log entries and *tut-tut*. She couldn't fault me technically, so she homed in on my handwriting and spelling. I came on duty one afternoon to find two small dictionaries on my table – an English job, and a Polish–English equivalent. I flogged them to a schoolteacher in the pub that night and got threatened with five days' CB and my pay docked after Lucy found out. But she told me she couldn't be bothered with the paperwork a charge sheet would have entailed.

'Get rid of me then,' I said. 'I've been here three weeks, so you must know by now whether you want me or not.'

'*Ma'am.*'

'. . . ma'am. Pass me or fail me.'

'I passed you two weeks ago, Charlie. In theory you can go on to another unit, if you need more training, any time you like, but a Wing Commander Watson believes that once we let you go we'll never see you again. So I'm stuck with you, apparently.' Then she smiled, and said, 'You may swear if it will make you feel any better; I did when I was told.'

That made me smile too. I didn't hate her. Not any more than I've hated any other authority figure, anyway.

'My work's still OK then?'

'Of course it is. Keep it up.' I nearly offered the Art Mistress saying that to the Gardener, but bit my tongue. I didn't think her indulgence would stretch that far.

Then she added, 'They've laid on a bit of entertainment for you this week, anyway. It will help break the monotony. You've got to report to Lydd on Wednesday morning for a Course 42.'

'What's Course 42, ma'am?'

She shrugged. 'God only knows. But 42's the designation they use for anything they haven't a proper name or number for. It can mean absolutely anything. Good luck.' She looked down at the file on her desk, just like the first time I had met her. Dismissed again. I think it was still the same file. It was only as I was walking away I remembered that she had called me *Charlie*. That must have counted for something.

We drove over to Lydd airfield, which looked pretty empty before we arrived. No aircraft, no activity . . . another bleeding ghost station, although everything was being kept in pretty good order. You noticed the *we* of course! I wasn't alone. Ivy was on a day's stand-down, bored out of her brains, so I hid her under a blanket on the back seat as I went through the gate. The boy with the Stirling sub-machine gun was back. His hands and fingers looked as blue as his greatcoat. It was a still, clear, blue sky with not a puff of cloud, and as cold as nuns' tits. I've never liked Decembers, even although I was born in one.

After a hundred yards she scrambled over into the front passenger seat, and gave me a peck on the cheek. 'Thanks, love.'

'What for?'

'Rescuing me from Lucy. She's determined to get my knickers off before I go.'

'You mean she's . . . ?'

She laughed at me. 'Christ, Charlie, didn't you know? Where have you been all of your life?'

'Not around people like her, that's for certain!'

'Sure?'

It was the way she said it that left a question in my mind: I'd known one of Lucy's friends, remember.

'What are you going to do while I'm working this morning?'

'What will *you* be doing?'

'Haven't a clue. Course 42 can mean anything, apparently. They haven't told me yet.'

'Maybe it's better you don't know.' She gave me another little peck on the cheek, which caused me to swerve into the path of a small Ford milk float. We left the driver with a face whiter than his bloody milk. Ivy said, 'Sorry,' and, 'I'll probably go for a walk.'

But life's never quite that simple is it?

I saw two guys standing by a C-type hangar so we trundled over there. A sergeant and a corporal. Both very smartly turned out and obviously impervious to cold. This did not bode well. The corporal held the door open for Ivy; she probably gave him a bit of leg as she slid out, because I saw him grin immediately.

The sergeant asked me, 'Pilot Officer Bassett, is it, sir?'

Someone had asked me that not too long ago. I've never had all that much bother remembering my own name, so I took the piss, 'I think so, Sergeant. That's exactly who I was the last time someone asked.'

He smiled a smile I didn't like, and handed me a sheet of paper from his big mitt. His big mitt seemed to be covered in old scars: some things count more than rank. It was a class list headed up *Course 42*, and the date. I was the only student listed, and in the column headed *Comments*, alongside the student's name, someone had printed *Comedian*. Time to beat the retreat.

I said, 'Sorry, Sergeant. I've been on Civvy Street too long.'

His big lumpy face broke into a friendly smile. The sort of smile that conceals a Mills bomb. 'Don't worry, sir; you'll find a sense of humour helps a lot where you'll be going . . .'

'Where *am* I going?'

'About five thousand feet up, sir, for the one o'clock jump – first a small-arms refresher for a couple of hours, and then we're going to stick a 'chute on your back and fling you out of an aeroplane.'

'I've already done that once,' I wailed, 'and I'm still here. I passed. I don't want to try it again!'

'Then hard luck, sir. Someone up there must think it might be useful wherever you're going next. They want to know if you can still do it.'

'What happens if I make a mess of it?'

The corporal put on his most funereal of faces and told me, 'Service burial, full blues and a firing party. Don't you worry, sir; we'll do you justice.'

The bastards must have known that I'd baled out of a

disintegrating aircraft high over France in 1947, but it wasn't going to make any difference.

Ivy thought it was all a bit of a hoot, and asked them, 'Can I stick around and watch? Nothing like this ever happens to me.'

Amos 'n' Andy drew away for a few secs, before the sergeant replied, 'Don't see why not, miss. You can even come up with us if you like, as long as you signs the blood chit: there's no one watching today.'

Inside the hangar I learned to strip and fire the Stirling sub-machine gun. The bloody thing jammed twice.

'Prone to jamming,' the corporal told me, 'usually at inconvenient moments. I prefer the good old three-o-three meself, with a fucking great bayonet on the end to make my point.' Then he looked at Ivy and added, 'Begging your pardon, miss.'

She smiled, 'No problem, Corporal. Can I have a go myself?'

I'd seen this coming: she'd started to scuff her feet on the floor, and already looked bored. Ivy was better at it than me, of course, and it chose not to jam on her. Maybe it preferred women. Then we moved on to the .45 automatic pistol. It looked large enough in my small hands to club an elephant to death with, but I managed better with it. When Ivy took her turn, the kick of the damned thing threw her hand holding it vertically above her head and the explosion closed her eyes. She could still hit the target though, and I wondered if her fiancé actually wanted a girlfriend trained in small-arms firing.

Eventually the sergeant said, 'It's a bit parky in here.'

We didn't disagree – my toes felt numb – and he led us away to a small Nissen hut which had probably been a ground-crew rest-room. It had a new electric stove, and he had the makings of our lunch: tea and bacon sarnies – no butter. It would have been nice to have had a bit of butter. Ivy flirted with the other two like it was going out of fashion, but I wasn't up to responding to her. Once I started to think about the afternoon, my stomach started to churn. In my book anyone choosing to jump out of an aircraft must be a bit of a maniac.

We went back to work at twelve-thirty. Sergeant Hickman — that was his name; I knew it would come back to me — and his neophyte stuffed me into a pair of grey overalls three sizes too large for me, and strapped a parachute pack around me. They made me jump off a table a couple of times, onto an old sisal exercise mat. It was supposed to cushion my fall, but had about the same amount of give as a battleship's armoured deck. They told me all the usual scary stories about what can go wrong with parachute jumps. I was, however, particularly worried by a statement that one in ten jumps go wrong one way or another. I'd already got away with one jump safely, so I calculated that I'd shortened my odds to one in nine. But *which* of the nine, I wondered.

We were waiting outside in the cold sunshine when our lift turned up. I heard it before I saw it, and thought I recognized the engine note. Twin Cheetahs that buzzed like a swarm of bees. When I saw it minutes later I even recognized the bloody aircraft as well: it was one of ours . . . an old Airspeed Oxford painted as red as a pillar box. It belonged to Halton Air, and a few weeks earlier I had been the one giving its pilot his orders. I suspected immediately that Old Man Halton's refusal to defer my recall to the colours was tied to some sort of deal he had made with the WD to keep his fleet in the air. It led me to wonder if Elaine knew that as well.

The pilot was Randall Claywell Junior, an American journey-man flier I'd known since 1945. He was so big that the aircraft shifted from side to side as he moved back from the office to its side door. He stepped down back first. We had all trooped out to meet him and when he turned around, he looked genuinely surprised to see me.

'Hiya, Charlie, what y' doin' here?'

'Jumping out of your fucking aeroplane I think,' I muttered bitterly. 'Did they send you over here to make me feel better?'

'Do you know anyone who cares that much? Naw, I'm doing a coupla these stunts every week. The RAF's short of appropriate aircraft. They've committed their jumpers to the Paras, and we get to pick up the small stuff. Never thought I'd see you here.'

Appropriate was a big word for Randall: seeing me trussed up like an Egyptian mummy must have thrown him for a minute.

The sergeant didn't waste time with an intro – they all knew each other. He just said, 'No point in hanging around, folks. The sooner we're up there, sir, the sooner you'll be back down on terra firma.'

'That's exactly what I'm worried about,' I told him.

Randall unshipped the door, which was an odd, off-centre shape and not very big, and stowed it at the back of the cabin. Then he clambered in, and moved forward to the driving seat. Hickman and the corporal followed him, and sat in the next two seats. Then Ivy climbed up, and then me. We two took the next row back; I sat nearest to the space where the door should have been. Both the regulars turned back to look at us and talk, while Randall taxied out. The corporal shouted to me, 'When it's time for you to go, sir, I want you to squat on the door coaming with both your hands on the door frame, but with your fingers outside.'

'OK.'

'When I pat you on the shoulder, roll forward and dive out and down, pushing back hard with your hands. You've got to dive *down* to avoid the tail: if you hit it you'll break your back.'

'Thanks for that. What about the toggle?' In fact the pull was a hard leather handgrip on a piece of cable: I hadn't seen one like that before, which either meant that this was a museum piece, or something new undergoing test. I do so love the way the RAF cares for its people.

'Hold it between your teeth; grab it and pull as soon as you like, once you're outside the aircraft, sir, but don't leave it too late.'

'No. *I'd* thought of that as well.'

'The other thing you gotta know, sir, is that once you're in the exit position, I can't get you back into the aircraft. If you don't jump, I'll have to *kick* you out.'

I said, 'Thanks.' My voice sounded just a bit shaky.

He grinned, and showed all his front teeth. They were improbably white. Falsies. I still couldn't work out why he and his boss were looking back at us all the time, instead of ahead, where we were going. Randall gunned the motors and got us really rolling, cold air smashed into the cabin, and Ivy's skirt blew over her head.

I couldn't make out if her shrieks were of laughter, anger, embarrassment or fear. She had pale stockings, a white suspender belt and a lovely pair of pink knickers – so she looked like a girl on a roller-coaster ride at a funfair. Every time she pushed her skirt down again the slipstream took it out of her hands. Eventually she gave up, and scrunched it down around her hips, and finally I worked out what the noise was. Ivy was laughing: this was fun. I also worked out why the regulars had turned back to look at us – they'd pulled this trick on a girl before.

By the time we'd sorted ourselves out, Randall was airborne, and so were we. So far, so good. All I had to do now was get down in one piece.

Piece of cake. Trouser-filling piece of cake, but a piece of cake all the same. Randall seemed to take for ever to make height in lazy circles over Lydd, but eventually we were up there, and it was time to go. I was so cold I didn't care.

If you ask me now why I did it, I would have to answer that it was something to do with *the power of command*. It's what they teach NCOs. Once Hickman and his man had begun to boss me about, it never occurred to me to question what I was being told to do. It's all about the way an order is framed, and how it's delivered. Once you understand that, you'll understand how they convinced millions of Tommies in the First Lot to get up out of their trenches, walk on to the German machine guns and commit suicide — because suicide is what it was. *Power of command* has a lot to fucking answer for.

Let me tell you a bit about making a parachute jump. What it *isn't* is a gentle sailing down to earth under a silken canopy wafted on the zephyrs of a peaceful sky. It's actually a controlled bleeding fall. When I made my first jump in France I wasn't scared, because I didn't know what to expect. This time I *knew* what to expect, and the only reason I didn't shit myself on the way down was because my buttocks were clenched so tightly with fear you couldn't have got a whistle between them. I fell out of the Oxford without clouting it, screamed, and of course dropped the grab handle from my mouth. There followed a couple of nervy seconds with the pull drifting around in front of my face, and dodging out of the way each time I grabbed for it. Then it gave up and let me catch hold of it. I was upside-down when I pulled the 'chute. Then I screamed again, because the opening canopy wrenched both my arms from their sockets, and my man's favourite bits were pulled north to somewhere above my belly button. You'd scream too. Believe me, you would.

Oddly enough I touched down exactly as Hickman had shown me. Knees bent, and a single roll. It was just like jumping off a table. If the table was at five thousand feet, and moving forward at about 100 mph, that is. And I hadn't a fucking clue where I was, either.

*

63

I hit the deck on shingle, which, curiously, cushioned my fall, and between the largest and silliest concrete sculptures I had ever seen in my life. They were enormous. One must have been at least two hundred feet across and twenty feet high. It looked like one of those curved flat radar scanners you can see on the mast above the bridge of a warship. That was odd: *radar* was the first word to pop into my mind. Concrete radar? Bloody silly.

There were two others, both circular dishes angled slightly back from vertical – maybe twenty or thirty feet across. All three were grouped together, and faced across the Channel. Maybe they were new beam weapons focused on France; that thought cheered me up no end. I hadn't seen them until the last minute, and somehow I'd managed to avoid the lot. I leaned back in the small depression in the shingle that my arrival had caused, popped the parachute straps, and got my breath back. The khaki silk parachute immediately rolled away on an on-shore breeze which had sprung from somewhere, and wrapped itself around one of the dishes.

That's when a voice said, 'I'll have that if tha' don't want it.' An old man was sitting close to a line of scrubby gorse bushes, which is why I'd not seen him at first. One of his companions barked at me, and another *baa-ed*. A mangy collie dog and three sheep: a shepherd then.

'I think I've used it all I want,' I told him.

He was smoking a curved pipe, and looked a very contented old shepherd. Maybe he was so old that John Clare had once written a poem about him. I turned towards him, and felt inside my breast pocket to find out if my fall had broken my own straight briar.

It hadn't, and my new friend said, 'Tha' wants a fill?'

'I'll exchange one for the parachute. OK?'

He took his pipe from his mouth, and lit up his face with a huge toothless smile. I guessed it was going to be OK. Then

Randall flew over at about a hundred feet. Ivy waved at me through the missing cabin door, and then her face was lost under her skirt again. I knew exactly where the two instructors would be looking.

I asked the old fellow, 'Is there an airfield near here?' as I handed him back his tobacco pouch.

'Ten minutes. Over tha'.' He used his pipe to gesture over his shoulder. The red Oxford came round again. I was able to wave because my hands had stopped shaking. Ivy's skirt was still over her head. I could imagine her delighted shrieks.

My new friend scowled and said, 'Noisy beggars.' He wasn't wrong.

I sat with him for ten minutes before I moved. His dog came over and sniffed at me. I could see the fleas moving in its coat. Then it went over and lifted its leg against the base of one of the concrete dishes. I asked the old man, 'What the hell are these things?'

'They call them "The Listening Ears" these days, son. They wuz secret when they built them. They collect sounds from across the Channel and force them altogether like.'

'So you can hear people speaking in France?'

'No. Aeroplanes. So you could hear aeroplanes before you saw them. They were supposed to give an advance warning of an air attack.'

'Did they work?'

'Never in a month of Sundays.' He said all this with his pipe in his mouth, but removed it to give a great spit. 'Nothing ever bloody does any more, do it?'

He pulled down the chute and rolled the silk, the shrouds and the harness into a ball which can't have been much more than eighteen inches across: I got the feeling that he'd done this before. I recalled that the Yanks had flown Thunderbolts from near here after D-Day, and had dropped them all over the shop

. . . so maybe my shepherd had had some practice. The dog snarled at me as it followed him away.

I took my time walking in. The Oxford was already on the ground. Sergeant Hickman asked me to go back and get the parachute, and I told him I'd lost it. The corporal looked worried, and said he thought I'd have to pay for it. I observed that if I had to explain what had happened to the parachute, we all might have to explain what a girl was doing up in an aircraft chartered to the RAF, with her skirts around her ears. They got my unsubtle point. The corporal looked even more worried. The onshore puff had disappeared again; it was absolutely still.

Randall told us, 'I think your parachute got blown to shreds in the gale, Charlie. I guess you were lucky to get down.'

'You're right, Randall. I probably owe my deliverance to the fine training these two gentlemen have given me today.'

Ivy butted in and said, 'I don't understand what you're talking about.' Then she asked the sergeant, 'Can't I have the parachute, after all?'

At least he had the grace to blush until Randall rescued him with, 'No you can't, honey. It got lost. We'll catch you another time, OK?' and we all shook on it.

The corporal explained, 'You were supposed to land in the middle of the airfield, but everyone freezes the first time they jump, so we tell them early, count to five, and then shove them out. I touched your shoulder, shouted *Go!* . . . and you went straight away. That's never happened before. It's why you nearly ended up in the drink.'

'I wasn't going to let any bastard push me out of an aeroplane.'

Honours even, I supposed. I was an NCO myself once and liked the breed, so I didn't prolong the agony for them. They gave me an A Pass certificate for falling out of aircraft, and another for firing sub-machine guns in empty hangars, and I shook their hands and watched them go.

Ivy and I waited to wave Randall off. It was still early afternoon, and the sun had a couple of hours in it. I told Ivy about the Listening Ears, and she didn't believe me, so I had to walk her over to see them for herself.

I've often thought that big strange-shaped objects have a profoundly odd effect on young women. That's probably why most of the girls I've really fancied chose tall boyfriends instead. Ivy and I tried out the body-sized dip in the shingle where I'd arrived. I lifted her skirt for a slow and detailed reconnaissance, and thought I'd arrived all over again, but eventually she pushed me off and said she was saving herself for her wedding night. You can't argue with that, can you? I ached, but it didn't stop us laughing a lot, and walking back in the twilight arm in arm . . . which isn't too bad a way to end a day.

Lucy was inspecting the guard when we got back. I wondered what authority a Wren officer actually had over serving airmen, CO or not – but this lot were all national service heroes from grammar schools, so they wouldn't have known any better anyway. She had three of them in a line, and was giving them one of her evil little bawling-outs. We had to wait the other side of the compound gate until she dismissed one of them to open it. He grinned, and mouthed *old cow* as I drove past him. Lucy spotted Ivy, and waved me down – but she went to Ivy's side of the car.

Ivy beat her to the draw with, 'Mr Bassett passed me as I was walking in, ma'am. Offered me a lift.'

'That was kind of him.' Then she bent down, and looked across Ivy at me. 'How did it go, Bassett? Any problems?'

'No. Not once I got over the shock, ma'am. Parachute training.'

'Always comes in handy.'

'You've done it yourself, ma'am?'

'I'm not that damned stupid, Mr Bassett.' That was me told, wasn't it? She re-addressed herself to Ivy. 'You're off back to your factory in a couple of days, aren't you?' Ivy nodded in response. The CO continued, 'Would you mind doing the early shift this morning – two till six? One of the other operators has reported sick. I'll come on myself and relieve you for a break.' They'd be on their own: the rest of us would have our heads down. *Ho hum*, I thought.

Ivy looked down at her feet and nodded. Then she said, 'Yes; fine.' There was no *ma'am* – perhaps the civvies didn't have to – and no emotion in her voice, one way or the other. Ivy risked a glance at me. She knew I could have got her off the hook by volunteering for it myself. But I didn't, of course. We didn't speak as I drove the Singer into the black shadow of the blockhouse. She got out without a word.

I leaned across the passenger seat, and called her back, 'Ivy love . . .'

She turned and bent down; stuck her head back in the car. 'Yes?'

'Leave your knickers off tonight . . . it will save time.'

She slammed the door so hard she nearly turned the car over. We never spoke again, although it wasn't the last time I saw her.

Later I was having a smoke with Rob, in what they called the Off-Duty Ward Room. I casually asked him, 'Where will they work the early morning shift tonight? The two till six.'

'Number seven on the top floor: that's at the very end, under the slit window.'

'Any way I can watch the operator?'

'Sure, just turn up – I'll fix it for you.'

'. . . I meant without the operator knowing I was there?'

He frowned but didn't ask the obvious. He said, 'Sure,' again. Then, 'We can get into one of the curtained alcoves before they come on duty, stay there and leave after their shift ends. Who is it, a he or a she?'

I had noticed the *we*.

'A bit of both, I suspect.'

'Would it be worth my watching too?'

'Probably. But you'd better be able to keep your mouth shut afterwards.'

'Mum's the word.' He was closer than he bloody realized, wasn't he?

I know that you'll think that was pretty sneaky of us, but I excused it as a necessary extension of my education, and it *was*, too. If I'd been able to take photographs I'd have been able to make a fortune flogging them off to the blokes in my next barrack. As it was Ivy went back to her man with more skills than she'd arrived at Dungeness with, and small-arms drill wasn't the half of it. After an hour on stag (which means observation or guard duty for those of you who weren't around in the Fifties) and watching the action, I'd have given her a certificate myself.

Elaine phoned me a few days later. I was allowed two calls in, and two out each week, although they couldn't control who I called when I was outside. I made sure the boys got a couple of them. Dieter was dead keen on me working alongside a light-house, and made me promise to send him a postcard of it. He was thirteen now, I thought – we weren't exactly sure – and had talked a lot about ships and sailing recently. It might be just a phase he was going through, or he might be inclined towards a Navy career. I'd wait and see. Anyway, I told you; Elaine phoned me.

'Mr Halton just left. Someone told him you'll get a posting soon – and at least a week's leave before it. Will you be coming back?'

'Of course I will.'

'I've something to tell you.' My heart flipped over. Most of the other organs in my body did as well. It wasn't the first time she'd done this to me: I had been holding a telephone receiver to my ear in Germany when she told me she was pregnant the last time. She'd let me sweat for days before she let drop the fact that the new apple of her eye had been legitimately conceived in her marriage bed.

'What?'

'Terry's taken the Watford job.' Somewhere at the back of my mind the *All-Clear* sounded. Men can be bastards; you don't have to tell me.

'You mean you'll be seeing a lot more of him. That's a good thing, surely?'

'I'll also be seeing a bit less of you – when you come back, I mean. Or when you're on leave . . .'

'I understand; I won't make things awkward for you – don't worry about it.' I was making it as easy as possible for her to drop me again.

At first she didn't say anything, and then she sighed. It was a sigh as deep as the world's end. Then she said, 'Don't worry, I won't . . . but at least you could have had the manners to sound sorry about it!' Then she slammed the phone down. Oh, Charlie: another fence to mend! I thought about what she'd said about my posting: I'd got used to Old Man Halton knowing more about my life than I did, but it still teed me off.

I took a two-bob bit from my pocket and made Dolly heads, and June tails. June had a nice tail, if I thought about it. It came up heads, so I phoned Dolly. Dolly didn't answer: a man I didn't recognize picked up her phone, so I hung up before I pressed the button.

June did answer. Without preamble I asked, 'Could you get a few days off, and come down to the seaside with me? I have two young sons I didn't tell you about, and they want to meet you.'

'Who is this?' She knew, of course, but was just making a bloody point.

'Charlie. Charlie Bassett. We . . .'

'I remember you, Charlie.' Then she didn't speak for so long I thought I'd lost the line. I played 'Minnie the Moocher' in my head, and got to the second verse. Then she said, 'You've got a bloody nerve, Charlie!'

'I know. Part of my charm?'

Another pause; not so long this time. If it carried on like this, my two bob would run out without anything getting settled.

'Negative, Charlie; I should probably hang up.'

'You still can.'

'You took me for the most enjoyable meal in my life, romanced and bedded me, then didn't return my phone calls. Even your secretary told me to bugger off, as if I was a naughty schoolgirl. It's been at least a month.'

'She was probably being protective. I'm sorry.'

'She was protecting her own bloody patch!'

'Maybe that as well. Wait while I put another tanner in, then I'll have to be quick – it's all the change I have.'

After the coin dropped she asked, 'Where was it you wanted me to go again?'

'A small place on the coast, named Bosham. I have a prefab there alongside a pub owned by one of my best friends . . .'

'. . . and sons, you said?'

'I have two boys. I told them about you, and they asked me to bring you down.' That was stretching it a bit, I know, but all in a good cause. 'You'll have to be careful if you do come; they're always trying to marry me off.'

71

Another long pause; I began to worry about the money again. Her voice sounded different when she asked, 'When?' Lighter maybe, or interested . . . or had I imagined it?

'I'm not quite sure, but very soon. With a bit of luck I'll be up in London in a few days' time . . . to start my embarkation leave. I'll phone you as soon as I get in.'

This time I heard a smile in her voice, I'm sure of it, 'OK, Mr Bassett, but you'd better not fail this time. Last chance.'

'I won't need another.'

We both replaced the receivers at the same time. My hand was shaking. That was interesting.

Lucy asked to see me an hour later. When I walked into her office she had the brown envelope for me. I hoped I could dispense with the *ma'ams* at this stage. I also hoped I smiled.

'Arctic or Antarctic?'

'Neither. I thought they'd send you back to RAF Padgate, to teach you how to dress and drill again – you really are a bit of a shambles – but the signal here says you're off to RAF Abingdon, after a ten-day leave.' She handed it to me. Then she sat back in her chair and smiled a cat's smile. I wondered what nasty little time bombs she had written into my PR – my personal record. 'We never really got to know each other, did we? That's almost a pity; I thought you might be a bit of a challenge . . .'

I couldn't avoid the *ma'am* this time.

'I think I learned something from you, ma'am.'

She was looking down at that bloody file on her desk again. I had already been dismissed. Without looking up she asked, 'What was that, Charlie?' I liked the *Charlie*. It made what happened next even better.

'What it would be like to have a really nice black mole, ma'am; halfway between my belly button and, well . . . you know. Now I can imagine what it would look like.'

She looked up quickly. Her face was suddenly bloodless, and her mouth dropped open. It was a nice little mouth, but I'd seen far more of her than that when I'd watched her getting off with Ivy. Including the mole. I gave a smart salute even although I was still in my ragbag of uniform bits, about-turned and marched out.

Her secret was safe with me. Until I needed it, that is. Gross insubordination, strike one: nice one, Charlie.

Chapter Five

Goodbye, goodbye, I wish you all a last goodbye

That was Benatzky, wasn't it – the soldier's song from *White Horse Inn*? I don't know why, but it was the tune that popped into my head as I marched away from Lucy's office. I whistled it under my breath. Rob must have been earwigging outside, because he fell in beside me, whistling a full octave lower. We gave the room a demonstration of sharp synchronized marching and whistling until we reached the far end: my original drill instructor would have been proud of me. He would have liked it less when we collapsed with laughter, and had to prop each other up. I guessed, with what Rob had learned about Lucy, he'd be on easy street from now on. I was out of there by the afternoon.

Corporal Baxter was loitering beside my car when I slipped out into the cold. He took off a glove and held out his hand for a shake, which startled me.

'Good luck, sir.'

'Thank you, Mr Baxter. Good luck to you too.' A thought occurred to me – I'd never paid any attention to his flashes, and couldn't see them under his greatcoat now. I asked, 'Are you SP' – service police – 'or are you in the Regiment?'

'The former, sir, for the next forty-eight hours. Then the latter. I just got my posting – I've being trying to get in for two years.'

'Well done. So you're not here to arrest me for anything?'

'No sir; nothing like that.' Then he grinned and added, 'So you'd better go while the going's good.'

We shook hands again, rather awkwardly this time. He was only out there to say goodbye to me, though we hadn't exchanged over a dozen words since I'd arrived. People never fail to surprise me.

As I watched him dwindle in the car's rear-view mirror when I drove away from the bloody place, it began to snow.

At Lympne, an hour and a half later, I called Wing Commander Watson. He didn't sound all that sober: that was my kind of Watson again. I wanted to know what was at RAF Abingdon.

'Cyprus is, old boy. Good luck.' I wished people wouldn't keep saying that to me.

'Cyprus has come to Abingdon?' *Sir*; remember the *sir*, Charlie. You're back in blues.

'It's your *lift* to Cyprus. Transport Command. You can cadge a lift from the York Flight Specialist Unit there – they have those big polished shiny things: you like Yorks, don't you?'

As it happened I had a love–hate relationship with Avro Yorks. Halton Air had a big red nasty one, and it was always going tech on us. I doubt that we ever made a decent operating profit on her.

'Yes, sir; I'm familiar with the breed.' It was depressing how quickly the *sirs* came back to you.

'. . . not that you're in a hurry any more. Your ten days' leave just grew to seventeen.'

'Why's that, sir?'

'It's Christmas next week, you fool. It's impolite to invade a country at Christmas time.'

It must have been my time of life, because it seemed that everyone was putting down the phone on me. I hoped that the word *invade* had been a proper mistake, not just a slip of the tongue. Maybe we'd let the success of D-Day, eight years ago, go to our heads.

Elaine was standing at my office door with some papers in her hand. She'd got my job off to a T all right, but was dotting the i's and crossing the other things with a question here and there.

'Why didn't you tell me it was Christmas?' I asked her. 'I suppose I must have known, but I'd forgotten.'

'Your boys won't have.' Bugger it! Then she softened. 'There's a big new toy shop opened in Hastings: you can stop on the way through. And don't forget a new satchel for Dieter; he's worn out that army pack you gave him.'

'How did you know that?'

'He phones up every week when you're not here – checking up on you.'

I said it earlier, didn't I? People never fail to surprise me.

Flaming June was still in Halton's office – either working out her notice, or having had second thoughts about quitting. I rather hoped it was the latter. After she picked up the phone with a brisk 'Halton Transport', I said, 'I'm glad you're still there.'

She didn't ask who I was this time.

'I came to a new arrangement with Mr Halton. He agreed to let me buy a bigger size of uniform. I look less like a Shepherd's Bush tart now.'

'You never looked like one.'

'Have you ever been to Shepherd's Bush, Charlie?'

'No.'

'Then we can have this conversation again once you have. Did you want me or Mr Halton?'

'You.'

'Good – because he's away. He took the Auster up to Birmingham this morning. Something to do with meeting a car manufacturer, I think.'

'I just phoned to say that it was dumb of me to expect you to drop everything and come down to my place the weekend before Christmas. I'm sorry, I forgot.'

'It's fine. I've fixed up my Christmas already. Mum and Dad don't expect me until Christmas Eve.'

'Really?'

'Really. It's absolutely OK. How old are your boys by the way?'

'Thirteen, I think . . . and seven. Why?'

'Never you mind. You can meet me off the train at Chichester on Friday evening.'

Ah . . . an organizer. When I thought about it, I realized that an organizer was exactly what I needed. I wondered if she would stick though, or get tired of me like the rest of them.

'That was the new girl in the boss's office, wasn't it?' Elaine asked. 'I've spoken to her a couple of times this week. She seems to be pretty level-headed.'

'Are you trying to tell me something?'

'Me? No, I wouldn't dare.' A month ago she was in my bed; now I was pretty sure she was trying to fix me up with someone else. 'Fancy a cuppa?'

'Oh, all right.'

I don't know what I was so bad-tempered about. Maybe it was just the fact of change. Maybe I've never been so good when things change around me.

*

I phoned James's pub; the boys were just back from school. After a few minutes of this and that with Mrs Maggs, who actually ran my life and his without telling us, I got to speak with Dieter.

After a few more minutes of this and that – he always insisted on giving me progress reports for both of them – I said, 'Can you give Carlo a message for me?'

'You can speak to him yourself, if you like, Dad.' I think the fact that he and Carly both called me *Dad* now, as if it was the most natural thing in the world, may have swung it with the adoption people.

'In a minute, but I think you'll want to give him this message yourself. Tell him his dad's coming home for Christmas.' You never can tell with kids. I knew he was pleased, but Dieter had been a self-controlled type since I'd picked him up on a battlefield in Germany.

After a pause he asked, 'Can we still go to Mrs Maggs's party?'

'If I can come with you.'

'Of course you can, Dad. You know she loves you.'

That's another thing. Talking about love is something that's difficult for me. It took me a few seconds before I could answer, and a few more before the conversation returned to an even keel.

'Remember that girl I told you about?'

'The one who might have a bit of a temper?'

'That's right. She's coming down for a few days before Christmas. That OK?'

I stopped off at Hastings the next day, bought enough presents to fill a kitbag, and arrived at Chichester in time to pick the boys up from school again. It was a routine they quite liked. If we went into a shop afterwards, Carly would always make a point of holding my hand at some time. I didn't mind: it was his way of showing his classmates that he had a father too. He still wouldn't talk about his mother, Grace — a woman I'd known for about three years — or agree to see his grandparents. That was a pity because they were as rich as Crœsus, and his mother, although not much of a mother, was, in my eyes, a genuine heroine. He'd have to come to terms with both eventually. The next day was a Friday, and I drove back into Chichester again to meet the late London train. June tottered out of a Third Class carriage on big heels, and with a plain old trench coat thrown over her red office suit. She looked exotic, but cold.

The first thing she said after she kissed me was, 'Sorry, I didn't have time to change. I almost missed the train.'

'Don't be. You look fabulous.' I got another kiss for that. The next thing she said was, 'I have a suitcase and a box in the carriage. Can you help me?' I kissed her again. The train was waiting to go, and her compartment door was still open. The station master was bearing down on us looking station-masterful. I decided to keep the third kiss for later, and nodded to him. Thinking about it, my usual drive to get a woman's clothes off had been wholly superseded by the simple urge to just kiss her again, and carry on kissing her. That was interesting.

June took her suitcase. It was a small well-travelled leather affair with a bracing strap around it. I've always liked women who can make do with a small travelling case.

I almost buckled at the knees when I lifted the box down. It was about a yard cubed, and made of very heavy-duty cardboard — the like of which no one had seen since before the war started — and weighed a hundredweight. The name *Frank Hornby* was overprinted in a huge flowing signature on one side.

I know that a *hundredweight* as a measure of weight will be difficult for some of you — but don't go blaming me for your lack of a decent education. If you look in the front of your pocket diary, you'll find its equivalent set out in kilograms. My generation still doesn't like kilos, because they were the weight descriptors the Jerries used to grade the bombs they dropped on us. We still prefer the old Imperial measures we used for ours. The phrase *ten-thousand-pounder* still sounds like music to my ears, although I accept that a resident of Hamburg might have an entirely different opinion. Anyway, June's cardboard box was heavy enough for me to wave in a porter, and his trolley. It was the only way we could get it to the car without a crane.

'Strewth! What's in here?'

'Wait and see.'

I got number three then. Things were definitely looking up. The last woman to be this pleased to see me had been my mother, the time I came home on my first leave.

The barber's shop in East Street was still open as we drove past. June said, 'Stop a min. There's a love.'

I was, and I did. I can cope with quick decision making,

'What's up?'

'Go over there, and buy something for the weekend, will you?'

She was looking down, but smiling broadly at the same time.

'You mean . . . ?'

'I mean that being unprepared the first time was all very well, but one of the things I'm *not* going to do on Sunday is go back pregnant. Understand?'

I probably gaped, and I know I asked a stupid question. 'How many?'

She looked up at me, still smiling. 'I rather thought I'd leave that up to you.'

Sometimes you fall completely on your feet. The boys, Maggs and the Major liked her right off the shelf. On Saturday my friend Les drove down from Banstead to give her the once-over. It was beginning to look like a conspiracy to me. At the fag end of the war, Les, the Major and I had driven from an airfield in the

North of France, through Belgium and Holland and into Germany. That's where I found Dieter, and where Carly was dumped on me after his mother ran off. To be honest, Les did most of the driving, but he and James – the Major – and Maggs the Major's woman had been a club of three at the core of my life ever since. I suspect that the Major had phoned him and said enough about June to pique his interest. For one reason or another, my little gang was gathering around me.

You will want to know what was in June's cardboard box, of course, but if you're over fifty you won't have missed the clue I left you. The box contained the biggest O-gauge clockwork train set I had ever seen in my life. Three locomotives, with carriages, a dozen goods and guards wagons, a station and a signal box, and enough rails and scenery to fill the boys' bedroom several times over.

'My father's,' she explained. 'He was going to give them to a charity, I think, but when I told him about you and your boys, he insisted that I brought them down for Christmas.'

'They're wonderful.' We hadn't seen Carly or Dieter since they began to unpack them. 'I'm not going to be able to get them into bed before midnight at this rate. Your dad's family must have been very wealthy to have bought him a train set that size.'

'Not really. Grandfather was a country doctor. Dad's the same, but there's not as much money in it as before the war. If we're still going out, after you come back from wherever they're going to send you . . .'

'Cyprus to begin with . . .'

'If we're still going out, then Dad will want to meet you. We're still that kind of family I'm afraid.'

'Don't worry. So are mine, only I didn't realize it until today.'

This level of quick intimacy was all very odd. The strangest thing about it was how natural it all seemed. I felt as if I had known her all my life, not just for an evening and a night. June went to bed soon after the boys had agreed to retire. I wasn't too shy about where, because I've never hidden anything from them. After I joined her we lay for hours whispering before we made love.

Before we slept she told me, 'You have to take care of yourself this time, Charlie: you have to come back.'

'I always have before.'

'This is different. This time I am relying on you.' That was a thought, and I sensed a shadow in the background. She continued, 'I had someone before who didn't come back.'

'I'm sorry.'

'We say that so often about dead men that we don't mean it any longer.'

I showed her my back, because that either angered or hurt me; I couldn't make up my mind which.

She spoke again a few minutes later. I was dozing off, and was startled by the sound of her voice.

'He was out in Korea – in the Gloucesters.' The Gloucesters had covered themselves in glory, but maybe too many of them had been lost to have made it worthwhile. It's hard to explain, but in the 1950s I still didn't like talking about my war, and I wasn't all that interested in other people's. I knew, however, that I'd have to listen to this, or it would always lie between us.

'I'm sorry.' I rolled back towards her, and let her lift her head on to my shoulder.

'Killed or captured?'

'He was wounded, but afterwards some of the others saw the Chinese going around the trenches killing the badly wounded. Nobody actually saw him killed, but nobody saw him at all after that. I've spoken to people who knew him, and who got away. They say he's dead.' After a pause she asked, 'Did *you* lose people you were close to?' When I didn't answer immediately, she sniffed, and said, 'Sorry: stupid question.'

'No, it's all right. I lost a few. Most people did, didn't they?'

'Will you tell me one day?'

'Can we make do with a *maybe* for the time being?'

'OK. Do you want to . . . you know . . . again? I've quite woken up now.'

I had never wanted to kiss a woman more. So I did. What happened next seemed to do the trick because we slept soon after.

I've told you before that my prefab was built alongside James and Maggs's pub — and that the boys lived there with them when I was away. That morning Dieter slipped across to the pub, and came back with two plates of Maggs's 'death by fried breakfasts' — he served them to us in bed, then went into the kitchen to brew some tea.

June looked fabulous in the mornings — it was something I hadn't noticed the first time. She yawned, stretched. 'Is that a good sign? Do you think he likes me?'

'He's thirteen years old,' I told her. 'He wanted to see your tits.'

She pouted, but she was smiling. 'Sometimes, Charlie, you can be perfectly foul.'

'Best you learn that now, before you get stuck on me. Can I have your fried bread if you don't want it? It's no good once it gets cold.'

Had I said the wrong thing again already? I was only joking of course, but the upside-down smile slipped across her face, almost as if I had slapped her.

When I told her that I was falling in love with her, as I put her on the train on Sunday afternoon, it was as if I'd mentioned that I liked fish for supper on Fridays.

She just nodded, and said, 'Mmm.' And after a pause, 'I'll remember that.'

I suppose that I had asked for it. Both the boys had come to say goodbye to her. We left them in the car, and I walked her to the train. When I returned to the car Dieter piped up from the back seat.

'I don't know what you said to her yesterday, Dad, but this time you definitely blew it.'

'Where did you learn to talk like that?'

'From the Americans. *Superman* on the Saturday-morning pictures.'

This was a bit of a trial of strength so I tried embarrassment. 'Did you like her tits then?'

Dieter didn't buy embarrassment: he was thirteen going on thirty. I should have remembered that. 'Not as nice as Marilyn's.'

'Who's she?'

'Marilyn Monroe. She's another American. Martin's selling pictures of her at school. Hers are wonderful.'

I chanced glancing round to see his face before delivering some sort of rebuke . . . but was arrested by Carlo's instead. Carly hadn't said much as usual, but was looking out of the side screen with tears streaming down his face. I could see that I had some work to do.

I *coped* with Christmas; that's the best that can be said for it. I've never felt comfortable at Christmas time – old-fashioned guilt about an excess of pleasure, I expect.

I was best taking the boys for walks, flying kites and gliders with them on the strand, and serving in James's bar after they had gone to bed for the night. I've always felt strangely out of place sitting at a table groaning with food, with a paper crown on my head. At least we weren't going to run short of booze, and that got me by, although I should be ashamed to admit it.

I played with the boys and their new trains – the rails circled and crossed their room several times – but that only made me miserable. I was aware that I hadn't parted from June on the best of terms, and definitely hadn't appreciated the efforts she made to get to know the boys. Carlo understood that even better than Dieter, which is why he had cried. We made plans for our first holiday together after I returned, and then it was time to get into my Singer and face life's next great adventure.

'I loved the idea of the British Empire when I was a kid,' I had told Maggs one night before I left. 'In Sunday school they used to give us magic lantern shows of happy piccaninnies climbing palm trees, and throwing down coconuts to benevolent white masters in exchange for Christianity and a school uniform – barefoot, mind you. Now I know that all we did was steal other people's countries.'

'So did all the other Imperials. Spain, France, Germany, the Dutch . . . you name it. The Yanks and Reds are at it now, aren't they?'

'That's no excuse. What did we need an Empire for?'

Maggs blinked, and looked at me as if I was a bit thick. 'Money, of course, and soldiers to fight all those bleedin' wars against the other Empires.'

'My old man thinks that we've done enough wars, and set out to stop them last month. I thought he was crazy, but he's probably right as usual. I'll have to tell him so before I go.'

'Whatever you do, Charlie, don't talk like this once you get overseas. They'll think you're a Conchie an' lock you up.'

'I promise to take care, Maggs.' That's not the same thing, is it?

Three more days at Lympne. Elaine was more than capable by now – she probably had been from the very start – so I took the opportunity to give her a few days off: she'd get precious little leave once I was away. Then I overnighted with Les and his family in Banstead, on the way to Abingdon. I loved spending time with Les and Kate and their boys – and there always seemed to be another one each time I visited. I liked the way their family seemed to interlock with each other, and doubted that I'd ever be as good, no matter how hard I worked at it. We went down to Les's local after supper, and talked about it.

'Being a dad is like swimming,' Les told me. 'All the time you worry about it, you can't do it properly. Then you wake up one morning, and the first thing you think about is yer wife an' kids . . . an' all of a sudden you're good at it. It's suddenly like you've been doing it all yer life.'

'How does it work?'

'I don't know. It's a mystery.'

'I say the wrong things all the time: to the boys, to my girlfriends – even to friends like you.'

'You're much better than you were.'

'Thanks. You think so?'

'Yeah; you're more than halfway there. All you need is a decent woman to complete the picture. Was that June any good?' Les would have been an ace interrogator: he always slipped in the crucial question before you saw it coming.

'I'm in love with her, I think. She fits me like a glove.'

'Told 'er so?'

'Yes.'

'What d'she say? . . . This is like drawing teeth, Charlie.'

'Nothing much. I think she was already pissed off with me by then.'

'See 'er before you go. After all, you got nothin' to lose.'

Straight for the bleeding jugular. Don't worry about the pun.

I took a chance and drove out to Halton Transport's office and shed, at Heathrow's Cargo Side. Everything was fogged in and there was no flying. The warehouse was shut down; no one was there. Except June, that is. She looked neither pleased nor displeased to see me. Unmoved.

I asked, 'What are you doing here?'

'I came in to check the mail – I live nearer than anyone else – and maybe type up the delivery chits for the start of the year.' She sounded as happy as an undertaker when the doctors announce a miracle cure, but I was determined to try.

'I'm sorry I sounded less than enthusiastic about you when we were in bed that morning. I was just trying to be funny, that was all.'

'I worked that out eventually.'

'I think you're fantastic; the best.'

'You could have told me that, couldn't you?'

'Yes, but you didn't try to contact me either.'

'*Your* job.'

'I didn't have your parents' telephone number.'

'I worked that out eventually . . . as well.'

This was like a duel.

'Will saying *sorry*, and asking if we can start again, work?'

'I doubt it. I've never done that before.'

Most of the other unforgiving people I'd met before had been NCOs with parade-ground manners.

'Look, I'm sorry I upset you. It wasn't my intention.' That sounded stilted, even to me. 'I didn't mean to. Sometimes I'm clumsy with words. Now it's your turn.'

'I'm glad you're sorry. I'm glad it wasn't your intention, and I'm sorry that you're clumsy with words.' That was it. Somewhere along the line I'd ended up with the losing cards again. If this was Thermopylae, I was one of the six hundred Spartans waiting for the sword. I didn't know what to say next because she was being too guarded to get close to.

I asked her, 'Can you drive?'

'Pardon?' At least that got a reaction.

'Can you drive a car?'

'Yes, of course. Daddy taught me.'

'But you don't have one?'

'No. Where's this leading us, Charlie?'

'I can't take my car to Cyprus, can I? If I leave it with you, you can have the use of it. I'll get the insurance switched over, and it's been taxed for a year.'

'Why?'

'I'd like to think of you driving it while I'm away.'

'Try again. Another reason?'

'Sitting unused for a year will do it no good at all.'

'Better. Will you be away for a whole year then?'

'I have no way of knowing. I'm the last person they'll tell.' At least that pulled a small grin from her. 'So, will you look after my car for me?'

She thought for a few seconds. She looked just as desirable in town-and-country civvies as in her Halton outfit, but this definitely wasn't the time to say it. She had a flat brown spot, like a large freckle, in the small of her back, but this wasn't the time to remember it, either.

Then she said, 'Yes; you can leave your car with me. But it doesn't mean anything.'

My turn to think. I ran the first few bars of Cole's 'Ev'ry time we say goodbye' in my head. It seemed appropriate at the time.

Then I said, 'OK, I'll show you how to start her. She can be a bit of a bitch – sorry – in cold weather. Then you can run me to the station.'

What I couldn't understand – even if I had been less than sensitive a few days earlier – is why she shied away from me so absolutely now. I was Charlie Bassett, not Albert Pierrepoint, the government's hangman. I looked into her eyes, and there was nothing there for me at all. I wanted to shout, *What was it, exactly, that I did so wrong?* But all I could think was that I'd let Carlo down. That was interesting.

She continued to look steadily at me from behind her desk. There was something else going on here that I didn't understand: like a conversation that I wasn't a part of. She held a brown card, and was turning it around in her hands as if she could read the words on it by touch. Braille.

She suddenly said, 'I'm not being deliberately cruel to you, Charlie; and whatever you think, I'm not getting my own back.' When someone says that, they bloody well are, aren't they? You can be sure of it.

'No?'

'No.' Then she sighed, and handed me the card. 'You'd better read this. It was waiting for me at home when I got back.'

Her family address was on one side, and the other was headed up with those friendly old words *The War Office*. Maybe she was being called up as well. No. It was a simple pre-printed postcard which told her that the International Red Cross had informed the Minister of the identity of a certain corporal from the Gloucesters presently in a prison camp in North Korea. He was slowly recovering from wounds, and his repatriation was being negotiated.

It took a few seconds for the penny to drop, 'This was the man you told me about?'

'Yes. Anthony; he's a good person.' Being a good person trumped being a Charlie, I suppose. What do you say? I was too gutted to react with anything except the truth.

'Good. I'm pleased for you.' Then I offered, '. . . but a little sad for me.'

She smiled a sad brief smile which matched my words, I guess.

'That was a nice thing to say. What about your car now?'

'The offer still stands. I've nothing else to do with it, if that's all right?'

'OK. Until you get back.'

'Why don't we go down to the station now? We can talk in the car.' I just wanted to get away.

I think we had made peace, but now I was left standing on a railway platform in my old flying jacket, propping up a kitbag containing nearly all I owned, while she drove away in my lovely old car. I felt like a sucker. Why was everyone else better at this sort of thing than me? The train to Abingdon was freezing, and zigzagged all over Oxfordshire before it found it. I turned up at the RAF station guardhouse at nightfall, tired and dispirited. Even a posting to the Arctic Circle would have been a better idea than this.

The guard commander was an elderly flight lieutenant. We called them 'French Letters' when I had been a sergeant, but I was too weary to be disrespectful – that's how they get the discipline to you eventually. I put my heels together, pulled in my stomach and reported, thinking but not saying, *Sieg Heil*!

He looked vaguely amused, and said, 'Wait a mo'. I think you'll find you're booked into the guest quarter.' He went back inside, and came out with a thin, grey, card-covered file with my name, rank and number on it. If we were waging our wars with files and paperclips these days it was OK by me.

'I haven't had a fresh uniform issue yet. I'm a bit short of kit,' I explained. Understatement of the bloody week.

'I think you'll find there are several large boxes up in your room already. I remember them arriving yesterday: someone will have organized them for you. Anything else you need you can get from the Stores Officer in the morning, OK? And welcome back, by the way.' When I didn't respond immediately he asked, 'Do you want me to organize a lift up to the Mess, chum? You look just about all in.'

He was so far from what I'd expected that I nearly cried.

Chapter Six

Jack o' Diamonds

The guest block wasn't big. From the outside it looked like a larger version of the brick air-raid shelters they built in some school playgrounds in 1939, but with windows. A long, low, narrow affair, but there were double doors at each end, like an airlock — so the first thing you noticed was that it was warm, and it smelled of fresh paint. One corridor, six rooms on either side, followed by a large washroom and toilet area on either side, followed by another twelve bedrooms. You didn't need to be a mathematical genius to work out that they could accommodate twenty-four officers. Each residential room door had a paper-card nameplate on it. I wandered along until I found my name neatly typed: Bassett C DFM, 22602108, Pilot Officer. Leaving the door open I dumped my kitbag alongside the narrow bed, and stretched out for a moment. I could hear music playing from a radio at the other end of the corridor. Fuck it, I was back!

When I opened my eyes it was dark. Someone knocked on the open door again, and then switched on the light. I rolled away from it, and then sat up, shielding my eyes. A small dark-haired WRAF stood at my door with a tray. She had a plate of sandwiches, and a steaming mug of something.

'Aircraftwoman Lorenzo, sir. I let you sleep, but you missed the evening meal. I took the liberty of having these made up for you. Aircraftwoman Francis and I look after these quarters. If you want anything there's a bell above your desk.' There was, too – a small electric bell push on the wall, above a desk just about big enough to write a letter on. She put the tray on it.

I ran my hands through my hair and said, 'Thank you,' then asked awkwardly, 'What am I supposed to call you? I've been away a long time.'

'Lorenzo will be fine, sir, or Aircraftwoman . . . but sometimes that's a bit of a mouthful.'

'I'm Charlie.' I helped myself to a sandwich, suddenly starving hungry. The mug smelled like strong tea.

'You're Pilot Officer, or Mr, Bassett, sir.'

I smiled and shrugged. 'Suit yourself. Do you have a first name, Lorenzo?'

Silence, then, 'Amanda . . . Mandy.' She could smile politely when she wanted to.

'Well, thank you for the sandwiches and tea, Lorenzo. They're going to save my life.' Cheese and tomato, and corned beef and tomato – Officers' Mess style: no crusts.

'Hardly, sir. Have you anything in the kitbag that needs washing?'

'Most of it, probably.'

'I'll take it with me; if you have time to try on your new issue tonight, I'll get the alterations you need done before you leave. You'll know that your flight was put back, and you are booked in here for four days. They'll want you to sign in to the Mess.'

'No ruddy fear. I won't go near the place. I never asked to be an officer in the first place. I still think it was a joke that they played on someone else.' She laughed. A little whinnying sound. 'We can look at the clothes in the morning, if you like.'

'Fine, sir. It's our job to see that you're properly turned out, if you understand?'

'You mean that you get a bollocking if I look a shambles?' I remembered Lucy's description of me.

'I might, sir.'

'I'd better pull my socks up then.'

I still had that Communist Party card in my pocket. It was mine, although it wasn't in my real name. I wondered how many other Commies had a servant as pretty as mine. I read a Nigel Balchin novel for a couple of hours: his hero was an awkward cuss like me. Then I slept until breakfast, to be awoken by Lorenzo with a cup of tea. Someone must have spirited the tray of empties away during the night, but I hadn't heard a thing. It was a brand-new world.

Even the bath and shower rooms were centrally heated. After I washed, I opened my hanging cupboard, and couldn't believe what I was looking at. I actually counted the clothes, like a schoolboy counting up his collection of Dinky Toys: formal mess kit, a full set of walking-out blues, two working blues and a greatcoat . . . and everything to go with them. Shoes, and boots (flying) . . . and two sets of KDs, including shorts that fell below my knees. I'd need a lorry to move my bloody wardrobe around with.

'What will they expect me to wear today?' I asked Lorenzo.

'A working set; just like when you were a sergeant. It hasn't changed that much.'

It hadn't taken her long to find that out. 'Both jackets will need to be taken in, and the greatcoat's too long. I'll get them done.'

'I tried on the shorts – I look like something from a *Beau Geste* film. Could you get someone to turn them up an inch or two?'

'Yes, but not too much. You won't want your new station commander getting upset. Have you had any breakfast yet, sir?'

'No.' I didn't meet her eye.

'Why don't you come along to the galley? Frances and I usually have a fry-up and a smoke around this time, after we've got our officers away . . . unless the SAC is around.'

'Frances?'

'Aircraftwoman Francis, sir. Frances Francis. She still can't work out if that's amusing or cruel.'

'Lead on Macduff.'

As I followed her trim figure along the corridor to a small kitchen, she looked back over her shoulder and asked me, 'Did you know that's a common misquotation, sir?'

'I don't even know where it comes from.'

'*Macbeth*. It's actually "lay on, Macduff" . . .'

'Is that important?'

'It *was* to Macbeth. It was the last thing he said before Macduff killed him!' Then we were at the galley. The woman already sitting in it was plain and lanky. She had a wide mouth and a great embarrassed smile, and tried to get up.

Lorenzo pushed her back into her chair, saying, 'Frances this is Charlie.' To me she said, 'This is *our* place. You can be Charlie here if you like, but not outside.'

Bacon sarnies, of course: the service ran on them. Fresh doorsteps of bread, a bucket of butter, and bacon salty enough to preserve your tongue while it was still wriggling. On the radio they played a record of Billie Holiday singing along to Lester Young with the Count Basie Orchestra. Time rolled back: I remembered the RAF girls I had known at Bawne during the war, and wondered if I would do better with women if I simply kept to my own kind. Within minutes I felt at home, relaxed and happy.

What had I told Elaine weeks ago? *I could cope with that.*

*

I couldn't get away with it for ever.

'Mr Bassett, is it?' This was after a rap on my door. A rather neat but otherwise unmemorable warrant officer stood there. I was lying on my bed reading a rather horny Hank Janson paperback I'd filched from one of the empty rooms. I stood up — reluctantly.

'Yes, WO. Can I help you?'

'Thought it might be the other way round, sir. I'm the SWO. New arrivals usually look me up for a bit of a brief.' Ah. He'd called me *sir*, but it was obvious which of us was really in command, and it wasn't me. In his heart, even the commanding officer of a RAF station knows that the station warrant officer is the person really in charge.

'I didn't think it worth it, WO. I expected to ship out today.'

'But you're stuck here for a few days instead — I take it that someone's told you? Mind if I come in and sit down, sir?'

'Help yourself.' He shut the door behind him, and sat at the desk. I sat on the bed and picked up my pipe. I said, 'Smoke, if you like.'

'Thank you, sir.' It got us through the next minute. He offered me a fag from a packet of Black Cat, but I shook my head and lit my pipe. 'Will you be going off-station, sir?'

'No. I saw Abingdon from the taxi I took from the railway station. I didn't like any of it.'

'Don't be like that, sir. The older part is quite picturesque: historic. So you won't want a brief on which bars to avoid, and which are definitely out of bounds?'

'No. Thank you.'

'. . . and you haven't signed in with P2, or visited the Mess either?' *Ah* again: so that was it. Someone from Admin had sent him to see what I was up to. P2 was the pay and admin branch . . . I'd thought that signing on here would have been the equivalent of opening a new bank account for less than a week. What the hell for?

'Has someone said something about me?'

'The PMC's staff mentioned something. If you haven't been issued with your Mess number yet they can't account for your keep. I know that it seems inconsequential, but little things like that keep the cogs turning. Why don't you wander over with me now, and I'll show you what's where.' And the next most important person on a RAF station is the President of the Mess Committee.

I couldn't help smiling, 'You're bloody well telling me to, aren't you, WO?'

'Pierce, sir. SWO Pierce . . . and no, I would never presume, sir.'

Two things had changed since my Bawne and Tempsford days. The WOs had been taught exquisite manners, and they could use words as long as *inconsequential*. I wasn't sure I liked it. Ten years earlier a flight lieutenant would have probably battered his way in and pinned me to the wall with righteous blasphemy, but at least then you knew where you were.

I pulled on my greatcoat and my fore-and-after, and followed him into the cold light of day . . . and for once that phrase is factually accurate. As we walked up to the Admin Block and Mess Building, behind its curved approach road, I tried to make conversation.

'When did you get concrete runways? This was all grass when I was in training.'

'Did you fly from here then, sir?'

'No, but I flew over it a few times.'

'I believe they started to put the concrete down in 1944, sir. It was an OTU, and a Gunnery School. Then the Parachute School came along of course.'

That reminded me of the jump I'd just done. I didn't thank him for that.

He left me in an office that reminded me of a bank. Decent counter, desks, a mixture of uniforms and civvies, and an overall air of quiet efficiency. I had to ask myself, with staff as calm, courteous and obviously as bright as these, why the Brass had made the god-awful decisions that littered my service history. A keen civvy type produced a file of papers, each marked with pencilled Xs where he wanted my signature. Dozens of the bloody things.

He smiled and observed, 'You can read them if you like, sir, but no one else does.'

'What are they?'

'Bumf – what else? But with them you promise to repay anything over the odds we spend on you, and you're indemnifying the Crown if you happen to kill yourself while you're here.'

'Thanks for that!'

'My pleasure, sir. We aim to please.' I glanced around; several of the men and women were smiling as they earwigged the chat. They seemed a cheerful bunch.

'Frightful, isn't it?' This was from a man who had moved up behind me so silently I hadn't heard him. When I turned it was the officer of the watch from the night before. He yawned, apologized for it, and held out a hand for the ritual touch. 'Alec Holden.'

'Charlie Bassett. You passed me in last night.'

'I know. Not my usual spot, but I was filling in for some bod on leave. I like to do that now and again – get to know more people. You're a reservist, right – recalled for Queen and Country? We've seen a few of you lately.'

'I wasn't all that keen to return, to tell the truth, sir.'

'Don't blame you son; nor am I. I even hate coming back from leave these days. I sometimes think it was more fun when Jerry was shooting at us.' *You were younger then*, I thought. I had kept my pipe in my hand throughout the ceremony of the hundred signatures. He asked, 'Pipe man?' I nodded. 'Why don't we sit outside in the sun, and have a jaw?'

He had magically produced a pipe of his own from somewhere – a stained, curved meerschaum. What I know now, but didn't know then, was that you don't *own* a meerschaum pipe; you have a love affair with it. Despite what today's tobacco Nazis tell you, the Brotherhood of the Pipe was once a great leveller; our inclusive modern society started with it.

We sat on a bench in the garden, and smoked in the sun, which had just enough warmth in it. I was twenty-eight years old, and felt about eighteen. I smoked my Wills Sweet Chestnut, whilst he packed his with Erinmore – that brand was a little hot for me.

He asked, 'When were you commissioned, Charlie?'

'In 1945. I was in hospital after a crash at Tempsford in the last few months. I'd flown as a sergeant.'

He was too canny to ask about Tempsford or the crash. 'So you've been an officer for about eight years now?'

'That's exactly the point: I don't see it that way. I've only been an officer for three days actually. Before I was demobbed they posted me away for six months – to the place that became GCHQ. It was very informal: most of the time it wasn't like being in the services at all. No real officering there.'

'Under David Watson, was that?' Full of surprises, Mr Holden.

'Do you know him, sir? I saw him a couple of months ago.'

'Went to school together. *Frightful* chap.' But it was the way he said the word: there was a lot of affection in it. I chose not to tell him about haring across France and Germany behind our armies' advance in 1945, and my year of wandering around Europe after that. Now I suspect he knew all about it. 'How do you manage to calculate your officer service to just three days?'

'I spent my first night in an Officers' Mess at Waddington in 1947,' I told him. 'I was on a weather flight that was delayed a day – because of the weather.' That made him smile. 'Then in 1948 I spent another night, after I had been discharged; but at Bawne that time – it was under Care and Maintenance; we were the only bods there. The third day was yesterday.'

He grunted, and asked, 'So what's the trouble then?'

I suppose that I had to tell someone, so I ground it out slowly – a bit ashamed of myself, and looking down at the gravel path in front of us.

'I . . . don't . . . know . . . how to behave. I don't know what's expected of me. I don't know the little signs and code words that let me into officers' company without sounding like a prat.'

He tamped down his pipe, because he'd let it out, then relit it from a box of Swan Vestas, which he then offered to me. I copied him.

'That's all there is to it,' he told me. 'Just copy everybody else. Why don't you let me show you round the place. You can see how it works. There's just time before lunch.'

'Very kind of you, sir, but I'm supposed to contact someone from the Mess Committee, and get *that* sorted out.'

'Which is what you're doing at this moment, old fellow. That's me. I'm supposed to support the PMC in my spare time.'

'Just exactly what do you do around here, sir?'

He waved his pipe around. 'Masses of stuff, old chap: masses of stuff. Shall we go? It's a nice walk when the weather's with you.'

*

I don't know how long the RAF takes to make an officer these days. Months and months probably . . . if not years, and that's after they've earned fifteen Honours Degrees at some obscure university near Huddersfield. Alec Holden did a pretty thorough job on me in just four days, by the end of which that phrase came back to me again: *I can cope with this*. A few months later I bought him a great curved meerschaum from a side-street bazaar in Port Said: it was carved with the face of a grinning camel. I parcelled it up with printed silk scarves for Mandy and Frances, and sent it back to Abingdon for them on a homing flight. That was because the most improbable people can change your life.

I was at Abingdon for five nights, and left on the sixth day. On the last evening I put on civvies and joined Lorenzo, Francis and WO Pierce – also all in civvies – for an impromptu going-away bash. We sloped down to a pub named the Prince of Wales: they called it the Three Feathers. You work it out. I suspected that non-commissioned ranks getting rat-arsed with an officer probably broke one of Pierce's rules, but he didn't let on. A bunch of my new officer pals stood in one corner and pointedly ignored us. Then they tried to chat up the girls after we were all turfed out at closing time. Some things never change, do they?

There was a big shiny York parked near the Watch Office when I walked out the next morning. Even with my old flying jacket over my new duds I felt cold. My fellow passengers milling around it all wore more rings than a gypsy fortune teller: I was moving – literally – in exalted company. I should have guessed, of course. The SWO intercepted me before I was close enough for any of the gods of the RAF to turn and look at me.

'Not that one, I'm afraid, sir. Your original transport's been requisitioned by the top brass. Your new aircraft is now over the

far side – I've organized a crew bus for you. Over there.'
Everything must have been done in a hurry, because the crew
bus still had cobwebs in it; an old Commer that hadn't been used
for months. It was cold inside, and its engine rattled: I doubted
it would get us to the other side of the airfield. The AC driver
was one of those cheeky chappies it's impossible to like: he
whistled as he drove – pitch-perfect. It was just a pity that the
tune was the Sailors' Hymn about those in peril on the sea. There
was one other passenger; a flying officer a bit older than me. He
was wrapped in his greatcoat but still shivering. We touched
gloved hands – not a real shake.

'Charlie Bassett.'

'Hector . . . Heck. The rest is Macdonaldsmith, I'm afraid.'

'Hyphenated?'

' 'fraid not.'

'You poor beggar. How do you ever fit it in when you get a
place on a form which says "*Your full name*"?'

'I don't. I write M apostrophe Smith. Everyone who reads it
then thinks I'm stuck up, and hates me instinctively.'

I think he'd been laughing in between the words since the
conversation had begun. A comedian, obviously. With a handle
that long you'd have to be.

'I'm glad of your company,' I told him.

'. . . and I of yours. There's another dozen on the transport,
and I understand they're not Pongoes, thank God.' Pongoes were
the Senior Service – sailors – and notoriously delicate air
passengers. So we had aircraftmen or Brown Jobs. He could have
meant either.

'Seeing as the Air Board's nicked our aeroplane, do you know
what type we've been bumped on to?'

'I do, Charlie, but I'll leave it to be a surprise.' He looked
away from me, out of the side screen, and smiled. I glanced at

the passenger-side door mirror. We were leaving a trail of black smoke you could see a mile away – I was surprised the fire tenders hadn't been scrambled to us. The erk still whistled.

'Oh for God's sake shut it!' I told him irritably.

'Sorry, sir.'

I regretted that immediately, 'No, carry on – it's not your fault . . .'

'Don't worry, sir. You'll love the *Jack o' Diamonds* – she h'ain't let us down yet. Never.'

The *Jack o' Diamonds* came into sight seconds later. It was squatting close to the ground in front of one of the old blast pens. If ever an aircraft looked as if it was taking a shit, this type did. Her fat belly looked as if it was scraping the floor. She was silver in colour, but that was where the similarity to my stolen ride ended. The York I'd been promised was silver because her metal surfaces had been lovingly polished. *Jack o' Diamonds* was silver because her fabric had been painted silver. Yes, that's right – *fabric*. She was an old Wellington bomber converted to the transport role. She had our nice new RAF three-ring roundels, a large black letter J on her flanks, and a neat picture of the Jack of Diamonds playing card under the sliding clear screen beside the pilot.

One of the things I've never told you before is that I'd flown a dozen training trips in Wimpies – that's what we called them – from my OTU before I was posted to a squadron. I didn't tell you because I wanted to forget them. I wanted to forget them because every time I had flown in a Wellington I had been violently sick. I leaned towards M'smith and whispered, 'I feel sick.'

'I know what you mean. We're certainly going to be.'

Oh well, at least he'd been around the block a few times.

Wellington bombers are not like other aircraft. They are not made of nice metal sheets riveted onto a nice firm metal frame.

They are made of a metal latticework of narrow spars and tubes stitched together in diamond shapes, like a lace doily, and then covered in painted canvas. In flight the whole fuselage – which is where we had to sit – flexed. It flexed from side to side, end to end, and up and down. And the wings flapped like a pregnant bird. Some people, I'm told, learned to love the Wimpy. I never actually met one. Bollocks.

After we had stepped down from the Commer, it made a turn but only managed about a hundred yards, trailing thicker clouds of black smoke, before the engine gave way with an enormous crash and a clatter. I should have felt sorry for Whistling Rufus, but I wasn't.

There was a small mob of aircraftmen being contained by a patient SAC close to *Jack*'s fuselage door. They were all dressed for travelling. Our fellow passengers looked young and excited. National service types I guessed. I wondered if any of them had flown before, and if they knew what they were letting themselves in for. The SAC said in a voice loud enough to echo among the dreaming spires miles away, 'The officers are 'ere, lads; let 'em through, let 'em through. Mind outta the way. Now we can get off.' After a rather smart salute, he asked us, 'Where would you care to sit, sir?'

I told him, 'Up the front. As near to the main spar as is humanly possible.'

'It can be a little noisy up there, sir. Between the engines.'

I wasn't going to be taken in. 'We'll take a chance on it, OK?'

'Ridden the Wimpy before, 'ave you, sir?' I liked the way he said *ridden*; as if the Wellington was something you mastered, like a bucking bronco, rather than something you rode in.

'A few times; a few years ago.'

I might have been mistaken but maybe the ghost of a smile crossed his face for a second. 'Very good, sir. If you'd care to mount up now, I'll get the men loaded after you.' There it was again: *mount up*. Maybe the SAC knew Wimpies even better than I did. No looking back now. As I climbed up into the belly of the beast I asked M'smith behind me,

'Any idea where they're taking our original transport?'

'Yes; Stanstead, apparently.'

'Stanstead?'

'Yes.'

'That can't be more than thirty miles away.'

'That's right.'

'You mean that because the gaffers have to get to somewhere they can see even before they've taken off, we have to fly halfway round the world in a twenty-year-old aircraft made from hair-nets, pipe-cleaners and brown paper?'

'That's right. Ain't peace wonderful?' If he saw the funny side of everything, he could probably get on your nerves.

The SAC got his mob seated, in equal numbers on bench-type seats on either side of the aircraft. The kitbags were stowed neatly beyond them, nearer the tail. His briefing was about as far away from the flight-safety briefing you get from a bored stewardess today as it was possible to get.

'Listen up, lads, and pipe down. These are the things you need to know. The small box on the fuselage by the hatch you came in is full of brown paper bags and pieces of string. They are paper bags, airsickness for the use of. Once you have used them, and you *will* use them, tie them off with the string and place them beneath your seats. The reason you will be sick is that you have the honour to be riding in a Wellington bomber, and a Welling-ton bomber is not a fixed platform like other aircraft. If you look to the rear when we are in flight you will gain the impression that the fuselage is moving independently up and down, and from side to side. Your impression will be correct, and when you dwell on that fact, and you *will* dwell on that fact, you will be airsick. There is an Elsan for other forms of bodily evacuation the other side of your kit. You can begin to use it once we reach our operating height, OK?' He looked around his charges and was met with a few nods. A couple of them looked distinctly white around the gills already. 'Now . . . settle down and buckle your lap belts.'

One of the aircraftmen held his hand up like a child in a classroom.

'Yes, lad?'

'What do we do if we land on the sea, SAC?'

'Wellingtons do not land on the sea, lad; they *crash* into the sea.'

'I can't swim, SAC.'

'Then you will drown, lad. Just try to do it quietly.'

He took the seat next to mine. 'If you don't mind, sir?'

'Not at all, chum. That was a smashing brief: I wish I'd written it down.'

'All in the book, sir, providing you knows where to look. And if you wouldn't mind . . . the lap belts as well, sirs. I need you to set the boys a good example.'

M'smith met my eye. We both grinned and complied. A green light came on over the bulkhead door between us and the flight crew. *Jack o'Diamonds'* twin engines coughed asthmatically, one after the other. I could see the props through a long window in front of me – the latticework of the construction made it like seeing them through diamond-shaped Tudor glass window panes. The props dissolved into round shields shimmering in the air, and she began to move. The two-striper had been right: the noise was tremendous.

He winked at me, and produced a ball of cotton wool from his battledress pocket – then he handed us enough to fashion ear plugs for ourselves. The pilot opened the taps, and *Jack* made her bid for the air. I think we came off sideways. Just like old times.

At just about ten thousand feet *Jack* gave up; leastwise, that's what it felt like. After a lurch we stopped climbing and levelled out. I know the height because there was an altimeter on the bulkhead alongside the crew door. The pilot then went into cruise mode and the noise level dropped. I removed my plugs, but kept them. M'smith and the section leader did the same. The first sprog lurched towards the paper bags.

'What's your name?' I asked the SAC.

'Bates, sir, and I've heard all the jokes. The teachers used to love my name when I was a nipper.'

'Where have you been posted, Mr Bates?'

'Abingdon, sir; I'm just along for the ride. I have to deliver this lot to Valletta. Then I go back.'

'Malta?'

'That's right, sir. Luqa via Munich: a couple of long hops.'

'I thought I was going to Egypt.'

'You are, sir, but you're not in a particular hurry, are you?'

'No. Why?'

'I think you'll find you're routed Munich, Luqa and on to Cyprus. We have a service airfield near Limassol. That'll take you the best part of three days. Cyprus will send you on; they have cruises to the Holy Land and the Land of the Pharaohs every week, on Thursdays. In fact you may not get into Suez for a week, so I hope you brought something to read, sir.' He had a bit of a wicked grin. Three of his blokes were clutching bags now.

'Why are we taking such a roundabout route?'

'Mountains, sir. This old bitch — begging your pardon, sir — can't fly over them, and the cabin's not rigged for oxygen anyway. We have to go round.'

'I could have worked that out for myself, couldn't I?'

M'smith was sitting facing me. He said, 'Don't worry: it'll all come back. Coffee?' He opened a decent-size pack he'd lodged between his feet. It was khaki so he'd probably nicked it from the Brown Jobs. I spotted at least three thermoses among all the greaseproof packages. He must once have been a Boy Scout.

Munich was under civilian command again and, as airfields go, it looked pretty smart. They'd even had time to cut the grass and dig flower beds. Or maybe they'd just left the old ones there because, as we banked in the circuit over the end of the main runway, eight empty flower beds came magically together in a large dark swastika. The bastards never learn.

We'd flown six hundred and fifty miles in just over four and a half hours: not bad for the old Wimpy, I guessed. I wanted to stretch my legs and get some air, but there wasn't much time. We taxied straight up to a refuelling bay, and started topping up. There was a misty bitter rain in the air, so it didn't feel much warmer than England. I stood in the open door and looked north. Somewhere up there, near Frankfurt, I owned a big house that was rented out to the Americans. I hoped they were taking good care of it. I had acquired the place and a couple of neighbouring farms in a shady but fundamentally legal deal at the end of the war. It was amusing to think that I owned somewhere in Germany before I did in England.

Most of the lads took the opportunity to piss in the grass before we fuelled up. The Fraus driving the fuel bowser cracked up over it, pointed out the best specimens, and began cat-calling. The boys didn't mind: most of them would have promised their dads and elder brothers to piss all over Germany if they had the chance. It was one of the things we still did then. Everything stopped when we were taxiing out for take-off. A Dutch DC-4 had conked out at the junction of the taxiway and the runways, and a queue built up behind it. We were about sixth in line. A smart old civvy tri-motor behind the Dutchman was apparently in unfamiliar colours.

I know this because the bulkhead door was open, and I heard

107

our pilot ask someone near him, 'What's the white job up ahead, Stevie?'

'That's the new Jerry airline, isn't it? They call it Lufthansa, just like the old one we broke for them.'

'I thought they hadn't started up yet? They haven't any aircraft.'

'They're poncing about inside Germany in an old Junkers 52 with a new paint job, until they get a proper fleet up and running – just to make a point.'

Our radio was on open broadcast so the crew could speak over it, and we could now hear the flap that Control was getting into. Apart from that, it was peaceful sitting there on the taxiway with the engines off.

It was just about then we heard a very American voice from somewhere in the line behind us say over the air, 'Ahm fucking bored.' He must have pressed his transmit button.

Before the Tower had time to respond, the German aircraft up ahead joined in. I heard, *'Wie lange muss ich warten, bis dieser niederlandischen Narr?'* after the new Lufthansa call sign and flight number.

Our pilot called back into the cabin, 'Anyone speak any German?'

I did, a bit, so I shouted back, 'I think he asked, *"How long must I wait for this Dutch fool?"* or something like that.'

'Thanks.'

That gave the Tower a dilemma, because the Lufthansa pilot was obviously looking for some Teutonic solidarity here, but English is the international language of flight, and the poor sods in Flying Control had a host of international witnesses earwigging the exchange.

Control played it straight: after calling back Lufthansa's identifier, he said, 'Lufthansa flight; you know the international language for flying is English. You *must* speak English.'

The German pilot came back in heavily accented English with, 'Control, control; I am a German pilot, in a German aircraft, in *Germany*. Why can't we speak German?'

Then the American who started it all chimed in before Control could respond,

'Because you lost the fucking war!' and all hell broke loose.

Control made a final attempt to restore order, 'Unknown aircraft, unknown aircraft – identify yourself!'

'Ah may be fucking bored,' the American drawl came back, 'but ahm not fucking stupid.'

Twenty minutes later a tractor towed the Dutchman away, and we all began to move.

Malta was only another five hours away.

I slept, missed the vomiting competition and the turbulence that spilled the Elsan, and only woke up when we were in the circuit at Luqa. I hadn't felt sick, so I began to like the old Wimpy after all. It was dark. Early evening. Valletta was a ring of lights and the harbour was full of illuminated grey ships, and of purposeful little launches that trailed white tails in the mirror of the sea. As the pilot slid *Jack* down towards Luqa, I could hear the murmuring voice of the radio operator talking to the ground: he sounded like a Westcountryman. It was like going back ten years.

Chapter Seven

The Beguine

We had a day in Malta.

You've heard all about the George Cross island, haven't you? Plucky little Maltesers holding out against the full might of the Luftwaffe for a year or more? The *Pedestal* convoy and all that guff, and that oil tanker which saved the day – the *Ohio*, I think she was called. An island, we're told, more British than Britain: more English than the English.

Well, fucking forget all that.

M'smith and I got off the Navy bus from Luqa to Valletta in front of the cinema. On our one night in town we'd come to see a double bill from last year: *Ivanhoe* because M'smith was in love with Elizabeth Taylor, and *Man Bait*, because I wanted a gander at that new girl, Diana Dors, all the squaddies were talking about.

The first things we saw as we stepped down from the bus were four paper posters plastered on the cinema wall. Two, on either side of the door, read BRITISH GET OUT. A small one high above the door read HUMANITY IN CHAINS, and the whopper below it read MALTA WANTS INDEPENDENCE. This last one also had the picture of a fiery torch, which was the symbol of an independence party. We'd already read in the papers about British soldiers being beaten up in bars, and spat on in the street. Our friendly Mr Bates hadn't cautioned against leaving the billet; he just told us to keep our wits about us.

'Look on it as a bit of practice for Egypt,' he'd told me. It was more than eighty degrees F in the early evening, so maybe he had a point.

Most of the Brits were in mufti, but they stood out because of their short hair, and pale faces. A few were in crumpled KDs, like M'smith and me – and probably for the same reason, our civvies were still stowed away. The Shore Patrol was outside in a jeep as we left the cinema. Someone jostled a Malteser who drew a knife, and a riot sprang out of absolutely nowhere. For ten minutes it was like World War Three. M'smith kicked open a locked office door behind the ticket kiosk, and we hid there in the dark until the fight moved down the road. It wasn't until we decided to go that the person under the desk gave themselves away by moving.

A girl crawled out: quite a looker in a dark way, although nothing on Elizabeth Taylor. And I was still quite gone on Diana Dors, who had hair like a platinum-gold waterfall, and tits like Mum's steamed puddings. This girl wore a simple dark blue shirt, and voluminous black trousers.

She pushed her black hair back as she crawled out and said, 'Please don't rape me.'

I've heard better chat-up lines than that.

M'smith laughed. I think he laughed at everything. 'Don't be silly. You're the ticket girl aren't you? You sold us our tickets.' She nodded. He stuck on, 'We're not rapists, or anything like that.'

'British sailors want to rape Maltese girls. It's in all the newspapers. Everyone knows.'

I haven't really got a lot of patience with fools; never had. I told her, 'Only stupid people believe that. Anyway, we're airmen: RAF.' I watched her face. I don't think that reassured her.

M'smith said, 'You're better off with us here than with that lot outside, but you can go if you want.' He stood aside from the door, and I copied him.

She looked undecided, asked, 'What are you going to do?'

'Smoke a cigarette, wait until the coast is clear, and scarper. You can wait too if you want.'

She nodded and she waited. She accepted the cigarette M'smith offered her – Woodbine Exports – and smoked it like a true professional. I filled and lit my pipe, so we had a nice little fug building up in the office. At least she smiled timidly a couple of times, but made no attempt at conversation.

We left together. I wanted to head straight for the Navy's military transport back to Luqa, but M'smith asked her, 'Will you be all right? Where do you live?'

'Less than ten minutes' walk away.'

'Would you like us to walk with you?'

She was obviously reluctant, but looked up the road to where the sound of the riot was no longer diminishing. It might have even been drifting back our way. Glass breaking, and wild shouts. I suppose that the alternative to us might have been worse.

'OK. Thank you. That would be kind.' I think she said that more from hope than conviction. 'This way.'

The streets were cobbled, steep and unlit. Some had more rubble in them than houses. The war had left Malta scars that were bigger and longer-lasting than many of the towns I had seen in Germany.

'I'm M'smith,' he told her, 'and this is Charlie. He's not a bundle of fun tonight because he doesn't like fights and he wants Diana Dors.'

'At last, a sensible Englishman; but your M'smith is a peculiar name.'

'Yes, and I can't seem to do anything about it.'

She laughed at that, and some of her tension seemed to blow away with it.

'My name is Suyenne. Suyenne Hansen.'

'Is that a local name?'

'No, I'm from Gibraltar.' She must have been about twenty, and already wore an engagement ring. 'I came with my father soon after the blockade was lifted.'

I calculated back: she must have been about twelve when she arrived, and this smashed-up garrison town must have scared her half to death.

'What is your father?' M'smith tried. She didn't react. I'm not surprised because it was a stupid question. He tried again. 'What work does he do?'

'He's a policeman.'

'He'll be glad we escorted you home,' I said.

'No. No, he won't. He'll think you wanted to rape me.' Full bloody circle, but we were now outside a tall old tenement on a narrow street and she stopped as if it was her destination. She said, 'Thank you. It *was* kind of you – I was frightened.'

M'smith chucked that away. 'Don't be silly; we were frightened too. Anyway; it wasn't far out of our way.'

'What will you do now?'

My turn. 'Walk down to Grand Harbour, and catch the military bus back to Luqa. Tomorrow we'll be in another country.'

'Which one?'

'If we tell you that, we'll have to kill you.' I told her. At least she smiled, but I know she'd heard the joke before.

'You know how to get to Grand Harbour?' she asked us. 'It's like a maze up here: you could get lost.'

'If we keep following the roads leading down,' I responded, 'we're bound to get there eventually.'

She suddenly froze, and stared at my face as if she was trying to look into my very being. I actually saw a decision being made; it was in her eyes. She pointed down the road, the way we'd come.

'Why don't you walk down to that corner, and wait for the civilian bus instead? It will only be about five minutes, and will get you to Luqa quicker.'

'I'm not sure . . .' I started.

'It will be empty at this time of night, and the driver won't charge you, but will be delighted if you tip him with English money.'

'. . . I don't know.'

She shrugged, and added, 'It's what I would do in your shoes, but it's your decision anyway. Now I will say goodnight and good luck. I didn't expect to be rescued by two Englishmen.' Then she surprised us by giving us each a kiss on the cheek, before slipping into the dark.

M'smith made a production of lighting another cigarette, and asked me, 'What do you think?' while glancing at the street corner she had indicated. 'Shall we take a chance?' One of those decisions that change your life.

I shrugged just the way she had, and said, 'Why not?'

So we slouched down to the corner to wait in a doorway for one of the island's ancient buses.

Two hours later I was lying on the bed in my temporary accommodation, trying to slow myself down to sleep with that Hank Janson novel. I felt nervy; just like after some of the long trips while I'd been on the squadron in '44. I gave up on the book and lay back, calculating the odds against being able to date Diana Dors . . . then gave up on *that* when I reached the several hundred million to one against.

The Navy bus we had been supposed to get wasn't in yet. The

114

Pongoes had been running the blue Off-Duty Personnel bus around Malta for some time, and called it the Liberty Bus – that's because the Navy has always been crap at naming things. When I heard a bit of commotion outside, I yawned, stood up and went to the door. A RAF Regiment bod was going down the corridor from door to door, doing a quick head count.

'What's up, chum?' I asked as he hurried by.

'The bastards blew up the Liberty Bus: four dead so far.' Ah.

Jack lifted off at a quarter to ten for a leisurely five-to-six-hour drag to Cyprus. It would depend on the head or tail winds. I stood with our pilot as he smoked his last fag: he explained that he usually got tail winds in the Eastern Med at this time of the year – it could give him another 30 knots. Only two of the AC conscripts were left now, and Mister Bates looked hung-over. They'd replaced the other erks with packing cases for the base at Akrotiri. I didn't like the look of the way they were stowed, and made the Luqa handlers do it again. That had given them another half-hour's work, and they gave me the look as they sloped off.

Bates said, 'You seem to know what you're doing, sir.'

'They would have shifted with the first bit of turbulence, and started flying about all over the shop. I ran a small freight outfit at Lympne before they invited me back to the RAF. I know how to stow aeroplanes.'

'And will they use your expertise in that when you get to Egypt, sir? No, they'll probably put you in charge of motor spares or something. What were you in the war, if I might ask, sir?'

I turned so that he could see my half wing.

'Sparks.'

'Big jobs or small jobs?'

'Big ones. Lancasters at Bawne. And you?'

'I missed it. I joined from school in 1948. Now I'm a

nursemaid.' It wasn't his fault but it seemed to me that half the RAF we had now had managed to miss the war.

He seemed curiously bitter towards the system this morning. Might as well be direct: so I asked him,

'What's the matter, Mr Bates?'

'A couple of the lads we brought out yesterday were on that bus last night. Blown to pieces. Their great adventure didn't even last a bleeding day, did it, sir?'

'Not your fault.'

'That's what the CO said – I'd already handed them over to the base here. Doesn't make a blind bit o' difference though, does it?'

I knew what he meant. There were a couple of mornings on the squadron in '44 that I looked around the empty chairs in the Sergeants' Mess after particularly bloody raids, and felt guilty at still being there. I leaned over, and squeezed his shoulder.

'No, it doesn't make any difference. Some are lucky and some aren't, and that's all there is to it. Nothing to do with us. I fancy sticking a waxer in Mr M'smith's coffee once we've settled down – how about you? You can ask those two lads to join us, if you like. They look scared to death.'

He nodded and said, 'Thank you, sir,' before he turned away.

We droned east. The sea was a dark, deep blue and sparkled in the sun. We saw one large trooper gliding smoothly west, cutting the water and leaving a wake a mile long – full of lucky buggers going home, I thought. I went up to the office and talked to the crew for a while. The radio operator was an old sweat from Bristol. He'd done two full tours in the Forties, and had finished the war in his second OTU. We had some acquaintances in common, and had even flown on the same raid once.

M'smith slept with his cap over his face for a couple of hours. When he woke up he leaned over and tapped me on the knee to distract me from my book.

'That girl, Charlie . . .'

'Which girl?'

'That one last night. She was a bit of a cracker, wasn't she?'

'She was a terrorist, Heck.'

'Surely not, old fellow.'

'She told us not to get the Liberty bus, didn't she? Then some bastard blows it up. She was paying us back with our lives: one good turn deserves another.'

He thought about this for a few minutes, and then he tapped me on the knee again.

'Don't you think we should tell someone?'

'I already did. You can go back to sleep.'

I liked M'smith, but fervently hoped that he would be posted to one end of Egypt while I got the other. He would be a great fellow to go on the skite with now and again, but not to work with. I didn't want *him* watching my back. Then it occurred to me that I didn't even know what shape or size Egypt was these days, or the fucking Canal Zone to which I was bound. I'd have to find a library somewhere, and some old Brit who'd spent half his life there. There was bound to be someone who could tell me what was what.

Two hours later we were letting down over Cyprus in clean air: that odd staggered ber-bump as the main wheels dropped down – never together – and the odder moment when the pilot selects a hefty degree of flap, and the Wimpy seems almost to float motionless above the ground as he throttles back. I had been right about the stowage, although I felt no satisfaction about it. An hour out of Malta we had skirted one of those sudden Mediterranean squalls that come from nowhere, and *Jack* had been bounced about like a shuttlecock. Both the erks were sick, but their recovery times were short. They'd have a story to tell their families if they made it home.

We were collected from *Jack* by an AC2 in a strange six-wheeled wagon with ten seats and a canvas top; prewar I'd say. He had his own idea about what should happen next, but M'smith soon put paid to that. He gave him a friendly poke in the shoulder and said, 'Bars please, my man. Theirs first . . .' indicating Bates and his two strays, '. . . and then ours. OK?' He did seem to have a *way* about him.

The Officers' Mess was a double Nissen hut with a bar running down one side. It was empty when we walked in, except for a solitary barman flicking away the flies with a wet towel – they were as big as wrens I'd seen in Blighty. He brightened up when we presented in front of him.

'Mr Bassett and Mr Macdonaldsmith, sirs?'

Both of us said, 'Yes,' simultaneously. It was nice to be wanted.

'Just some bumf for your attention, sirs, and then I can serve you a drink.' Bollocks.

'Where's everyone else?'

He looked on me with the benevolence of a father to his youngest son. 'Asleep, sir. It's half past three.'

So it was. I walked back to the door, opened it and listened to the sounds of a working airfield: absolutely fuck-all. When I shut the heat out again all I could hear was the slow beats of an overhead fan. Yeah, you guessed it. I could cope with this. I initialled the forms the barman put in front of me – I could have signed away my pay for the next three months for all I knew.

When he took them back from us he wished us very gravely, 'Welcome to Cyprus, gentlemen.' Then said, 'The bar is now open.'

If you haven't noticed it by now, I should probably make it plain that drink has a moderately prominent role in my story. You meet a nice class of person in a bar. Two long glasses of Stella, produced now, without a fuss, confirmed in me the opinion that bar staff are God's real representatives on Earth; bugger the Pope.

'When will everyone get up from being asleep?' I asked the steward.

'When it's time to eat usually, sir – about seven.'

'I could get to like Cyprus.'

'It's a fine island when the Greeks aren't shooting at us. They don't want us here any more.'

'Cyprus too? Something has gone terribly wrong with the world,' M'smith remarked. 'I'll have another please.' He pushed his glass forward. The foam clung around the inside in discrete rings. Something else had been bothering me.

'Any idea how long we're likely to be here before we move on?'

'Two days, I believe, sir. The SWO says to tell you he'll touch base with you this evening, and the Adjutant asks that Pilot Officer Bassett presents himself at Hut 7 tomorrow morning; after breakfast. You'll find we're quite relaxed here, sir.'

'What's in hut number seven?'

'They don't tell me that sort of thing, sir.'

'Where is it?'

'Alongside Hut 6 I'd imagine,' said M'smith. 'Don't worry, you'll find it.'

'You can take me to supper in the Mess tonight,' I told him, 'and teach me how to eat like an officer.'

'Easy, dear chap. Just grab everything in sight, spill grub all down your shirt, throw up when you've drunk too much, and don't pay for a damned thing. No one will notice.'

Promotion was a bit like being mentally raped; it corrupted you utterly. I never forgot that, or M'smith's advice.

After he left the bar, I sat down for half an hour with the January *Picturegoer* magazine. There was a girl called Monica

Lewis on the front cover. I'd never heard of her, but she was showing bags of leg. She had a nervous smile, and I hoped she hadn't given away too much to get a front cover. I took it to my cabin, which was a room in a square building like an electricity substation, with four bedrooms and a large sitting room. It was where the RAF parked their transiting officers. There were snores coming from three of the rooms – one would be M'smith, I supposed.

I couldn't settle, and found it was pleasantly cool on the shaded veranda. I smoked my pipe, drank water from a new cooler inside, and watched a Varsity arrive. One engine sounded horribly rough to my tutored ear. The troops who trooped off it looked around as if they didn't know what was going on. They had pale skins, and carried their gear awkwardly. I was glad that I wasn't a national serviceman and knew more or less what was expected of me, and how to avoid it most of the time – which was the important thing. There was a big black Bakelite telephone clinging to the wall of the common room. I decided to try it out.

I told the base operator who I was, and where. He sounded pretty cheerful; I was beginning to suspect that Cyprus was the place to be . . . when the Greeks weren't shooting at you, of course.

'Can you give me your service number, please sir.'

'22602108. Bassett C.'

'Have you a mess number yet, sir?' I gave him that as well.

'Can I make a call back to Blighty?'

'Not a personal one?'

'No, a WD number in London.' I gave him Dolly's number. If I didn't make it plain before, I will now. Dolly worked with RAF Intelligence. When I met her she had been a driver in the car pool. Then she worked her way up. Then she worked her way back down to the car pool again. I didn't know what ebb her career was at now, but from the way she'd treated me earlier

I guessed that she would be bossing people around again. I had to wait for five minutes for the call to go through, and then another five for someone to run her down. When she spoke, she sounded as if her mouth was full. I asked, 'Why are you stuffing your face in the middle of the afternoon?'

'Because it's not. It's lunchtime over here, and that means you're no longer in the country.'

'That's very clever Dolly; you should be in Intelligence.' Dolly didn't like me talking about her job on the telephone. She liked me taking the piss out of her even less. I waited while she decided whether or not to hang up. '. . . Dolly?'

'Yes, I'm still here. What do you want?'

'Something odd happened to me in Malta yesterday. I told a whitetop about it, but I'm not sure he understood the significance, so I wanted to tell someone who knew what she was doing.' Dolly would have liked that, but I was telling her the truth for once. Another one of those pauses as long as the intro to a decent jazz number . . . 'The big noise from Winnetka' maybe . . . da,da, da – de-da, da . . . da, da . . . But she wasn't buggering me about this time. The noises I could hear communicated someone searching for a confidential pad to write on, and a pen to do it with.

Dolly said, 'OK. Sorry about that. Shoot . . .' I'd actually shot her last boss when he went crazy, but it wasn't the time to go into that. I told her about the riot, and the policeman's daughter who had steered us away from being blown up in a bus. I was right. Dolly was interested despite herself.

'Did you get her address?'

'Only the street, sorry.' I gave it to her.

'Thank you, Charlie. That sounds quite interesting. It would be nice to put one over on the Pongoes for a change; they think they own the bloody island.' When Dolly was in work mode she rarely used proper nouns herself. 'It was nice of you to think of me.' I often thought about her, because we'd counted one another's freckles a few times, but it wasn't the time to remind her of that either.

She asked, 'Was there anything else?'

'Do you still have the Major's phone number down in Bosham?'

'Yes, it's in my book as an alternative one for you.'

'Could you give them a ring, and let the boys know I'm OK? So far so good.'

'Of course.' It was the real reason for my call, of course, and Dolly didn't mind. 'You haven't finished your trip out yet?'

'No, I'm in Cyprus. And I'm here for two days. It's warm and the beer is very, very good. I might even get to paddle in the sea.'

'Please take care, and call me any time you want. Let me know as soon as you're back.'

'Does that mean we're reconciled, then?'

'We were never anything else, stupid. You're my favourite little man, even when I hate you.'

'Really?'

'Truly. You always have been; didn't you know?'

That was a bit of a yorker: I didn't know quite how to respond, so I asked, 'Didn't you get married?'

'No, not quite. I went out with some of my girlfriends the night before, and got rather sloshed. I'm afraid I was still asleep when I was supposed to be getting hitched.'

I laughed, and then apologized for laughing.

'Wasn't that a bit of an irresponsible thing to do?'

'No, Charlie. It was exactly the *right* thing to do, as things turned out. Mother hasn't spoken to me since, but Daddy thinks it is all rather amusing.'

'Dads usually come up trumps.'

'Yours too?'

'He's never let me down; even when he should have. What happened to your fellah?'

'At the moment he's driving a car in the Monte Carlo rally, and doing rather well. I saw him on the Pathé News at the flicks last night. His co-driver is a Guardsman, and someone told me they're in love. I don't expect I'll see him again.' I'd heard those rumours about the Guards as well.

'I miss you, Dolly. I always forget that I'm going to, and then I always do.'

'And that is exactly the right place to end this chat, Charlie. Don't worry: it's only seven months, and it will flash by.'

'Bye to you too!' We were both giggling a bit when I put the receiver back. At least I knew how long my posting was now. But how the hell did Dolly know that?

I once remarked that these bastards were so far up each other's arses that only their feet were showing. How did Dolly know that? She knew it because David Watson knew it. And how did David Watson know it? He knew it because he was waiting in Hut 7 for me when I sauntered in the next morning. His old prewar KDs looked threadbare, and the soft-peaked cap on his desk was the type I'd seen pictures of Lawrence of Arabia wearing. I pulled myself quickly into a semblance of the shape assumed by a junior RAF officer.

He was in a mellow mood as usual, so he didn't notice. 'Come in, Charlie, pull up a pew. You've met M'smith.'

I had; but I didn't know where he fitted in.

'Good morning, sir.'

He almost nodded when I said *sir*; as if he'd been waiting for it. Hut 7 was more or less square – just the one room. Charts on the walls, old-fashioned blackout curtains drawn, and an old 1154/1155 radio set up on a table in one corner. We were playing the Aussies in the Test at Adelaide soon, so perhaps that's what it was for: you always got great reception on the old Lancaster radio sets.

Watson sat behind a desk. M'smith at another working on some charts. He looked back at me over his shoulder, and grinned. He looked as if he knew what he was doing. Bloody nav.

I asked Watson, 'When did you get in, sir?'

'A week or so ago.'

'What are we doing here?'

'Same as before. Same as you were doing at that dreadful place on the South Coast . . . where was it again?'

'Dungeness, sir.'

'That's right.'

'So . . . I'm going to be flying about, or sitting on my backside in a place like this, listening to the Reds all over again? I didn't even know they were out here.'

'Not exactly, Charlie – but for your information the Reds are everywhere.'

I had learned to distrust his *not exactlys*.

'Tell me, then, sir. Tell me the worst.'

'Do you know what I wrote in your B107 the last time we served together, Charlie?' Whatever it was, I wasn't going to like it, was I? So I didn't reply. Watson shoved on. 'I wrote *almost insubordinate*.'

'Thank you, sir.'

'Knew y'd like it. We're going to be driving around all that sandy stuff in North Africa and the Sinai, eavesdropping on the wog army and police force. They mean us no good.'

'When you say *we*, sir, you actually mean poor buggers like me, don't you?'

He turned to face M'smith, and told him, 'See, I was right. *Almost* insubordinate.' Then he looked back and said, 'Yes, Charlie. I mean poor buggers like you.'

'You're sending me out into the desert?'

'Yes, Charlie. It's not *our* desert really; but the bold British Army is out there holding the foe at bay. You will be a passenger on some of their patrols; all on account of your skills with the old knobs and switches. Your training CO at, where was it again . . . ?'

'Dungeness, sir.'

'Yes, Dungeness. She wrote that you were the best she'd seen, and recommended you specifically for desert-penetration patrols to the most dangerous places. Did you upset her? She seems to have it in for you.' Ah, the revenge of the dark blue woolly knicker brigade.

The radios against the wall suddenly started to chatter Morse. Watson said, 'Get that, will you . . . then acknowledge.'

Whoever the sender was he was quite handy. He had a fast, musical signature. One of the immaculate hands. I relayed to Watson, 'It's from someone good called Broadstairs. He reported it as a positioning reflex, and then signed off. What do you want me to send?'

'Just acknowledge, and sign off Harrogate. As fast as you can, please, Charlie. The Gyppoes are listening to us back.'

'Broadstairs?'

'Field radios are all seaside resorts, and controls are inland spa towns . . . I shall find you something suitably plebeian. *Morecambe*, maybe. I never liked Morecambe.'

Personally I've never had a problem with Morecambe, so maybe it was a class thing.

Less than a minute later, the green telephone on Watson's desk rang – he always managed to get green telephones – and he listened to it, wrote something on a pad, grunted and put the telephone down. Then he got up and passed what he'd written to M'smith, who stood up in turn, went across and made a pencil mark on one of the charts on the wall. Somewhere southeast of

Tripoli. In bloody Libya . . . I wondered if their King Idris knew about that. I also wondered why the king of Libya had a Welsh name. Maybe he was a secret Taff.

'Triangulation,' Watson explained to me. 'The patrols have a broadcasting schedule, rather like the BBC. They just send the words we've briefed them with, which tells us they are still in contact . . . but we've got a sub and surface vessels off the coast who tell us where they are.'

'But if we can do that, so can the opposition!'

'I know; that's why we lose an operator from time to time. The man you're replacing went off the air more than a month ago.'

Bollocks – or probably without any, if half what I'd been told about the Arabs was true.

'Who knows that we're doing this, sir?'

'Apart from the wogs? Not many people. Careless talk still costs lives, you know.'

Idiot. My dad was right about us; not content with winning one decent war, we'd been losing others ever since, and it was time to stop. The reason I'd asked Watson the question was because he'd already implied that we were wandering all over other people's countries again, provoking the neighbours and pretending we weren't doing any harm. Police action my arse; we were the ones who needed bloody policing.

As if Watson had read my mind he said, 'Ah yes, your *father*.'

'Yes, sir?' What now?

'I had a call about him yesterday. I was asked to tell you he'd been arrested in London.'

'Again?'

'They didn't tell me that. I assumed that it was for the first time.'

'No. The same thing happened a month ago. He's become a militant pacifist.'

'Contradiction in terms, Charlie boy. Anyway; I've arranged that you'll speak to the police officer involved. Privately, from here this afternoon. OK?'

'Thank you, sir.'

'. . . and you'll let us know if we can help?'

'Yes, sir.' I just needed some time to think. 'When do I fly out?'

'You don't. You leave for Port Said in three days. It should have been two, but the Navy's been late for everything since Trafalgar, and it even almost missed that.'

'The Navy?'

'Yes, Charlie, the Navy. Port Said is a *port*, as its name implies – so you will travel in style in one of Her Majesty's ships. I understand that this one is called a corvette, and it's probably very smart.'

'A corvette . . . ?'

'You've begun to repeat everything I'm saying, Charlie. Are you all right?'

'I don't like boats, boss, and I can't swim.'

'Soon do something about that . . .'

Later I asked him, 'So what *is* going to happen to me for the next few months, sir? Can't you give me any more details?'

'No. But when you get to Port Said, you'll be allocated a camp up-country, which in Egypt is *down* – somewhere in the south . . . probably RAF Fayid. But before that you'll have a week's Middle East acclimatization training – that's like a school for surviving Egypt. After that you'll be in a camp with the other wallahs, but listening to whom I tell you, *when* I tell you . . . and occasionally you will going out into the blue with a patrol, or on a scheme . . .'

'. . . and on those?'

'Yes, I'm sure you've already got it. You'll do whatever I tell you to, whenever I tell you. Couldn't be plainer, could it?'

'No, sir. What do you want me to do while I'm waiting here?'

'Don't go off the base, but otherwise enjoy yourself. Relax. There's a half-decent beach club, a couple of bars, some sports facilities . . . even a bit of motorcycle scrambling if that interests you.' It didn't, although the beach club and the bars sounded all right.

'Thank you, sir.'

'Come back at three to make that call. OK? . . . and take M'smith with you. He works all the time: I can't stand the sight of the beggar already.'

Before we'd got through the door he'd retuned the receiver to British Forces Network. David Whitfield was still singing that silly bloody soldier's song. They played it a lot in those days. Watson pulled open a lower desk drawer. I heard the bottle clink. He was back on it again.

The telephone hissed and crackled for half an hour, and then I heard someone clearing his throat. It wasn't me, and the office was empty. The Wing Commander and the rest of Cyprus had retired for their siestas. I'm sure the *Daily Mirror* would love to know how we were spending the taxpayers' money.

I spoke, 'Sergeant Pike, is that you?'

'Sergeant Pry, Mr Bassett. *Pry*. Did they tell you that your father was in trouble again?'

'Only that he'd been arrested. What was it for this time?'

He paused, as if ordering his thoughts. 'Are you familiar with a delicacy known as a Scotch Pie, sir?'

'Yes, Sergeant. I've even eaten a few. Smashing. Round hard pastry pie crust with a filling of mince, onions and loads of really sloppy gravy. The Jocks eat them with chips . . . pie and chips. I'm babbling, aren't I?'

'Only a little, sir. It would appear that your father made

another of his special little excursions down here, with half a dozen of the tasty little beggars in his rucksack.'

'What for?'

'To throw at people, apparently. He got both the Chief of the General Staff and the First Sea Lord on the steps of the War Ministry. It was the gravy that did all the damage – it went everywhere.'

'Is it in the papers?'

'Not yet.'

'That will disappoint him. What can I do from here, though?'

'If you can find someone to stand for him, he'll probably be let out on bail and sent back to Glasgow, with his tail between his legs. The bail conditions would banish him from London. That would be a start.'

'He's been charged, I suppose?'

'Assault, threatening behaviour and damage to government property – to wit two uniforms, one gravy-ed door, and mince all over a nice set of granite steps. But I wouldn't be surprised if it didn't come to anything, provided you can get him to stop.'

'I'll try.'

'That's the style, sir. No one wants the publicity of a trial, do they? What about a bail surety?'

'I'll make a few calls, OK?'

'Good. I'll wait until I hear from someone. If you don't get him out, we'll need to find him a solicitor.'

'A psychiatrist would be more use. What did I do to deserve this?'

'Have a father who worries about you, I think, sir. Shall I tell him that you're safe and well?'

'Yes, Sergeant. Thank you.' I didn't apologize, because deep in my heart I knew the old man was right.

I put the receiver down, and then lifted it again to ask the switchboard for another number. Then I took a deep breath before speaking to Dolly. I needn't have worried: she thought it was terribly funny.

For the Beach Club, the military had probably nicked Cyprus's best bathing spot. No wonder the buggers wanted us off the island. I headed down there in an old pair of KD shorts I thought I could wade in if I had to, an even older KD shirt open and flapping, and a pair of new plimsolls. The Hank Janson I hadn't finished was in my back pocket and a towel over my shoulder. I couldn't help reflecting how people pay money to do this sort of thing on holiday. There was a row of gaily painted Billy Butlin beach huts, like a terrace of small houses, and anyone who wasn't sleeping in their billet was probably in a deckchair under a sunshade here. There were a few empty ones, so that was all right. Occasional stewards, with trays of glasses of cold beer beaded with moisture, moved among them. That was all right, too. The Brown Jobs had managed to make a nice set-up here on the quiet.

I hadn't gone ten yards before a voice from the 1940s spoke to me. It was just as I was passing a big beach shade. There were two deckchairs. One was occupied by a woman.

She spoke again. 'Hello, Charlie; small world.'

Adelaide Baker was Grace's mother, and Carlo's grandmother. I couldn't see her eyes behind her sunglasses, but her legs and arms were firm and tanned. Tennis? She must have been nearly fifty but her body, under an inappropriately white swimming suit, was still as good as money could buy. Millionairesses seem to have this system that defies the ageing process: it's called cash.

At first I couldn't speak. Then: 'Hello, Addy. What are you doing here?'

'Visiting someone. How about you?'

'Passing through.'

She took a great gulp of cold beer from her cold glass, and then pressed it between her tits. It left a damp patch on her costume. Then she offered it to me – the beer, I mean – which was a surprisingly intimate gesture. 'Thirsty?'

'Yes. Thanks.'

I drained it, and then scooped two more from the tray of a passing steward, pausing to sign the chitty with a Mess number I made up on the spot.

It was her turn to say, 'Thank you.'

We had absolutely nothing to say to each other, and a million things to say, all at the same time. She smiled like royalty.

'Passing through, Charlie . . . for how long?'

'A few days.'

'Have dinner with me tonight?'

I didn't have to think about it. 'Why not? Where, and when?'

'There's a restaurant run by the NAAFI for waifs and strays and in-betweens like me – about ten minutes along the beach. It has the really tacky name of Casa Aphrodite but their fish is the best you've eaten since the war.' It was funny, but for hundreds of thousands of us the war was still our touchstone: our reference point.

'OK,' I told her. 'I'll see you at . . .'

'About half past eight. Jacket and tie.'

'What about socks and shoes as well? I suppose it's a posh sort of place.'

She pulled a face. 'Stop mocking me, Charlie: you were always too good at that. Go away and lie in the sun for an hour; your body is excessively white. We can talk tonight.'

I probably regarded her steadily for a moment, then said, 'Yes. Yes, we can.'

'You can tell me about my grandson.'

'OK.'

As I walked off she began to hum 'The Beguine'. I took it away inside my head – the Tommy Dorsey version that is.

Was this an accidental meeting? From the moment she'd spotted me Grace's mum had made all the running. That was interesting. She wanted to talk about Carlo: so was this where I would begin to lose him?

Chapter Eight

That old feeling

She wore a floaty, cream linen summer dress which had never been near the clothing ration. It left her tanned shoulders bare.

I remarked, 'I don't know how you do it, Addy.'

We drank Stella from cold glasses. I can forgive a woman anything if she knows when to drink beer.

'How I do what?'

'Stay young: you look like a film star.'

'Why thank you, Charlie.'

'I mean it.'

'I know you do. Cheerio.' She raised her glass to me.

'Cheers. I was twenty when I first met you, now I'm twenty-eight. I've aged eight years – probably more. You haven't aged at all.'

'When you talk like that, Charlie, I know why Grace fell in love with you.'

'Grace never loved me at all. I think I was just some sort of light entertainment.'

'Grace loved you. I think she still does.'

'Bollocks.'

'There, just when it's all going your way, you have to break the spell.'

'Sorry. It's just that it's easier for me to believe that she didn't

133

love me – not in a way that I would recognize, anyway. Why would you think she did?'

'Because she told me.'

'When?'

'This afternoon; after I mentioned I'd seen you.' I've said it before, and I'll say it again: *Bollocks!* 'And if you close your gaping mouth for a few seconds, she might even tell you herself.'

She was at my shoulder. I heard her before I saw her. That slightly breathy girl's voice which melted resolution.

'Hello, Charlie.'

Nothing trite. Nothing smart. Nothing funny. Just, *Hello, Charlie*, and I died. I didn't know what to say, and for the first time since I'd known her, neither did Grace.

Addy laughed, and said, '. . . Oops!' and looked away embarrassed, but then she always had a cruel streak.

Grace bent down, and kissed me on the side of my neck, between my ear and my shirt collar.

Dead in the water, Charlie.

Grace was wearing faded KD pants and one of those washed-out khaki cotton vests she'd got from the Yanks years ago. They were freshly laundered. The only concession she had made to an evening out was her shoes. I was used to seeing her in battered brown field boots, but this evening she wore a pair of light white slip-ons. Every other woman in the place was in full war paint, dressed for dinner and dancing, but it was Grace all the men looked at. She drew glances the way a magnet captures iron filings. There wasn't a man in the place that evening who didn't want to be me.

Addy went onto the dance floor with an Artillery captain, and didn't come back. Either she was being tactful, or just giving us space to fight. I had once fallen for Grace as hard as any twenty-year-old can. Then she'd left me, and crossed Europe with a motley group of medicine men, healing the sick and tending the wounded. But I had pursued her, which had been a bad thing to do. So she ran again, but not before leaving me holding the baby who had grown into Carlo. I met her again in 1947 and, just as I had begun to fall for her once more, she scooted again. This time for the embryonic State of Israel. She sailed up onto a beach on a tramp steamer with a group of illegals, and I hadn't heard of her since. There was a candle inside a glass funnel on the table between us. She held her hands on either side of it, and they became translucent.

I asked her, 'How did you know I was here?'

'I didn't until Mummy said she'd seen you.'

'She's very interested in Carlo.'

'She's his grandmother, but don't worry – she won't take him away.'

'I did wonder.'

'You're turning into too good a father, Charlie. The boys worship you – they'll miss you when you're away.' How did Grace know that?

'I miss them too. That's funny, isn't it?'

'No.'

The windows were open: a sea breeze cool on my sunburned arms. After a comfortable silence she said, 'Sometimes I envy you; but not always.'

She lit a cigarette – untipped as always – and the smoke she breathed out momentarily encircled me. American: maybe Luckies or Camel.

'It's not too late to be a mother,' I told her awkwardly. 'I haven't ever lied to Carlo. He knows all about you . . . and I think he's rather proud.' Then I changed the subject. 'I always forget how lovely you are. You're like Addy: she never seems to age either.'

135

Grace looked away. Then she picked up one of my hands and examined it like a fortune teller as she spoke. 'I got married, Charlie. Did you know that?'

'No, how could I? It doesn't matter.'

'It was the only way to stay in Israel. After all I'd done — conning that bloody old ship across the Med for them, full of the arms and ammunition they needed to stop the Arabs — they were going to kick me out. The only females they wanted were those prepared to spread their legs and think of Israel: breeding stock. Weren't the Germans like that under Hitler?'

'I'm sorry. Who did you marry?'

'A gang leader who gave me a dose on our wedding night. I walked out a month later, and divorced him exactly a year and a day after the wedding . . . with my new passport in my hand.'

'Poor Grace.'

'Poor us. I should have grabbed you while I could.'

Pause. How would it have worked out if she had? The band was playing 'That old feeling', which could have been just plain sentimental, or simply one of God's bad jokes: suit yourself.

I meant to ask her to dance, but found myself saying, 'I'd like to sleep with you again.'

I don't know whether the smile she shot me was sad or cheeky. Maybe both.

'I'll settle for that.'

I didn't want to smuggle her into my hut as the others would be bound to hear us. Grace was sharing a room with her mother, but they had a key to one of the beach huts, and Grace, being Grace, had it with her. We spent the night there. After we had made love, we sat on a thin mattress on the floor at the back of the hut, and through the open door watched the reflection of the moon on the sea. I hugged her to me. Her body was as spare as I remembered, and she had made love like a tigress. I had remembered that too.

It was round about then I asked her, 'What are you doing over here?'

'Having a couple of weeks off from making a new country, and enjoying a holiday with Mummy.'

'That's probably a load of bollocks.'

'. . . also unofficially negotiating favours between the State of Israel and the lords of the British Army. My new Israeli friends have found they need me, actually – I'm the stepdaughter of a lord, after all; and you dear Brits are still madly impressed by a title and a double-clanger.' That was a bit of slang we used in the Fifties – it could mean either a double-barrelled name, or a bicycle's derailleur front gear change. Take your choice.

'Negotiating what kind of favours?'

'If I told you that, I'd have to kill you.'

We didn't speak for a minute or two, and then I asked her, 'Did I teach you that, or did you teach me?'

She squirmed around to face me, said, 'Does it matter?' and then, 'Kiss me again: we're still very good at it.' Everywhere my hands ran over her was naked and cool and tanned. She was almost olive-green in the moonlight, like a bronze statue of a pagan goddess. Grace's small body had never failed to overwhelm me. Her sensuality was a real thing.

She spoke into the hollow of my shoulder, 'Don't start falling for me again, darling. Not allowed.'

I think I murmured, ' . . .'s too late.'

I never bleeding learn, do I?

Exactly the same thought that later came to mind as I was leaning over the lee side of Her Majesty's corvette *Wallflower*, vomiting into the Med. The friendly CPO who had been detailed to look after me had protested, 'You can't get seasick in the Med, sir! Nobody can.'

'Just you bloody watch me, Chief,' I told him, and made

another dash for the rail. The curious formality of the Navy demanded that I was in day uniform, but they made me wear my plimsolls underneath so as to not scratch the paintwork of their shiny ship. After a day I realized that ninety per cent of the life of a sailor consisted of cleaning his bloody ship. The nasty cow was spotless.

Corvettes started their lives as cheap anti-submarine escorts for convoys; they should have ended them there as well. Whoever had been given the job of designing them had been asked to produce a vessel that would roll alarmingly, and pitch and toss in even the calmest of seas – and he hadn't made a bad job of it. I reckon you could get seasick in a corvette tied up alongside, while resting on the harbour bottom at low tide. She was, in three words, *an utter bastard*. Corvette crews, of course, loved their vessels with a passion that passed all understanding, but that's the Navy for you: as mad as monkeys.

They spent the best part of three days bouncing around the Med looking for Port Said – I think we passed it twice during the night, but to be honest I was too sick to care. One odd occurrence was the smell that we steamed into on the last night: a sort of invisible fogbank of fetid mustiness. I understand that I was not the first to remark on it.

'What's that smell, Chief?' I asked the CPO. 'It's horrible.'

'That, sir, is the smell of Africa – more specifically, it's the smell of Egypt.'

'It's horrible! Is it always that bad?'

'Usually it's worse: we're still half a day away.'

I wandered back to the rail: just in case. You ask any veteran the first thing they noticed about Egypt and they'll tell you it was the stink of the fucking place. I know someone who was there just last year – she tells me it hasn't changed a bit.

When I rolled out of my bunk in the morning, the dear old *Wallflower* was pitching less – in fact she was rubbing herself to pieces against an endless stone wall that stretched as far as the eye could see in both directions. As I began to stuff what little I had unpacked into my kitbag, the friendly CPO put in an appearance. He definitely had that *And where the hell do you think you're going?* look in his eye.

'Problem, Chiefy?'

'Don't think so, sir. Hungry?'

'As a matter of fact, I rather am. I'll find my way to where I have to report, and pick up some grub on the way.'

'You won't want to be doing that, sir. This is Egypt, the land of cockroaches and diarrhoea; you wouldn't know what you were eatin'. Besides; you *can't*, actually.'

'Who says so?'

'The Queen, sir. Her Majesty.' And when I looked gratifyingly blank he informed me, 'Navy regs, sir: unless she's been paid off a naval vessel will have a commissioned officer standing by her at all times. The rest have scarpered for the weekend, begging your pardon, sir. That leaves you.'

'But I'm in the RAF!'

' . . . know sir. The gentlemen did 'ave some discussion about that before they left, but the Captin opined that leavin' you in charge would be in order, sir, so long as you 'ad a senior hand to advise you.'

'You?'

'Exactly, sir.'

'Hard bleeding luck.'

'My thoughts precisely, sir: it's very irregular.'

I followed him on deck. The sunlight dazzled me and the heat roasted me. And then there was the smell of Egypt, of course.

I was still half inclined to think that the Pongoes were playing a trick on me: revenge for my being sick all the way across the Med. It wasn't a trick though: a corvette, small, nifty and, above all, exceptionally cheap, does not have all that many officers. I think I saw three the whole time I was on her. The bastards had abandoned me. As had about three quarters of the crew. It did occur to me to protest the legality of this dodge, but who was there left to protest to?

'How many of us are left?' I asked him.

'You, me, eight hands and the cook, sir.'

'And I'm in charge?'

'Theoretically, sir . . . although if you orders me to sea, or to move ship, I think you'll find we have an engine breakdown.'

'You realize that this is completely nuts? I know fuck-all about ships and sailors: I'm a radio man.' I tapped the half wing on my chest.

'Glad to hear that, sir. The signallers went ashore as well. They left their schedules for you.'

'Where have your people *gone*, Chief?'

'Down the Treaty Road to Ismailia, sir; except for the skipper. He'll have gone on to El Kirsh. His wife's in the married compound there. Gives him a chance to see her for a weekend.'

'What's in Ismailia?'

'Arab persons, sir. The rest of our people have gone to the Blue Kettle. That's a club. There's a rumour going about that a very special lady dancer is putting in a bit of an appearance.'

'Is this lady an agriculturist, by any chance? A bit of an animal-lover?'

The CPO looked uncomfortable. 'You might say that, sir. I'm surprised you knew about her already.'

'You bastards! She was about the only thing in Egypt I was looking forward to.'

'She gets about, apparently. You'll get another chance if you stick around long enough.'

It was blisteringly hot, and it stank – all manner of Port Said's debris and refuse was being pushed up against the wall by the tide, and *Wallflower* was squatting blithely in the middle of it. A wallflower in a shit heap.

'What about my report? Won't they miss me?'

'They don't know we're in yet, sir. That's why the skipper stuck us this far up the eastern mole. No one will notice us for days. We'll report in on Sunday night, and organize some transport for you next day.'

'Got it all worked out, your skipper?'

'That's why they made him a skipper, sir.'

Oddly, I wasn't all that bothered. My well-ordered little life had been out of control ever since David Watson had reappeared in it . . . this was no madder than anything else that had happened to me since then.

'So what do we do for the next two days?'

'I thought we'd all eat together in the Petty Officers' Mess, sir; seeing as there's just the few of us?'

'OK by me.'

'Brekker's in about twenty minutes, then. You might wish to familiarize yourself with the radio shack, sir, in the meantime.'

'I suppose I might,' I sighed. 'By the way, shall we switch off the Navy and the RAF for the weekend? My name's Charlie . . .'

'And they call me Taff, sir.'

'Pleased to meet you, Taff.'

'And you, sir.' You could never tell these bloody Regulars anything.

The port may not have known that we were there, but the bloody Gyppoes did. When I came back on deck from the radio room a quarter of an hour later, having mastered nothing other than the cooling fan on the ceiling, a large friendly Arab was beaming down at me from the mole. My first wog: Wog One. He was smothered in a long dirty robe – thick white and rust-coloured vertical stripes. It hadn't seen the inside of a wash tub for about a year, or maybe that was just my prejudice showing. He showed his teeth as he smiled. There weren't many of them, either. He gestured to a handcart of fruit behind him: both he and his wares had appeared as if by magic. His eyes sparkled.

'Buy oranges?'

'No thank you.'

'Dates. Fresh dates: no flies.'

'No. *Thank* you.' Firmer this time, Charlie.

'HMS *Wallflower*. Flower-class corvette. One thousand and thirty-one tonnes. Eighty-five crew. One brave captain. I love the British Navy.'

'Good for you, chum.'

'You buy oranges now?'

I was to learn that this was a reasonably characteristic conversation between a British serviceman and an Egyptian entrepreneur. A matelot saved me: he climbed through one of the bulkhead doors and onto the deck, wiping his hands on a grey dishcloth that looked filthier than Wog One's outfit. He smelt like a cook. In size, the Egyptian outnumbered us both by about two to one.

The AB squinted up. 'Wotcha, Ali. Wotcha got?'

'Oranges, Captain. Fresh dates. Figs . . . and olives. Good olives. Greek.'

'Firty oranges.'

'Five piastres.'

'One piastre.'

They settled for two . . . and that was a characteristic transaction. Two lessons on my first Egyptian morning, and I hadn't set foot on shore yet. Cookie also bought most of the man's olives.

I turned to ask him, 'You call him *Ali*. You often buy from him?'

'Never seen him before in me life, sir. I call all the wogs *Ali* – saves time. *Ali Baba*, see?'

I looked back at my first Egyptian again, but he was gone. Simply vanished. There was half a mile of empty narrow stone jetty on either side of us – it was like a bony finger pointing from Port Said into the Mediterranean. It was now completely empty, and there was no cover.

'Where did he go?'

The cook shook his head. 'They do that all the time.'

'How did he do it?'

'I don't know. It's a mystery.'

The Captain came back on Sunday afternoon. I happened to be on deck as he stepped on board. He turned to face the bridge, put down his suitcase, and saluted rather smartly. I happened to be in his way so I saluted back.

He smiled and said, 'No, *you* don't have to. It's what we do every time we board a commissioned ship.'

'Why, sir?'

'Damned if I know. I must have been told once, but I've forgotten. Feeling better?'

His tropical whites were immaculate: they almost gleamed. One of the benefits of a trip home, I supposed. He had a wavy line beside the straight gold ones on his epaulettes: so, a reservist like me.

'Yes, sir. I'd make a very good sailor as long as we stayed tied up alongside.'

'And *I* get sick each time I climb into an aeroplane. Odd, what?'

'Most people do, sooner or later: it depends on the type, I find.'

'Thanks for minding the shop. My wife sends her thanks as well – promises you tiffin if you find yourself down there. I always say *An unexpected home leave is an unexpected pleasure*: points all round. Anything happen?'

'Egyptians trying to sell us things; no one else came near us. I've put copies of the radio signals in your cabin. You've been warned for some time next week.'

'Good. We'll move up to the basin tomorrow, and declare our presence.'

'Did they really not know we've been here all weekend, sir?'

He produced a gentle smile. Apparently he approved of whoever was running the naval side of the port. 'Oh, they knew all right. Just looked the other way. It's accepted practice – it suits everyone.' I thought about Cyprus; that seemed to be the way things were done out here. 'Thought we'd have a little party tonight: welcome you to Egypt and thank you for our weekend off. I know my people are keen.' Party. Now that was a word I understood.

I was hung-over the following morning. The *Wallflower*'s ward room wasn't short of pink gins, and then before I turned in the NCOs wanted to toast me in grog . . . which is over-proof rum diluted with water until it has the consistency of a sweet-tasting paint stripper. It's absolutely fucking deadly. When I woke up the clothes I had passed out in were sticking to me, and we were already alongside the quay in the Port Said basin.

I needn't have worried about reporting because a young Navy medic came to collect me from the ship. It was already hot, and he drove his jeep fast. With the windscreen laid flat on the bonnet we were cooled by our own passing. There was a thin steel girder with a cutting edge mounted vertically on the jeep's front bumper, supported by a couple of metal stays. It must have reached clear six feet above the ground.

'What's that for?' I shouted.

He shouted back. 'The fucking wogs string wire across the roads neck-high to a motorcyclist. We've lost several dispatch riders that way. A major hit one in his jeep last month, and took the top of his head off: he drove into the base hospital with his brain showing.'

'Did he make it?'

'Yeah. He was a Brown Job major, like I said, so the general consensus is that although he lost most of his brain, nobody will notice.'

'Where are you taking me?'

'PMO, sir: Port Medical Officer.' Balls, had I caught something already?

I hadn't, as it turned out, and what's more the War Office didn't want me to. The old PMO, a kindly-looking retread with tufts of white hair and wire-framed glasses, had to explain:

'We had a signal about you, Pilot Officer. Although you were given your Tab One and Tab Twos, and most of the rest in the UK, before you left, some dozy doctor forgot to check your medical record. You haven't had the separate yellow fever vaccination, and we can't let you loose until you have. Roll your sleeve up now, there's a good chap.'

While he was preparing me for the ordeal he observed, 'I was in the Royal Veterinary Corps once. Before the war, that was . . . in Afghanistan and Iraq. I learned my trade injecting donkeys' bums, and whipping their goolies off.'

'You came down-market, then, sir. What happened?'

'I transferred to the RMC because soldiers and sailors don't kick or bite as much as donkeys. It's noticeably safer.' And while he was saying that he gave me the jab in my upper arm. He had a nice touch, and I didn't even feel it. At the time. Then the orderly took me out to a sand-coloured bus devoid of regimental flashes, and as I got on, pulling my kitbag after me, an RASC lance jack handed me my transit order in a sealed envelope.

'Where am I going?' I asked him.

'Down Treaty Road and Canal Road, sir . . . about seventy mile.'

'Where to?'

'Spinney Wood Camp, sir, just outside Ismailia. It's the RAF Comms HQ. I expect you'll be posted on from there. Most of the RAF lads end up at Deversoir or Fayid. You aircrew, sir?'

'Sometimes – if I can't get out of it.'

'That's the style, sir: you shouldn't have joined up if you can't take a joke. Don't worry; the Army'll get you there.'

Whenever someone feels the need to offer me reassuring words before I've asked for them I get a sinking feeling in the pit of my stomach. I accepted an old aluminium water bottle from him. I could hear fluid that I hoped was water sloshing about in it, and something else that rattled. I'd heard tales about the Army putting chemicals in the water to suppress men's natural inclinations, so I hoped it wasn't that. Meanwhile I had a headache which was not improving – I ought to have asked that doctor for an aspirin. On the upside I was heading for Ismailia, closing in on an exotic dancer with a reputation for improvisations that could bring a tear to the eye. So life wasn't all bad.

I was wrong, of course: it bloody was.

They tell me that your first visual impression of the sweep of Egypt seen from the Treaty Road stays with you for ever. Mine didn't.

The road is a dark thread of tarmac parallel to the Canal, and literally within spitting distance of it. It runs as straight as a Roman road, skirting the salt beds of Lake Manzala, and on south to Canal Road and Ismailia. To the west – that's on your right if you are travelling south – the desert stretches off as far as you can see. The sky is a washed-out blue, because the intense sun robs your eyes of their ability to concentrate colour. It looks like a place where nothing normal can live. I didn't see much of that, though: after about ten minutes I began to shiver. I wrapped my flying jacket, which I had been toting over my shoulder, tightly around me and squeezed into the corner of my seat. I probably passed out soon after that.

Nobody noticed, because my few fellow passengers – mainly old Canal Zone sweats – had settled down to sleep themselves by then. Apparently someone finally pointed out to the driver, after the stop at Gordon Camp was behind us, that an RAF officer at the back was stubbornly resisting all attempts to rouse him. Gordon Camp was about fifty miles south of Port Said – the last stop proper before Ismailia, and the complex of camps around it. I suspect that my driver wasn't alerted before then because nobody wanted the bus delayed before it reached their own stop: your British squaddie is nothing if not practical. The driver decided to press on: any other decision would have probably earned him a thick ear anyway.

My next proper memory – and there are a few others, mainly fragments of faces and murmurings – is of waking up in a white room with a curved ceiling, and knowing immediately that all was not well. It felt like the inside of a long Nissen hut, because it *was* the inside of a long Nissen hut. I'm not that fond of Nissen huts: they remind me of being forced to get into a Lancaster bomber and fly all over Germany while our German brothers were meanwhile doing their level best to kill me. I was aware immediately, though, that this wasn't a bad dream or a flashback. Nearly everything else in the long narrow room was white as well. I knew that white: I had woken up in a bloody hospital before. After twenty minutes, a woman came to stand alongside the bed. I felt too ill to even care whether she was plain or a looker. She took my pulse. Why do nurses always do that? Even when you roll them on their backs they can't resist the urge to take your pulse. It must be some sort of programmed reflex they develop when they're still in training.

147

'Welcome back, Pilot Officer. The doctors were worried about you.'

'Did they blow up the bus?' My voice was cracked and hoarse, and my mouth was dry.

'No. Why do you think that?'

'I missed one in Malta, and the Maltesers blew it up. I thought this might be God having a second go at me.'

She smiled. 'Nothing as dramatic as that, I'm afraid.'

'Then what happened to me?'

'The doctor will explain. Are you thirsty?' I nodded my head. 'I'll get you something to drink.' It was cold water sipped slowly through a straw: the best drink I ever had in my life.

I said, 'I'm tired.'

'Why don't you sleep then?' She picked up my limp wrist again, and I knew exactly what she was about to do. Maybe they just like to keep in practice.

The next morning I was lifted onto a trolley, and my bed sheets and mattress changed. Two male orderlies sponged me down with cool water: they can't have enjoyed it as much as I did. I drank a cup of very thin tea, and ate half a slice of bread and jam. Then I went to sleep again.

I awoke feeling reasonably alert, and because I was reasonably alert quickly noticed the Port Medical Officer from Port Said standing alongside the bed beaming happily down at me.

'Good,' he said, 'you're not dead. I haven't killed a patient yet, not even a donkey . . . and didn't want to start with you.'

'I would find it hard to disagree with that, sir.'

He pulled over a chair. It creaked when he sat down. An overhead fan nearby clicked as it revolved.

I asked, 'What happened to me?' My voice was stronger.

'I nearly did for you with a yellow fever jab, that's what.'

'You gave me yellow fever?'

'I hope so. That's the principle of the whole process.' He grinned and looked younger. 'We give you enough dead yellow fever antigen for your body to produce the necessary antibodies against the real thing. The dead virus wasn't a problem, but what we had it in was.'

'Please explain.'

'The vaccination you were given wouldn't last ten minutes after it had been manufactured unless there was a preservative in there to stop it going off. We need it to live in a fridge for at least a year. There was something in the preservative that your body didn't like. You had an allergic reaction to it that nearly killed you.'

'What was it?'

'A compound of mercury.'

I reached over to a small bedside cupboard, and took a swig from my water through a straw. It didn't taste anything like as good as the day before – now I fancied a beer.

'When I was at school, we were taught that mercury was toxic – a poison.'

'It is, but in minute concentrations it is also a magnificent preserving emulsifier for vaccines, and it doesn't do most people any harm at all.'

'But I'm allergic to it?'

'Right. If ever you spill any of it on your skin in the future you have to promise me you'll run for the nearest nurse.'

'Will they know what to do?'

'Probably not, but at least they can hold your hand while you die.' It's curious, but I miss those old service doctors now: they called it the way they saw it. 'Have you seen your arm yet?'

I shook my head. He unwrapped a mile of bandage from around my left upper arm. Nothing hurt up there, so I had been wondering about it. My newly exposed arm was half as thick again as nature intended, and bruised to the colour of uncooked liver. There was an open abscess the size of a joey – a threepenny bit to anyone as old as me – at the injection site, and visible cheesy pus inside it. It smelt bad.

'That's not gangrene, is it? You won't have to cut my arm off?' I asked.

'No. It's fine. It's just pretending – looking for sympathy.'

'It won't get much.'

'It will tomorrow – when it will itch like hell, and you will be unable to scratch it. I'll get one of the nurses to dress it again, and then I'll toddle off. Must be close to lunch time. I'll come by again in five days.'

'I won't be out by then?'

'No, but near enough. Ta-ra.'

Welcome to Egypt, Charlie.

The nurse was a tall, well-built young thing – a Queen Alexandra's: one of the famous Grey Mafia. She was in her twenties. She had dark hair bleached several shades by the sun, luscious lips and broad shoulders. Taller than me; but, again, that's not difficult. She must have just come on duty because she still smelled of soap, and not perspiration or stale perfume. She could also tie a pretty mean bandage.

I asked her, 'When can I get up, and wander around?'

'I put your clothes into the laundry. They should come back tomorrow; you can get up then.'

There was a row of tall metal lockers across the room; I reckoned one would be mine.

'That's all right. There's a couple of spares in my kitbag. I can get up today.'

She shook her head, 'I'll make some inquiries, but nothing came off the bus with you. I'm sure of that. Certainly no kitbag.'

It took a couple of seconds for the penny to drop. Then I realized that my fellow bus passengers had not only kept me on the bus long enough to nearly bloody kill me, they'd robbed me blind into the bargain. My third lesson from Egypt taught me never to turn my back on a fucking soul. Charlie would be turning up at his next station the way he'd arrived at several others – with just the clothes he stood up in. My flying jacket was draped over the back of a nearby chair; at least they'd left me that . . . I wondered if they'd found the small pistol in it yet. Then I began to laugh.

Florence Nightingale went all po-faced on me, and asked, 'Did I say something funny?'

'No. Sorry. I just realized that all of my kit's been nicked. I almost went out of this world as naked as I came in, didn't I?'

She gave me a funny look and said, 'The PMO told you how touch-and-go it was then? I didn't think he would.'

'He didn't; *you* just did . . . but don't worry – I won't tell on you.' She must have felt foolish, because she blushed. 'It just makes me even gladder to wake up and find people who look like you around. Dead and gone to Heaven.' Her blush was even deeper now, but I thought I might have made a friend.

Before she walked away from me I asked her the old classic, 'Nurse, where am I?'

She smiled. Everything back under control. 'Not dead and gone to Heaven for a start. I've lots to do, so stop messing me about.'

'I'm not. I mean it . . .'

'You really don't know where you are?'

'No: nobody told me.'

'El Kirsh.'

'Which is?'

'Probably the most heavily protected camp we have: we've married quarters here – although a woman would have to feel really desperate to follow her husband to Ismailia, wouldn't she?'

'What else?'

'A satellite base hospital – meaning us: mainly for the dependants, and a few other small units, including a motor unit . . . and a load of very unpleasant regimental policemen who are supposed to look after us. Do you know anyone here?'

I probably smiled. 'Not quite. The wife of the skipper of the ship that brought me here promised me tiffin, whatever that is, because I got him a weekend off with her. Captain Holroyd – first name Neville or Nev. She lives around here somewhere.'

'I'll ask. Anything you need?'

'Something to read when you have a minute.'

'OK. Why don't you lie back for a few minutes; you're beginning to look a bit seedy again.'

'And I feel it, too.'

'This is going to happen a lot to you in the next few days. You're going to feel suddenly very tired – bone-weary.'

'What should I do?'

'Why fight it? Your body knows what it's doing.'

She was right. My eyes were closed before she was out of sight. The last thing I noticed before my eyes closed was a poster on the wall. The ward had been decorated with BOAC posters to cheer everyone up. This one showed a girl in colourful clothes dancing a samba at the Carnival at Rio. It was where I would have rather been.

When I awoke, there was a Bible on the bedside cabinet. It wasn't exactly the reading I'd had in mind. Maybe they were trying to tell me something.

PART TWO

Into the Blue

Chapter Nine

Am I blue?

Her name was Susan Haye, 'Hay with an *e*' . . . and within two days I was soft on her. She told me that men always get soft on their nurses, as long as they're not other men. She was the first paid-up member of the Grey Mafia I had exchanged more than a dance with. In case you're wondering, both their uniforms and berets are grey; there's nothing more to the nickname than that. Mind you, whenever you see one walking towards you with a syringe big enough for an elephant in her tray, and two hefty male orderlies to hold you down, you are reminded of the phrase that bloke used a few years ago – '*an offer you cannot refuse*'.

In a ward that could take twenty there were only five others beside myself, and I think they all had the terminal trots. I only seemed to meet them hurrying to and from the bogs, and at night it wasn't unusual for one of them to shit in his sleep. That resulted in the usual ring of white screens, 'tut-tuts', and the inevitable noisy morning blanket bath. Whatever they had I wanted none of it. Staff Nurse Susan told me not to worry – they were well past the infectious stage.

The food was good, but not as good as the paper bag of home-made ginger biscuits I found on my bed one afternoon: crisp on the outside but soft and peppery once you bit into them. I asked Saucy Susan (who was anything but, of course) where they'd come from, and she pretended not to know. I wanted them to be from her, but perhaps I had a secret admirer. Who knows? There's a first time for everything.

There was a small, deep veranda at one end of the ward, and I was the only one who used it. It was too far from the bogs for the others. I sat there smoking gifted cigarettes because I'd run out of pipe tobacco, and sometimes I read the Bible for something to do. I loved the rolling language of the Book of Revelation, but it had a sad ending. Come to think of it, almost everything in the Bible has a sad ending: it's a handbook for manic depressives, and I don't know why so many folk are keen on it. There was room on the veranda for just two cane chairs; Susan came and sat in the other, lit a cigarette and we smoked in companionable silence. Smokers do that, you know. Smoking together is what the words *companionable* and *silence* were coined for.

Then I moaned, 'A fag never lasts long enough.' – I know that wouldn't mean the same thing today, but I assure you that in 1953 we were only talking about cigarettes – 'I miss my pipe.'

'Was it stolen with your other things?'

'No, I've only run out of tobacco.'

'I smoked de Reszkes back home, but I learned to like Turkish cigarettes out here; now I smoke Abdullahs: would you like one?'

'Thank you.'

Half a fag later she bent to pick up the Bible which I had dropped by the chair. 'Would you like to come to church on Sunday?'

'God's not all that keen on me.' The last time I had been to church was with Dolly, in Chelsea in 1947. We had gone home afterwards, and straight to bed. I'd often suspected that God has had it in for me since then.

'God's keen on everyone, silly.'

'Going to church is like getting married. I only go to church with women I'm going to sleep with.'

She breathed out the last of the smoke from her cigarette, dropped it under a foot and extinguished it. Then she gave a low laugh. 'Nice try, Charlie, but my boyfriend wouldn't like it.'

'Is he out here?'

'Yes. He's out in the blue; due back next week.'

It was the first time I'd really paid attention to that phrase. It means far away, out deep in the desert.

'He's a lucky man.' They are the words we men use to signal that we won't try it on again. Not until the next time, anyway.

'Sometimes,' she said, 'I wonder about that . . .' and sounded wistful. I added the only word that fitted: '*Don't*.'

'Time I went back to work.'

'. . . I've bums to jab, and floors to sweep, and bedpans to wash before I sleep . . .'

'That's from a poem.'

'Not quite,' I said.

The next day when I came in from my afternoon smoke, and a slow perambulation around the outside of the hut, a two-ounce tin of RN Navy Cut tobacco was on my bed, along with three paperback books. Two were by an American I'd never read. It was that guy Mickey Spillane, and if the girls on the cover were anything to go by, I was going to enjoy them. The third was by a maniac named Charles Hoy Fort – *The Book of the Damned*. Things were looking up. I still have that last one.

The day before David Watson came to see me I woke up from my afternoon nap to find a woman standing alongside my bed. Her back was to me. It was a nice back. She was leaning out of the window making smoke. We were quite good at smoking in the Fifties; pity the next lot made such a mess of it. Like I said, I liked her back. Most of it was clad in a summer frock, but the skin above her plunging backline, arms and calves was tanned, with a faint golden fuzz of hair. What I could see of the hair on

157

her head was also blonde, and pulled back into a pony tail with an elastic band. Most amazing of all was the finest of gold chains around her right ankle.

I yawned, sat up and swung my legs over the side of the bed. 'Sorry. Was I snoring?'

'No. You looked as peaceful as a baby. I didn't want to wake you.' Her front looked just as good as her back. It must be one of God's tricks. I tried two no trumps.

'Are you Mrs Holroyd?'

'No: I'm one of Mrs Holroyd's neighbours. She told me there was an RAF boy stuck up in the hospital, who didn't know anyone in Egypt.'

'I'm trying.'

'I know. Nurse Haye told me. She said that you were obviously recovering, and for me to stay out of reach. I brought you a book: I know you men like war stories.' It was about Navy frogmen.

'That was a kind thought. Thank you. I do get very bored. All the other men here have got the shits. I think they get to talk to each other in the lavatory. So I get to talk to no one except the nurses and the orderlies. Then I say the wrong things.'

'I thought that you would be younger.'

'So did I. It's what I think every morning when I wake up . . . and then I look in the mirror. Disappointed?'

She didn't answer immediately; then, 'Not yet.' So far she'd stood up to me like one of those dames in a Hank Janson book. She hadn't disappointed *me* either.

'I'm Charlie. Charlie Bassett: last in a long line of liquorice allsorts jokes. I'm also an optimist.'

'Jill Paul. Pessimist.'

There were several ways on from there. 'Married lady or unmarried lady?'

'Both.' That was interesting.

'It's kind of you to visit someone you don't know.'

'Service tradition. Don't think about it; it's expected of us.'

'Is it too early to say that the chain around your ankle is driving me wonderfully insane?'

'Definitely.'

'When can I say it?'

'After you've had tea with me. Tomorrow afternoon, OK?' I probably gave her the dumb-show nod. 'This is my address. In the married lines; you'll find it easily.' She handed me a small white card on which she had written an address with that kind of small, clear handwriting that always makes you jealous.

'Thank you. When?'

'Say fifteen hundred.' She picked up a small white purse from my bed. I hadn't noticed it. 'I'll be off, then . . .'

'OK.'

I watched her walk down the ward. She didn't look back. Her hips swayed from side to side under the floral print. Even one of the squitter merchants hauled himself upright to speak to her. Then he ducked, because she'd scooped something from a medical trolley, and shied it at him. Then I realized that she hadn't smiled much. Yes; interesting, and at least I knew where the ginger biscuits had come from. All that, and she could cook too?

Later in the day – in the early evening – I sat on the veranda with Nurse Haye-with-an-e: she was about to go off duty. The smoke from her cigarette mingled with smoke from my pipe. I thought that was very romantic. I asked her, 'Who *was* that woman?'

'Just one of the wives. They visit from time to time; to keep morale up.'

'She was friendlier than I expected, that's all.'

Long pause and intro . . . Tommy's 'Smoke gets in your eyes'.

Then she asked, 'Have you ever heard that phrase the Yanks

159

use about long-term prisoners, Charlie? They say they go *stir-crazy*.'

'Yes, I've heard that. Someone used it on me not long ago. I forget who.'

'Well.' Deep breath. 'One way or another, we're all stir-crazy down here, Charlie. You shouldn't forget that.'

Watson sat with me on the same veranda, and we both smoked. The morning sun was so bright that the dirt of the parade ground looked almost white. I hadn't realized how quickly you could fixate on a woman who replenished your tobacco stock.

'Am I shallow, sir?' I asked him.

'Exceptionally, old fruit.'

'Really?'

'Really and truly. You are about the shallowest person I've ever met.'

'So why do some people like me?'

'Because they know exactly where they are with you, Charlie. It's very easy to have low expectations of you, at a personal level.'

I thought that was unfair. 'I don't think I've ever let you down, sir.' He was already beginning to piss me off.

'That's because my expectations were always low. Can we now talk about when you're coming back to work?'

'They haven't told me yet, but I'm feeling almost a hundred per cent, and I'm bored beyond belief. Why don't you ask them?'

'I have done, actually. I've arranged for you to get a medical in two days' time if that's not inconvenient. If they say *yes* you'll be ready to come out to play again.'

'I lost all my kit.'

'I know. But Daisy got your measurements from the records, and re-indented for you: a lot of it's already arrived.'

'Is she over here with you? If so, she must be madder than you are.'

'You said that before, Charlie, and it annoyed me then. Say it again, and I'll lend you to the Brown Jobs for permanent guard duty, and painting coal. They have *vays of making you squawk*.' In his part of England they would have found that very witty. I made a job of refilling and relighting my pipe – you tend to make a bit of a pig of yourself if you've been without it for a couple of days – and kept my head down.

'Where will my permanent station be, sir?'

'Probably Deversoir, down on the Great Bitter Lake. But some of the time you'll be not far from here, at Abu Sueir . . . it depends which direction I'm sending you in.' I didn't respond, just raised an eyebrow. He waved a hand to show it didn't matter. 'Out into the blue, old boy, out into the blue – just up your street; you'll love it!'

Then he leaned over, and poked a nice flat quarter-bottle into my KD jacket pocket. I liked the old soak really.

He asked, 'This really is a cushy number: any worries?'

'Yes, sir. I have one. I'm wondering if I'm allergic to anything else. I don't know exactly what happened a few days ago, but I think it could have killed me.'

'I asked them that too: I thought you'd want to know.'

'What did they say?'

'That they'd think about it. Rum bunch these doctors. Cheers.' He'd pulled another quarter-bottle from another pocket. Neither of the bottles had a label on it. He took a swig, and then offered me one. Over-proof rum. God bless the Navy!

I know you'll find this difficult to believe, but I know what you're thinking now . . . and it simply didn't happen. I brassed myself up for my afternoon tea. Haye checked me out before I left, looked me up and down and gave me a small nod of approval. Going over to the semi-detached bungalows on the Married Lines was the furthest I'd walked since I'd moved in to the hospital, and it was no problem. Jill Paul wasn't a problem either: dressed as I'd seen her the day before, maybe a bit more relaxed and smiley. Barefoot too. She handed me a clear drink in one of those flat cocktail glasses. A few bubbles drifted up to the surface.

She said, 'I should wear shoes in here, but I can't bear to. So I have to watch out for the scorpions.'

No one had told me about the scorpions, 'I didn't know there were any.'

'One rule of Wives' Club: anything with more than four legs is likely to be a scorpion, and anything that looks like a boot lace or piece of rope is more likely to be a snake. Another rule of Wives' Club: avoid both because they're poisonous.'

'Really. What's Wives' Club?'

'It's really the Lost Wives' Club. It's what we women do to avoid being driven round the bend by life in a prison cage on the edge of a desert.'

'Does it work?'

'No, not really.' She took the glass from me before I had a chance to try it. 'Would you like to dance?' She turned on a big old Bakelite box radio. Billie Holiday came from the speaker. She was doing 'Am I blue?' I've had the record for years: Grant Clarke and Harry Akst. Do they still write them like that? We danced slowly, and very close . . . for about a minute. Her back was cool against my hand. Then she stopped abruptly – there might have been the real thing glistening in the corners of her eyes – and said, 'This isn't going to work, is it?'

I understood her completely, although I wouldn't have had that sort of courage, 'No. Sorry . . . I don't know why.'

She walked away from me, turned the radio off, and gave me my drink back.

I said, 'Thanks. What is it?'

'Absolute alcohol from the hospital, with tonic and a slice of lime. It's a make-believe gin-and-tonic. Ethanol and tonic: the old expats call it E and T. Don't worry – we dilute the alcohol before we pour it.' Then she smiled the first genuine smile I had seen from her. Perhaps it was from relief. 'What shall we do now?'

'Seeing as I haven't been in here long enough to misbehave, why don't we sit on your veranda and sip our drinks in full view of your neighbours. That way they'll know you haven't anything to hide. You never know; the curtains may even stop twitching, they'll get curious, come over and join us.'

We sat out in the shade. I wondered if it ever rained on this caustic earth.

She said, 'I get the feeling you've done this before.'

'Mmm.'

'But *I* haven't. I don't know why I came on like that.'

'I realized that. We're all a bit crazy when our lives get too dull to bear – it's the most endearing and stupid thing about people. Tell me about Mr Paul.'

'Neville, you mean.'

'Neville Holroyd?'

'Yes.'

'You told me . . .'

'Jill Paul: my maiden name . . . sorry. I suddenly didn't feel very married. I never know when he's coming back.'

'In that case you've entertained me just as you promised him, and nothing bad happened . . . although it was a close-run thing.'

Then she grinned at me, and I rather began to like her. She

said, 'No; it wasn't.' When a woman looks you in the eye and tells you that you never stood a chance, it can actually be quite a liberating experience.

Twenty minutes later one of her neighbours crossed the street to give me the once-over, and then Haye dropped in on her way off-duty. We drank their pretend gin, and the stories they told me of the other wives in the compound made the place sound like a Shanghai cat-house. I don't think now that one hundredth of it was true; just desperate people and wishful thinking. In return I told them everything that had happened to me since my call-up, making it sound as silly as possible. We laughed a lot.

Before I left them I asked, 'My boss told me he'll send me up here from time to time to work out of Abu-somewhere-or-other. Would you mind if I dropped in?'

'I'd like that, Charlie,' Mrs Holroyd said.

'We *all* would,' Haye said firmly. I think she was marking my card.

The third woman was named Evelyn, and the others deferred to her. I'd known an Eve in a previous life. This one looked like a well-marinated Lauren Bacall, had a raucous laugh and a ribald sense of humour. Her skin had tanned as dark as a gypsy's. Lord knows how long she'd been in Egypt. She had two children at the Base School, and a maid who came from Asmara. She left us for ten minutes, and when she came back brought me a Navy kitbag – dirty white with a couple of blue bands around it. An old spare of her husband's, she told me he'd never miss it. Something to start again with. By the time I left them I felt as if I had been initiated into a secret society.

I was collected by an aircraftman in KD shirt and shorts driving an odd boxy jeep. It had small side doors. If even the jeeps had doors these days then the services were turning soft.

He announced, 'The Wing Commander sent me for you, sir. Short drive to Deversoir.'

'Thanks. I haven't been here long enough yet to find out how the transport works.'

I only had my old jacket – and they'd either not found my pistol, or had decided to let sleeping dogs lie, because it was still in a pocket – and an empty kitbag. I also had a full kitbag: the one I'd started with was sitting in the rear foot well. The erk was wearing a side arm. That was interesting.

He said, 'Your kit was handed in at Moascar after the bus got there, sir. I thought you'd want me to collect it en route.'

'Thanks again. What's this thing called?'

'Land-Rover, sir. Haven't you seen one before?'

'I think I saw pictures of it in the *Motor*.'

'We're trialling this one, but I've heard the Army has bought a load of them. I like the old jeep meself, but this is lighter – made of aluminium – and very good in sand.'

'. . . and the pole sticking up in front is for cutting cheese wire strung across the road?'

'That's right, sir. Very good. Your Gyppo terrorist is very brave when he doesn't have to hang around and watch. No problem when you're face to face though. They all have that American disease: what's it called?'

'I dunno.'

'Givinitis. They drops their weapons, throws up their hands and gives in.' He made me laugh. Maybe the Yanks *were* like that now. Certainly in general terms they appeared to have gone home and left all the fighting to us.

'Er . . . what worries me is my kitbag you so thoughtfully retrieved. We believed it had been nicked, so the CO's secretary has been getting replacements in for me.'

'Miss Daisy?'

'You know her?'

'I drive her sometimes. Handsome woman.'

'Yes; I knew her years ago . . . I suppose she is. I'll have to give it all back to her.'

'You don't want to be doing that, sir. She won't ask, so why don't you see me once it's all in, sir, and we'll find something creative to do with it?'

The bastard was taking a chance, but, there again, maybe I had the look of someone not terribly good with regulations. Or maybe all junior officers were always short of dosh. I suppose it was a fair bet. I let him sweat for a couple of minutes before replying, 'OK . . . what's your name?'

'Tobin, sir.'

'OK, Mr Tobin; fifty-fifty. I'd shake on it except I want you to keep both hands on the wheel.'

We were driving into a town which had ramshackle mud shanties scattered around it, but grander old buildings with verandas on its main streets. And avenues of shady trees. I don't know why, but after Port Said the last thing I expected of Egypt was more trees.

'Where are we?'

'Ismailia, sir . . . and seeing as the alert's only red-amber, it's safe enough to give you the Cook's Tour, if you'd like to look around.'

'Yes please.'

He saw me swivel to look at a boxy white building with the words Blue Kettle emblazoned on its façade, and said, 'Hard lines, sir: she's gone back to Alex. But she'll be back in a couple of months if yer still here.'

I intended to be; but I didn't tell him that.

Just outside Ismailia is a military cemetery. Tobin stopped the car at its main gate. A church poked its head above the trees. He turned to me.

'Don't mind me asking, sir, but did you get the dos-and-don'ts lecture from the Service Police or someone in the Regiment?'

'I didn't get anything. They gave me a yellow fever jab, and I passed out. I'm allergic to something they preserve it with, only we didn't find out until after they'd tried.'

'That's what someone told me. Did you get the *Never turn your back on a wog* handbook?'

'No.'

'I'll get you one. It's about eighty pages of dos and don'ts and useful Arabic phrases, but it all boils down to *Don't turn your back on a wog.*'

'Thank you. I shall remember that.'

'But all you needs to know is right in front of you, sir.' He indicated the cemetery with a sweep of one hand. There were the usual discreet white services gravestones, and a number of more recent wooden crosses. Too bloody many of them. 'All you needs to know, sir, is that if you fuck up, this is where you'll spend the rest of your life.' There was maybe a mixed metaphor in there, but he'd made his point.

'How many people do we have out here?'

'Mr Churchill says about fifty thousand, but if truth be known it's never less than eighty-eight thousand, and when things brew up sometimes twice that many.'

'And how often do things *brew up*?'

'Every few months, sir.'

'. . . and how many people do we lose?'

'Two or three a week isn't all that unusual, sir . . . and we don't often get the bodies back. When it brews up, we lose two or three at a time . . . sometimes more. Do you mind if I get going again, sir? I doesn't like to sit still for too long when there's not many people about.'

I nodded, and we set off south. He'd certainly given me

something to think about. On the way he pointed out Lake Timsah and a couple of beach clubs. He said that sailing and swimming were usually safe there. I hated the word *usually*. The road was brutally hot, and decided to teach me my next Egyptian lesson . . . I'd lost count of them by then.

Just as we reached a place where two telegraph poles straddled the road, driving at about sixty, I caught a brief flash of light at about head height, and then there was a strange twanging sound – like a violin string breaking – as writhing bright sections of wire snaked by in the air on either side of us. The vehicle was tugged a few feet to the left, but Tobin held it, and floored the throttle. I noticed that he'd instinctively crouched down. So had I.

A mile later he breathed out and said, 'Bastards!' He must have thought me quiet, because he asked, 'You OK, sir?'

'Thank you, yes. I just have to get used to people trying to kill me again.'

'Don't worry, sir. That was Mile Twelve. They often strings those telegraph poles at Mile Twelve. What I'm worried about is that one day there'll be a couple of bastards with Stens dug in alongside them; then we'll cop it.'

'These terrorists have got machine guns then?'

'These *terrorists* are often off-duty Gyppo soldiers and policemen, sir. Sometimes I think they have more guns than we do. I does picket duties with a .303 and ten rounds; the wog trying to get through the wire has a Sten and thirty. The Gyppo cop guarding our gate one day will be trying to stab you in the bazaar the next. They *are* proper bastards, believe me.'

'Why don't we just knock down all the poles alongside the road?'

'The ambassador doesn't want us to do anything to annoy the Gyppoes, sir. It's complicated, but you'll quickly get used to it.'

'Sounds stupid.'

'Some Navy wag painted up a big sign on the dock at Port Said, where the big troopers come in. It read "Welcome to Wonderland". *Alice in Wonderland*, geddit?'

'What happened?'

'They shipped him home in irons fer embarrassing the wogs. Surprised you needed to ask, sir.'

'So am I. But don't worry; I'm a quick learner.'

I'd bloody need to be at this rate.

The last time I saw somewhere that looked anything like RAF Deversoir it had been a concentration camp in Germany. The only difference from a superficial glance was that the inmates looked marginally better fed. It had a guardhouse, a functioning lift-arm gate and oil drums filled with concrete that Tobin had to weave around. There were two Egyptian policemen lounging under a scrubby tree outside. I committed their faces to memory in case I ever saw either of them coming up behind me in a bazaar.

Apart from that, Deversoir had a few unhappy flower beds lining its main internal road, some runways in the distance, and about thirty miles of barbed wire around it with the occasional lookout post. I don't know why they bothered: no one could police a perimeter that length with anything less than a brigade. There were the usual workshops and garages, accommodation huts . . . and rows and rows of bleeding tents. I assumed that the tents were where the enlisted men lived, and pitied them, until Tobin brought us decorously to a stop alongside one.

' . . .'ome sweet 'ome, sir.'

'It's a bloody tent!'

'Most of us live in tents, sir. I share mine with five other buggers; begging your pardon, sir.'

'What's your point?'

'This is a four-man tent, sir . . . and there's only two of you in it. You don't know when you're well off.' Then he repeated, ' . . . begging your pardon, sir.'

I suppose that, as tents go, it wasn't a bad tent. It was probably twelve feet square ridged up to a central pole, and didn't have too many repair patches. There was even height enough to stand up inside. All four sides were brailed up to the ridges to let the air and the sun in. Two camp beds, assorted low lockers, a low table and a couple of camp chairs. A cheap radio wired to an old car battery, and a pack of cards.

As I got down and lifted out my clobber I asked Tobin, 'A few questions . . .'

'Go ahead, sir.'

'Where do I find Mr Watson when I need him, and where do I find you?'

'Along the main drag another hundred yards, sir, and take the first on the right – the Wing Commander's office is right in front of you. It's made of wood so you can't miss it.'

'And you?'

'Either the MT workshop, or in me tent – that's the big job behind the Wing Commander's office.'

'Who's your immediate boss?'

'LAC Raynes, sir. He also runs the tent.'

'What's he like?'

Tobin looked quickly in either direction: evasive. Then, 'Tosser, sir. No use at all. Anything you want you'd better ask me.'

'What's your other name?'

'Patrick, sir. The lads call me Pat.'

'Then thanks, Pat; for the ride, and the advice. I'll be in touch.'

'I'm sure you will, sir.'

As I walked into the tent space, perspiration running down my back, Oscar Wilde was lying face-down on one of the two beds, wearing a pair of shorts too small for him, and no shirt.

His back and his legs were the colour of a Cherokee Indian's. He had ignored me while I was still in the Land-Rover. He ignored me now, except for saying, 'You won't like it here. Nobody does.'

There was a concentration of scents drifting high in the tent. I couldn't make out if it was incense, wacky baccy, or an overdose of very expensive aftershave. Maybe there were the traces of all three up there.

'Can I take any of the lockers?'

'As many as you want, dearie, but if I was you I'd only put in them what you need day to day . . . anything else will get nicked. Pat will rent you out a locked cupboard in the MT section for your decent stuff. Only an acker a week.'

'An acker?'

'Local currency: worth bugger-all.'

'I'm Charlie Bassett.'

'I know: the bad news preceded you. Oliver Nansen: Olive or Nancy — I answer to both. I sleep naked; I hope you don't mind.'

Nansen reminded me of a pilot I'd known on my squadron at Bawne during the war; but at least Quelch could fly. I wondered what this limp-wristed nitwit could possibly have going for him. You probably don't realize how prejudiced my generation was — I would have happily flown with Quelch, you see, because he was bloody A1 at his job . . . but I'm buggered if I would have slept in the next bed. Forgive the pun. It's just the way we were. That's why I didn't even bother to unpack.

'I am not living in a fucking tent!'

'. . . tent, *sir*.' Watson corrected me. He didn't seem particularly worried by the omission, but he waited for my acknowledgement.

'Sorry; *sir*. Your driver dropped me off outside a tent with a

queer in it, and said it was where I lived. I am not a fucking
Arab, sir, and I won't live in a tent in the desert with a queer.
My mother wouldn't like it.'

Watson sighed. 'Your mother's dead, Charlie. Which is it that
offends you, the tent or the queer?'

'The tent.'

'This is Lawrence of Arabia country, son. Half the world lives
in tents here, and thinks it the fashionable thing to do. You too.
We haven't any hard billets to spare; in any case my small mob
comes right at the bottom of the pecking order. Even *I* haven't a
separate cabin – I live here.' *Here* was a wooden shack that looked
like a small cricket pavilion of bleached wood. That was odd: the
last time I worked with him at Cheltenham in 1947, he operated
out of a virtually identical building. I now suspected that he
moved it with him wherever he went. Like a tortoise.

'I'll swap you, sir. You can have my tent.'

'No I can't. Make do with what you've got. Stop bloody
bellyaching, and get yourself sorted out. You'll be going out in a
few days' time.'

'. . . the queer then? I'm objecting to sharing a tent with a
homo. He says his name's Nancy, which figures, and he's cut his
shorts back so far that the cheeks of his arse are showing. His hair
reaches his shoulders, and he's draped across his camp bed like
Jane Russell saying *Come up and see me sometime*. He's a bloody
monstrosity.'

'That was Mae West, actually . . . but I think you must have
him wrong. He can't be a homo. Homosexuality is illegal in the
armed forces: he'd be cashiered for it. He *is* in the armed forces;
therefore he cannot be a homosexual. QED; you must be wrong.
Anyway his name's not Nancy, it's Nansen, like the explorer;
you shouldn't jump to conclusions.'

'The tent smells like a Berlin brothel: he has incense burning.'

'Good idea: keeps the flies down. I saw one the size of a golf ball once. Don't worry about Nancy. He has a useful function in the RAF, or he wouldn't be here. Get used to him, get unpacked, and get yourself ready for the blue. Find out which vehicle you're going out in – the Army leaves the radio vehicles here for us to maintain. Make sure the radios are OK, and that you have sufficient spares for a long trip. Ask Tobin to get you anything you need, but don't give him money for bribes or he'll have the shirt off your back.'

'What about the little things, sir? Like food, fuel and water?'

'Leave that to the Brown Jobs; they'll be conducting you, doing all the rough stuff and carrying the cargo. All you have to do is listen. You'll get bored, so take a book. Piece of piss.'

I hate it when people say something like that. It's almost an invitation for the shit to begin flying. OK, time to eat humble pie, and make peace with my new room mate. Maybe he could give me enough tips to get me safely through my first patrol.

'I'm stuck with you, aren't I?' Those were the words Nansen re-greeted me with. 'The old man wouldn't let you move on. That's because everyone else who fetches up here asks to move, and there's nowhere left to move you to.'

'How many others?'

'In the last few months? Four.'

'What happened to them?'

'Johnson lost his head; you've been told about clearing your throat with a line of telephone wire?'

'Yes: someone tried it on me on the way here.'

'Then there was Johnson Two . . . that's Johnston with a t . . . he got VD from a girl he met in the Blue Kettle and is still *hors de combat*. A cultured Scotch git named Donnie something broke his arm and leg out in the blue, and was shipped out . . .

and Denny is still here, but got himself shifted to a tent near the wire . . . no one else wanted it.'

'Why was that?'

'Why was what?'

'Why did no one else want his tent?'

'. . . because, dearie, when your wog comes through the wire, looking for something to steal and a nice white boy to slice up, he makes for the nearest tent, doesn't he? Just don't go visiting Denny after dark – he sleeps with a loaded revolver in his hand. You don't come from the East End, by any chance?'

'No. Surrey. South of London – why?'

'In that case, dearie, you are going to see things out here for which your experience has not prepared you. The Gyppoes have taken the art of the knife and the cut-throat razor to entirely a new level. If Jack the Ripper had fallen asleep, and awoken in the Canal Zone in 1953 he would have been as happy as a pig in shit.'

'I was in Lancasters in the war. People got cut up in those as well.'

Nansen blinked. It was the first thing I'd said to give him pause. 'Ah . . . sorry. Sometimes my tongue carries me away.'

'Don't worry about it. Somebody has to tell me these things if I'm to achieve my ambition.'

'Which is?'

'To get through these next months, and then get off home again with all my important body parts still attached.'

Nansen sat up, and held out his hand for a shake. He had a rather charming smile when he chose to use it, and a hard handshake.

'At last: a realist! Welcome to my humble abode – and you *are* welcome to share it.' Then he destroyed the words by adding, 'You've already stayed ten minutes longer than any of your predecessors, anyway.'

'Thank you. We can start by you showing me what to keep, and what to take to Pat Tobin. After that you can take me to a bar . . . I take it there is one around here somewhere?'

'Several actually. The RAF is trying to recreate the Raj on the banks of the Great Bitter Lake, and no one has told them yet that it is about a hundred years too late for that.'

'What do I call you? And it will be neither Nancy nor Olive, I can tell you for a start.'

'Oliver, then. Pilot Officer Oliver Nansen; lost but not forgotten.'

'Oliver then . . . and Oliver, can we agree that if you don't call me *dearie* again, I won't try to make your life a misery in return?'

'Yes, master.' He suddenly reminded me of Bozey's three-legged dog, and I realized that my life was about to become a little more interesting. The other thing you need to know, and I know that this has taken longer to write than I intended, is that that occasion was my introduction to one of the best men I ever met. Life deals you funny cards, and then it's up to you to play them as well as you can.

Chapter Ten

*

Blue skies

A few days later I was out in the blue, riding the passenger seat of an old Austin K5 radio wagon. The driver was a short, tough Ordnance lance-jack who looked as if he'd been in the desert since puberty. Like Nansen's, his flesh, where it was exposed to the sun, was a deep coppery red. He also appeared to know what he was doing. What surprised me was that most of the bull disappeared once these types drove off into the sand. I called him Roy, but he never called me Charlie. Everyone else called him Trigger, but that was because his last name was Rogers: you work it out. We deferred to the sergeant in charge of the patrol – only we all called him Sergeant; even me, although I technically outranked him. Like my driver, he knew what he was doing; I didn't.

The K5 had a steel cab, but what Roy referred to as 'hollow legs' – he meant that she had a lightweight three-ply body on top of her chassis – which meant that all of her weight was in the right place, even if the radio shack on the back wouldn't stop a bullet. I had a Sten on the floor between my feet, and above my head was an open observation hatch: I could stand on my seat, and fire my gun from it if I had to. I practised a few times scrambling from sitting to standing, looking out with my gun in my hands.

That amused Roy. He said, 'Full marks for trying anyway, but don't do it until I say so, and try not to shoot the Sergeant: he's the only one who can find his way around out here.'

Sergeant Clare: just like the countryman poet John Clare, who I mentioned earlier. The sort of man you respect before he even opens his mouth. I had been standing beside the K5 in the Deversoir compound when Clare and his little convoy drove up. He was a passenger in the old jeep that led it. I had my pack and bedroll at my feet, a pipe in my mouth, and had been looking the other way. First impressions count, so I hope I didn't look too much of a tosser. I was protecting my bonce with my oldest service peaked cap – it had faded to an indecent light grey by then – but I couldn't hide the fact that I'd spent too long out in the Gyppo sun already. My elbows, knees and forearms were peeling.

I returned Clare's salute sloppily – I've never been any good at them. He slid smoothly out of the jeep with, 'Sergeant Clare, sir. Would you mind if we got cracking? You've had your station briefing; I can give a field briefing the first time we stop.'

'Fine, Sergeant. Do I drive this thing, or just ride in it?' I put my hand on the K5's flank, and speedily took it off again. You could have boiled a kettle on it.

Clare smiled. 'Ride in it for the time being, if you don't mind. Have you driven a four-by-four before?' I liked the alliteration, but shook my head. He continued, 'I'll show you how it works later on, but for now Driver Rogers will take her.' A small man not much bigger than me had jumped down from the back of one of the two Bedford QL lorries that made up our company. 'Mount up with him, and we'll talk later. I want to be across the Canal by midday.'

He turned away, but walked back to me as I was about to climb up into the cab – it was nearly four feet off the ground.

'Just one last thing, Mr Bassett. In a normal army in normal times, we would be said to be going out on what would be described as an armed patrol. This is not a normal army, and these are not normal times. We are not officially at war with Egypt – it is just an unfriendly power – so what you are about to be engaged on is called a *scheme*, not a patrol, goddit?'

'Yes, Sergeant. I understand.'

His voice dropped about ten decibels. I think that Rogers was probably the only other person in earshot. Clare continued, 'No, sir; I don't think you do. What I am saying is that you are definitely not to kill anyone until I tell you to. Understood?'

'Yes, Sergeant. Now I understand.'

It was as I climbed up into the cab that I saw the Sten that Corporal Rogers had placed in the foot well.

He said, 'Welcome to the Sons of the Desert, sir. I'm Roy Rogers.'

'Pleased to meet you, Roy. I'm Charlie.'

'OK, sir.' He nodded to where Clare was getting back into his jeep. 'Don't take any notice over what the Sarge just said. Just start shooting as soon as I tells you to; and I want good body shots every bleedin' time, *capisce*?' We were all using the word now. Too many bloody Eyetie film stars in the world, weren't there?

We could have driven an hour up the Canal, and crossed on a swing bridge, and been seen by all the world and his mother, but Clare turned out to be too canny for that. We drove out of Deversoir, down to the Bitter Lake shore, and loaded up onto two landing craft. LCVs they called them, and I managed to cross the lake without getting seasick. It took about twenty minutes to load the two lorries onto one of the LCVs, and the jeep and the K5 onto the other. I got the feeling that Clare was not going to let me out of his sight for a while. I didn't blame him. I wouldn't have trusted a desert novice not to fuck something up, either. We passed two flat-tops moored about fifty yards apart. One of them had about thirty bored-looking squaddies in shorts sitting on it. They waved and jeered as we chugged past. We got a few of Winston's salutes as well.

'Swimming lesson number six,' Rogers informed me. We'd just been given the OK to smoke, and were leaning over the side.

'What?'

'It's how they teach you to swim out here. You get a week's light duty, but you're expected to attend the swimming pool – like the RAF pool at Abu Sucir – for five consecutive days. Then they take you out to two barges – usually on Lake Timsah – and get you to swim from one to the other in PT half kit. That's swimming lesson number six. If you don't drown your record is marked that the Army's taught you to swim.'

'You won't catch me doing that. I can't stand water. I can't breathe in it.'

'You don't have to. Your head's underneath it most of the time, so all you have to do is remember to keep yer mouth shut.'

I had never been any good at keeping my mouth shut. That was probably written into my record somewhere as well.

The Sergeant was sitting in the well of the craft with his back against its side. His beret, already thick with dust and the other shit in the air, was tipped over his eyes, and his easy breathing suggested he was asleep. He'd adopted this position as soon as he was satisfied that the jeep and the K5 were properly lashed down. He didn't even stir when I joined him. After about five minutes of the gentle buffeting of the vessel, my chin dropped to my chest too, and my eyes closed. I could cope with this: like a bleeding holiday camp. I opened my eyes again when he spoke to me. I don't know how long I'd been dozing.

He suddenly asked, 'What do you think of Egypt so far, Mr Bassett?'

'It stinks.'

Then he surprised me by asking, 'Literally or metaphorically, would that be?'

'Both, Sergeant.'

He grunted and stopped speaking. Had that been a test question? If so, had I given the correct answer? My eyes closed again. When I awoke Trigger was whistling Irving Berlin's 'Blue skies'. I still have the Josephine Baker recording of that, and when I play it am immediately transported in my mind to two small ships bobbing up and down on the Great Bitter Lake. Three quarters of an hour later everyone started to move around again, and ten minutes after that we were driving up onto a stony shore with a few scrub trees. Then I realized why Moses led his people out of Egypt. It had nothing to do with the persecution of the tribe of Israel, and nothing to do with God promising them another land. It was because Egypt is such a horrible fucking place to begin with.

There were ten of us. Two in each vehicle cab and two spare. The others were all Ordnance Corps according to their flashes, but the RAOC conceals a multitude of sins; these bastards could have a hundred homicidal skills or none at all. The two spares did most of the domestics.

The land rose and fell, but always in gentle slopes, and even the valleys were shallow stony places. We ground along open scrub desert and old camel tracks – sometimes where they crossed each other was marked by an old rusted oil drum: once one was even holding up a canted original English country road sign. It had three arms. One read *Ifold 3 miles*, another *Loxwood 2⅓ miles* and the last one said *Horsham*. All this in the middle of the fucking Egyptian desert, east of Suez. What joker had carted it all the way here? I've wanted to go to Loxwood and Ifold ever since, and never made it. I wonder what's there.

We stopped in some low ground after noon, and rigged tarps out from the sides of the lorries, for a little shelter from the sun.

'You pays your money, sir, and takes your choice,' Clare told me. 'Either we sit on the top of a ridge and can be seen for miles around, or in the troughs, which are a degree or so cooler, but from where we can't see anyone creeping up on us.'

I asked myself who could possibly want to creep around out there anyway, but wanting to appear interested, observed, 'You could always put a lookout up on the ridge.'

Rogers looked up from his char, suddenly alarmed. He shook his head, but it was too late.

Clare said, 'That's what I usually do, Mr Bassett. I was wondering if you and Rogers'd do first stag when you've finished your char. I'll send someone up for you after an hour.'

Trust me to bloody well walk straight into it.

As we were trudging up the slope, toting a Bren gun and two spare magazines, I apologized to Rogers. We had a half canteen of water between the two of us, and that was supposed to last an hour.

'My fault. Sorry about that. I should have kept my gob shut.'

His upside-down smile turned quickly to a rueful grin, 'You'll know better next time, then, won't you? You'll have to watch the Sarge; he can be a bit cute.'

He had dipped his handkerchief in a water bucket before we set out, and wrung it out over the same container so's not to waste the stuff. Then he spread it over his neck and tucked it under the back of his black beret. I copied him. The damp cotton clinging to my neck, as we climbed, was bliss. We were only twenty feet or so above the trucks when we settled down. I'd always imagined deserts to be dunes of rolling sand. Not this stuff, however – just staggered low ridges of stone and coarse ground rolling away to the north and east for ever. It was an uninviting grey plain of absolutely fuck-all. A few scrubby plants looked dead until you were close to them, and then realized that they were still just clinging on to life . . . and it was so hot I thought I couldn't breathe.

'Breathe through your nose,' Roy instructed me. 'That will cool it just enough for you.'

At the far end of my line of sight, the desert shook and shimmered in a haze that joined it to the sky. A snake moved from under a stone about six feet away from us. It was less than a foot long and as thick as a finger. A brown, rough-scaled body and a flat triangular head. I'd had a decent relationship with a snake once: this one looked meaner.

'Desert viper,' Trigger told me. 'Bad buggers; they can kill you.' When I raised a large rock to crush it he held my hand back, with, 'But that ain't no reason to go killing it. Watch.' He tossed a small round pebble close to its head. The snake arched its neck and hissed violently, but then beat a hasty retreat. I eventually lost sight of it. He continued, 'They're as short-sighted as fuck. It probably never even saw us; so it never meant you no harm.' We settled down to keep watch in opposite directions, propped up against a couple of the larger stones. 'Tell me if you see any flies,' Trigger told me.

'OK. Why?'

'Show you later.'

Clare was as good as his word. We were relieved within the hour.

Trigger sat under one of the awnings with an old copy of *Tit-Bits*. I crawled inside the wooden radio room on the back of the K5. It was shady in there, but even with the back door and the vents open it was as hot as hell. I felt exhausted and quickly dozed. Maybe sleeping a lot was what Egypt was about. The last thing I heard before I dropped off was Roy sniggering at some of the dirty jokes.

Clare got us moving again at 15.30. If there was now coolness in the air, I hadn't noticed it yet. He had me call in before we set off. My call sign was *Morecambe*, just like Watson had threatened, and the Morse strip I had to broadcast was D980BETT571. On the second day the 1 was to change to a 2, and so on. I wasn't in for one of Watson's listening watches until the next night, when we were up closer to the old Palestine border.

I wanted to leave the radio pre-set for the next scheduled call in, but the Sergeant cautioned against it. He had me scramble the tuning after each session, in case the truck was captured by the opposition, and they could see at a glance what profile we were using. I suppose that was more professional, but to tell the truth all they had to do was sweep the wavebands until they found us anyway — time-consuming, but more or less fool-proof. I wasn't all that sure who the opposition were anyway. The wogs or the Israelis? We'd fought both in the last couple of years. If they both decided to come after us at the same time, I couldn't see us remaining in the Canal Zone for all that long.

Each of the vehicles had a roll of barbed wire hanging in front of its radiator. I found out what it was used for when we stopped at dusk a few hours later. We were on one of those messed-up camel tracks, going through a wide flat depression, when Clare called a halt. He pulled the group off the road, and they parked the vehicles up like a wagon train circling against the Red Indians — only about ten feet apart. And that's exactly what we were, so perhaps the old tunes are always the best ones — because they proceeded to string the barbed wire between the trucks. One of the spares — a young national serviceman named Cyril — dug a latrine in looser soil a few feet outside our mobile fortlet, and the other lads dug a few shallow 'scrapes' in the surface inside it.

These might have just provided a bit of cover if the bullets had started in at us. After an hour, Clare inspected our defences, and declared himself satisfied. Everyone relaxed, and Roy lit a desert stove to start a cook-up.

The desert stove is a small, cut-down oil drum full of sand, doused with petrol and oil and allowed to burn: you can boil a billycan on it in minutes. Desert rations were eight tins of bully chopped fine, with an onion, and dropped in a saucepan with eight tins of baked beans . . . and each plate accompanied by a couple of doorsteps of bread without butter. All washed down with a bottle of warm Stella we weren't supposed to have. We sat around the stove as the air cooled. I hadn't expected such a wide variation in temperatures, and was now glad of the sweater that Nansen had told me to take along.

One of the squaddies remarked, 'Roll on tomorrer. I can't wait for me egg.' This seemed odd, because I knew that we had none.

The sky went black, and you could see a billion billion stars. A tall, thin 24-monther picked out the constellations we were not familiar with – he was going back to be an astronomer – and Clare eventually chipped in to explain how to use some for desert navigation. Rogers sang a folk song called 'The Lincolnshire poacher', and revealed he had a singing voice as pure as a choirboy's. A couple of guys told bad jokes; another described his home town in Devon on market day. Clare was going to have us away early the next day; not long after sun-up, so we soon began to get our heads down. The Sergeant was the only one to sleep in the open, under the sky. The rest of us split for our transport. Rogers slept in the K5's cab, and I bunked down in the radio shack.

I was one of the last to leave the warm shroud of the stove. As I did, Clare looked up, gave a twitchy little smile and said, 'You did all right, Mr Bassett. I think you have the makings of a soldier.'

All I did was wave back to show I'd heard him . . . and I had one of those odd moments when your brain suddenly notices *I'm happy here*, and says, *Don't forget this*.

I was awoken the next morning by a persistent buzzing noise. When I opened my eyes I registered that I was bunked on the floor of the radio room, and that half a dozen flies were formation-flying close to its roof. They were noisy little buggers. I watched them doing half-rolls to land upside down on the ceiling near the ventilator. The laws of physics tell us that is an impossible manoeuvre, but flies never study physics, do they? They only fly.

Then I remembered something Roy had told me, yawned, stood up and hammered on the wall of my shack, which was also the back of his cab. He opened the sliding window between us and yawned back at me.

'Yeah, what is it?'

'You asked me to tell you when I saw any flies. There are some in here with me now.'

I have to admit old Roy could move when he had to. By the time I had climbed down, he was standing stark-naked, Sten in hand, at the wire between the K5 and the next truck in the circle – one of the QLs as it happened. His bottom was absurdly white. He was studying the progress of an Arab leading a donkey, who was approaching us along the valley floor.

'You can cover your cock up, Roy.' That was the Sergeant's voice. '. . . I've watched him coming. I'm sure he's on his own.'

'Yes, Sergeant.'

'And hurry it up, there's a good lad. That big black bag on the back of the ass probably contains his woman.'

I'd been sleeping in my shorts anyway, so it was less of a problem to me. I joined Clare at the wire to greet our visitor. He was a tall, thin million-year-old Arab man in an unusually immaculate djellaba.

He smiled at Clare and said, '*Salaam aleikum*, Sergeant.' He had a wonderfully modulated English drawl: right out of the top drawer. Wherever you go, they speak better English than you do. George Sanders sounded like him.

'*Salaam*, Abdul. You are well?'

'I am well, Sergeant. You want my eggs?'

Clare laughed. It was then that I noticed that though bare-chested, he was still wearing his pistol belt, and that the flap of its canvas holster was undone. His right hand didn't stray far from it. Trigger had left me the Sten. My hands holding it were suddenly sweaty. The old man's black eyes glanced at me from above his hawk nose – almost as if he knew what I was thinking and didn't care. He smiled. His teeth were stained.

Clare asked, 'How many?'

'Two dozen; English measure. All fresh. Young hens. Grade one.'

'How much?'

'Twenty-five ackers.'

'Twelve.'

The Arab shrugged, and turned away. He picked a cloth sack from the ass, put it on the ground, and carefully counted out twenty-four eggs – also onto the ground. A couple of the other squaddies had wandered over by now, but they didn't crowd the transaction.

Clare handed him a few coins across the wire. The old man bowed his head slightly as he accepted them. Clare nodded at the big black thing on the back of the animal. It was a human being dressed in a voluminous black garment. Dark eyes stared back at me from a narrow slit at face level . . . 'You have a new wife?'

'No, she's just a woman. I bought her from the Bedou last week. You will not like her: she isn't obedient yet.' Then he spread his hands and offered, 'But, just for you . . . five piastres for the whole camp. I collect her tomorrow.'

'No thanks, Abdul . . . you break her in first, and we'll see you next trip.'

'She's a Nubian. Very beautiful. Queen of Sheba.'

'You told me that last time, and she was probably as old as my grandmother and very bad-tempered.'

The Arab cackled, and then he smiled. No one could refuse a man with a smile like that. His smile was as trustworthy as that of the Jesus you see in pictures in the *Children's Illustrated Bible*.

'This one is different.'

'Thank you for the eggs.' There was no mistaking the finality in Clare's voice. The Arab shrugged, smiled and they *salaamed* each other all over again. It went on a bit. Then he led the donkey away the same way he had come. When they were fifty yards away the person in the black bag turned to look at us; I felt her eyes on me.

Clare said, 'She might have been a young Nubian after all. What a pity.'

'How do you know?' That was me: always asking the bleeding questions.

'No ordinary Arab woman would have looked back.'

'I met a Navy cook in Port Said. He called all Arabs *Ali* because he said it was easier than trying to remember their names. Do you call them all *Abdul*?'

Clare looked momentarily thrown. He said, 'No . . . That *is* Abdul. I've known him well over a year.'

'How did he know we were here?'

'I don't know.'

'And where are his hens?'

'I don't know. All I know is that one moment you're out in

the middle of fuck-all, with a hundred empty miles in any direction, and the next moment there's a cloud of flies, followed by an Arab riding up to you offering you eggs.'

'How do they do that?'

'I don't know that either. It's very mysterious.'

'That's what a Navy bloke told me.'

Clare grinned, 'Then it must be true, mustn't it?' He looked around at the others, and barked, 'Hasn't anyone got the char on yet?' I was amused to see how quickly they moved, although there were a couple of downcast faces among them.

'Was that really a young girl he was offering us?'

'Told you already: who knows?' I made the Sten safe; his eyes followed my hand movements. As I did that he said, 'Well done, Mr Bassett. You can come out with us again.'

The woman in black could so easily have been a man with a hidden machine gun, of course, and that's exactly what we didn't say. The other thing we didn't say was that if a man with a donkey could track us into the middle of nowhere, then every other bugger out here probably knew where we were, as well. It induced a curiously vulnerable state of mind.

When we stopped for a quick mid-morning brew-up I was standing between Clare and Trigger near the stove. I asked them, 'That Abdul. Do you think he's a spy?'

Clare looked amused. He said, 'No, Charlie; he's an egg salesman – that's his job,' and he threw the lees of his tea on the hot sand, where it sizzled for a second before it disappeared. Time to mount up. As we walked back to the K5 I recalled that he had said *Charlie*. Maybe I'd just joined the Army.

I didn't draw a stag when we had our midday rest stop, because I had one of Watson's radio sweeps to perform. I got two different signals somewhere out to the northwest, but they weren't talking to each other. I copied their clumsy Morse into a small notebook Watson had given me. It was supposed to live locked in a hidden compartment under the floor of the truck.

Clare came in while I was homing in on the second, and he listened in one earphone. I showed him what I'd written down: as far as I was concerned it was gibberish, but, strangely, it didn't look like any code form I'd seen before either. Almost immediately I found a voice transmission, but I only caught the last minute. The language sounded high-pitched with some guttural sounds thrown in for good measure. When it died, Clare leaned forward to my pad and marked an extra four word spacers in places I wouldn't have recognized.

I asked, 'What was it?'

'Yiddish.'

'What were they talking about?'

'Us, probably.' That put a bit of a different complexion on it. So I decided to miss my call in – which I was entitled to do – and run it at the fall-back time in the evening. I don't know why. When I informed Clare of my decision he nodded in approval before he turned away. As we set off again Trigger handed me a beige cotton ski-cap with a big peak; I'd already seen most of the other guys wearing them. They had come out after the first brew stop after the Bitter Lake. It had a diamond-shaped cloth badge sitting above a cloth eagle carrying a swastika.

'What's this?' I asked him.

'Best desert hat ever made; so say thank you. It will never let you down.'

'Thank you . . . but it's Nazi.'

'The cap's not Nazi, is it? – only the bloke who wore it once. Anyway it was Afrika Korps, and they weren't all that bad. Cut the badge off, if it bothers you.'

'Thank you.' I said it again.

'Just take it off and sit on it if we run into a Yid patrol, OK? It upsets them.'

'Shouldn't the Israelis stay their side of the border?'

'Nobody knows where the border is any more, sir. Why else do you think we're up here?'

I remember two things from the evening that followed. One was that we climbed up, for the umpteenth time it seemed, out of a low stony wadi – but instead of being faced with more of the same there was now sand. Beautiful deep orange sand lit up by the setting sun as if it was on fire. It stretched for a hundred miles, and was so beautiful that it took my breath away. Clare turned us round, and we camped for the night around a lonely, stumpy-looking tree. The odd rusty can dotted here and there said we weren't the first Boy Scouts to spend the night here. The second memory is that when we were settled round the stove with a bottle each, taking the smallest of sips to make the beer last, one of the kids asked me to tell them what it was like flying over Germany in 1944.

I talked for longer than I intended, and at the end of it no one said a word for several minutes. Then Trigger asked me to tune one of the radios so as to pick up some music. I got something from Port Said or Cairo. Arab music. Drums, tambourines and small cymbals; the gentle wailing of pipes and flutes. That was why the guys began to compare the dancing girls they'd seen in clubs and bars up and down the Canal Zone. Flat bellies and big tits seemed to be the combination they recalled best. When I asked about the girl and the pig I'd been told about, Clare said, 'She must be a European; even English maybe.'

'How do you make that out, Sarge?' That was one of the young national servicemen: I never properly learned his name. Carter maybe?

'No Muslim woman would be allowed to do that. They'd lock her up; maybe even worse. Stone her or cut bits off her – just like in the Bible. The pig is religiously an unclean animal for them . . . they can't even touch it. It's because we allow that sort of thing to go on in our clubs, *and* build churches every-where, that they don't take us seriously when we say we want to negotiate an end to the troubles out here.'

'Have you seen her, Sarge?'

'Yes; as it happens.'

'What was she like?'

There were a couple of low guffaws before he responded. I looked up: a billion billion stars like the night before. I could feel the heat radiating from the oil-drum stove on my legs, and cooler air off the desert curling around my back.

'Bloody formidable, as it happens . . . but my mother wouldn't 'ave been all that chuffed to see me there.'

We broke away soon after that. Every man to his own blanket and his own thoughts. I tried to think about Dolly and Grace . . . they were so much part of my world, but I found thoughts of my boys instead, and the girl Flaming June. Maybe she was still waiting for her wounded hero. Maybe she had married him. I remembered Dieter telling me off for blowing it with her, and Carlo crying. I resolved to send her a letter or a card when I got back. Cast my bread upon the waters.

In the morning the Sergeant sat me down at the radio, and made me stay there. We didn't break camp. I had a two-hour listening watch for Watson in the middle of it, so it didn't make that much difference. Clare himself set off into the desert with one man, a pole about six feet long, a shovel, a map and a compass – but they only went about fifty yards.

The men lazed about watching him, but no one seemed to think it odd behaviour. Those who'd been in the blue with him before had seen it already, and those who hadn't had learned to trust him anyway. From the small side window of my radio wagon I watched him prospecting around in the sand. After about an hour he straightened from the latest hole that he had scooped, turned back to us and waved. Five or six of the lads lifted spades that had been dumped in a heap from one of the wagons, and trudged up the nearest sand dune to join him. Then they began to dig in earnest.

Clare and his helper returned to us. Trigger put on a brew. When he had an ally mug of strong tea in his hand the Sergeant climbed into the radio room.

'Anything?'

'No, Sergeant. Even the static sounds pretty uninspired. What am I listening for?'

'Anyone. Friendlies and unfriendlies.'

'What's the difference?'

'Friendlies are the ones we allow to be out here, and the unfriendlies aren't. At the moment the Israelis are classified as *friendlies*, but only four years ago they were blowing up hotels full of our nurses, weren't they?'

'So even the friendlies are unfriendly, as far as you're concerned?'

'Yeah, so yell if you hear anything. Goddit?'

'Yes, Sergeant.'

'I'll get Trigger to bung you a cup of char; I should ha' brought you one.'

'Thanks.'

'. . . and one last thing.'

'Yes?'

'That cap really suits you: you look like a proper little Nazi.'

'I knew someone clever in the War Office a few years ago . . . he said that *we* are the Nazis now.'

'He should know.'

'He died.' Actually I shot him, but let's pass over that one.

'Well; he can't have been all that clever then, can he?'

Thinking about it, being deemed *not all that clever* is an epitaph that Piers would have absolutely hated. It cheered me up no end.

They dug up a lorry. Well, half a lorry anyway. The rear end of an old AEC Matador buried deep in the sand. Clare had found it eventually by watching the compass swing as he moved around it, and by drawing intersecting vectors in the sand. The wagon was under the place where they all crossed. It had a steel box body with rear doors, having probably been an artillery tractor in an earlier life. Trigger had them all stand back, and then screwed about it a bit for booby traps. Apparently it was one of his specialities, but he didn't find any. Then he rattled up and down its metal side with a big screwdriver for a bit. The noise set my teeth on edge.

'Gets rid of the scorpions,' Clare told me later. 'They scarper when they get the vibrations.'

'What about snakes?'

'Yeah. There's always a couple down under the frame, but the noise usually sends them about their business as well. But, you're right – when the bold boys start working on it I make sure they're careful where they step, and wear leather gauntlets.'

A bright kid called Muzzard spelled me for an hour so I could get some grub. He was a complete novice, but he picked up the principles of the sweep very quickly . . . I thought he showed promise. He was supposed to yell for me or Clare, of course, as soon as he heard something. He didn't though, and I got some lunch and a cuppa in peace. I wandered up to the excavation before I settled down again. The Matador's cargo space was filled with ordnance, motor spares, petrol and water. Clare's team were checking the *safe* date on the metal cases and wooden boxes, and replacing those that were out of date with fresh stores from one of our trucks. The stores being replaced were detailed by entries onto about thirty different forms.

'CIO – CII. That means count it all *out*, and count it all *in*,' Trigger sang out, when he dropped in for a chat. '. . . a good military principle.' The radio wagon was as hot as hell. I sat in my shorts and boots, and the perspiration poured off every inch of my body. My shorts were as wet as if I'd just come out of the sea with them on.

'Want me to give you ten minutes?' Roy asked.

'No, I can manage, but thanks.'

'OK. Just shout.'

I saw him slogging up the dune with a spade. They were nearly all up there by then, burying the fucking thing all over again. By the time they finished smoothing out the sand with mats dragged behind them, it was difficult to know anyone had ever been there: the first breath of wind would do the rest.

There were a couple of times in the next few hours when I was tempted by Rogers's offer. No signals. Or nearly no signals anyway. There was a bleating in the distance I could barely make out, so I yelled until Clare ducked his head into the shack.

'What is it?'

'Dunno. It comes on, and then fades.'

'Can you read any of it?'

'No.'

'Let me know if it comes back.' I saw him look down at his watch and trigger the sweep hand on the stop. That was interesting. Exactly half an hour later I called him back.

He asked, 'Same signal?'

'Yes. Probably a hundred miles away, unless he has a dodgy battery.'

Clare stopped the sweep arm of his watch, grinned and said,

'Good. You can secure; then clean yourself up, and let's get out of here.'

The penny dropped a few minutes later. I had heard the recall, and the content of the message was immaterial. The interval between the end of the signal and the beginning of the next was everything: a thirty-minute gap to tell Clare to clear off. I rubbed down with sand, and changed my clothes. At Trigger's insistence I piled so much foot powder between my toes that my boots and socks puffed smoke with each step I took.

He said, 'You'll lose all the skin between your toes, but if you can keep them dry at least they won't get infected. Stick it under your arms as well.'

'Why doesn't it happen to you?'

'Who says it don't? We just learned to live with it.' Uh-huh? 'Smoke break?'

Clare swapped over with Rogers, and kept his promise. He taught me how to drive a four-by-four. It was like heaving a tank about, but I liked that odd grab of extra traction from the front wheels when you least expected it. He had me drive into some softer stuff, just in order to prove the wagon could pull itself out again. I was sweating again, but only in the small of my back. Clare had three days' growth of beard – all the others did as well; it made them look like pirates.

'What have we been doing out here, Sergeant?'

'On a scheme. In the RAF you'd call it an exercise.'

'In the RAF we'd call it replenishing a stores dump, and I'll bet it's one that's not supposed to be there.'

'You know, Charlie . . . mind that rock; you might have 4WD but things that size can still break your springs . . . where was I?'

'. . . You know, Charlie?'

'Yeah, there's such a thing as seeing too much.'

We camped thirty miles from the buried Matador, and the Arab came in that night with his eggs and his woman. We bought more of the former, and Clare firmly declined the woman again.

'Has the Sarge ever said *yes* for the woman?' I asked when Clare was out of earshot.

'No,' Trigger told me, 'but I think about it a lot.'

We didn't see the Arab again.

Three nights later we drove over one of the swing bridges, and on to the Treaty Road. My skin was dry and salty – and suddenly brown: the sun had caught up with me without my noticing. I felt as tired as if we'd been away for weeks. Arab kids were chasing chickens with sticks in the Ismailia suburbs, and in the town centre watchful military patrols armed with pick-axe handles were looking for Arabs to beat up. This could only end in tears.

Chapter Eleven

Blue kettle rag

Oliver shook me awake. Perspiration had run down my chin and pooled in that hollow at the base of the throat.

'What is it?'

'Nothing. You were shouting.'

'Sorry, I was dreaming.'

'What about?'

'Snow. Isn't that silly? I was dreaming I was in a snowball fight with my boys.'

I propped myself up on the camp bed, and he handed me a bottle of Stella. He always seemed to have a supply. We clinked bottles. 'Thanks. What time is it?'

'Past eleven. Time you got up anyway – you've slept fourteen hours.'

'Christ! Has Watson been asking for me?'

'He knows better. The desert really takes it out of you until you're used to it. Anyway he'll give you a few days' leave after you've reported. A week in the blue always gets you time off. Tell me about the snow.'

'It was crisp and new: the sort that moulds together for great snowballs and snowmen.'

'I remember that. I was in Blighty in 1949 and I joined a party of volunteers digging trains out of snowdrifts up in the Pennines.'

197

He looked around with a rueful smile. The cheap thermometer hanging from the tent post had already hit 130 degrees, but I didn't know if it was to be trusted. 'Seems supremely surreal to be sitting in this bloody oven talking about snow, doesn't it?'

I noticed that although he had hoisted the sides of the tent to allow whatever breeze there was to cool us, he'd left the side alongside my bed down to shield me sleeping. Considerate that, and not what I'd expected. There was a half-wing, not unlike my own, on the shirt he had dangling on a hanger in the tent eave, but it bore an 'O' for Observer. Mine was an 'S' for air signaller – which always conjured up the ridiculous image of some bod trying to communicate between aircraft by waving semaphore flags.

'What do you do for Watson?' I asked him.

'Photographs mostly. I take pictures of rock formations, wadis, desert crossroads and way points.'

'Can't the Army do that?'

'They tried, but they always came back with the wrong things. The RAF needs things they can identify from the air, not when they're looking up at it.'

'Do you do some of your stuff from the air, then?'

'Most of it. You can expect to go up there as well, from time to time.' He must have seen my grimace, because he asked, 'What's the matter? Gone off flying?'

'Not entirely. I've just gone off flying the way the RAF does it – far too fucking uncomfortable.'

As I finished the beer, and put the bottle in the box of empties under the table he observed, 'Very good time of day for taking a shower, if you don't mind me saying it: you won't need to queue. But you'll have to break out a change. I gave the clothes you came back in to the dhobi man.' For a moment I was startled. That wasn't a familiar word, and I wondered if he meant something like a rag-and-bone merchant. Again he picked this up from just my expression, because he added, 'No, don't worry. You'll get them back later, washed and pressed better than you've ever seen them before . . . and it'll only cost you an acker.'

'Are you telling me that I stink?'

'The scent of the desert, old son. It was just a hint.'

'And one I'll take. Thanks.'

I'll tell you something. It was in Egypt I learned to love the simple act of taking a shower; I still think of it as a luxury I haven't really earned.

Watson offered me tea. That was a first. It came thin and boiling hot, with a sprig of mint floating on the surface.

'Good trip?'

'I feel I've learned a lot in a hurry, sir . . . if that makes sense.'

'Egypt does that to you. I completely understand. Did you get anything?'

I handed him the small notebook of radio traffic. He scrutinized the numbered pages. I had used eight in all. He tore those out neatly against the edge of a ruler, and then took the next two blank sheets as well, explaining. 'You can recover your last message as an impression from the pages that follow it. Better safe than sorry.' Then he signed for the pages he'd removed on the inside cover, before handing the notebook back to me.

'Thank you, Charlie.'

I knew him well enough not to ask what he would do with them. He'd tell me if I needed to know. That might sound like a bit of a cop-out to your modern ear, but it was actually strangely comforting.

'Is this what I'm going to be doing out here, sir? Going out with small expeditions and monitoring hostile radio signals?'

'. . . and providing their comms when they need it. Yes,

you'll often be doing that. The average scheme from here is five or six days long.'

'And what will my other duties be?'

'Bugger-all most of the time, my boy. The Army and the national service contingent will probably be very jealous, and may give you a hard time. I might ask you to do a bit of training, if the RAF Regiment has anyone promising, and occasionally you'll pull a bit of stag. You won't mind that, will you?' It was a rhetorical question of course. I sipped my tea and waited for the next barrel. '. . . and you can have a week off. You could learn to swim. We're good at that over here.' Only the British would think of waiting until you were surrounded by desert before teaching you to swim. I definitely was having none of that.

'Didn't I tell you already, sir? I can swim. My school was famous for it. Most of my class were medallists, although I was never that good.'

'OK. Take a ninety-six then, and take care of your bloody self. Keep your eyes on the alerts wherever you go.' He wrote out and handed me the ticket, and said, '. . . and keep this in your bloody pocket; if the SPs pick you up without one they'll think you're a deserter, and with your reputation I don't think you'll be able to talk yourself out of twenty-one days at Moascar. Toddle along now.'

I walked around his pavilion to find Pat Tobin – I needed a decent set of KDs and a couple of spare shirts out of my secure storage. Between the MT Section's tent and the pavilion was a small square area screened off on three sides by striped wind-breakers – the kind you see on the beach at Southend. Concealed in it lay a woman under a sunshade, face-down on a cheap sunbed. She wore a white swimsuit with the shoulder straps pulled down and a floppy white hat.

She lifted her head and looked over her shoulder when she heard me. 'Hello, Charlie.'

I loved her body, but it took me a minute to recognize it. I'd never seen her with her clothes off.

Then, 'Hello, Daisy. Day off?'

'Half-day. He worked me hard last night.'

'There are a thousand bored men confined behind the wire here . . . and most of them probably have their binoculars trained on you. What you're doing is either dangerous, or cruel.'

'. . . probably cruel.'

I wouldn't bet on it, love, were the words that went through my mind, but all I said was, '. . . see you.' Light touch, Charlie: if she was playing silly buggers it was her own fault, wasn't it?

'What would you do with your first ninety-six?' I asked Nansen, as I threw what I needed into a small canvas crew bag someone had given me at RAF Waddington years before.

'I'd ask my outrageous tent mate if he would like to join me.'

'Would you?'

'Love to, but I'm flying over the Delta tomorrow photographing Gyppo installations.' Military installations, that is. There had been a few incidents reported in the papers. The Egyptian Army was getting very touchy about our reconnaissance flights.

'*What* then?'

'Ismailia, I suppose; but draw a pick handle from the guards before you go – it's either a red-amber or an amber alert again, but the Arabs still hate us, and will stuff you if they can. Personally I always feel safer in Port Said. There's a lot more of *us* about because of the port and the transit camps, and hence a lot more of our coppers on the street . . . and it's more cosmopolitan in many ways. More of the locals speak English, and there are more clubs and restaurants, old-fashioned hotels and even an art gallery.'

'I know some people in Ismailia. From when I was in hospital there.'

'Well, then; pay your money, and take your choice . . . and don't forget to wave as you see me flying over.'

'Could you get away after your job?'

'Mm . . . Charlie. Maybe. That sounds suspiciously like a date.' Then he laughed, turned away and picked up an old copy of *Picture Post*. The girl in a swimming suit on the cover looked like Daisy. I noticed he had reverted to shorts of a more or less standard pattern, and wondered if that was because his streamliners were in the wash, or was it because of me?

I paid a visit I had been putting off. The SWO at Deversoir was surprisingly difficult to find. He was in an office behind an office behind an office behind an office, and everyone I asked had a different way of getting there. I found him in a large room at the end of a corridor in a long wooden hut. A big bald man with a hanging black moustache. He looked like the walrus's father, and twice as fierce. A notice facing me on his desk top read *SWO Cox*. I've always distrusted people who need their own name on their desk: I suspect it is there because they are in danger of forgetting it, and therefore shouldn't have been trusted with a desk of their own in the first place – I'm sure you've met the type. An aircraftman typed at a table behind him, and a relentless fan stirred the air slowly above them. Overweight flies rode on it like kids at a fairground. I wondered where the Arabs were. Then I caught my own thought – *bloody well all around us, of course.*

'Pilot Officer Bassett,' I told him. 'I wanted to see you earlier, but they sent me out almost immediately.'

'Good afternoon, sir.' He was right. It was afternoon already. He was probably one of those sad types who always get that right. 'I was wondering where you'd got to. Take a pew.' My chair was rickety. I didn't trust it.

'What do I need to know?'

'More than I can teach you, sir, but with a ha'p'orth of common sense you'll get by. Would you like a glass of lemonade?'

'Thank you.'

The AC brought two over without being asked.

'In the first place keep your wits about you at night – and being inside the wire is no guarantee of safety. There are incidents every week . . . most of the wogs who break in are just stealing, but if you get between them and what they're after they'll slit your throat first, and call themselves a hero of the resistance afterwards. Don't take any chances – OK?'

'I understand.'

'You might feel like a bit of a girl, but even if you're going to the karzi after dark take someone with you. You're one of Mr Watson's staff, aren't you?'

'That's right.'

'Then my advice to you, sir, is to get in a bit of guard duty as soon as you can – get used to moving around the compound in the dark. Get used to what it looks like.'

'OK. Tell me about the states of alert, SWO . . .'

'They are *levels* of alert, sir . . . for that read danger – for British personnel in the Canal Zone. That is anywhere in the Canal Zone, got it?'

'Yes.'

'*Red* is danger – meaning you won't leave camp until you're ordered to, and when you do you carry a fully loaded side arm at all times. Please understand that the bastards out there will try to kill you. Usually mob-handed, so we can't pin down the killers afterwards. Soldiers and airmen have been kicked to death, beaten and drowned, shot, carved up . . . you name it. Couple of months ago they kidnapped one of our bus drivers, and tossed his bits back over the wire later that night. They even raped and killed a nun for being a teacher in an English school. Your Egyptian is neither a stable nor a nice man, and never will be in

my opinion . . . and this is serious stuff I'm telling you. Got it?'
I nodded. I wonder if he noticed my involuntary swallow. He
probably did, as SWOs don't miss much. 'Red-Amber is only
one notch down . . . you're usually going to be OK outside the
camp, but if anything happens to you I'd probably say it served
you right for being out there. Amber is more or less OK . . . but
you're expected to carry a pickaxe handle with you outside the
wire at all times, and if you see a British soldier in trouble,
you're expected to wade in with it. Got that? Green is OK. It
means that some silly bugger has decided that the British serviceman will be safe out here, wherever he goes. If you believe
that then you're thicker than you look, sir.'

'I've just been given a ninety-six, and had decided to see a bit
of Egypt, Ismailia or Port Said. Now you've almost changed my
mind.'

'Good, that means you may be safe out there, sir, and I've
done my duty.'

'Anything else?'

'Yes, sir. In Egypt you *never* ask a policeman, despite the old
song. On-duty policemen are off-duty terrorists. They'll direct
you up a dark alley to get a good kicking or worse . . . and don't
follow a Gyppo offering you a young virgin, or cheap gold
jewellery, as you're bound to end up in the Sweet Water with a
knife between your ribs.'

I leaned back in my chair. It creaked, reminding me of my
earlier doubts.

'Someone else told me that about the cops. You make it sound
more dangerous down here on the Canal than out in the desert.'

'I'm glad you've worked that out, sir, because it is. Lastly,
keep your papers and your wallet buttoned into a pocket. The
clubs are full of girls with long fingers, and while one hand's in
your fly the other will be robbing you blind. End of sermon –
sorry.'

I grinned. Grinning is one of the things I'm good at, so I do it a lot. 'No. It's exactly what I needed. Are there areas of Ismailia or Port Said out of bounds?'

'I'll give you the street maps we've xeroxed; they're clearly marked. I've made them up into a small booklet – with Cairo, Suez and Alex as well.'

'OK. Thanks. Today's alert is actually amber – it said so on your noticeboard outside: so where do I collect a pick handle?'

'At the gate. And there's a big box of johnnies there as well – make sure you take a pocketful.'

As I left him, I recognized a feeling I'd had since I'd landed. It was as if I was being watched all the time, and not by the Brits. It was a feeling that I'd met in Bremen at the end of the war, and I hadn't liked it then either.

I went up to Ismailia in the back of a three-tonner which had come forward on a milk run from one of the Army bases. There was no cover on the wagon bed and we sat with our arses on the floor and our heads below the level of the cab so the wires couldn't reach us.

Oh yeah, the guy I squeezed in alongside was Roy Rogers. He said, 'Hello, sir. Off for a few days?'

'Yeah, Roy. What about you?'

'I drew a forty-eight after that little lot.'

'They gave me ninety-six.'

'Yer an officer. You need it.' He had a wicked grin himself. 'You meeting someone tonight?'

'No, I thought I'd get a look at Ismailia or Port Said.'

'I'm not doing anything; I'll show you round Ish if you like?'

'That would be great: get me started.'

The pickaxe handles carried by the Brown Jobs were bigger than mine. I resolved to swap one as soon as I could, and keep it. What made me laugh was that they all had a WD stamp and a painted number on them, and that upside-down arrow. Somewhere some poor clerk would be busy tallying them up. It was a smooth old road, and because I couldn't see a horizon from my seat on the truck bed, the heat soon began to get to me. My head began to nod, and my eyes closed. When I opened them again we had stopped outside the Blue Kettle club.

Rogers said, 'C'mon,' and hopped over the tailboard. We handed our packs up to the driver, with an instruction for him to drop them off at a billet near the Families Club at Abu Sueir.

As we watched the truck drive off I asked Roy, 'D'ye reckon it will be all right? Our bags won't get knocked off?'

'I knows that driver, Charlie, and he knows that I knows him. That's all it takes to move things around safely in the British Army.'

'So, what next?'

'Seen yer first belly dancer yet?'

'No.'

'Time to complete yer education then.'

She was small, much smaller than I'd imagined, and I was entranced. The two Egyptian pounds she cost me was worth every piastre. I was glad that I'd taken the SWO's advice. This is the sort of encounter a soldier doesn't tell his girl or wife about, or if he does, it's not until after he's an old man. I still have one of the filmy blue pieces of material she made me keep for a souvenir. I pull it out from time to time, and remember it low on her hips as she moved in the shadows, and the smell of limes from our drinks.

We took the last British night bus from Ismailia's geometric government centre to the accommodation. Roy didn't want to walk past the Arab quarter in the dark. Waiting for the transport with a noisy group from the Ordnance Depot up the road, I caught an unexpected rich seam of flower scent on the air. That was when colours and scents first began to overlap in my mind. These flower scents were blue, of course: a fine thin veil of aquamarine carried on the night air. There was the sound of a motorbike starting near the Army HQ, and a rowdy crowd of Kiwis being turned out of the NAAFI a block away. Somewhere a donkey brayed, and then another animal coughed. Camel. From where I stood I could look down a narrow boulevard overhung with trees. That was where the scent breezed in from. I distinctly saw a large shadowy lion cross from one line of trees to the other. She paused momentarily on the roadway, and looked directly at me. Eye contact. The hair stood up on my neck.

I told Roy but he only laughed. 'They haven't had any free lions in Egypt for over a hundred years.'

'I saw it.'

'Then you saw the past.'

I didn't tell him that that had happened before, either.

I lay under an awning at the Abu Sueir swimming pool the next morning sweating off a hangover. I was getting good at being under sunshades in the sun. Susan Haye with an e lay within arm's reach, but she would have torn mine off if I'd made a move, and I didn't feel strong enough for that yet. She wore one of those new two-piece swimsuits that look like matching but substantial pieces of underwear. It was a dull pinky-red, with big white printed flowers. I could see the fine hairs on her stomach, and wanted to touch it.

She said, 'I'm going to have a swim. Coming?' There weren't that many couples around at that time of the morning: mostly just families.

'I can't. I never learned.'

207

'You will out here. It's one of the substitution therapies the services dreamed up to take our minds off each other. Everyone learns to swim; has to. Even you.'

'That'll be the day.'

'Bet you. Bet you a fiver?'

'That I learn to swim? That's not fair on you. All I have to do is avoid it.'

'I still bet you.'

'OK.' We shook on it.

'At least come in the pool, and wash away that awful perspiration – you smell like a brewery.'

I wasn't sure that the families around us would have given me top marks for hygiene, but I complied. Susan swam a slow breaststroke; each time her arms thrust forward, her head sank beneath the surface and then popped up again like a seal's. I stayed at the shallow end hanging with my arms along the bar. Each time she came back to me she paused before the turn, and held her body touching mine. I got a hard on, of course, and she knew it. What had she warned me about? *We are all stir-crazy here*. Something like that.

'You're a horrible flirt,' I told her. 'You're just trying to embarrass me.'

'Am I, Charlie?' Her voice sounded very close to me.

'Everyone can see us.'

'. . . and so they know that nothing is really happening. Not in front of the kids, anyway. All the women know that I'm only ever going to tease you, while the men misread my intentions and are jealous. They'll hate you.' It was more like torture than tease. Then she turned, and did another couple of lengths. I had to wait on for five minutes in the pool after she climbed out, and she was rubbing her hair dry as I walked back.

I asked her, 'Do you want me to do that?'

She laughed. 'You really don't get it, do you, Charlie? Then they would *know* something was going on.'

'But it isn't.'

She laughed again. 'You need some lessons. I'll round up the Lost Wives' Club to teach you.'

'Did your fellah come back?'

'Yes. Now he's gone away again.'

My headache was lifting, and I fancied a beer again. Maybe that's why I asked, 'Are you sure you don't want to sleep with me?'

She said, 'Almost,' and giggled. It was almost like her brushing up against me in the pool.

'I'm going to get us a couple of beers then.'

She nodded, turned on her stomach, and pulled a big straw hat over the back of her head.

I took that as a *yes*. For the beer, that is.

Up at the bar I found myself alongside a man who'd nearly killed me. The Port Said doctor was smoking a large cigar, and had a self-satisfied look on his face. So would I with seven or eight empties lined up in front of me.

I greeted him, 'Hiya, Doc. Who've you come to poison today?'

'That was almost funny,' he responded. 'For some reason everyone's greeting me with the phrase *What's up, Doc?* this month, and then breaking into peals of laughter as if I was a bloody comedian. What d'ye think it means?'

'Probably that they've seen a film you haven't. I wouldn't worry about it. Can I get you a drink?'

'I like patients who buy me a drink; it restores my faith in medicine.'

'Do you have a regular clinic down here, or are you in danger of losing another patient?'

'Neither. Autopsy. Some poor sod got himself murdered again last night.' I ran the words in my head, and felt that maybe someone who managed to get murdered *again* had cracked the secret of eternal life.

'Who?'

'A Kiwi who missed his last bus – in more ways than one. Fancy spending the last night of your life in a bloody NAAFI – too depressing for words.'

'What happened to him?'

'Gyppoes, my boss tells me: they're getting worse every day. They broke his neck with a heavy blow, and then defaced his body. The Chief Medical Officer says it was intended to make it look like a ritual killing.'

'How?'

'There were groups of parallel slashes on his shoulders and back. Four at a time. I told him I'd seen something like that before – on an animal out in Iraq, which had been attacked by another animal – and he told me to bugger off. So I did. Now I'm going to get drunk.'

'You think it was something else?'

'No old boy; I *don't*. Not allowed to think. We're in the Army now.' He drew a finger across his lips in a zipping motion, and then tried a shaky salute. For a moment it looked as if he would fall over. I steadied him. 'Thanks; think I shall toddle off for a slash myself. Toodle-oo.' It must have been the word association that triggered his need.

Outside I asked Haye with an e, 'Did you hear that someone was killed last night?'

'Drunk, and lost in the Arab quarter; what do you expect? Thanks for the beer by the way.' I rested my beer bottle on the small of her back. She said, 'Oh, that's lovely.'

'I want to put my hand on your bum.'

'If you do I'll creep up on you in the night with a scalpel, and cut it off.'

'My hand?'

'That too. Go back in the pool and cool off.' *Yes ma'am.*

She had come down to Ismailia for a weekly early-morning clinic, but had the rest of the day off. When I asked her what the clinic was for, she had replied *spontaneous pregnancies, and VD*. I didn't ask any more.

Late afternoon, she borrowed my room in which to shower and change. I didn't follow her there, and I don't expect she was disappointed. When she brought me back my key she was every bit a foot soldier of the Grey Mafia again. If anything, I fancied her even more in uniform, but that's the way it goes . . . You lose some, and you lose some.

That is probably why I was back in the Blue Kettle on my own an hour later.

It was empty. Which is probably why I tried a bit of bad poetry, doodling on the beer mat up at the bar.

> '*twas empty,*
> *and the Arab girls did twist and tumble like the wave.*

But there were no Arab girls either.

There were four-bladed fans on the ceilings. They beat slowly to the rhythm of a New Orleans funeral band. There were flies too. They circled like a squadron of Stukas, spiralling down to feed from the sweat on the back of your neck if you turned your back on them. There was a barman with a flyswat who did his best . . . and his best was far from good enough. He moved like a sleepwalker. The room had the smell of all bars before you are too drunk to notice: disinfectant, stale cigarettes, spilled drinks and last year's perfume. The disinfectant smelled a livid yellow — the colour of strong urine. The perfume was a ghostly violet. If you need to be told the colour of the smell of stale cigarettes you've been living on the wrong planet for a few years: it's the colour of cancer.

And the joint wasn't completely empty either. A big man detached himself from a table in one of the shadowy alcoves. He nodded to the bar boy, who reached for another beer from the cold box. This man had a round, olive-coloured face with a small black beard and moustache, a tailored linen suit in need of a dhobi, and an ancient fez on his head. He had six inches on me, but was twice as broad. In fact he probably weighed as much as three of me. He wiped his hand on a handkerchief before offering it to me.

Glancing at my effort on the beer mat he observed, 'Ah, an English poet.'

'Hardly. Just a bored Englishman doing a bit of scribbling.'

'The first word in your first line is incorrect, I think.'

'Yes?' I recognized that he was a chancer, but at least he was trying. He made me smile.

'It should be *twat*. Soldiers, and even the RAF, come here looking for a bit of *twat*, not *'twas*.' He laughed as if he had made a joke.

'Twat?'

'Yes: an old word. It means cunt: vagina. Woman. You are looking for a woman.'

'The place was full of them last night.'

'That was before your unfortunate colleague went to meet our maker. This is the notorious Blue Kettle, after all. Every time something bad happens in Ismailia your Military Police close us down.'

'For how long?'

He shrugged and smiled, as if the answer was of no account, 'Two weeks; three . . . who knows? Until a visiting colonel wants a dancing girl, and then we are miraculously safe again, and open for business.'

Another bottle had appeared before me. I hadn't even noticed the bar boy move. How did he do that?

'How did he do that?' I asked the fat man. 'How did he serve me a beer without my seeing it?'

'Who knows?' he said again. 'It is a mystery.' I liked the way he shrugged. It was as if he was denying responsibility for something.

'Everybody's always saying that to me.'

'That is because Egypt is a mysterious country. Shall we sit down? My feet are hurting.' We sat at a small round table under a fan. You've seen round tables like it in bars all over the world. Were they created for bars; or were bars created as places to accommodate round tables? If I asked anyone here that question I knew the answer I would receive. As soon as we were seated, the boy came around the bar, and brought us another two beers. This time I saw him move.

We rattled the bottles together. I said, 'Cheerio.'

The fat man said, '*L'chaim.*'

'What language is that?'

'Israeli.'

'Your English is also very good.'

'And we are very fortunate, because your Arabic is . . . ?'

'Non-existent, or *shite*, as my Scottish friends would say. I was hoping to find a girl to teach me a little tonight.'

'Did you have a particular girl in mind?'

'One was called Yasmin.'

'No good: most of them are called Yasmin.'

'She is a dancer.'

'Also no good. Here they are all dancers.'

'She is small. Very small. Smaller than me.'

'. . . a *child*?' I wasn't too struck with the note of relish in his voice here.

'No, of course not. Older. Maybe nineteen or twenty.'

'Then maybe I know her. I will ask for her to be sent to you.' He barked an imperious string of gobbledegook at the barman, who in turn barked it into a telephone behind the bar. He then beamed at the fat man, and the fat man beamed at me. I should have picked up on it earlier.

'You own this place, don't you?'

He shrugged his exaggerated shrug, smiled a trader's smile and spread his hands. 'Only partly.' He swallowed most of the beer from his bottle in a oner, and clicked his fingers for another.

'Somebody I met told me that one reason the Egyptians want us out is that we show no respect for your traditional Muslim values. One of those values is refraining from drinking alcohol . . . and yet, here you are, drinking beer with me. Curious.'

He leaned forward to pat me on the shoulder like you would an old friend. He actually laughed aloud.

Then said, 'So: I cannot be a Muslim, can I? I am Lebanese, Mr Bassett, and a Christian. I am David Yassine.' Bollocks: the bugger had called me by name. He must have seen my face. 'Don't worry, Mr Bassett. All my girls are good Christians also; you are among friends here. Welcome to the Blue Kettle.'

He took me up polished white stone stairs to a large room that overlooked the bar through a huge arched pane of glass.

He said, 'Don't worry. It is mirrored glass. You can see out, but no one can see in. Once we are dealing with each other again, your wonderful Military Police will come up here and film men downstairs with the girls.'

I had a thought. 'Were they here last night?'

'No; and I shouldn't have let them film you if they had been.'

214

'Why not?'

'Because you are a friend.'

The conversation faltered for a second. 'I was going to ask you about that. How come you know my name?'

'I knew it twice, Mr Bassett . . .'

'You may as well call me Charlie; everyone else does.'

'Charlie; thank you . . . I knew it twice, Charlie: once by accident almost, and once from a deliberate information.'

'Who told you about me deliberately? I'll have a word with the bastard.'

He shook his head and smiled. He knew I wouldn't.

'Mr Watson – you know him?' I nodded. 'He gives me the name and description of his officers. He asks me to look after them.'

'. . . and pays you for it.'

'Of course. So when you come to Ismailia or Suez you are insured.'

'You said you also learned of me by accident?'

'Yes, only two weeks ago. I was in Europe – I need to consider investing in a club in developing Europe; somewhere safer than Egypt. One of the owners I dined with named and described you. He also asked me to take care of you if we met.'

'. . . and paid you.'

'Of course not. One doesn't pay one's partners.'

'Berlin.'

'Precisely . . . and hearing your name twice within a few weeks kindled my interest in you, Charlie Bassett.' Bloody Bozey. 'I made an investment in all three of your clubs, Charlie. We cannot hold money in Egypt now. Since Farouk left, every time there is trouble the exchange rate crashes. So I invest in the business I know.' *Three* clubs? What the fuck was Bozey doing with our money?

The room was like a large study in a stately home, or maybe

the reading room of a gentleman's club in Knightsbridge. It smelt of rich old cigars, and was lined with hanging carpets and books. He came in on cue with, 'Cigar? I always smoke one about now.'

'No thank you. Do you mind if I put this on?' I waved my pipe at him.

'Of course not; I would say *be my guest*, but you are not really a guest. When my agent's negotiations with Mr Borland are successful, you two, and I, will be partners in this very establishment. He has asked for ten per cent.' I spluttered my beer. 'So I will say it again: welcome to the Blue Kettle.'

I stared at him. I hope it wasn't an unfriendly stare. That set Bob Crosby used to play came into my mind . . . the panicky opening bars of 'Can't we be friends' . . . then I reached over, and took his hand for the second time.

'Thank you, partner . . .' I paused before asking, 'Will the British authorities, or Mr Watson, have to know anything about this?'

'I don't think so, Charlie, do you? They are not as discreet as they should be. Would you like to recommence your lessons in Arabic now?'

The last thing he showed me was a door in the corridor behind his office. It led directly onto a fire escape, and the back yard. There was always a bicycle beneath it, in case the unfriendly British raided the club, he said. It had happened before.

I waited in a sumptuously appointed lounge. Deep low couches, antimacassars and carpets for wall hangings. A Roman tribune would have felt at home there. A cloudy smoky scent clung to the drapes. Like rich, sweet cigar smoke. When the girl walked in I was surprised to find her in Western clothes: a short white skirt and a skimpy grey top. A three-inch gap between them showed off her stomach: olive-skinned and flat, but with that slight womanly bulge that sends men mad.

I asked her, 'What's your real name?'

'Mariam. Mariam Sfeir. Last night you said you were Charlie.'
I nodded. 'And you are also from Lebanon?'
'Beirut, yes. Have you been to Beirut, sir?'
'No.'
'It is the most wonderful city in the world: full of millionaires.
Are you a millionaire?'
'Not yet.'
'David says that I may be able to go on holiday to one of your
bars in Germany, if one of your German women comes here as
an exchange. Is that right?'
It was an odd definition of holiday perhaps, but I said, 'Yes, I
am sure that will be arranged. You will be a star in Europe. Men
will stand in line to watch you dance.'
She giggled. I thought she looked impossibly glamorous. A
mere shadow of lipstick, and a vague suggestion of an expensive
perfume. Her hair just brushed her olive shoulders. It was neither
brown nor blonde; some magical combination of both which
swung whenever she moved her head. Oh Charlie.
'Famous film directors maybe?' She went over to an American
fridge in one corner. It was as big as a telephone box. When she
came back she had two beers for us. I hadn't paid for anything
that night, and didn't know how this worked.
'I don't know,' I told her honestly.
'I'm sure David could arrange it . . .'
Twenty minutes later my education in the Arabic tongue
recommenced. I found that Lebanese Arabic was an inventive,
playful and tactile language. You sleep exceptionally well after a
lesson, and I can recommend it to anyone.

I had breakfast with David Yassine.
He asked, 'You slept well?'
'Terrifically, thank you.'
'You weren't awoken by the noise?'

'What noise?'

'There was a demonstration outside. The Muslim Brotherhood wishes me to close my club to British soldiers.'

'What happened?'

'I pushed someone out to explain to them that it was already closed to British soldiers, so they sent me a present of fruit and dates, and then went to burn some cars in the Old Town.'

'Nobody was hurt?'

'Not as far as I know. Breakfast?'

Breakfast was a large juicy orange, dates, slices of fried goat's cheese and flat baked bread with honey. Turkish coffee sweet enough to strip the silver from the EPNS. Bloody wonderful. We sat cross-legged on large cushions in front of a low table, and were served by one of his women. She danced for us as we ate. Belly dancing for breakfast: that was one for the diary. I wondered if my dad would believe it when I told him. Yassine asked me where I got my Egyptian spending money, and when I replied, 'The base,' he shook his head.

'Far too expensive. The British government is charging you an extortionate rate to change money they already owe to you, into local currency. In future please come to me. How much do you have at present?'

'About forty Egyptian pounds.' Again he shook his head.

'Not enough for a man of our business stature. I will give you . . .' From a small safe in the corner he took out two small bundles of notes. The thing looked stuffed with them. '. . . two hundred pounds Egyptian. Here.' He offered them.

'I have nothing yet to exchange for it.'

'I take it from your ten per cent. Your Mr Borland will be happy now: he was worried about you. Easier for me too: less currency to get out of the country.' So that was all right then.

'OK. Thank you.' I buttoned them into my KD shirt pocket.

Someone had told me about that, hadn't they? 'Did I tell you I saw a lion a couple of nights ago?'

'No. In a cage in a club? They used to do that in the old days.'

'No, loose on the street not far from here.'

'Not possible, Charlie. No lions in Egypt for many years.'

'Someone else told me that.'

'So now two people have told you. Maybe you will believe?' It sounded sarky, but it wasn't. He was smiling. He was also shovelling away a second breakfast, so I was left in no doubt where his bulk came from.

The last thing I asked him before making my plans was, 'Could I make telephone calls from here? The military base exchanges are expensive, rationed and monitored . . . and I was warned that the MPs listen in.'

'They sometimes listen to me as well; hoping to catch me spying for the Egyptian police. You can tell because the phone clicks when you lift it. Once their technician left his microphone open, and I heard him snoring.'

'Would you do that? Spy for the Egyptian police?'

'If I didn't, they would put me out of business: maybe worse.'

'Who else do you work for?'

'Egyptian Army if they ask. If I said no to *them*, then some night a hand grenade comes through the window. Anyway, they pay well.'

'Your business affairs seem very complicated, David.'

'I would say *interesting*. Anyway – safer now that I have two English partners.'

'I wouldn't bet on that.'

'Ah, but I am, I am. These calls you want to make; they are also business?'

'Some business; some private . . . to my family.'

'You have a family . . . nice. Children?'

'Two boys.'

'Wife?'

'No, just the boys.'

'You are a widower . . . sad. Wife dead . . . you get a new one. Mariam is healthy: a woman like her would work hard.'

'Thank you, but no. Not yet, at any rate. My wife is not dead; I just never married. Just a couple of phone calls would do for now. I would appreciate it.'

'Of course. Whenever you please, but whatever you do remember the clicks.'

'I will remember the clicks.'

'And come and go across the courtyard. There is a British policeman at the front door now. It would be impolite to embarrass him.'

Ever since my pal Tommo had bought it in an air crash in '49, there had been something missing from my life. Now I knew what it was: that special sense of danger and unpredictability he brought, hanging about at the periphery of my vision. God had now sent me David Yassine to fill that gap. Bravo, God.

I borrowed a pool Standard Vanguard from the commissariat, and drove over to El Kirsh. Finding the gears on its worn column change was like stirring the Christmas pudding. Haye was on duty, pleased to see me, but not pleased to be still working.

'Call me next time; then I can swap for a couple of hours, and take you somewhere.'

'You're not the only person I came to see.'

'. . . and telling me that will get you nowhere fast.' But she was smiling, and that counted for a lot. I wondered if I'd get to see her in her bikini again. She handed me four letters that had come into the BFPO, had been sent on to the hospital for me, but arrived after I'd moved on. 'These came yesterday. I was hoping you'd catch them. You can sit on the veranda and read them if you like. I'll bring you a mug of tea.' The British race has an unnatural fixation with tea; have you noticed that?

Two were from Elaine, one was from Dieter, and one from a person whose handwriting I didn't recognize, but when I turned it over the return name and address were Flaming June's. I decided to keep her for later. I read Dieter's first. He had a superb, clear, small hand which put mine to shame, and wrote on pencil-ruled lines on airmail paper. It took me about twenty minutes to read, and told me enough for me to imagine their lives in Bosham in detail. After I had finished it, I let it lie in my lap while I stared out across the ugly camp and into the desert in the distance. Susan came out, touched my shoulder, gave me the tea and left again without saying a word. That was very clever of her.

Elaine's letters were a mixture of news, gossip and technical questions that she hadn't mastered before I left . . . and, in case I had forgotten, she signed one with a very suggestive drawing. I'd seen the same symbol in the sky before: fighter pilots can draw it with their vapour trails. I decided to call her at work tomorrow. I read recently that some sod thought he'd now invented a new business style which he cleverly called *remote management*, and probably got a knighthood for it. Give him a call somebody, and tell him we were doing it back in the 1950s.

Half an hour later Susan came out with her own tea, and sat alongside me. She asked, 'Everything OK at home?'

'Fine, but it slows you down when you read about it. There's a whole life back there going on without you.'

'I know. The services say it's good for us to stay in touch, and encourage our relations to write . . . but sometimes I wonder.'

'Wonder what, pet?'

'They just couldn't imagine what it's really like out here; not unless they've been here themselves. I had a boyfriend in Nottingham who expected me to save myself for him . . . stupid idea!'

'How long do you have to do?'

'Two and a half; but they often extend that by six months, and you get no choice in the matter.'

'How long have you been out?'

'A year.' I realized that, with a bit of luck, I would be home long before her, but didn't say it. She added, 'I finish in half an hour; do you want to come down to my place for a long, cold drink?'

'. . . *come up and see me some time?*'

'Try, *if you don't like my peaches, why do you shake my tree?* That was Mae West as well, I think.' She was smiling a sad smile that came of us talking too much about home. Egypt had taught me another lesson.

'I'd love to come down to your place for a drink.'

'And please make a pass at me; so that I can say *no*.'

'OK.'

Chapter Twelve

Blackbird blues

'I met a friend of yours in Ish.'

'We are forgetting something, Charlie. Try remembering the *sirs* now and again.'

That was Watson of course. We were sitting under the fan in his office, with a Sundowner each, jostling for a foot of floorboards a degree cooler than the next.

'I think this had better be a completely confidential conversation, sir. Sort of a chat between two old friends, before one of them fills the other in for compromising him.'

'Ah, *that* sort of a conversation.'

I had surprised the pair of us by coming off leave a day early. The truth was, as a reservist back in Watson's private air force, I didn't actually feel as if I was in the services again, or subject to its bizarre vagaries. It felt more like being a member of an easygoing criminal gang. Ninety-six hours might have meant ninety-six to them, but it had only meant seventy-two to me. I'd take the other day when I felt like it, although I was old soldier enough to know that could lead to trouble. After the New Zealander had been murdered, they shut down all traffic on the road south for a day anyway, so I travelled back with Roy Rogers, whose leave had been extended a day. What goes around comes around, even in the armed services – I've told you that before. We travelled in a sand-coloured motor coach with a small RAF roundel on its wing, in a sand-coloured dust cloud in a small sand-coloured convoy. Some god with a paintbrush had clearly had a severe deficiency of imagination in the colour department on the Treaty Road. The convoy had a fore-and-aft escort of heavily armed jeeps. Three Comet tanks were parked up around the Mile Twelve telegraph posts. Their main guns pointed purposefully back down the road to Ismailia. I was already beginning to call it *Ish*, by the way, the same as Trigger's mates.

We passed a body on the road. Tossed into a gully by the wayside, like a piece of discarded rubbish. He had been a man once. I could clearly see the dried bloodstains on his dirty djellaba. He was surrounded by a cloud of flies, and a bizarre scattering of fruits; some of which were mashed into the road surface; we weren't the first to drive past him.

Trigger yawned and observed, 'That's 'ow you know we're more civilized than your average wog. Our boys often vanish without a trace; as if they'd never been on the Earth. But *we* always leaves them the bodies to bury. It's because of differences like that the wog's not to be trusted to run the Canal.'

'Maybe he was only a poor fucking greengrocer after all . . .'

'Then he shouldn't have argued with a Bren gun, should he?'

I'd already heard that there were revenge killings and beatings of Egyptians after a murder of one of ours; some divisional commanders were even rumoured to encourage it. When would that nonsense stop? When we were simply tired of killing each other, or when the politicians realized that it wasn't going to work any more? Maybe it would go on until there were no longer any of us left on either side to die – I really didn't deserve to be in this bloody madhouse.

'Why don't you get some kip?' Roy asked me. 'You've 'ad a busy weekend. I'll wake you up when I have to start calling you *sir* again.' There it goes again: what comes around goes around. What we need is a world where *everyone* calls each other 'sir', or else no one does it at all. Believe me: if they ever make me dictator of the British, the only bullshit left will come out of creatures with four legs and a bad attitude.

Watson was always uncomfortable with what he called *that kind of a conversation*. He was better at bludgeoning the uneducated to death with public-school vowels than coping with the meeting of two equal minds which comprised *that kind of a conversation*.

After a pause into which I could have played a rumba he asked, 'What's on your mind, Charlie?'

'A greasy fat bastard called David Yassine is on my mind.' I had already decided not to say anything about my personal and unexpected connection with the fat man. I was sure that he wouldn't have told Watson yet – he would surely save that titbit up until he could make use of it. 'When I walked into his club he already expected me. He knew my name and description, and as much as admitted that you had given them to him.'

Watson looked shifty. That was interesting. He called Daisy before he replied to me.

'Another couple of the same if you don't mind, old dear; Charlie's thirsty.' Then he told me, 'It's just a little arrangement we have. He keeps an eye out for my lads on his premises, and keeps them out of trouble. It's a shocking place, really; you've got no idea what goes on there.'

'And you buy information from him; and route duff intelligence to the Gyppoes through him when you feel like it.'

'Hang on, old son, that's a bit stiff. You've no reason to say that.'

'Yes I bloody have, sir. I know exactly what *you're* like, and I spent an evening getting to know Yassine. I've met people like him all over Europe. They're the Clapham Junction in human form: information in/information out – and the bell on the cash register never stops ringing. I'd hoped I was clear of all that when I came out here.'

'Maybe I should have told you to be careful,' he admitted grudgingly, '. . . seeing as we've worked together before.'

'Have you told any of the others?'

'No, as a matter of fact.'

'Then bloody don't. They'll lynch you – boss or not.'

Daisy came in with another couple of drinks. I don't know what I expected, but it wasn't the quick on-off smile to grimace I got – as if she'd gone off me in a big way.

After she left I asked loudly, hoping she'd hear, 'What's up with her?'

'Don't know, Charlie; funny creatures women . . . she's been giving me the silent routine for a couple of days. I would have minded if she hadn't been doing the same to everyone. It looks like Little Miss Sunshine has gone on holiday, and left something dark in her place.' That was interesting – and you know what I'm like by now, I was going to make a point of finding out what was what.

'Is that the end of *that sort of a conversation* for the time being? Can we get back to *sir* and Charlie?'

'If you like, sir.'

'Good, after you've got yourself sorted out, nip over to the Doc's and make sure you have all the Istanbul and Tehran inoculations. You're rejoining the RAF, and getting back into the air tomorrow.'

Bollocks.

'Doing what, sir?'

'Would you believe that you're showing the flag?'

'No, sir, I wouldn't.'

'Sightseeing then; you'll have Nansen with you, so try to keep him out of trouble for once.'

The MO declined to make any more puncture marks in me, but gave me some thick sloppy stuff to drink, and some ointment. I had seen the ointment before in 1944. It had the consistency of the stuff Castrol sold for greasing cars.

'What's this for, Doc?'

'The trots. Everyone gets them in Istanbul. Don't panic when your shit turns a khaki dark-green colour with yellow streaks, and starts running out of you like Emil Zatopek. Just dose yourself up and stay close to a bog for a day. After that, normal service will be resumed as soon as possible . . . probably.'

I didn't like the *probably*, but, generally speaking, I don't like doctors either. Just like coppers, they all fancy themselves as comedians, and these days it's remarkable how many of them manage to get on to the telly or the radio — once they realize that they're no good at doctoring, and not corruptible enough to make it into Parliament.

'Somebody stole your fore an' after,' Oliver told me. 'I must have had my back turned.' It wasn't what he said, you see; it was always the way he said it that made you look up. Anyway, it was the narrow RAF forage titfer he was talking about. It sat on the top of your head looking like a fanny waiting for a kiss, and made you look like an air cadet. I hated the bloody thing — so I wasn't going to report it.

He changed the subject. 'Good leave?'

'They murdered someone while I was there. A New Zealander.'

'I told you that you weren't going to like it over here. See any dancers?'

'I met one in the Blue Kettle.'

'Just the one?'

'I met the same one twice.'

'Hope you've been to the Doc for some of the old cock wash.'

'Just come from him, if you must know. Have you got a beer? I've just been drinking something obnoxious with the Wing Commander.'

'You have the words in the wrong order, Charlie, but yes, we have some beer. It's about time you contributed some of your own.'

Who would I have to see? I asked myself. Pat Tobin? I rearranged the words I had last used. The best I could come up with was *I've just been drinking something with the obnoxious Wing Commander.* Maybe Nancy was brighter than he looked.

The next day we climbed back into an aeroplane.

In some ways the aircraft was a miracle. It was a miracle because most of the things the RAF had stuffed me into so far had been beat-up and falling to pieces. One of the things you are almost certainly unaware of is that the bright, shiny war planes you see dancing in the sky at air shows are not typical of RAF equipment. Most of the real kit it uses needs a fresh paint job, has bits missing and several essential systems that won't work. The Varsity sitting on the strip for us at Deversoir looked brand-new. RAF Transport Command at its very best: a polished and beautiful passenger aircraft. All we needed was a couple of those BOAC trolley dollies and I probably would refuse to get out of her again.

The problems started when we climbed up inside, because if this was a Transport Command ship then I was a Dutchman, *mijnheer*. The pilot and his oppo hadn't shaved for a couple of days – they looked like thugs. There was a bang-up-to-date-radio rig behind the pilot, for me . . . although a bulkhead separated us, and across the walk space from me was a decent navigation table with bloody M'smith already seated at it.

He said, 'Hi, Charlie. Good leave?'

'Fine thanks. I didn't know you were here.'

'Fayid. The old man likes to keep us spread about a bit.' Were Nancy and I being billeted closer to Watson so he could keep an eye on us?

There was a radar station behind M'smith, still facing forward, but anything portable was missing. Nansen slid into the seat, and began to sort out his cameras. We stowed our small packs beneath him. Oh; I forgot the policemen. There were two RAF policemen wearing side arms sitting up close to the tail. Sightseeing with guns in their hands. Who knows – perhaps it will catch on? Bung on the old earphones, Charlie.

In my ears I heard the skipper's voice ask, 'Everyone nailed down?' . . . and the acknowledgements he received one by one. Then he opened the taps and we were airborne in two shakes of her tail. I was impressed by her speed and nimbleness, compared with the *Jack o' Diamonds* from whom she had been developed. A stressed-skin fuselage can make all the difference. Apart from the occasional instruction the skipper was a man of few words. In fact, practically none. I eventually worked out that he was an Australian, so he probably didn't know all that many words anyway – you know what Aussies are like. The co-pilot/engineer came back for a chat now and again, and he and Oliver went down to the tail occasionally, to share a smoke with the coppers.

It was while they were doing this that I asked M'smith, 'What do we need coppers on board for? Are they frightened we won't come back?'

'Nothing as sinister, Charlie. They'll guard the aircraft when we're on the ground – keep Johnny Foreigner at arm's length.'

I didn't even have all that much to do. Once the pilot had set course I flipped a couple of switches on a newish piece of kit. It looked like a wire recorder, but used a spool of plasticky tape, and all of the radio traffic was automatically recorded. It even self-triggered as soon as it picked up a broadcast. I still had to do a few manual sweeps on infrequently used wavelengths, but for the most part this new gear did everything itself. Nansen told me that he also had two wide-angle-lens fixed reconnaissance cameras in the aircraft's belly. All he had to do was make sure the ports covering them were opened before the pilot commenced runs along pre-set coordinates, at briefed heights. Piece of piss.

'So what looks like a Transport Command troop transport is actually a pretty sophisticated spy plane?'

'Technical, or electronic, surveillance is the term we use these days, Charlie. She's a Q plane. Call sign, as you know – *Queenie*: something pretending to be other than what she actually is. Someone in Command has a sense of the ironic.'

'And who are *we*, then?'

'*Queenie*'s courtiers,' M'smith leaned over and told us. 'She's Watson's pride and joy, so we're not even allowed to be sick in her. If you feel ill, we'll hang you out the door by your ankles until you feel better.'

I remembered something then, that I'd forgotten to ask Nansen earlier: 'Where do we buy our beer, Oliver? From Pat Tobin?'

'. . . thought you'd never ask, old dear. No, Pat's too dear, dear. I'll introduce you to a braw young lassie from the NAAFI: you'll love her. If Robert Burns was alive today do you think he'd write some of his doggerel about a lassie from the NAAFI?' Then he sang, '*I love a lassie, she works in the NAAFI, she's the apple of her mother's old glass eye . . .*'

He sounded a bit like Harry Lauder. 'What else rhymes with lassie?'

'Chassis,' I told him.

'I'm sure we can do something with that . . .'

'Don't worry about Oliver,' M'smith butted in. 'He's Watson's Q airman, just like *Queenie* here. He looks like a queer and sounds like a queer, but actually he's not. He's just like you and me, and when he puts his mind to pulling a bird I've never seen one turn him down. You'll find that living alongside him is quite depressing.'

'Bloody fine photographer too,' Nansen said. 'Don't forget that. Sandwich anyone? I brought enough for you two too, because I knew you'd forget.'

'One last thing,' I asked them, '. . . and then we can talk rubbish all the way to Turkey if you want.'

'What?'

'What?'

They'd obviously flown together before.

'The pilot and his mate; they're not regular RAF either, are they?'

M'smith got in first.

'Australian Special Forces,' he told me. 'If we crash in the desert they'll slit your throat, and drink your blood to stay alive if they have to.'

I was glad I still had my small pistol in my pocket.

Queenie droned north. Sometimes we gained height, and sometimes we lost a bit. Periodically, Oliver would unsheathe his belly cameras, and photograph a strip of land that would one day be strategic to some poor sod or another. Two Israeli late-model Spitfires came up for a look at us. The pilots smiled and waved, and took our photographs with hand-held cameras. More for souvenirs than anything else I think. In 1948 and 1949 we and the Israelis had been killing each other on the quiet, as we Brits got in the way of the creation of the new state of Israel. Something had happened between then and 1953, because now we were acting as if we'd always been best buddies. Ask the politicians; they're the ones who order and direct all the killing, aren't they? And they're the ones who tell us when to stop. And then they pretend it was nothing to do with them after all, and ask us to vote for them all over again. I don't know why we're always stupid enough to do it.

The Arabian states came and went under the starboard wing. I can describe them in two simple words: mainly brown. They looked brown, sounded brown, and smelled brown. Not one of my favourite colours. When someone comes back from Saudi these days, and tells you it's shite, I promise you that they will be speaking from more than one perspective. Whenever a red light came on over the nav's table Oliver had to open the camera ports, and when a green came on alongside it he triggered the belly cameras.

Three hours into the flight we were over mountain ranges in southeast Turkey.

'They used to call this Kurdistan in the old days, I think,' M'smith told us. 'The native people underneath us have had at least half a dozen masters in the last thousand years. No one managed to break them . . . they're as bad as the Afghanis on the North-West Frontier. We have to look for something which was spotted during an overflight a few months ago.'

Our piratical pilot was letting us gently down towards the peaks and valleys. Too many bloody peaks and too few valleys for my liking. The air got a bit lumpy. There was even some snow on the high ground. I had never imagined snow out here, and we were nearer to the bloody stuff than I was comfortable with. There were very few radio signals. Not many people up here to send them, I imagined. They were all probably tucked up in their igloos for the winter. We started a run. Red light. Nansen's camera ports opened with a slight rumbling sound. Green light. About three or four minutes.

Then I heard Oliver's voice in my earphones. 'Cameras, Skip . . . can you come round again, and get us any closer?'

'. . . give you another hundred feet, OK? I wouldn't want to get any nearer to the pointy things than that.'

Queenie's twin engines roared like lions — which reminded me of something — as he pulled her around in a climbing turn to starboard. It occurred to me to wonder what her stalling speed was, but this guy seemed to know what he was doing. As we banked around a 360 Nansen pointed out the target to me from one of our round glazed windows.

'*There* — down there. Like a small dark cross on the ground.'

As we lost height towards it I could see it quite clearly. But it wasn't a dark cross: it was an aircraft. A bigger, blacker aircraft than the thing I was sitting in. It was a four-engined bomber type, from the war half the world had just been engaged in; parked neatly on a flat grassy plateau as if it had grown there. Oliver was also snapping away with his hand-held cameras for all he was worth.

M'smith peered over my shoulder and asked, 'What the fuck's *that* doing down there? I didn't think that the Turks had anything that big.'

They didn't. It was a big black bastard of a Stirling bomber, and I knew in my heart I had seen her before. A rage as black as her peeling flanks rose in me. Now I knew what I had been called up for, and for once I couldn't wait to see Watson again . . . and then get my hands around his treacherous fucking throat.

I had to wait as it turned out, because our lord and master had been called away. I didn't find that out until the morning after we had returned from our flying four-day scheme, introducing Turkey and Iran to the best the RAF could offer. That meant trying to drink the clubs dry in Istanbul and Tehran.

Istanbul was my sort of place: poky small bars where the coffee was so sweet you could stand your spoon up in it, and bazaars you could get lost in. I had never thought of Constantinople as one of the great walled cities of the world, but it is. Our Aussie flew us on a circuit of the massive walls, before putting us down at a very rudimentary airport where the Varsity was promptly surrounded by policemen in dark outfits and dark red fezes: they looked like a Toy Town army. The purpose of the Turkish police was to stop the locals making off with essential pieces from the outside of our transport. The purpose of our *own* two policemen was to prevent the Turkish cops getting inside the aircraft and stripping it bare. If we had left it unattended we would probably have found it for sale in component parts in the Grand Bazaar the very next day. The Turks are the greatest thieves in the world.

'Who looks after our two guys?' M'smith asked, as we stepped down into a temperature like a Sussex spring. 'They have to eat, and all that.'

'I do,' answered a world-weary-looking young man from the front of one of the police jeeps. He wore a crumpled linen suit and a battered panama. When he took it off his prematurely thinned hair clung to his pink scalp like seaweed. He handed me a card. It was as crumpled as his suit. Why do these ambassadorial types all have to dress like something from a Graham Greene book? 'Lance Love; British Embassy. I'll make sure that your men are accommodated. If you'd like to do the Customs thing in that small building over there, I'll give you a lift into your hotel. I've booked you for two nights, OK?'

Oliver gave him a grotesque come-on con of a smile, and said, '*Lance*? Nice name . . .'

Love blushed. Men who've cultivated world-weary should be told not to blush. Our pilot looked from one to the other and said, 'Why don't you two fairies just fuck off, and leave us to find our own way around?' I don't think there was an insult intended. The words just flowed in a very conversational tone.

Nansen turned on him. 'Oh no, dear; couldn't do that. You'll need someone to protect you from all these naughty Turks. Didn't anyone tell you?'

The Aussie grimaced. He may have bunched a fist. I thought we might be in for an interesting evening.

The next day I had a hangover. We all did. The flight crew looked like wounded bears. M'smith had heard that the best way to cure a hangover was a Turkish massage. Nancy, who knew better, cautioned us against it, which sort of made our minds up.

In a massage joint that looked like the inside of a synagogue, my small and naked body was covered in a soapy, oily concoction, and flipped around on a marble slab as if I was a piece of fish. Then the fat Ottoman doing the flipping stood on me and dug his feet in. His toes burrowed into my back like moles, and I knew what poor old HMS *Victory* must have felt like when the Death Watch Beetle started on her. After that I felt too ill, and was in too much pain from the massage, to protest. I just wanted to die.

I left the place an hour later with every joint in my body dislocated, every muscle pounded into useless jelly and with no feeling in my fingers and toes. Maybe they had been playfully wrenched off by the monster appointed to me. Chastened, we headed for the nearest bar, smelling like poofs. When I looked around it, every other patron seemed in the same state as me and pouring light beers down their throats as if the world was about to end. The lesson I learned there was that if you want to own a really successful bar, open one as near to a massage parlour as you bloody well can.

I didn't get the trots, but M'smith did. I gave him my stuff. He took the linctus, but gave me a funny look and handed back the ointment.

Nansen grabbed it, 'I'll have that if you don't want it.'

'What for, Oliver?'

'I can sell it, you dummy . . . worth a bloody mint over here.'

I wasn't empty-handed when I climbed wearily back into the aircraft. Four large sacks of spices I'd bargained for at the Spice Bazaar followed me on to it. The smell wasn't all that bad, but the cops complained. Cops always seem to be able to find something to complain about, don't they?

M'smith asked me, 'What are those for?'

'A place in Berlin I'm involved with. Someone over there told me that you could ask what you wanted for spices in Germany – although that was a couple of years ago. It may not be as good now.'

'How will you get them there?'

I was tempted to use that phrase they'd taught me about Egypt, but said instead, 'I haven't worked that one out yet.'

After Istanbul, Tehran was a cinch. It was in the most Western-ized Arab country I'd been near yet, even if their prime minister was well known for telling ours where to get off. The Aussies disappeared for twenty-four hours, and when they came back they were in high spirits. That meant they'd shafted someone. I got round to asking the skipper his name.

He told me, 'Hudd.' When I put the same question to the co-pilot he replied, 'Hudd's man.'

I'd ask Nancy about that later. M'smith sniggered. Hudd's man looked at him, and he stopped sniggering. I would have done the same.

Because our take-off was put back nine hours until a local sandstorm blew itself out, I had a beer alone with Hudd at the airport bar. We'd rigged tarps over the engines in a high wind, and were experiencing that odd high that men get from achieving a difficult task successfully together. Wrestling twenty feet of old tarpaulin into a Force 8 just about comes under that description. He blew the froth from a large glass of beer, then passed it back to the barman for a top-up.

When the barman had moved away he said from out of nowhere, 'They've handed you a shit of a job, haven't they?'

'How did you guess that?'

'I didn't. I heard you sucking your breath in the first time we banked over that old aircraft down in Turkey.' He must have heard me over his head set.

'Why did you think it was me?'

'Oh, I always know.'

'. . . anyway, the answer is that I don't really know yet. I last saw that aircraft on the ground in England in 1944 – just before it was stolen by its crew. Later I was accused of helping them to get away. It can't be coincidence that you just happened to fly me over it, can it?'

Hudd laughed. Then he asked, 'They can't seriously want it back, can they? It will be fuck-all use if it's been standing out there for nearly ten years.' He took a huge swig at his beer, and emptied half the glass.

'You know the War Office . . . it has a memory like an elephant. What are you doing out here anyway? You don't look like the bus-driver type to me.'

'You heard of Operation Ajax?'

'No.'

'Good. Forget I said it then.'

'What is it?'

He shook his head, but after a pause said, 'Ike wants to lose a prime minister an' make a new friend. We're gonna help him.'

'Why?'

'Where you bin these last coupla years, son? This Persian bastard nationalized the oil over here, an' wants to sell it to the Reds.'

'And we're going to *kill* him for that?'

'. . . would if I was asked to, but no . . . jest gonna convince his Arab brothers to choose another prime minister. The guy left in charge will be like a king, and he'll love us for it.'

'How do you persuade a people to replace their government?' He didn't answer. He looked away and smiled.

I told him, 'I used to know a girl who went out with Ike whenever he was back in Britain. They used to go up to some Scottish castle, and dance the night away with eightsome reels or something.'

'Why are you telling me?'

'Because she's an Aussie too.'

'So was Ned Kelly, but I don't see no reason to boast about it.' This was as close to polite as he got. He was telling me to shut up, and get another round in. Or maybe he was trying to tell me something else altogether: you just don't know with maneaters.

That night, as we were taking off into the twilight, the centre of Tehran exploded with riots. Over the 'phones I heard one of the Hudds whistling 'When Johnny comes marching home again', and then 'Waltzing Matilda'. I'm glad someone was happy.

We staggered out of the aircraft in the early hours, and I had nothing in my mind other than getting a shower and falling on my bed. The shower block was dark – the bloody lights had blown again – and to cap it all the last bastards through there had forgotten to run the pump to refill the shower cistern. It was as empty as a Mother Superior's dreams. Something flat and dark and long moved along the floor in one of the stalls, so I decided to pass up on that as well. *Bollocks*. My bed was still there, and I dropped onto it fully clothed. Nancy was already snoring.

I awoke looking at a calendar tacked high on one of the tent posts with a drawing pin. There was a pink lady pictured above the grid of dates. Not that dreadful Pink Lady cocktail our infantile thirty-year-olds are drinking these days, but a painting of a cheerful pink lady without her clothes. Her nipples looked like strawberries. She was advertising the capabilities of a company named Ralph W Folk, from Milton, Wisconsin.

I yawned, and asked Nancy, 'Where did you get that?'

'I bought her from a man in the souk in Istanbul. Ten bob. I thought if I stuck her up here no one would get the wrong idea about us.'

'Thanks.'

'We'll have to hide her whenever we're both away or she'll get nicked.'

'What do Ralph W Folk and friends do?'

'They advertise things.'

'So she's advertising advertising by advertising?'

'I suppose so. Do you want to give her a name?'

I said, 'Grace,' and regretted it immediately.

'I like that: if we get bored with that we can change that to her lesbian friend Mary.'

'Come again?'

'Hail Mary full of Grace – just like Tuesday's child.' I suppose my face showed that he'd touched a bone, because he immediately asked, 'What's the matter?'

'Nothing.'

'Bollocks. What's the matter?'

'I knew a *Tuesday's Child* once – a Lancaster bomber I flew. She crashed and burned first time out with her next crew. I suppose she still worries me.' He didn't respond, which was a reasonable thing to do. Then I observed, 'It's odd, but the further I get from the war the more it seems to matter. It didn't matter much at the time; we just got on with it. What do you think?'

'I think you've shared a tent with me for too long: it's making you sensitive. Why don't you get up and wash, and then go down and tear a strip off our governor . . . it's all you were talking about on the trip in. He'll probably CB you for fourteen days, and we can all get back to a normal life complaining about the wogs.'

I had slept so well that I had forgotten. Bollocks.

Daisy had a tiny office alongside Watson's big office in the cricket pavilion. I suspected that most of our work was done in her small office, whilst Watson sat with his feet under the desk in the big one, sloshing whisky and chatting to his cronies on the telephone. It's the way you have a good war. Watson's office was currently empty of Watson, but Daisy came through to find out who was making the noise.

'Where is he?' I asked her without preamble.

'Gone over to Cairo for a meeting and a conference. He said that you were going to be awkward when you got back, and that if you were *too* awkward I was to call the police. Are you going to be too awkward, Charlie?'

'Yes: I want to brain the bastard.'

She immediately reached past me for the telephone on his desk. I put my hand on it first to prevent her, and she slapped me. I think it shocked both of us. Daisy's mouth dropped open, and she rushed back into her den and slammed the door.

I had to follow her, didn't I? I'm not sure whether that was because I was concerned for her, or to make sure she wasn't phoning the cops from in there. She wasn't. She was crying, and I, of course, lost all my resolve. Men are so stupid. I went over and put my arm around an aircraftwoman who had technically assaulted a senior officer. That meant that I technically assaulted her. Again: stupid. Daisy was having none of that. She pulled violently away, but accepted my handkerchief – one of those horrible light khaki issue jobs with the broad dark stripe down one side. There was a packet of Passing Cloud, and a box of B&Ms matches on her desk, alongside a glass ashtray. I lit two fags for us, and passed her one. I enjoyed the swift hit of the

Turkish tobacco, but this was hardly the time to start discussing that. Daisy stopped shaking, and began to drag heavily on the fag. I think it calmed her as well as me. I went and sat on the edge of her desk, leaving yards of sea room between us.

Eventually she asked, 'Will you have to report me?' I hated the way that she wouldn't meet my eye.

'Don't be daft; I've known you for years. I just want to know what I've done wrong.'

She laughed a bitter little laugh. It was as if the Daisy I'd known had completely disappeared, and an entirely different unpleasant person was looking out from her body at me. 'Nothing. Nothing at all, Charlie. You've done nothing.' She'd just said the same thing three times. Did that mean anything, or was she simply losing her marbles?

'I still don't understand. You really were going to phone the cops and make some sort of report about me. Why?'

This time she did make eye contact, and there was nothing good in there. It was enough to make you believe in those silly old Catholic tales of demonic possession.

'Because I *could*, Charlie.'

'But why?'

'Because I loathe you, and I would enjoy seeing you taken down a peg or two.'

'Again . . . but why?'

'Because you're a man.'

I felt like saying *Is that all?* And then *Situation normal*, but it was too serious for that. I headed back out to Watson's office. Don't ask me what I was thinking about, because my mind was spinning. His cupboard was unlocked. The Dimple Haig had been finished, but there was a half-decent Black Label Johnnie Walker. I didn't think he would begrudge it me. Daisy came and stood alongside me, reached over and poured us a glass each. A hefty glass of whisky at this time of day was definitely a trespass into

Watson's territory. This time it was she who sat on the edge of the desk. She had a nice pair of pins but, again, it wasn't the right time to notice them.

'He's not really a drunk you know: it's all an act. He rarely touches the stuff unless there's someone here to see him do it.'

'Half the people I know spend most of their time pretending to be someone other than they are . . .' and I wasn't prepared to let her off the hook . . . 'Look at you: you've spent years pretending to be someone I liked . . .'

'More bloody fool you, then.' She was still at it.

'Are you going to tell me what it's all about?' I took a sit-up-straight chair by the door that led out onto Watson's veranda. I just had this sense that out of her arms' reach was a sensible place to be. 'Why have you changed from one of my friends, into someone who *loathes* me?' I used her word. 'What did I do?'

'I told you. It's nothing to do with you. Stop being so vain.'

'Then stop hating me.'

She looked away, and said quietly, 'I can't.' But there was no weakness in the words.

Stalemate. I think I've told you somewhere before that God created me specifically to break stalemates by giving me all the stupid questions to ask. When I'm dead it's probably what people will remember about me.

Now I asked, 'What if I came over there, put you over my knee, and slapped your arse until you told me what the hell is going on?'

That got her attention. 'Mr Watson has a loaded service revolver in his right-hand desk drawer. He always forgets to take it out with him. I'll reach over, take it, and shoot you.'

I don't only have a problem with stupid questions: I also have a problem with the stupid answers I usually get to them. I stood up, and took one pace towards her.

'Go on then. Why don't you do it? There's no one else here,

so you can tell them what you like. Tell them I attacked you.'
Without taking her eyes off me she leaned away from me,
reached back and opened the drawer by feel; then placed her
hand inside. I could see that she was trembling. I held my breath.
Then she paused – I was gambling on her not being totally
doolally. Then she pulled the drawer shut, stood up stiffly and
walked in silence back into her own space, taking her drink with
her . . . and shut the door between us.

I gave my lungs permission to breathe again, and my heart
permission to start beating. My shirt was sticking to the small of
my back. I'd been silly again.

I swallowed the whisky in a oner, not even feeling it go down,
went over to the cupboard, and poured another. Then I went
over and sat behind the Wing Commander's desk. What the hell
had I let myself in for this time? All I knew was that I shouldn't
leave. So I didn't. After five minutes, I heard Daisy begin to
weep again. She cried and cried, and I didn't go in there. After
another twenty minutes she stopped, and a little later came out
mopping her face with my handkerchief. I know that you're
supposed to tell people how great they look, but Daisy looked
dreadful so I didn't even try.

Her back was to me – she was pulling herself another whisky:
I couldn't remember ever having seen her drink much before –
when I said, 'You're still going to have to shoot me . . .'

'Why?' She didn't turn.

'Because I'm going to sit here, or follow you around until you
tell me what the hell has happened.'

She turned this time, her eyes were watery again. She said,
'You're a fool, Charlie.'

'I know. Tell me something I don't . . .'

I've told you before that there is an exact length of a pause in
a conversation when a speaker is about to say something important: you can just fit the intro to Major Glenn Miller's 'String of

pearls' into it. Eventually she said, 'I had a fight with a couple of men.'

'Fight?'

'More of a tussle really; they didn't hurt me.'

'What do you mean, Daisy?'

'Don't be so bloody dense, Charlie. One held me for the other, and then they changed places. They were careful, considerate even. They didn't hurt me: they just had me, cleaned up, and went away again.'

Why was that the last thing I had expected? *Shit*. My mouth went dry.

'When?'

'The day before you went away.'

'Where?' There you go again, Charlie. Why did it matter where?

'Here. On the very desk you're sitting at, if you must know.'

She went to sit at the chair I'd vacated by the door. It was as if her legs could suddenly no longer support her. When I started to rise, she held her hand up to fend me off, so I stayed where I was.

'Where was Watson?'

'Out. They must have waited until they had seen him leave, because they came in soon afterwards.'

'Who have you told?'

'No one, stupid! It was probably my own fault: lying out there in the sun where anyone could walk by. Didn't you tell me that yourself?'

'Maybe. But that's not the way to look at it, Daisy.'

'Why not? What *is* the way to look at it?'

'My dad told me about the three ways of sex between ordinary people, when I was still a kid. There's sex between two people who don't know what they're doing – which is embarrassing.

244

There's sex between two people who *do* know what they're doing, and want to, which is terrific . . . but between people, one of whom *doesn't* want to, sex is rape. He reckons that they are the only three varieties for people like you and me.'

'What do *you* reckon?'

'I reckon he's right . . . don't you?'

She didn't answer me. She said, 'I'm getting a bit drunk, Charlie, I'm sorry.'

'Never say you're sorry for being drunk; it's a sign of weakness . . .'

'Who said that?'

'John Wayne almost said it.' That won me a twitch of a smile.

'. . . but I want another drink.'

'That's OK. The boss is away. I'll pretend to be him, and give us permission.' I held my own glass out as well. I asked her, 'Are you telling me that you've done nothing about them?'

'Yes. I couldn't think of anything to do.'

'Report them. Lay charges. You can't mess around with people like that.'

'And have everyone talking about me and sniggering? How would you like that? I told you; most people will say it's my own fault.' She looked out of the window and carried on speaking almost as if I wasn't in the room. 'Anyway one of them came back later, and apologized. He said they couldn't help it, because I was lovely and they hadn't seen their girlfriends for over a year . . . something like that. He said how sorry they were, and even offered me money. He asked if I was all right; he was very concerned.'

'I'll bet he was. What did you say?'

'I said I was all right, and asked him to go away. They weren't brutal with me, Charlie. One just held me down while the other had me.' Then she started to cry again, but very quietly – like a whisper, if ever a cry can be a whisper. 'They held a hand across my mouth so I couldn't even say anything . . . so it was almost as if it wasn't happening to me.'

I found that I was almost whispering as well. 'Tell me who they were.' And at precisely that moment something odd occurred: I remembered something similar happening to a woman at RAF Bawne during my bombing tour . . . and I remembered how badly the Boss class had dealt with it then.

'Why?'

'So I can do something about them.'

'No . . . oo . . . o.' It was an odd, drawn-out sound. 'That will make it worse.'

Anyway I took a chance again. I went round the desk, and stood closer to her. 'Please trust me. Just this once, please trust me.'

'Why?'

'Because I'm not sure what to do either.' I took her small nod for a *yes*, and made a decision on the strength of it. I had told her the truth: I didn't know what to do, but you'll remember the old advert, I'm sure – so perhaps I knew someone who did. I picked up the telephone. The person I was looking for wasn't at work, but they gave me an alternative number. It was the number of her quarter.

I said, 'Hello Haye with an e. It's me, Charlie.'

'I knew it. You sound like Charlie.'

'I have a problem, Haye, and I need your help . . .'

I had noticed before that Watson was much more assertive by telephone. When I answered it, he barked, 'Where's Daisy?'

'She's not well,' I lied smoothly. 'I sent her up the road to the hospital at Abu Sueir. They didn't have the right people down here.'

The sharpness went out of his voice. 'What's up with her?'

Bad choice of words maybe, but then mine was worse. I'd promised not to tell anyone else. I wasn't sure it was a promise I was going to completely keep, but I thought it covered the boss.

'Women's problem, sir.' That's right, I thought numbly, sometimes men *are* women's problems.

'Oh God! How long's she going to be out of action?'

'Possibly a couple of weeks, sir.'

'Who's running the shop?'

'Me and M'smith. Nancy's giving us a hand. The army has another scheme planned for a week's time: out into the sand in the northwest this time.'

'Get yourself sorted out for it then.' Then he paused and asked, 'Should I send her something?'

'That would be a good idea, sir. She wouldn't let us alert you – didn't want to worry you.' I wondered where he'd find a bunch of flowers in camel-dung country.

'Silly woman – so you *don't* tell me, and as soon as I find out I'm worried sick!' I thought she'd like to know that, but doubted he'd ever tell her. 'I could always come back via the hospital, I suppose.'

'That sounds like a good idea to me, sir, but you had better probably check with them first.'

'Good thought. Anything else?'

'Yes, I have a bone to pick with you about this last trip, sir.'

'. . . and that can bloody wait . . . you got a three-day swan out of it, so don't be an ungrateful little swine. Stop bellyaching.' And then he put the phone down on me. When you're my height, they can't resist saying *little*. I try not to let it get to me any more. Sometimes I understand why other nations aren't all that keen on the Brits. I put my feet up on his desk and resolved to drink him dry before he returned. Then I decided to keep my options open with the SWO, and volunteered for a night as duty officer.

Chapter Thirteen

Blues my naughty sweetie gives to me

I was surprised the SWO was there to bat me in. Usually a guard commander just got what they called 'the hand-over' from his predecessor. I'd borrowed a pushbike, and ridden around the compound in the afternoon. As the sweat dripped off me I told myself that it was doing me good – my skin even felt hardened enough to try it without a shirt. Daisy was right; I was vain. I just wanted to be the same colour as all the old-timers. Flying had been shut down because of the heat of the afternoon. It was nice to be somewhere you couldn't fight a war because it was too hot. At one of the runway run-offs a corporal was drilling a squad of defaulters. They looked half dead. He saluted as he doubled them past me, and I wondered how he knew the half-naked fool on a bicycle was an officer. Maybe I had the look. I hoped to Christ I hadn't.

At its best, the camp perimeter consisted of a ditch in the fucking desert surmounted by a high fence of barbed-wire strands, followed by a second internal ditch. A patrol would have to be careful not to fall into it at night. Rubbish had accumulated in it in places: I didn't like to think of what lurked underneath. At its worst, the defence was no more than several tangled rolls of rusty barbed wire that looked like something from the First War: my old man would have felt at home here. Pieces of paper had blown on to the wire and fluttered like white flags in the breeze. They gave off a weird, hushed rustling sound. You could be forgiven for thinking that was the sound of rodents, or the snakes that hunted them down, moving along the ditches beneath the rubbish. There were small, directed lights on poles in a few places. These gave the wogs some light to see what they were doing. I still couldn't believe it was Daisy who had brought me to this, but it was: I wanted to have the SWO firmly on my side when I decided to do something about her attackers, so I'd volunteered.

That night I relieved a flight lieutenant in the Regiment. He looked amused when I breezed in a few minutes before twenty-three hundred.

'I heard you volunteered. You must have been out in the sun too long.'

'The SWO advised me to get some time in as quickly as I could, and, with respect, there seems damn-all else for me to do.'

'Camp Cinema?'

'It's turning out just about now, isn't it? Besides, I saw them in Malta a month ago.'

Then he smiled, and held out his hand, 'Just so. Sorry, I was being sarky: we don't get many of Watson's Wankers over here at this time of night.'

'Is that what they call us?'

' 'fraid so. Can I take you over the maps before I go?'

The SWO clomped in a few minutes after my predecessor had left. The area was outside his direct realm of responsibility, so I did wonder what he was doing there. They obviously didn't trust me to run the show on my own.

He shook hands, and looked down on me.

'Good evening, sir: I thought I'd come and make the introductions, seeing as it's your first night.'

'You just didn't trust me not to make a mess of it.'

He gave me that up-and-down look: I suppose that I could have been better turned out. 'When did you last stand guard, sir, if you don't mind me asking?' He had me there.

'I think that would have been at Padgate in 1942 – at the end of my induction weeks.'

One of the erks in the room sniggered, and Cox bit him like a rattlesnake. I've seen a rattler in action – in fact I was once rather fond of one – so I should know. Cox spun round and snarled, 'What's that, Hoskins?'

'Nothing, SWO.'

'See me tomorrow morning – 0830. I'll find a cure for it. Understood?'

'Yes, SWO.'

I have a piece of advice for you. Something I learned in the Forties. Never get between a Warrant Officer and his men. It's not far removed from an act of suicide. So when he asked me, 'Would you like me to show you the ropes, sir?' I surrendered immediately.

'Yes, please, Mr Cox. And shout at me if I'm too rusty.'

'Wouldn't dream of it, sir.'

He had me strap on a .38 revolver, and drove me along my section of the perimeter in a jeep which had seen better days. Hoskins rode behind us with a Stirling on his lap and a miserable expression on his face. I reckoned he'd be polishing silverware in the Officers' Mess by mid-morning. We were responsible for one side of the giant quadrilateral compound. Luckily it was one of the utilitarian wire fences I'd reconnoitred that afternoon. I wondered if anyone had seen me doing it and told Cox, and he'd made his deployment accordingly.

Apart from a full mile and a half of wire, I had a couple of two-man foot patrols, who met in the middle for a fag before they turned back, and two ramshackle observation posts. One of those was on top of a water tank, standing about twelve feet off the ground — it was supposed to cover a couple of stores buildings. *I* sat in a satellite guardhouse in touch with the outliers by a twenty-year-old radio telephone. Naturally, it was a useless piece of junk: because you wouldn't send the British serviceman into a hostile country with decent equipment, would you? He might win a battle or something, and that would never do.

When I looked at the home receiver set — it was like a small, portable telephone switchboard — I could actually see the sharp blue flare of sparks from two of the wires at the back. They were continuously shorting across. I was surprised that the fucking thing hadn't electrocuted someone.

Before he left me Cox pointed at it and said, 'You can talk to your people on that if you like, sir, but you'll find there's massive interference, and you have to listen very sharply. It's often difficult to make out what's said. One of the squadron technical officers says it's the atmospherics in this part of the world.'

After Cox left, Hoskins told me, 'I wouldn't touch it if I was you, sir. You get electric shocks off it all the time.'

I could hear the generator wheezing away outside: if the bloody system was connected to that they'd black the entire camp out one night.

'That's why you can't hear what you're saying to each other on the bloody thing. Do you want me to fix it for you?'

'*Can* you, sir?'

'Piece of piss.'

Hoskins visibly winced: I'd have to watch my language. He was a tall, gangly-looking man in his early twenties. He wore round wire-rimmed spectacles, and spoke with a plummy apologetic tone . . . you knew instinctively that he'd been a clumsy git all his life. He looked too old for a national serviceman. I remarked on that, and he replied, 'I finished at university first. Then I had to do the call-up, sir. Only six months left to do.'

'What did you study?'

'I read English Literature and Divinity, sir.'

We all read English Literature, you prat, but what did you *study*? Then I remembered that *read* and *studied* meant the same thing to these educated types. I was surprised he'd lasted out here so long.

'What are you going to do with it when you get home?'

'I want to be a novelist, sir.'

'No money in it,' I grunted, '. . .'. and one *sir* every ten minutes will do, if that's all right with you. I'd join an advertising agency if I was you, and write advertising copy for them. It's the future of literature.'

'Does it pay better, sir?'

'Not necessarily, but you do get to look at pictures of naked girls a lot of the time.' I was thinking of the calendar hanging in our tent. The only thing the girl was wearing was a sailor's cap. Hoskins seemed to brighten up a bit after that. I didn't. I turned away from him, and made a job of filling my pipe and lighting it. I'd need some tobacco from the NAAFI before long.

The reason I was suddenly a little downcast was that it had occurred to me to set what I'd just said to Hoskins alongside what had happened to Daisy. Don't get me wrong. It wasn't as easy as cause and effect; at least, I hoped not. But there was something there. Some connection that made me uncomfortable. Something to do with the way we talked about women, and our attitude, and what sometimes happened afterwards. I decided to talk to Haye with an e about it the next time I met her. I remembered the old-stager at Padgate who had taught us how to take care of our kit. *Attitude*, he'd say, holding up a shining pair of boots. *Attitude, gentlemen, is everything. Attitude makes things happen*. Maybe he was right. But that went for bad things, as well as good things. Maybe that was it.

I asked Hoskins, 'Did I get you into a spot of bother with the SWO?'

'No, sir. It's just that I've never been able to stop myself noticing the absurd side of service life. Some of the things we say and do are just plain silly, but we are expected to stand there, and not even smile. Even with two years in, I can't do that. The NCOs hate me; I'm always getting caned for it.' Not literally I hoped; they'd been supposed to stop flogging soldiers years ago.

'Can you drive, Hoskins?'

'Yes, sir. Do you want me to drive you?'

'No. I want you to drive yourself.'

A cloud drifted across his face as he adopted the expression that clever people use to disguise the fact that they haven't a bleeding clue.

'I don't understand, sir.'

'I want to make good this shit-heap of a telephone they've left us with. That will take me about twenty minutes, once I've got the stuff I need. During those twenty minutes the telephones won't work. It means that our patrols and the blokes on stag won't be able to call up help if there's an emergency. So I want you to drive up and down between them, keeping the comms open in the old-fashioned way – word of mouth. Do you understand?'

He gave me a sudden bright grin. 'Like Leonidas at Thermopylae, sir. He used runners to stay in touch with Sparta.'

He might have come up with a more encouraging simile.

'Wasn't he killed; and all his army with him?'

'Yes, sir. Sorry, sir.'

'So where can I find a pair of scissors, a small screwdriver and some insulating tape?'

It took us longer to find the kit than for me to do the job

itself. Once I'd scraped the wires back I could see that they'd been insulated before but that the tape had dried out, cracked into pieces and fallen away. I taped a hand-printed note to the back for good measure, advising them to replace the insulation every three months. It was nice to feel useful for once.

When I lifted the handset and threw the small toggle that connected me to the water tower, the loud and clear response I got from the other end was, 'Christ, who's that?'

'Guard commander, you fool.'

'But I can *hear* you, sir.'

'Of course you can sodding hear me; I've repaired your sodding telephone.'

'Sorry, sir.'

That is the ultimate tragedy of other ranks: they spend half their time apologizing for something they haven't done.

'Can you see the jeep?'

'Yessir.'

'Flag it down with your signal lamp, then climb down and tell Hoskins to come back; all is forgiven.'

When Hoskins came back in, bringing the smell of the desert with him, the first thing he asked was, 'Forgiven for what, sir?' One of these literally literary types.

We were sipping char from big ally mugs when the telephone jangled at me. It was the furthest patrol. Whenever anything goes wrong on a stag it's always at the place furthest from you. I flipped the right toggle and lifted the handset, but before I could hear anything being said we could both hear the man screaming at the other end. There were no actual words. Just screams. Fuck it. Hoskins grabbed the Stirling and ran for the door. He used the words that had just crossed my mind.

'Fuck it! C'mon, sir. Let's go . . .' Then he shouted back to an open door behind me in the office, 'Mind the phone, Toby.'

It was the first time I realized that there had been anyone else there; he must have had his head down all along.

I let Hoskins drive. He wasn't all that good, but he was fast, and that's what we needed. The only thing he said on the drive was, 'Fucking wogs!' He'd obviously been in this movie before.

At one point he clipped a guy-rope of a tent at the end of the tent lines, and dragged the damned thing with us for a few yards before it broke free. He was moving so fast that we were out of range of the shouts from the tent's occupants within seconds.

The field telephone was on a telegraph pole at head height, inside the wire at the inner ditch, at the northwestern corner of the camp. Beyond it was the wire, the outer trench and hundreds of miles of fucking desert, lit up by the occasional small circle of one of our lights. Not that it was dark: the black sky above us was a sea of stars. Hoskins was out of the wagon before me. He crouched by the jeep, making a very low target. I thought he looked as if he knew what he was doing, so I copied him.

He whispered, 'Where are they?'

There was a point to his question because the telephone handset attached to the box attached to the telegraph pole was dangling free. It had not been replaced. In fact it was even still swinging to and fro, although there was no hint of a breeze. The guard was not in sight.

'Where are they?' Hoskins whispered again. I could see he was scanning the desert for movement, and the wire for gaps. There were neither.

When he said it the third time he spoke louder. There was even a hint of exasperation in his voice. 'Where the fuck are they?'

'Down here . . .' a weak voice replied. It wasn't mine.

Hoskins and I were virtually on our knees by then. He because he was an efficient serviceman with a healthy respect for his own skin, and me out of sheer funk. We crawled over to the ditch that was on our side of the wire. It was about six feet deep at this point. Two pale faces looked up at us. 'Down here.'

'What are you doing down there?' That was Hoskins of course. He was probably command material but no one had bothered to tell him.

'Hiding from the lion. Can ye no see it?'

We pulled them out: two terrified servicemen who wanted nothing other than to go home. There was one named Scottie who sounded like one, and there was the other one. The other one didn't sound like anything, because he didn't say anything. He was shaking with huge tremors. When he dropped his rifle he let it lie there.

'Pick it up, son.' I hope I sounded kinder than the words look. He bent to pick it up, but still didn't say a word, and wouldn't look at me. '*What* lion?' I asked the other.

'A fucking great lion. It was in the compound. When I turned round, it was right behind us. Tell him, Daniel.'

The other man tried to speak, but his head was shaking and all that came out was a strange sound like 'Day . . . day . . . day . . .'

'Don't bother,' I told him, and asked the Scot, 'What's the matter with him?'

'He could have reached out, and chuffed it under the chin, sir: it was that close. When Daniel jumped straight inta the trench I don't know who was the more alarmed: me or the lion.'

'What did you do?'

'Jumped in after him. Sorry, sir, but I wasn't facing that fucking thing on my own.'

I let them sit in the back of the jeep and smoke a couple of fags. I called in from the telephone. Toby, whoever the hell he was, said nothing else was happening.

'What the hell do we do now?' I asked Hoskins. I know that it should have been the other way round, but you have to let common sense come into these things: Hoskins knew what he was doing; I didn't.

'Why don't you leave me here, sir? I'll patrol up to the other team, and tell them you said for them to change over with me and take this section.'

'They'll know something's up. They'll want to know why.'

'I'll tell them Dan's been taken sick; they don't need to know anything until after you've sorted it out. Then you can send Toby out to join me, and we'll finish the night that way.' I couldn't think of anything better. 'Old Tobe will moan a bit if you give him a chance, sir, so make your orders direct and unambiguous. Don't give him room to wriggle.'

The last thing I said to him before I drove off into the dark with my two Bravehearts was, 'I get the feeling that maybe I owe you a couple of drinks the next time we're off.'

'That would be a pleasure, sir,' and he saluted me. I'd have to get used to this saluting lark again.

The shaking man spoke to me for the first time before we left the jeep, right outside my office. He said, 'Daniel.'

'I beg your pardon?' He might as well have said *locomotive* or *coleus* for all it meant to me.

'*Daniel*, sir: my name. I knew it would get me into trouble one day.'

'I don't understand.'

'Don'cha read yer Bible, sir? Daniel in the fucking lions' den . . . sir?' He actually didn't look all that well: in fact he looked deranged. Maybe our excuse would hold.

'Er . . . why don't we all go inside and get some char?'

*

257

It wasn't quite that straightforward because SWO Cox was sitting in my chair by the telephone. I sent Toby whatever-his-name-was to link up with Hoskins, and the others through to the galley.

Cox said, 'Morning, sir. Spot of bother?'

'Good morning, Mr Cox. Do you always come out this often?' It was past four in the morning now; didn't the man ever bloody sleep? He was immaculately turned out, and looked as if he'd just shaved.

'No, sir. Only when I get a bad feeling. I had a good feeling about leaving you in charge, in fact, but then I had a bad feeling half an hour ago, and I woke up. I get a sort of pins and needles in my thumbs and forefingers whenever something's going wrong, sir.'

'*By the pricking of my thumbs, something wicked this way comes . . .* something like that?'

'Exactly like that sir. *Macbeth*. Now would you mind telling me what the hell's going on . . . sir?' I loved that pause he put before the *sir*; I've used it so many times myself.

'Certainly, Mr Cox, but first I want a cup of tea.'

I told him about Daniel in the lions' den. I told him that the guard had seen something that had spooked them. Something they thought was a full-grown lion.

He said, 'I don't think there are any lions left in Egypt. I haven't heard of any, sir.'

'That's what I was told when I saw one in Ismailia a few days ago.'

'Seriously, sir?'

'Seriously. The Army says that there have been no free-roaming lions in Egypt for at least a hundred years, and that I must have been seeing things. The Army is always right.'

'Yes, sir, it is.'

I could see something was eating him.

'What's the matter?'

'If our boys spend half the night looking over their shoulders for lions, sir, they won't see the wogs when they come creeping up on them . . . and the wogs are much more likely to do them harm.'

'So it would be better if they never found out about the lion our two chaps thought they saw. So it *wasn't* a lion: just like mine. They probably mistook it for a cover flapping in the wind, some loose paper and a feral cat. Something like that?'

'Thank you, Mr Bassett.' I could almost see the little wheels churning inside his head as he turned the implication over. 'The two lads will keep their traps shut, if they think their pals will laugh at them for being frightened into the ditch by a cat. 'Specially if I tell them.'

'Least said, soonest mended.'

'My thoughts exactly, sir.'

'Your man Hoskins was pretty useful tonight,' I told him. 'He thinks pretty quickly, you know.' I might as well try to get him off whatever Cox had planned for him. I needn't have bothered.

'He's the makings of a fine airman, sir, although he doesn't know it yet. It wouldn't be a bad thing for the service if he opted to stay. Maybe in the Regiment. I intended to speak to him about it in the morning.' I've already told you about these SWOs: you can never bloody tell.

'I'm going to step outside for a minute to have a smoke, SWO. You might want to inspect the telephone while I'm away.'

'I told you it was a useless piece of kit, sir.'

'Not any more, it isn't. I repaired the bloody thing in fifteen minutes . . . and I'd like you to make sure it never gets into that state again.' The boot never feels better than when it is on the other foot.

He grinned, and said, 'Yes, sir.' He even saluted.

I wasn't sure any more whether he was supposed to. Maybe he was just taking the mick. Was I still in the RAF? And, if so, what the bloody hell was it up to? Because there wasn't much bloody flying going on.

Late the next morning I cycled out to the ditch we'd pulled our bold boyos from, but SWO Cox had beaten me to it. I was there to see if I could find any lion tracks: I reckoned a ghost lion wouldn't leave any. He was already there with a broom in his hand.

I asked, 'I don't suppose that there were any big-cat footprints in the sand, Mr Cox?'

'Not one, sir.' He sounded very cheerful. 'You were right; must have been all in their imagination.' But I could see his brush marks; they stretched for at least twenty-five yards. I wonder if anyone had seen the SWO personally sweeping up sand in the corner of a camp that was full of the bloody stuff and, if so, what they'd made of it.

I didn't tell him what I'd found outside my tent when I crawled out of my pit at 1100. There in the dust was a perfect cat's imprint: four toes and a big central pad. When I bent down to it I found it was as large as my spread hand.

We sipped tea on the veranda of the Men's Ward just like old friends. Haye with an e and me.

Daisy had reappeared at Deversoir and taken up her duties, but not quite as if nothing had happened. She was still subdued; nothing like her old self. Watson was also back, and we'd both carefully avoided a showdown. I was tossing up whether to mention the Stirling bomber or not. Maybe if I ignored it, it would go away. He said he worried that Daisy's women's trouble might be some form of tumour – apparently a woman in his family had died from one. As far as I knew no one had told him the truth, but he could also be double-bluffing me, couldn't he? When I was around them it felt as if there was a fragile sort of equilibrium which might blow up in our faces at any moment – so I stayed away as much as I could. I got a chit for a day off from him, and bummed a lift up to see Susan.

I told her about my old man, and his three types of sexual relationships.

She said, 'My mother told me nothing about men at all. My father tried to, the pet, just before I went away, but I don't actually think he knows very much.'

'What did he say?'

'That I would meet nice men and nasty men, good-looking men and ugly ones, young ones and old ones, rich ones and poor ones . . . but that, no matter who, most of the time all they'd be thinking about was how to get my knickers off.'

I laughed, but it was a bit of a rueful one. 'Your old man might know more than you think. But since this thing with Daisy, I've been worried, so I came up to talk to you. I appear before you as a penitent.'

'What's worrying you?'

'The boundary. Where you draw the line.'

'Explain, Charlie. What boundary? Your last few words are not far from gibberish.'

'Do you know how men talk about women when women aren't there?'

'How could I? Women aren't there. You said it yourself.'

'I think you know what I mean . . .'

'Yeah . . . sometimes women can be almost as bad, you know. Have you heard the *A hard man is good to find* joke?' I hadn't: it sounded like Mae again. It's just the sort of thing she'd say. I shook my head, but she didn't elaborate. She said, 'Tell me about this boundary.'

'It's the one you shouldn't cross. There are some things you can do to get a girl into bed, and some you can't.'

'I agree, and if you think like that you're probably going to

DAVID FIDDIMORE

get it right most of the time. Are there any of these stratagems that worry you particularly?'

'All of them, now I begin to think about it. Dating a girl is beginning to feel like a transaction – maybe I won't ever ask one out again.' She offered me one her Turkish fags and I accepted. We plumed the air around us in scented smoke.

When she spoke again it was to say, 'Maybe both our fathers were brighter than we gave them credit for: yours told you how to look at sex through the eyes of a woman, and mine told me about it from the point of view of a man. They almost sound like warnings, don't they? The way I see it – and after this I want to change the subject – is that the difference between a man's attitudes and a woman's is that if you lure me up to your room when I don't want to sleep with you, and you lock the door, I still won't want to sleep with you. In fact I'll probably like the idea even less. On the other hand, if I lure *you* up to *my* room when you don't want sex, and lock you in with me, you'll soon end up changing your mind – maybe you'll even think it was your idea in the first place. I think it's what they call the sexual imperative. We have different priorities, that's all. Now change the subject.'

'That hasn't helped.'

'It wasn't meant to, Charlie. I'm on the other side. Are you going to buy me a drink later . . . before you go back?'

I agreed to meet her in the Families Club later on. It had big wicker chairs, cooling fans and long drinks.

With some time to spare I hitched a ride down to the Blue Kettle. David Yassine was on the steps outside smoking a big cigar, and chatting to an MP and an Egyptian copper. The place was obviously still off-limits. As he stepped back he met my eye, and inclined his head briefly towards the alleyway a couple of buildings down. It led to the Kettle's back courtyard. I had my

262

small automatic in my trouser pocket, and kept my hand over it like a wanker as I walked into the shade. I needn't have worried. The one Arab I met grinned, and touched his head; he was one of Yassine's boys who worked in the club. The Fat Man met me under the fire escape, led me past another Gyppo copper, and on through to the bar. There were half a dozen Europeans, all of whom looked the other way, and a sprinkling of wealthier Arabs. Altogether your usual Wednesday afternoon crowd, I thought.

'You're very good at this,' I told him.

'Blame the Welsh. You want a Stella?' He nodded to a bar boy. Two beers appeared as if by magic. I've asked it before, I know, but *how did they do that*?

'And what have the Welsh to do with it, pray?'

Amazingly, he switched to an outrageously ripe Welsh accent: he sounded like Lloyd George. Another bleeding David. Goliath can't have been too far away.

'When I was a boy – before your European war, see – my father sent me to Britain to finish my education. For a year I lived in a small Welsh town named Lampeter. That was in Cardigan I think, and Cardigan is a *dry* county, which meant that the bars do not open on a Sunday. No booze. So the local public house, the Railway Tavern, held Bible classes every Sunday . . . and the only difference between a Saturday night out-of-control drinking session and the Bible class was that for the Bible class on Sunday you entered the premises from the back door, and the local policeman was there to let you in . . . just like the Blue Kettle when your military policemen have closed it down. Blame it on the Welsh. Cheers. Another?'

'Yes, please. Can we sit at a table and talk?'

'Of course.'

Another beer, and another conversation. I agreed to try to find out when the MPs were going to lift the ban on the Kettle. Then I asked him, 'Tell me, David, if, theoretically, I wanted to have a couple of men punished – not severely hurt, but punished enough for them to always remember it – are there people through whom that could be arranged?'

He made a steeple of his hands, and rested his mouth behind them like one of the devout at prayer. 'Of course. Yes, it could.'

'Even if those men were British officers?'

He took longer to reply. His eyes were hooded. I couldn't read him.

'Yes. Even if they are British officers.' I hadn't missed the change of tense.

'. . . and you, *personally*, wouldn't be put at risk? I shouldn't want that.'

He smiled. When he smiled his face changed shape: became squarer. His beard and moustache framed his mouth like pubic hair.

'Thank you for thinking of me . . . but *no*, I would not be at risk. What would they be punished for; these two theoretical officers? What is their theoretical sin?'

'Using a woman as if she was their own; when in fact she wasn't. Not asking her permission.'

'Has the woman been damaged?' I realized that he was thinking in terms of commodity. I'd met men like that before.

'Not on the outside. But inside her head? *Yes*; I think possibly she has . . . and she is a friend. It pains me.'

'But that cannot be allowed.' It was something to do with the finality of those five words, and the way his decision related to me rather than to Daisy. It gave me a glimpse of what Susan and the rest of them might be up against. 'You have their names, and their stations – these men?'

'Not yet, but I think I can get them.'

It was another landmark on the road that led to the making of a proper Charlie out of me. Eight years ago on the squadron I'd met some real chancers. Before that I'd been wet behind the ears. Now, although they weren't going to get killed for it, I'd just called down a hit on a couple of guys. How the hell had I come to this?

Yassine shifted in his chair, and looked around the bar. There were a few more people in it now, mainly rich Egyptians with uniformly beautiful, Westernized Arab women half their age. He said, 'Are we finished now? Our beer is. We could sit up at the bar . . . one of the girls is going to dance soon.'

It was Mariam of course, and I was entranced again: so were all of the other guys in the bar. When she came and perched on a stool between us, after the show, they were probably jealous. What had I said to Susan about it feeling like a transaction? I gave Mariam a few Egyptian pounds for her dance, and hoped she felt a little sad when I left at 1800. I wanted to catch Haye with an e coming off duty.

As I stood to leave, David Yassine asked me one question. His eyes were twinkling, and his little mouth wore a mischievous little smile. 'These men who might be punished, Charlie: is it possible that they are the same two officers who Mr Watson has suggested might be punished?' Ah.

'Did he give you their names?'

'Yes he did.' Bloody Watson! Whenever you thought butter wouldn't melt in his mouth, you forgot the knife up his sleeve.

'Then leave it with me for the moment; I'll get back to you.'

'Come back and see me when you get back from the desert; some time next week.'

'How did you know I was going out?'

He shrugged, smiled and splayed his hands out. I knew exactly what he was going to say.

'There was one particular woman,' I told Haye with an e.

'Yes, darling?'

She leaned forward, and I lit her cigarette for her. She was pretending we were sitting in a club in Happy Valley in the 1930s.

'I think we'd been madly attracted to each other for weeks, and as a result ended up irritating each other beyond belief . . .'

'Yes?'

'So she came to my billet on the squadron one day, when there was no one else around, and just said *Well, you'd better have me then*, or something like that, and began to take her clothes off. It sounded flat; the way she said it. As if she didn't want to do it but didn't see that she had a choice.'

'Did you . . . sleep together, I mean?'

'Of course we did.'

'More than once?'

'Yes. She came back a couple of times. She was a bit of a tiger actually.' Jennifer. Another Jenny. I smiled at the memory of her. She was one of those women you could have married if they weren't married to someone else.

'Was she married?'

'Yes, how did you guess?'

'Ah . . .'

'What does that mean?'

'It means that there are some situations to which your father's rules don't apply, Charlie. When that happens you can only do your best. Now, are you going to get me another drink?'

'OK.'

'Then you can walk me to the bus, and make a pass at me on the way.'

'So that you can say *no* again?'

'Of course, darling.'

When I got back to Deversoir the base was shut down, and the bus I was in had to shuffle forward in a queue. An Egyptian copper rode the last few yards with us, and a burly sergeant checked us in one by one. A lot of nervous guys with Stens or Stirlings were hanging about.

When I got back to the tent I asked Nancy, 'What's all the fuss?'

'Red alert, old son. A couple of fellas went down to the Bitter Lake for a swim, and got grabbed by the Gyppoes.' He made the throat-cutting gesture.

'Are they dead?'

'For their sake I almost hope so.'

Chapter Fourteen

Wild man blues

Unusually, the terrorists returned the two swimmers alive. But in a terrible state. That was two days later. They were dumped at the main gate during the morning rush when the Egyptian trusties who worked for us were allowed inside. When the noisy, djellabaed, chitty-waving crowd had dispersed to their work areas, there were two bloodied bundles left in the road by the gate. No one saw where they came from.

They had been caned on their arses with barbed-wire whips, until their buttocks were literally flayed. Unconscious; probably through loss of blood. Nansen was down there, and saw it all – he'd been waiting for a laundry parcel from the dhobi woman. By the time he returned the word was already around, but when I asked him what was up he just waved me to silence, grabbed his notebook, and wrote down a few pieces of what could have been Arab script.

He said, 'Not now, old chap. I'm trying to remember these.'

'What are they?'

'Arabic words tattooed on the two guys they found this morning.'

He worked for about ten minutes, and then leafed through a small paper-bound dictionary of Arabic and English. You could get them free at the NAAFI, and in the Camp clubs. The first thing he said when he finished was,

''strordinary.'

'What is?'

'Your Gyppo.'

'Explain.'

'As far as I can make out, these Arabic glyphs include *hokm* and *maraa* or *marai*.'

'What do they mean?'

'As far as I can make out, it means *judgement by a woman*, or *has been judged by a woman*.'

'Meaning?'

'Look, Charlie, you've got to start seeing things like a wog – the way those of us who've been out here a while see things. Getting these guys back alive is *'strordinary* of itself. If we expected them back at all, it would have been as sliced-up bits of meat thrown over the wire, or dumped into the Canal. These two are given back alive, with arses they won't sit down on for a couple of months, and a message to the perfidious Brits tattooed all over their guts . . . and the message is simply *Leave our women alone*. 'strordinary.' He'd only just begun to use the word, and already it irritated me. It was one of those things we'd picked up from the latest Gainsborough film, and everyone was using it.

'So you think they'd been misbehaving with Egyptian women?'

'*Respectable* Egyptian women: the wog doesn't give a toss about his whores. They must have been cuckolding the local nabobs, who've sent them back to us with a forceful reminder. The bosses will panic, and for weeks we'll be buried in OODs about not tupping the local floosies.' OODs were Orders of the Day, which were pinned up on noticeboards in the most unlikely places; so you could never keep up with them.

'You're right: that must be it.' I muttered. I knew he wasn't bloody right, but I wasn't prepared to tell him what I *did* know.

I hope I was casual enough when I asked, 'What will happen to them?'

'Immediate evac, I should think: it's what happens to most of the casualties. They'll be on a hospital ship up in the Med by tonight, with paste all over their bums. Ouch. Never more to grace these shores. I wonder how they'll get the tattoos off.'

The Wing Commander wasn't in his office. I mooched around it, looking at the papers pinned to the wall. They were mostly stores lists. Anyone who didn't know any better would imagine that our section was an HQ repository of high-value radio spares. We did that as well, of course, which is where people like Pat Tobin and our MT section came in. Daisy heard the noise I was making, and came out of her den. When she saw it was me she put on a genuine smile, and walked slowly over to give me a peck on the cheek. That was a first. Bloody hell; maybe she really had gone doolally.

She said, 'Thank you, Charlie. I told you not to do anything, but thank you anyway.'

'I didn't do anything.'

'I know; but thank you for doing it anyway.'

'Does it make you feel any better?'

'Yes, surprisingly, although it shouldn't do, should it? Revenge never gets you anywhere. I also feel a little guilty.'

'*Don't*: you didn't do anything . . . and neither did I. *Really* . . . subject closed.'

'I know. Your secret is safe with me.'

Round in bloody circles. That sailor who'd been disciplined for writing up *Welcome to Wonderland* on Port Said harbour wall didn't know how right he was.

'How about I pass your thanks on to the person who might really deserve it?' I was only digging myself deeper.

'Only if you're careful, Charlie. They must be violent men. Don't get yourself into trouble.'

I gave up. 'Don't worry; I won't. When's Mr Watson due back?'

'This afternoon. He wants to see you before your next trip anyway.'

That was OK. I wanted to see him as well. I wanted to see just what kind of trap I'd walked into when I answered his summons to that little office in Kentish Town.

'Your holiday trip's been put off; you can put the bucket and spade away for the moment. The Brown Jobs have had a significant transport failure.' Watson was smiling like he'd just knighted me. The joke was obviously at somebody else's expense.

'What was that, sir?'

'The wogs whipped one of their lorries. Right from under the nose of the MPs I understand. There's hell to pay down there.'

'I don't understand, sir. The Egyptians want us out of Egypt so they can have the Suez Canal all to themselves . . . so how does stealing a lorry advance their cause? We'll need the lorries to go away in.'

'Do you know, Charlie, ever since I invited you to join us out here all I seem to have heard is you whining *I don't understand, sir* in my lug? Can't you shut up, and give it a rest for once?' He was on fine form, having reappeared with a case of RN gin. 'Anyway the Gyppoes who want us out of Egypt aren't the same Gyppoes who steal us blind. The latter want us to stay until we have nothing left worth stealing, then they'll join the chaps who want us out. Two or three years, that's my guess. That lorry will be repainted and modified already, and someone will have turned it into a one-man road transport company operating out of Luxor, or somewhere similarly romantic. Cheers.'

We were in his office, and M'smith was off to one side with a pile of message flimsies a foot high, leafing through them like a man seeking a winning pools combination. I lifted my glass.

'Cheers, sir, and thank you for the drink. Didn't *I* use to run a transport company myself before you got hold of me?'

'It was only an air-freight mob, Charlie. Doesn't count. You probably saved the company by volunteering to leave it, and rejoin the colours.'

'I didn't volunteer, sir. I am a pressed man, and we both know it.'

'I think you'll find you did, old son. I think you'll find your statutory retention as a reservist ran out about three months before you came to see me, and begged me to take you back. No one could have forced you to come, so you must have volunteered.'

'Christ.'

'Don't swear, Charlie. Daisy can hear you, and she don't like blasphemy. It's not my fault if you don't keep a note of important dates in your diary. If I had been you, I should have known when I could turn down the PM's kind invitation to go flying again. The thing to do is settle down, and make the best of it.'

'What about M'smith?'

'I found him. He was cooling his whatsits in a military prison in Germany.'

I was in an old swivelling wooden office chair, so it was easy to turn and look at M'smith, who frowned before he smiled.

'What did you *do*, Hector?'

Watson answered for him.

'A rather clumsy fraud in the Paymaster General's Office. M'smith comes from a long line of successful forgers and clumsy fraudsters. A family should always stick with what they're good at, don't you think?'

'Weren't you even in the RAF?' I asked Hector.

He shook his head, and told me, 'Nor are you, Charlie. None of us are. Haven't you worked that one out yet?' I probably had but I wanted to ignore it.

'OK. I know you can navigate. What else do you do?'

Watson jumped in for him again. He probably thought I wouldn't understand unless it was said in small words. 'Creative accounting for my military radio spares store, and he's very good at recognizing funny money, if ever I'm lucky enough to lay my hands on any . . .'

'. . . and what am *I*, in your private circus?'

'You're the gold prospector . . . and, before you start whining all over again, I'm going to send you to see an officer who works out of Fayid. He can give you the briefing now that your security clearance has come through. Although, if you've half a brain, you'll have it all worked out for yourself by the time you get there.'

'Where, sir?'

'The Officers' Club on the Great Bitter Lake. He's expecting you for lunch; they do a good lunch there.' He waved a chitty at me. Watson had chitties for everything. He probably signed off one each time he went to the bog. A chitty for a shitty: that's not bad. 'Requisition one of those horrible beige Standards, and drive down right now. M'smith will give you directions.'

'Did my security clearance take a long time, sir?'

'Far longer than anyone else's that I've heard of. Even M'smith here was done in a fortnight, and he's a criminal. Yours has taken seven times as long as that – and even then it was touch and go. You've packed an awful lot of dubious characters into a very short life, haven't you, Charlie?' There is this well-known phrase about the pot and the kettle, isn't there?

'If I failed it, would you have had to send me home?'

'No . . . Either shot you, or tossed you into jail until it's all over. Wouldn't have risked you telling anyone.'

'Until *what* is over, sir?'

'What you'll be told about in an hour's time. Mr Levy is the man you're looking for. Captain Levy that is. Can't mistake him; he wears dark glasses you can't see through. Enjoy your lunch.' When I didn't move fast enough, he waved his hand at me like a man warding off flies, and said, 'Run along now.'

It's not like me to try to have the last word, but I tried . . . and bloody failed, as usual. I popped my head back inside the door from outside, and told him, 'By the way sir; there's a lion inside the compound. I saw it in Ismailia, and I think it's following me around.'

'No lions in Egypt, Charlie.'

'That's what people keep telling me.'

'Big lion, is it?'

'It is, as a matter of fact. Why?'

'I saw a James Stewart film once – *Harvey*. He was followed around by an animal in it: invisible giant rabbit as far as I remember. Perhaps you've got a touch of the same thing.'

I'd met Major James Stewart once; in Paris in 1945. In fact he'd got me out of a bit of a jam. But this wasn't the time to bring it up.

The road went ever on and on. That reminded me of something – *The Seven Pillars of Wisdom* perhaps. Half the guys you saw carrying books around for effect had that one. It was required reading for the desert warrior, which is how we all saw ourselves, of course. Another Lawrence of Arabia effect had been the proliferation of motorbikes, and endless motorcycle trials events in the desert. I blamed Lawrence for all of it, and none of our witless born-again motorcyclists seemed to recall that the only thing a motorcycle had done for the saviour of Arabia (and, incidentally, the architect of every problem we've had there ever since) was to kill him.

Maybe that's where all the new wooden crosses in the cemeteries actually came from.

I was passed by two motorcycle dispatch riders on the road down to Fayid, and hoped they'd learned to keep their heads down. I overtook a couple of small convoys trundling along at a snail's pace, waved past by their armed escort. The only vehicles I met on the road in either direction were British and military. If we owned all the bloody cars, it was no wonder the home-grown bastards hated us.

After half an hour I passed an Arab walking a string of pack camels parallel to the tarmac, and heading in the same direction as me. The camels didn't fancy me. They looked at me and sneered. One spat a gob the size of a cricket ball. Was it trained to do that, or did it just improvise? The Arab rode the lead camel of six. A small boy rode the last one. I slowed down, smiled, and waved to them. The boy flashed me a quick V sign, and then threw a stone. He had a bagful hanging from the wooden saddle. He was a good shot because it clattered off the boot of my car, and I prayed he would never get his hands on a decent gun.

People really were getting a bit twitchy. Two armed Egyptian policemen guarded the car park where I left the Standard Vanguard. I wondered if they were on our side, their side, or undecided. There's almost a pun in there if you look for it hard enough. It was a newer, less ill-used example of the car, and once I got used to the column change I was quite keen on it. At one point I had rolled it up to seventy, but was waved down by the wagging finger of one of our cops. A white-suited be-fezed Egyptian signed me in to the Officers' Club – which had been designed by someone who'd read too many Somerset Maugham stories for my liking – and pointed me to the Smoking Room where this year's fate awaited me.

I'd overtaken a blind officer as I went in; he had a tall Arab walking on one side of him and a guide dog in a harness like a baby walker in front of him. I guess he had it covered from all angles. *I* hadn't, though; because my brain wasn't working fast enough. Blind men wear dark glasses, don't they? . . . and he was the only man with shades in the whole bloody room. He sat down in a big cane peacock chair; his man stood beside and slightly behind him, and the dog was soon lying at his feet. It lifted its lip, and showed me its front teeth as if to say, when I approached, *I could bite you if I wanted to, you bastard, but I can't be arsed: it's too hot.* I have that effect on animals all the time. It also had one milky white eye. I had a thought that was simultaneously cruel and funny: about the blind leading the fucking blind. The blind man was wearing a nicely spruced tropical rig, with a one-word shoulder flash. I read *Intelligence.* I had travelled the country without finding much so far, so that was a nice change.

He said, 'Easy girl,' and bent to lay his hand on the dog's napper. The dog covered its teeth again. It almost smiled. As he bent to the dog I saw behind the dark glasses. Empty eye sockets. Ah, one of those. The Arab took half a step forward, and placed his hand on the European's shoulder. I used to do exactly the same in the office of our Lancaster bomber; it would signal to Grease, our pilot, that I was there. The blind man said, 'Pilot Officer Bassett, I presume,' and lifted his right paw for the ritual shake. Firm and quick; the way it should be.

'Yes, sir. I walked past you on the way in. Sorry.'

'Don't be, although if you make the *blind leading the blind joke* I'll have Chig knife you. Say hello to Chig. He's my boy.' I started to hold my hand out to the Arab, but he just bowed his head very slightly; a nod. He might have been smiling or he might not. He had a face which was impossible to age or read, and a square, black beard shot with grey. Your noble Arab. He belonged in the desert on a camel, with a hawk on his wrist, just like the King of the Riffs in *The Desert Song*: I'm sure you've seen the pictures. He did not, however, have a speaking part in this drama . . . and he wasn't a boy.

'Draw up a chair,' Levy said . . . 'and call me Peter. I can't tell anything about you except that you are either small, or that your mouth is somewhere between your tits, because your voice is coming from much nearer the ground than usual.'

'Less than five feet four, sir. Well done.'

'Nearer to five two . . . and don't bloody patronize me . . . and *Call me Peter* was an order by the way. Care for a gin and it before we eat?'

'Thank you. Love one.'

He addressed his Arab. 'Two long ones please, Chig; and bring yourself an orange juice.' The Arab gave his nervy little bow again, and cruised off to the bar. Dignified.

Levy told me, 'His proper name's Chigaru, which means *hound*. So I'm the first blind man you'll meet who has two dogs. Chig's dumb, by the way – some friendly tribesmen cut his tongue out, and all he can make is a gurgling sound. If you hear that, duck. He might have imperfect English in the understanding department, but he has acute hearing and I trust him, so you don't need to worry.'

'What about your blind dog?'

'Why do people persist in calling *guide* dogs, "*blind* dogs"? A blind dog would be no bloody use to me, would it? I need one which can see.'

'Yours has a bad eye . . .'

'. . . and also one particularly good one; don't overlook that. She belonged to some other beggar who traded her in when she began to go blind herself. The Society wanted to put her down. That seemed skew-whiff to me, so I took her on. After all, they didn't put me down when I lost my eyes, did they?'

'How was that?'

'Nothing heroic. Lost control of my motorcycle on the way

277

back to camp from Sidcup one night. I was loaded. When I woke up I had no eyes and no nose. They managed to rebuild the schnozzle, but no chance with the eyes – popped and gone to heaven.' I knew I'd been right about motorbikes all along. But after I heard him I winced, and instinctively said, 'I'm sorry.' It's almost a reflex reaction to apologize to the disabled for their own disability, isn't it? I don't think they love us for it.

'Don't be. They weren't particularly good eyes.'

'Your man is coming back.'

'How many glasses on the tray?'

'Five: two each for us, I think, and one for him.'

'Marvellous people these Egyptians. Great sense of anticipation. We'll drink one here, and take one through with us.'

'And we can talk in front of your man?'

'Christ yes; no problem. But be careful what you say in front of the dog though: I think she's a spy.'

The one-eyed Labrador lay under the table throughout the meal. Occasionally she'd let out a heartfelt sigh, and Levy would surreptitiously drop her a morsel of food. Her mouth of yellowing teeth was rarely less than nine inches from my naked leg, which unnerved me. Levy insisted on eating his lunch without talking shop. Fish, fish and fish, and all of it good. Better than good: memorable.

When I remarked on it he said,

'Surprised you haven't been here before. You're an automatic member; it's only an extension of the Mess.'

'Nobody told me about it.'

'Then you've something to thank me for already, and I love starting off relationships with the other person in my debt. I like to finish lunch with Egyptian-style coffee, by the way – all right by you?'

'Fine.'

'Some of the old wallahs disapprove, of course. They stick to English tea – something to do with a sense of empire.'

'Who are the old wallahs?'

'The nabobs? Generals, colonels and AVMs. We used to see the occasional admiral, but I think it's too far from the real sea for them: unless they're near something salty which drowns people, they feel insecure. We'll take coffee out on the veranda: your pipe smoke may keep the flies at bay.'

'You can smell my pipe on me.'

'. . . and the fact that you washed with Palmolive this morning, are wearing suede desert boots, and use neither an aftershave nor Brylcreem. The nabobs wouldn't like your boots in the club either.'

'How can you smell the difference between suede and ordinary leather?'

'I can't. I can't smell boot polish from you either, so the suedes were a deduction. Was I right?' He made me smile.

'Yes, you were, but what if I had no shoes on at all?'

'My dog would have smelled your feet, and set up a terrible howl. Within weeks of losing my eyes, my senses of smell and hearing improved until they were almost painful. Compensation I think, but a whole new world just the same. I'd probably make a better tracker dog than Mary.' The dog – that must have been her name.

We sat in the shade, in another couple of peacock chairs. His Arab stood about twenty feet from us at the end of the veranda, scanning the gardens, the Bitter Lake and the people around us. His eyes never stopped moving. More of a bodyguard than a bearer or a guide.

Maybe Levy picked up on what I was thinking because he asked me, 'Do you think he can hear us from there?'

'I didn't think you cared.'

'I don't. I just want to know how good you are.'

'He's about twenty feet away, so I'd say we were safe.'

'. . . and you'd be wrong. The conversational human voice can be heard easily up to thirty feet away by anyone who tries. Unless you are locked with one other person in a soundproofed room, or out in the wilderness with a clear view of what's around you, you are always going to be overheard. That's a fact, and you'd better remember it.'

I let that sink in. How many stupid things had I said in my life that would now appear to have been overheard? Millions.

I quietly said, 'Thank you. I will.'

'You dropped your voice immediately. Quick learner. I like that.' I wasn't sure that I did.

'The Wing Commander said you were going to brief me on what I'm doing out here – which isn't what the RAF originally told me, apparently.'

'Yes, that's right. I expected to see you earlier but there were problems with your screening. Are you really a Commie?'

'No, I'm a paid-up member of the Party, but that happened by accident in 1947. Do you need to know the story?'

'Yes; I think I do. Don't worry: we have all afternoon if we want.'

So I told him. If you've got this far, you've probably already read my earlier memoir, so I don't need to tell you again, do I? If you've forgotten the story, go back and read it again . . . and see your doctor about your failing memory: you have a problem. Levy thought it was highly amusing. Maybe you will too.

Then I said to him, 'Your turn, Captain. You can talk while I light my pipe.' He had been right; the flies had begun to pay amorous attention to us, and God did not create me to be copulated upon by hairy Egyptian flies.

'In 1945 you were posted to RAF Tempsford, weren't you? Some ground job after you'd got through your first tour.'

'That's right.'

'Smoke away. Let me do the talking.'

'OK.'

He frowned. I took the hint, and lit up. I was soon making as much smoke as the battleship *Warspite*. After two world wars she broke her back on St Michael's Mount in the Fifties I think; poor old girl.

'One of the wireless operators you retrained was a man named Albert Grost. His pilot was called Frohlich. Their whole crew was Jewish, according to the record.'

'They were pacifists. Claimed they were Buddhists. They flew without ammo in their guns, and delivered stores and people to the Resistance. I remember being amazed that the RAF was flexible enough to find a job for a bunch of conchies.'

'Shut up, Charlie; your pipe has gone out. These little bastards will eat us alive.' I took the hint, shut up and lit up again. 'Frohlich and his crew stole their aircraft; right?' I nodded, which produced puffballs of smoke from my pipe. I wondered if the Arab was any good at reading smoke signals. Back in the dining room someone had put a record on, Cab Calloway, and a couple danced urgently to it between the tables. I guess they wanted to be noticed. He asked me, 'Do you know what was in the aircraft when they stole it?'

I couldn't keep up with rhetorical questions for long. 'Apart from enough gas to get them to Israel, stores for the partisans, I suppose – that's what they usually flew. They parachuted them in in containers we called *containers*.' He didn't stop me that time.

'But what was in the containers when they went missing, Charlie?'

'I never asked. Guns, ammo and explosives. Detonators; that sort of thing . . .'

'And?'

'Uniforms? Clothes . . . or equipment the Maquis couldn't make for themselves?'

'. . . and?'

I gave up. 'Buggered if I know. I told you, I never asked and they never told me.'

'Money, Charlie. Oodles and oodles of dosh.'

I settled down then for a good old listen. As my dead pal Tommo would have said, Levy was speaking our language. I looked at my watch when he started, and again when he finished. It took him three quarters of an hour to tell the story. Chig brought us another drink when he thought it had gone on long enough, but it was only lemonade, so I was still supposed to concentrate. I ran the story back at Levy in short sentences, to make sure I had it right.

'When Frohlich and his band of Buddhists stole their aircraft in 1945, and flew it to Israel, they stole their cargo as well. That was enough Stens, .303s and ammo to start a small war . . .'

'They probably armed the Stern Gang.'

'. . . and enough plastic explosive to take down the Empire State building . . .'

'. . . or the King David Hotel.'

'. . . and a load of money intended for the Resistance groups mopping up Jerry in the Cévennes. How much?'

He paused for effect, which must be an officer thing. It never actually works, but nobody tells them that.

'One hundred thousand pounds in francs, and another hundred thousand in old English gold sovereigns – they had been requisitioned from the British Museum, which is still mumping on about it. I don't know why they expected to get through the war without us converting some of their collections into cash for the war effort.'

'Although two hundred grand is a lot of money to you and me, Captain, it's not the sort of sum to get too excited about, is it? Can't we just grab a bit more from the Jerries in reparations?'

'There is an *and*, Charlie . . .'

'*And* what, the Crown jewels?'

'. . . and millions and millions of American dollars. Maybe billions . . .'

'Where on earth did we get those in 1945? Weren't we giving everything we had left to the Americans by the end of the war, to pay for tanks, guns and aeroplanes? Whose mattress was that lot under?'

He did the pause thing again. He actually looked a bit sick. His tanned face definitely turned a shade paler . . . and he whispered, *really* whispered, 'We made it, Charlie.'

'*Made?*'

'Made it. Printed it. Good old De La Rue's.'

'The playing card company?'

'That's right. They print most of our money as well – except the Scottish and Irish stuff, which is a bit ropey.'

It was my turn to stop for breath. I did that thing I've told you about; whistled the intro to a jazz number inside my head. This time it was 'Caravan'; the Duke's version.

Then I asked him, 'You mean we forged billions of American dollars to pay off the French Resistance?'

'We couldn't do anything else. We'd put so much forged British and French currency out there that no one trusted it any more. We didn't have anything left to pay them with, and the French Commies wouldn't fire off so much as a single round unless we paid first.'

'Did our American cousins know anything about this at the time?'

'No.'

'Billions, you said . . . and it's still loose out there somewhere?'

'Possibly. That's what we need to find out. It just hasn't turned up anywhere yet.'

'Do the Americans know about it now?'

'No, not as far as we know. That's rather encouraging, I thought.'

'They are going to be very, very unhappy when they do . . .'

'Which is why we need to get it back, if we can. There is enough there to destabilize the almighty dollar, and if that happens we'll all go down the tubes with it.'

'Did you know that I was once accused of assisting Frohlich's merry bunch? Someone thought I must be in on it.' One of those little lights went on in my head: *money*. '. . . That's why an arrest warrant chased me all over Europe.'

'And that's why you're here. The RAF has been looking for the remains of that aircraft on the quiet, ever since the end of the war. They've photographed every square foot of its probable flight path. Palestine, Lebanon, Syria, Trans-Jordan – you name it. No one expected it to turn up in Kurdistan, but the hot candidate you saw a week or so ago was spotted from a lost Dakota fooling around in the mountains last year. It's taken us months to find the bloody thing again.'

'You really think it's Frohlich's crate?'

'It's black, and better eyes than mine say it's a Stirling bomber.'

I felt like saying better eyes than yours wouldn't be all that hard to come by, but the dog growled at me, so I thought better of it.

'What do you want me to do?'

'Identify the bloody thing, old son. You've been inside it before, and we can't find anyone else who'll admit to having been anywhere near it.'

Which is what I should have done if anyone asked me, shouldn't I?

'It will take us bloody weeks to trek up there, Peter. It's on a small plateau in the middle of exactly nowhere.' He didn't say anything, and I didn't say anything, so I repeated, 'It will take us bloody weeks . . .'

When I looked up Levy was staring at me. Except he wasn't, because of having no eyes. His sunspecs were looking at me. So was his dog, and so was the Arab.

Peter said, 'No, not really.'

'What do you mean *not really*?'

'Hudd reckons that once you're out of the aircraft, you'll be on the ground in less than five minutes.'

It was one of those odd moments when all the sounds of the outside world fade to nothing. People's mouths open and shut without speech: birds stop singing. I could no longer hear even the buzzing of the ruddy flies. Everything stops. It's happened to me every time I've been arrested. Then I fully understood what he'd just said.

He had to be bloody joking.

Chapter Fifteen

Blue moon

I didn't actually want to go back to Deversoir, and if you think about it for a minute, you won't bloody blame me. Charlie Bassett – nobody's fool. Play it, Sam. Play it again . . . these bastards were planning to fling me out of an aeroplane again, and I hadn't even seen a pyramid yet. The problem was that we were still on red alert, so there was nowhere safe to go. My authorization from Watson covered me for a journey to the Bitter Lake Officers' Club and back, not a Cook's Tour of Lower Egypt. Even so I took a chance, and drove past my base, and on to El Kirsh. Sod the lot of them.

When Haye with an e saw me she said, 'There must be a name for people like you . . . ghouls who can't stop themselves from hanging around hospitals.'

'I came to see you. Is your fellah in town?'

'No; he's on leave in Alex.'

'I'm not sure he exists. You may have invented him to put men off.'

'You may be right. It wouldn't be a bad idea. What did you want?'

'I told you: to see you. When are you off duty?' A passing doctor who was too handsome for his own good – one of those James Mason types – frowned to see his nurse talking to a humble airman as if he was a human being. She ignored him: I'll bet that did her career a lot of good.

She replied, 'I was going to go for a swim. Have you trunks with you?'

'I've nothing with me but my genius. Who said that?'

'Nobody did, except you. Oscar Wilde may once have said something like it, but probably didn't. I'll find you something to swim in.'

I drove her to the club at Abu Sueir, where we lay around the pool. She taught me a few swimming strokes. I could manage about six feet, say two strokes, of breast stroke before I rolled over on one side and foundered like a torpedoed aircraft carrier. It was fun. I suddenly realized that, apart from being with my boys and Maggs and the Major, I almost never had any fun any more. The thought quietened me, and Susan picked up on it.

'What's the matter?'

'I have two boys. I suddenly missed them.'

'Do they have a mother?'

'One each probably; I only knew one of them, and she didn't stick around for long enough.'

'That's sad . . .'

'Not as sad as if they had. We're probably better off without them. The boys are with my two best friends, who live on the South Coast. When I get back, I'm going to find ways of spending more time with them.'

'Do they know that?'

'No, not yet.'

'You should tell them.'

We drank limejuice with native lemonade: it was cloudy and bitter. Just the thing for a warm day.

Eventually she asked me, 'Why did you come up here, Charlie? It can't only have been to see me.'

'Technically I'm AWOL, I'm afraid; I'm getting rather good

DAVID FIDDIMORE

at it. I was supposed to return direct to base, but I suddenly didn't want to. Totally brassed off at being bossed about, so I came out here.'

'That was possibly a little stupid. I don't know whether to be flattered or alarmed. What about your boss?'

'He'll be having a hairy canary, but he won't do anything about it. I'll phone him later.'

'What brought this on?'

'Somebody told me something which scared me; *really* scared me.'

'Are you going to tell me?'

'No. Need to know.'

'Good. I hate other people's secrets, but we nurses get told a lot.'

'Can I stay with you tonight?'

'. . . another girl shares with me.'

'. . . and she'll mind?'

'Probably not. You're masculine and reasonably young; she's an Australian – the rest speaks for itself.'

We stopped at the RAF shops in Abu Sueir for a few things Susan needed, went on for a cool drink in Ali Osman's cafe. I bought a couple of dirty postcards – Edwardian style – from the travelling hurdy-gurdy man winding his music outside. She dozed on the drive back to El Kirsh, even though it was only a short journey. Egypt looked colourful, primitive and peaceful. Who could get into trouble here?

Haye with an e shared with a sheila named Sheila. I had difficulty with that myself at first. Like most Aussies she was a giantess, had big feet and a big laugh. She'd been contracted to the RAF from an oil company, and worked in a laboratory at El Firdan, testing aircraft fuels before they were pumped. She said there had been a problem with the water content of some of the stuff bought in from the Americans. It froze at high altitudes, and

288

blocked the injectors. She also made gin: gallons of the bloody stuff. So we had a gay old evening.

After an hour or so of drinking I walked out to a public telephone box on one of the streets of married quarters. It was identical to a phone box you can find on any London street. A woman in her forties had beaten me to it, and I had to spend ten minutes trying not to hear her arguing with her mother back in Blighty. When she left she gave me a nice smile, and raised her eyes briefly to the stars: she must have guessed my call wasn't going to be an easy one either. Life wasn't so bad.

Watson was in mild mode. 'Where are you, Charlie?'

'El Kirsh.'

'Seeing that nurse again? Anything going on between you two?'

'That's *our* business, sir, but *no*. And I am almost pleased to report it.'

'Good. Don't catch anything. We need you. When are you coming back?'

'Tomorrow.'

'Good.' Again. '. . . and don't lose that car: I can't afford another one. Change the date on your warrant, initial the change and overstamp it with the hospital stamp. I'm sure the girl you're with knows what to do. I don't want the MPs picking on you.'

'Fine.' I seemed to have lost all my words. Does that ever happen to you?

Watson had to make all the running. 'What's she like, this nurse of yours?'

'She can quote Oscar Wilde.'

'Don't tell anyone: they'd probably send her home.'

Maybe that was a tip to pass on. I offered to sleep on the veranda, but they said I'd be eaten alive by the creatures of the night, so I agreed to a bed made up from their sitting-room sofa. They showered and washed before they retired, and I followed them through the small bathroom. The feminine smells it contained made me almost as homesick as the memory of my boys.

After I had washed I braved the veranda for a last smoke. My tobacco was getting too dry; I'd have to find a way of keeping it moist. I was sure the old buggers out here had already solved that problem. The girls' small quarter was positioned midway between two street lamps, and as I smoked my eye was drawn to a tawny, dark shape sliding through the shadows cast by the houses opposite. Low and long, and completely silent. She paused to look at me, and then moved on. Eye contact. We'd have to stop meeting like this.

In the middle of the night Haye with an e tiptoed out of her bedroom, and woke me. I sat up and yawned. She squeezed in alongside. I put my arm around her, and pulled a blanket around both of us. During that season the days were hot, but the nights cool.

She said, 'I remembered something else that Oscar's supposed to have said.'

'What was it?'

'*Who, being loved, is poor?* Are you poor, Charlie?'

'No; not at the moment. I'm feeling a bit rich.'

'So am I.'

We didn't have to do or say anything else, so we didn't.

We went back to sleep like the Babes in the Wood. Susan slept still leaning against me. Sometimes life deals you very pleasant cards.

I was quite proud of myself for resisting the urge to drop into the Blue Kettle on the way back. I didn't even stop at Ismailia, thundered along the edge of Lake Timsah, heading south, but it was one of those days when the gods had it in for me, because I picked up a flat halfway between Gebel Maryam and Deversoir.

The road was dead straight before and behind me; the few palms shimmered in the heat haze. No water, unless you counted a bleeding great canal alongside me. One of those times when you realize that you could be in real trouble. I'd heard stories of Gyppoes spreading tacks on the road, and then gunning down the poor innocent who gets out to change his wheel. I scanned my surroundings from up close, right out to the horizons. No tacks. No Gyppoes. No anything for sodding miles. Not even a six-year-old stone thrower on the back of a camel, but if I wasn't worth their killing, I wasn't going to complain.

Just when you think things can't get worse, they always bloody do. When I opened the car boot there was no jack: so I had nothing to lift the bugger off the tarmac with. Half an hour later, when my depression was notching itself up into a nasty bit of panic, a three-tonner full of singing Brown Jobs came trundling down from the north.

They hadn't a jack small enough for the car, but they stood around and simply lifted it up and held it, until I had one wheel off and the spare on. One of the things the Army has always been exceptionally good at is training small groups of men to cooperate to achieve feats of strength beyond that possible by one on his own. The second lieutenant with them was sarky of course.

'Always pleased to help the junior service when it's in trouble, old son.'

'And I shall remember to buy a beer for the next soldier I see in the next bar I visit. Thanks for getting me out of a spot.'

' . . .told you: my pleasure. I'll be getting along now. Why don't you follow me, and stay out of trouble? If you're going abroad during a red alert you should at least carry a gun you know.' I didn't want to tell him that I'd completely forgotten to check the alert status again.

'I'll remember that, thanks. I've only been out here a few weeks.'

'Most of our casualties have been out here less than three months when they cop it. If you concentrate on getting through that period, you should be OK.' He touched his cap peak with his swagger stick. 'See you later.' He didn't though, even though he meant well.

Nancy was reading a copy of *Picture Post* that had a photograph of Marilyn on its cover. No one from my generation would ever ask you Marilyn *who*? He half rolled over when I ducked under the canvas. 'Where've you been? Old Bugger-Lugs is getting ready to send out a search party.'

'I've already reported, and given him his car back. I had a flat, and when I went to change the wheel found some bastard had nicked the jack. That's the last time I take out a car without looking first. Have you got anything to drink?'

'Water. I finished the Stella yesterday. We'll need to get in some more.'

Beggars can't be choosers: water it was. I looked over his shoulder. Marilyn smiled back at me from a picture spread. Most of her clothes were still on.

'I saw some original photographs of her that some tankies had taken from a German spy in France.'

'When?'

'In 1945. She was stretched stark-naked on a red velvet curtain, but still looked like the girl next-door. She's one of those people you don't begrudge being famous.'

'She is going to have an interesting life,' he told me. 'That's written all over her face . . . and when she's eighty she'll write a book that will lift the lid on what all those film stars and producers really get up to.'

'I'll be first in line to buy a copy. Can I have her after you?'

He flung the magazine at me, but in a good-natured way. 'Help yourself. I have to go and clean up anyway. Watson has

insisted that I look more *soldierly*. I respectfully observed that
RAF officers weren't supposed to look soldierly; that was for
soldiers . . . and then he exploded. I don't know what he expects
me to do – I can't help it you know.'

'Help what?'

'Looking like this.'

'Yes you can, Oliver. You can get your hair cut the same length
as the rest of us for a start . . . or at least have a decent DA.'
That's a haircut shaped like the feathers on a duck's arse, for those
of you too young to know better. My generation were good, but
crude, when it came to making up metaphors. 'Then you could
stop using perfume, and get yourself a bigger pair of shorts.'

'Do you think the Old Man would notice?'

'No, Oliver. But you would then conform, and he would *stop*
noticing. That's the point.'

'I'm glad you're back, Charlie: you understand these things.
You can take the flak for a while. I don't know why he's in such
a foul mood.'

'Nor do I; but I'm going to have a shower, and clean up, then
go back up there and find out.'

Watson was limping. I hadn't noticed that before. He moved
around the room like a hungry wolf.

'What happened, sir?'

'What happened when?'

'Apart from me, what happened last night or this morning to
make you so damned angry? We're a small team, so it's not as if
you can't find someone to let off steam to if you want. What
happened?'

He flung himself into his chair, and then he laughed, 'Napoleon
would have loved you, Charlie.'

'I don't think I would have liked him, sir: he was a fat French
git with piles . . . but why?'

'He always advised his officers, *If in doubt, march your men towards the sound of gunfire*. That's what you do. Everyone else has been tiptoeing around me all morning, whereas you blast in here and demand to know what's going on at the top of your voice. What am I going to do with you?'

'Send me home to Blighty?' That was the title of another music hall song my old man used to sing when he was drunk.

'Not a chance. Rather find you something else to do. Apparently you made a half-decent fist of the guard the other night, so it's been suggested that I supply a bit more manpower. M'smith and Nansen will be pretty teed off with you, when they find out. If you had made a complete cobblers of it nobody would have asked us again.'

'But that isn't what's pissed you off, sir?'

'No. If you must know, someone with more bars on his shoulders than common sense has suggested I use an intelligence source to find out what's been happening to all this kit that's being whipped off the Brown Jobs. He wants to impress them with our intelligence-gathering capabilities, and go one up on their CO . . . but I didn't join up to become a bloody policeman.'

'Ours not to reason why, sir. Couldn't Yassine give us a hint?' It wasn't the first time I'd acknowledged that we had, in the Fat Man, a genuinely mutual acquaintance. I was interested to see his reaction. He gave none at all.

'He could if I knew where the beggar was. He's not answering the phone in the Kettle, and his staff just say he's out.'

'I could go up there and find out?'

'Yes, Charlie, you could . . . but whenever you actually volunteer for something, I begin to get the willies. Let me think about it. What did you want anyway? There must be another reason for you presenting yourself so reasonably turned out for once.'

'Can I sit down, sir?'

'If you must.' Then he bawled at her open door, '*Dais-ee*: two mugs of tea, please.'

Her response was to laugh, and then I heard her moving about. At least things had improved at the business end of the department.

'If this unit isn't completely in the RAF, sir, despite your original assurances, then I presume that we don't always have to play by RAF rules . . .'

'Granted. That's why you have to do what I ask you, or end up in pokey. Continue.'

'In that case the same regulations about correspondence and telephone calls, which govern the hundreds of other poor sods lying around in tents out there, don't necessarily apply to me?'

'I follow you, Charlie, but I *don't* follow you. I don't see what you're driving at, so bloody get on with it.'

'Sorry, sir. It's just a long-winded way of asking if I can come back here when you are having your afternoon siesta, and make a few phone calls without the War Office listening in. I thought your green telephone must be worth something.'

'Why didn't you say so in the first place? No, of course you can't. Who d'ye want to call anyway?'

'My kids first, because I miss them . . . then my office back home to find out what's going on . . . also to a friend to ask what's happening to my dad, and another to a business partner in Germany.'

'And why should I say yes?'

'Because after I have discharged those duties, I can give my full attention to whatever madcap scheme you've dragged me out here for, sir . . . and incidentally, after one of those calls, it wouldn't surprise me to then be able to tell you where our Fat Man is. You'd like that, wouldn't you?'

'They bloody warned me about you, didn't they? Insub-bloody-ordinate all the bloody way,' he grumbled.

'I take it that's a yes then, sir?'

'Of course it is. Where's that bloody woman with the char?'

Daisy walked in on cue. Her KD skirt and blouse had been freshly laundered, and she looked . . . well, radiant. I was glad that it was working out for someone. She brought three mugs: one for herself.

'The doctor has told the Wing Commander to stop drinking,' she said, as if Watson wasn't there. Her old fondness for him was in her eyes again. 'He has gout in his right big toe. We're told that gout has a tendency to make people very ill-tempered, but I won't stand for that.'

'You told me he wasn't much of a drinker,' I told her.

'She lied.' That was Watson. 'I'm a drouth. It's having to put up with people like you which drives me to it. Now finish your tea, and bugger off.'

Before I went Daisy informed me, 'All of your uniform requisition has arrived now, Charlie. I've been passing it on to Mr Tobin for secure storage. Was that all right?'

'That was fine. I'll pop round and see him while I'm here.'

I found Tobin in our largest permanent shed. He had the wheels off our Land-Rover. His boss begrudged letting him away even for five minutes in the middle of his work. I don't know what the others were doing: the place looked three quarters empty to me.

'Where are all our bloody radio spares?'

'Most of them are out in the blue, sir.'

'Waiting for their buyers to pick them up?'

He put on a great injured face, 'Mr Bassett, you've got a suspicious mind.'

He waited until we were out of earshot of anyone else before he reached into his shirt pocket, and produced what looked like a Post Office savings book with a blue RAF cover. It had my name printed onto a line on the top, and *RAF Canal Zone and Arab*

Co-operative Bank. I had a surplus balance of fifty-eight quid already.

I asked him, 'What bank is this?'

'Mine sir. It operates inside any camp in the Canal Zone. I've taken the liberty of selling your surplus kit, sir, and crediting your account – hope you don't mind.'

I smiled because it was too bleeding late if I did.

'Of course not. What do you pay on deposits if I have any spare cash?'

'Four per cent sir. I follow the official bank rate.'

'. . . and can I draw out cash in local tender?'

'Of course, sir. Do you need any now?'

'No. It's just good to know. What I *do* need is a clean shirt to take out into the blue.'

'Take an old, soft one, sir: no sharp creases to wear yer skin away.'

Money or tailoring: Tobin, I thought, was your complete professional. I probably no longer had any new shirts anyway.

Daisy was out sitting on the step of Watson's veranda with a glass of cold water that afternoon. I could see it was cold from the moist cloudiness on the outside of the glass.

I paused, and asked, 'How do you get it so cold?'

'We have a fridge. It works overtime. I see the alert must has been lifted. We're either Red-Amber, or back to Amber again.'

'How do you know?'

'An Egyptian cobbler followed you up the road, pushing his cart. Didn't you see him?'

'Yes. Why didn't *I* work that out?'

'Because I'm a woman. Would you like a glass of water?' If she came on with cracks like that I'd soon go off her again.

'Yes, please. The boss said I could make a few phone calls.'

*

I didn't lie to them. I told them I hadn't written because I hadn't had the time, but would attend to that as soon as I could. Dieter wanted to know about crossing the Med in a corvette, and Carlo wanted to know about the desert. I told him about camels and shite-hawks, and that I'd met both his mother and his grandmother. He showed absolutely no curiosity about them, and I didn't quite know what to make of that. Something else to ask Susan about maybe. Both of the boys wanted Arab head-dresses.

Elaine told me that business had picked up. Old Man Halton had come back with some WD contracts in his pocket, and was bidding for an Army trooper run between Malta and the Canal Zone. Apparently they wanted old Avro Yorks for the job, and we had a horrible one of those currently under-employed. We called it *Dorothy*, after that dreadful child in *The Wizard of Oz* — God bless her, and all who sailed in her. The next thing Elaine said was, *Have you written back to me yet?* The next again was, *Do you still love me?* I had never said I did in the first place, but from two thousand and something miles away does it matter? *Would you like me to knit you woolly socks and gloves or maybe a balaclava — the way we did for the troops in the war?* This is fucking Egypt, Elaine, not the Crimea in winter. Even the snakes are so hot they can't be bothered to bite anyone.

'Have you seen snakes, Charlie?'

'Two . . . and a lion.'

'I didn't think that there were any lions in Egypt. Where did it come from?'

'I don't know. It's a mystery.' There, I was saying it myself.

My old man had been arrested again. This time it had happened in Scotland, where the police are less forgiving, and he was still nursing his bruises from the encounter. I got this from Dolly, who was still looking out for him.

I asked her, 'What did he do this time?'

'There's a Territorial Army camp site just outside Campbel-town. He painted something on the road outside.'

'What?'

'*Redcoats go home*. Then he chained himself to a lamp post. The police weren't terribly amused.'

'Is he going a bit odd?'

'Not as odd as his son. I miss you so much, Charlie, and I never thought I would.'

'I miss you, too. I dream of that beautiful mole in the middle of your back . . .'

There was one of the pregnant pauses which often happen in conversations between Dolly and me. Then she said flatly, 'I don't have a mole on my back,' and hung up. I said *sorry* to an empty telephone.

Sod it!

Bozey told me that business – both Halton's and ours – was brisk. I liked that word. Then we talked about David Yassine. When I put the phone down it was warm from my hand, and from my ear.

I walked into Daisy's closet to find another glass of water. She was asleep with her ankles up on the edge of the desk. An electric fan standing on a cabinet stirred the air around us. Her skirt had slipped back, and I could just see her stocking tops. My dilemma was that if I tried to pull it up over her knees, and she woke up, she'd think I was trying to get my hand up her skirt – so I moved quietly out again.

As I did so she spoke, without opening her eyes, 'It's OK, Charlie. Panic over.'

'Good,' I told her. 'Go back to sleep. I'll close the door on the snib behind me, and no one will come in.'

I reckoned I had a couple of days, and then I'd be back out in the blue.

It was the old torch-shone-in-my-face job. Someone came clumsily through the tent flap, and shone a light on me.

Nansen moaned, 'Whoever you are, fuck off. It's sleepy time Down South.'

Watson corrected him with, 'It's sleepy time, *sir*, and you're on a charge for being disrespectful to rank. See me tomorrow.' To me he said, 'Get some more clothes on, Charlie, we've got a job. I'll wait for you outside.' Then he turned back to Nancy and said, '. . . and start sleeping with some shorts on, or you'll be on another bloody charge for being a bloody unnatural: you look disgusting.' I was still tucking my shirt in when I went outside.

Watson observed, 'I don't know why you put up with him.'

'Haven't we had this conversation before, sir?'

'No. You must have imagined it.'

It was cooler than I'd reckoned, so I ducked inside for a jacket, and while I did so a vehicle drew up. It was an anonymous-looking 1-tonner, driven by Pat Tobin. He handed me the keys, gave us a sloppy salute, and made off for the darkness. I hoped the lion wouldn't get him. While Watson got behind the wheel, I climbed up into the other side – I should have made plain that it wasn't only an anonymous-looking vehicle, but a very old one. In the 1940s the military had a strange preference for vehicles that stood eighteen feet off the ground: you needed crampons to climb into some of them.

He drove out of the main gate, did a left and a right, and headed for the Suez road. He was a surprisingly fluid driver; much better than me. He belched, and told me, 'I always liked this old Bedford.'

'Is it ours, sir?'

'Pat says it is. That's good enough for me. Why don't you ask me what this is all about?'

'What's this all about, sir . . . or did the fancy for a moonlit drive just come on you suddenly?'

'Bloody funny, aren't you? This afternoon you told me that Yassine was in Suez and gave me a probable address, didn't you? I looked it up, and we're going to see if we can find him.'

'Why?'

'Because the wogs down there have stolen a Comet tank; fully armed and ready for dancing. If someone doesn't do something about it there's going to be a bloody war on.'

'Or a police action at the very least. I think those were the words you used, sir.'

'Told you before, Charlie; stop being bloody funny – not in the mood for it. I checked with the MPs and the address you had is in the Arab quarter.'

'What does that mean?'

'It means that there are two loaded .38 service revolvers, and a Stirling and two magazines, under your very seat. If you have a god, pray to him now that we don't need to use them.'

'Why us?'

'Why not?'

There was an early bit of moon – I hadn't been kidding him about that. The air whined in through a couple of tears in the canvas roof. To our left out on the Great Bitter Lake, a tugging little wind lifted small waves that sparkled in the moonlight. Billions of stars, of course – I've never seen starry nights like the starry nights in Egypt. They would have driven Van Gogh mad. Hang on a mo, he was half mad in the first place, wasn't he? From time to time I saw a flash of white as the sail of a Gyppo fishing boat caught the light. It would have been a wonderful drive if I hadn't been sitting on a small arsenal of things to kill people with.

We dropped further south every minute, passing Fayid and Abyad on our right and RAF Fanara on the left. Watson didn't speak much; occasionally he whistled, but it was stuff from shows – hardly my scene. At RAF Kasfareet you could see the aircraft lined up like toys – Vampires, and a few tired old Hastings transports. If you had parked up aircraft like that in the war, someone would have dropped out of a cloud and destroyed the lot in one low pass; but these were different times. We hit a shite-hawk feeding on a road kill somewhere south of Geneifa – I reckoned that made the score British armed services two, Egyptian wildlife nil – and trundled past Hodgson's Camp into the suburbs of Suez before dawn. I'd even managed an hour's kip along the way.

A wooden barrier across two oil drums and six MPs with side arms means *stop* in anybody's language. They had two of those brand-new Land-Rovers at a checkpoint. I know what Pat Tobin had said about his, but they looked a bit flimsy to me.

The sergeant in charge saluted Watson and asked, 'Wing Commander Watson sir?'

Watson yawned before he replied, 'Yes and Pilot Officer Bassett C. That's *Bassett* with two esses and two tees. Make sure you get the spelling right if all we get out of this is a couple of grave slabs.'

The sergeant visibly relaxed, 'It won't come to that, sir. The address you are interested in is on the very edge of the Arab quarter – quite classy actually – we won't need to venture in far. Are you allowed to tell me what this is about?'

' 'fraid not, Sergeant. The buggers don't even tell *me* half the time!'

'Very good, sir, but a word of caution if you don't mind.'

'Go ahead.'

'Things are a bit tense at present. We're getting a lot of pilfering by the wogs, and High Command is pretty fed up.'

'Thank you. We'll bear that in mind. What sort of things are they stealing?'

The copper looked round to make sure none of his team was earwigging. He leaned into the cab and whispered, 'You won't believe this, gentlemen, but they stole a battle tank, all thirty tons of it.'

'You're right,' Watson told him, 'I *don't* believe it. Shall we get on? My man is going to sleep here.'

I don't know why it is, but I've always found that having a boss who's a good liar is quite reassuring. Maybe that's one of the qualifications for becoming a boss in the first place. Either that or they teach you it in Bosses' School.

The address I had for Yassine was a villa in a wide, short cul-de-sac. If this was the Arab quarter, then I wanted to be a Suez Arab, not a pretend British airman living in a tent in the middle of a sandpit. The houses, behind high mudbrick walls, were big and airy, and had large cultivated gardens with specimen trees, and exotic flowers. *In Xanadu did Kubla Khan a stately pleasure-dome decree* . . . that's Coleridge, for the ignorant among you. I wondered how far we were from Xanadu. That brought to mind a soldier I'd once met who had hidden behind a poet's gravestone while a tip-and-run Messerschmitt machine-gunned him for fun. It's funny, the thoughts that run through your head when you're shit scared.

The idea was that we'd be accompanied by a Land-Rover and three men; they would remain with our truck, at the end of the road and out of sight, in a small open park. They were supposed to come in and get us if they heard gunfire. I'd heard better plans, but for the moment my mind would not come up with one.

One of the MPs confided in me, 'Not your usual wog houses, are they, sir? Most of them live in things made of dirt: they can fling them up in minutes.' He was being a bit hard, but I knew what he meant.

'What were these places?'

'Suez Canal Company villas, before the French pushed off. They look out over Port Tewfik and the Gulf. Really pretty. One of them used to be a nice brothel before that Free Church bloke got all iffy, and made us close it down.'

The Free Church bloke was a well-known brigadier who'd done some terribly brave things in the war, went mad and then found religion. He had been a pain in the arse wherever he'd served ever since. That last sentence contains a clue as to what eventually happened to him, and why he was dishonourably discharged in the end. You can't get away from the puns, even when you try.

Watson and I walked up the shadowy lane until we reached an old door set in a brick wall. The door looked far older than the wall itself. We had both strapped on revolvers, and I carried the Stirling. I didn't actually want to, but I couldn't leave it in the Bedford, and I wanted Watson with it even less. There was an Arab script for the number 5 – *khumsa* – above the door . . . and an iron bell-pull like a Victorian water closet.

'What's your plan?' I whispered. I thought we could dispense with the *sir* and *master* under the imperative of stress.

'Ring the bloody bell, you fool; what do you expect?'

What I expected, or rather *hoped* for, was the arrival of the 7th Cavalry if the Indians went on the warpath. I didn't say that; I tugged on the ironwork and was rewarded with a jangling loud enough to bring back Lazarus.

Watson frowned. 'Enough, Charlie.'

A dog barked, and then another. They were at least a quarter of a mile away. The bell jangled away to a sullen silence. Nothing: then more nothing. I liked more nothing. Then a door banged somewhere close, and after a minute the door in front of us was opened by a yawning seven-year-old boy.

In English he asked us, 'Yes?'

I asked him, 'Is your Master in?'

'My *Master*?'

'Is Mister David Yassine here?'

'I will look,' and, before I had time to intrude a friendly foot, he had shut the door in my face and bolted it. I felt very stupid standing there. Dawn was beginning to show.

'Well done, Charlie.' Bloody Watson.

'You weren't exactly much help either, sir.'

'What was I supposed to do,' he growled, '. . . pull a gun on a kid?'

That was one of the odd things, now I come to think about it. The child had shown no distress at finding a couple of fully armed Englishmen on his doorstep before dawn . . . he looked merely a little irritated.

Before we had taken the decision to heave the door in ourselves, Yassine opened it. In his sleeping robe he looked even fatter. The difference between the daytime djellaba and the thing they sleep in is that the latter has short sleeves. Men wearing them look like the seedy old transvestites you see at the Henley Regatta Ball . . . and before you ask, the answer is *yes*; go and look for yourself: the place is full of them.

He pulled us quickly through the door as if he was ashamed to be seen with us. That can't have been too far from the truth.

What he said was, 'I suppose you want breakfast.'

Watson replied, '. . . and a thirty-ton Comet tank, please.'

'That too, that too . . .' Yassine smiled, and turned his back on us. He waved his arms like a market trader in a bazaar. 'I'm sure we'll come to an arrangement. Do you mind if I leave you in the kitchen whilst I go and dress? I should, in courtesy, offer you the dining room, but I gain the impression that this is an unofficial visit.'

By then we were inside Yassine's seaside residence. The kitchen was large and hot, and I immediately felt sleepy. Watson noticed, and cautioned me.

'Bloody well stay awake, Charlie; this cove is as slippery as a fish.' I could have agreed *My new partner is as slippery as a fish*, but it wasn't the right time to bring that up.

'Don't worry, boss.'

'But I do, that's the problem.'

Yassine came back dressed like an Arab, and brought a plump, pretty, middle-aged woman with him. He didn't introduce her properly; he just pointed and said, 'Wife.'

Minutes later Mariam slipped down the stairs, wearing a blue silky robe that clung to all of the right places.

I asked Yassine, 'Your daughter perhaps?'

'No, of course not. Occasional concubine. She gets a few days away from the lustful clients at the Blue Kettle.'

'And you're not lustful of course?'

'. . . only on Christ's birthday, and at Easter – I am a good Christian. Didn't I tell you that?'

Before I could answer Mariam wriggled the fingers of one hand at me and said, 'Hello, Charlie.'

Watson gave me a look, but kept his trap shut. There'd be some questions to fend off later.

To begin with we sat at the table and drank coffee, and watched Yassine drink water. Then he watched us eat fried eggs as he picked at a little fruit. The women retired as soon as the food was before us.

I said, 'We didn't know how to contact you, David . . .'

'Are you your brother's keeper?'

'Stop pissing me about, and tell us about the tank.'

'Its new owners will be pleased that at last you have missed it, and that someone has come to ask for it back. They were getting worried.'

'What are they worried about?'

'What to do next. They don't know what to do with it, now that they have it. Acquisition is one thing: disposal another. It was a spur-of-the-moment thing – only a few boys.'

'And nothing to do with you I suppose?' Watson had shaken himself into life at last. I shouldn't have judged him; at least I'd slept for an hour in the truck.

'Nothing at all, Mr Watson. But I heard what happened, and am willing to act as the go-between – your agent, or an honest broker.' He used the words with irony and relish.

'Is it damaged?'

'Not as far as I know. Tanks are difficult to damage.'

'Where is it?'

'Exactly where your driver left it: at the end of a street of our poor native houses.'

'No, it isn't. The driver was merely moving it to the repair shop. He says he left the hatches open to ventilate it, that terrorists climbed in, drugged him with chloroform, and when he came to, he was outside the Land Forces HQ with a headache and no tank.'

'His recollection is very flawed. The drug must have damaged his memory.'

'What's your version?' I asked him.

'Not mine: the boys who found it abandoned.' I nodded for him to continue: I wasn't going to argue until I'd heard it all. 'Your driver stopped the vehicle outside the house of a well-known beauty, and cannot have believed his luck when she called him inside. When he came out an hour later his tank had completely vanished without a sound. Like the Indian rope trick – except in Egypt. Nobody saw it go. It was a mystery.'

'That's not possible. It weighs . . .'

'Thirty-three tons, yes, I know . . . it *is* possible if the street now has a new small house, and that house has a door, but no windows.'

He paused for dramatic effect. My brain was slow to pick up – I've never been a morning person.

When I twigged I asked, 'They built a *house* around it?'

'Yes. Very enterprising young men; they did it in less than an hour. I shall employ them all, once they have left school.'

'How old are they?'

'There are five of them, and the eldest is thirteen. Can we now pretend I haven't told you where the vehicle is, and negotiate a price for them? I thought ten Egyptian pounds each would be a fair finder's fee for returning a lost piece of valuable military equipment? But we will need to move fast – our honourable police force is also looking for it, for an entirely different purpose. It would be better if the British recovered it – we don't want another massacre on the Empire's conscience, like the one in Ismailia, do we?'

Watson asked me, 'Do you have fifty quid on you by any chance?' I had, but not much more. As I handed it to him, the Wing Commander told me. 'Congratulations, Charlie. You just bought a tank: the Army's gonna just *love* you.'

Watson stood up, and shook hands with Yassine.

He said, 'Thank you, David.'

'The house boy will take you to your lorry. And you can tell those three policemen they can go back for tea now.'

'How did you know about them?' That was my question.

He shrugged, and I knew that I was about to get the old Egyptian heave-ho again. Then he took pity on me and smiled, 'I watched you from an upstairs window. Very noisy. Half the neighbourhood will have known that you were here.'

'What will you tell them?'

'That I bribed you with a woman, and money, to let me reopen my club. All's well that ends well.' I bloody knew it. That's what Tommo always used to say after he'd had someone over.

I drove us back following the tail lights of the police Land-Rover. Watson looked all-in. The MPs were pretty perky after we told them where the tank was, and then let them relay the news on their walkie talkie. By the time they got back to camp they'd probably been persuaded that they'd found it themselves. Heroes. By then, of course, the High Command of British Middle Eastern Land Forces would have flung a ring of steel around their lost treasure in its new garage . . . probably one commanded by a general who had already convinced himself that *he'd* recovered the bleeding thing on his own. Yet another fucking hero: what goes around comes around.

They took us to Weston Camp, and after a bit of back-slapping led us to some decent guest quarters, and let us sleep. I don't know about Watson, but I was out of it before my head hit the pillow, and I didn't see him again until the next noon, when they fed us up and hurried us away. I thought their haste to see us gone us was all a bit ungrateful, but the Wing Commander explained,

'We're a bloody embarrassment, Charlie. They want to see the backs of us as soon as possible. How would *we* feel if we lost a Canberra, and a grubby little squaddie brought it back?' He concentrated on his driving, and I concentrated on seeing Egypt for once. I saw a few scrubby hills, loads of barbed wire, even more Army lorries, and a few aircraft. Not a bloody pyramid or sphinx in sight: maybe I'd come to the wrong bloody country.

After a while Watson asked me, 'What chance has the Empire got?'

'Sorry, sir.' – I'd yawned – 'What do you mean?'

'A hundred Brown Jobs searched that bloody street all day long yesterday, Charlie. All day! What chance has the Empire got if we can't even count the bloody houses?'

There were long spaces in our conversation that afternoon, but I do remember making one point with him. 'If David Yassine was our agent in this matter, what did *he* get out of it?'

'He got his club opened up again, didn't he?'

I played one of those jazz tunes inside my head. 'Sleepy time gal': I remembered Josephine Baker singing it before the war.

'Does that mean he organized the whole bloody thing?'

'Now why wouldn't that surprise me?'

I thought about it for fully five minutes before telling him,

'No: it wouldn't surprise me either sir.' Then I suggested, 'We could stop at the Officers' Club at Fayid, and get a glass of lemonade . . . I'm parched.'

'Good idea, Charlie. You can drive this old cow after that. I still feel like I've been up half the night.'

'When do I get my fifty quid back, sir?'

'When you tell me where you got it in the first place.'

I knew I hadn't heard the end of it, and he hadn't even said anything about Mariam yet. Give him time.

Chapter Sixteen

Kinda blue

I never felt more like singing the blues. Didn't Tommy Steel make a barrowload of dosh singing a song like that fifty years ago? Remember how I'd buttoned a letter from Flaming June into my shirt pocket to save it for later? I didn't. I sent the damned thing to the laundry instead, but even when I got it back it was just about readable.

The sergeant she'd been engaged to had not come back from Korea, apparently: it was just an impostor she didn't recognize wearing the same body. Three days after he got back he tried to murder a Chinese laundryman in Epsom. Now he was in a straitjacket locked up in Banstead, and Flaming June thought she might be in love with me after all. But we'd left it a bit bloody late, hadn't we?

If the letters from home got you down because you weren't there, the biggest problem for the serviceman in Egypt was that if you weren't working, and the alert was high enough for you not to be able to go visiting, then there was damn-all else to do. The camp cinemas tried their best, but there was a difference between the films the troops wanted to see, and the films the powers-that-be thought were good for us. I wanted to see *Macao*, not Groucho Marx. Bugger them. So I hung around Watson's office, and sometimes he threw me a bone, by giving me something to do. Pat Tobin ran a card school. Nancy learned to ride a motorbike rather well, and scraped both his knees. M'smith had cocked up somewhere and drew ten days' stag down at Fayid, so we never saw him.

Eventually I sat down, and answered my mail. The letter to the boys was the longest, and I learned that I'd found out more about Egypt than I'd realized. I embellished it with drawings of the pyramids I'd never seen, me being sick over the side of the corvette, and trudging out into the desert with a spade to do what a man's gotta do. You can't go wrong writing to kids about vomit and crap; they like that sort of stuff.

I wrote asking Elaine to tell Old Man Halton to start pulling strings to get me out of this madhouse, and wrote to Flaming June that I might love her too, but we'd have to wait for me to get back before we knew . . . never give a girl a complete knock-back, as you never know when you might want them again. That was another of my dad's rules, but one that I didn't share with anyone.

The truth was, as Watson had indicated, that the Charlie I knew in his twenties could have been mistaken for a pretty shallow person. That's as much as I'm willing to admit. I sent one of the dirty postcards to Bozey, and one to Dolly at her mews flat. After I dropped them in the postbox I realized that I no longer knew if she lived there. It was things like that which stopped you short. Then I wondered if the postcards would get past the BFPO censors, or would I get a couple of hefty service coppers knocking on the office door one day soon? I suppose the more likely scenario was that the censors would simply nick them, and stick them in their pockets.

I asked Daisy, 'When's this bloody trip back out into the blue supposed to come off? I don't want to do it, but I *do* want to get it over with.'

'Like a visit to the dentist?'

'Exactly like that.'

'I don't know. It's something to do with fixing up the transport. Do you want some of David's gin? He's away at GHQ for the day.'

'Yes please . . . and don't get cross at me for saying that you're looking better, and it shows.'

'No. I won't, and I am. The thought of those two bastards having to *stand* all the way home, and then having to explain away their tattoos, really bucked me up no end, although I've given up sunbathing except down at the Beach Club. I still don't know who – you or David – I have to thank for the dark pleasure of revenge; both of you deny it.'

'Maybe neither of us.'

'Or both?'

'Anyway, you realize now that *you* weren't to blame. That's the important thing.'

'I was to blame for being dumb, Charlie; but that was all. What did you come in for, anyway?'

'To shoot the breeze . . . isn't that what the Yanks say? I was bored, and didn't know what to do with myself. I was never any good at lying around doing nothing. I just begin to think too much.'

Daisy sat on Watson's desk, and swung her legs. She had a long G and T in her hand; tonic water is something we were never short of. I had a sudden vision of my kid sister Francie, who died when she was fourteen or fifteen. Would she have looked like this if she had reached her twenties?

'What do you think about?'

I found myself saying, 'You, sometimes. What happened to you changed how I felt around women – as a bunch, I mean – almost overnight.'

'In what way?'

'Less aggressive and more protective. Sometimes it feels a bit soft, but I think I can live with that.'

'Do you *like* women, Charlie? Outside the sexual thing I mean.'

I sensed that it was a serious question, and gave myself the time to think about the women I'd known. 'Yes; very much.'

'Well, maybe something good has come out of this after all. That's worth thinking about, too. Fancy the camp cinema tonight? Groucho Marx is in a film with Frank Sinatra.'

'I'm not sure.'

'And Jane Russell.'

'OK.'

The grin she gave me told me that she thought I still had some way to go.

'Who got the tank away?' I asked Watson. 'It must have taken them hours to dismantle that bloody house.'

'A little Scots tank driver called Fotheringham. It's one of those names you remember. He made a hole for the gun barrel to go through – like threading a needle – then he simply drove the thing out. He left them with only a pile of rubble where their new house had been.'

'When you said little, you meant *my* size, sir?'

'I meant smaller than you, Charlie: almost a dwarf, but much wittier. Explain to me why we always start off talking about anything except the reason I send for you in the first place.'

'I'd love to know, sir.'

'Then shut up and listen. You're going out *tomorrow*.' That had the effect he wanted. I was all ears. 'I'm not supposed to tell you, because the Brown Jobs are being all mysterious as usual, but you will be out with a scheme that will cross into the desert west of here, above Abu Sultan, go northwest up towards the

Sweet Water, then drop down towards Gebel el Girba.' He was facing a large-scale military map on the wall. The areas he was pointing out contained large amounts of absolutely fuck-all. I doubted that a flea could live out there.

'What's the ground like, sir . . . or is that a silly question?'

'It is – because this is Egypt. The bloody ground is changing all the time. If you go too far north you'll be in drifting sand, but further south there are some decent wadis . . . or at least there *were* the last time anyone looked.'

'What's the tasking?'

'Whatever communications the Army wants; they'll take one of their own signallers this time . . . and you'll be his relief. When he's not working you're to monitor any air traffic you can detect. We particularly need to know if their Lancasters are serviceable or are just heaps of junk sitting on their airstrips looking threatening. One more thing . . .'

'Yes, sir?'

'Take more underwear than you own; you're going to be working this time, and you'll sweat your bollocks off in that radio room.'

'Thank you, sir.'

'Don't mention it: I'm known for looking out for my people.'

It was already so hot that I was stuck to my seat. Before I got up I asked him, 'What was that massacre Yassine was so worried would happen again?'

'It wasn't a massacre, Charlie; it was a police action in Ismailia in January last year. The Army was ordered to disarm a group of Muslim Brotherhood policemen holed up in their barracks and in a clinic of some sort. At the end of the day they'd killed three or four of us . . . and we'd killed forty or fifty of them. We used Centurion tanks to winkle them out, shelled their building to smithereens, and even fired on the Governor's mansion.'

'If we killed fifty Egyptian policemen for the loss of three, it sounds a bit like a massacre to me. They were probably armed with bows and arrows. Is there anyone around who was there at the time?'

'Why, Charlie?'

'I'd like to ask someone how it happened, sir. Maybe it explains the strange looks most of the wogs have been giving me since I arrived.'

'And what kind of look would that be?'

'. . . as if they bloody hate me, and want me dead, sir.'

'Can't you just accept that they do, and leave it at that?' As I left his office he asked me to send Nancy over to see him – *that boy's going flying again* – and added, 'Don't go asking silly questions, Charlie. You don't want our side to end up hating you as well.'

That was exactly the sort of attitude that had put Hitler into the Reichstag, and I wondered why we had forgotten that so quickly.

With the erk who drove the runway sweeper I watched Nancy take off. I had cycled out to the edge of the strip like others used to do in the old days when I was setting off for Germany. Even when it was raining there had always been someone there to wave goodbye: we British can be a sentimental folk. Oliver was sitting in the back seat of one of those new Gloster Meteor trainers, which had a long glazed cockpit cover that looked like a humped greenhouse. The aircraft itself was unpainted, and in places the aluminium bloom had dulled its surfaces.

Nancy turned to look at me, and raised one hand in salute. So did the pilot. Nancy himself was wearing a canvas helmet and dark grey rubber ox mask, so I could only see his eyes. I think he was smiling, but I had that horrible feeling: *Ave Cæsar, morituri te salutant*. Then the noise level from the twin Rolls-Royce jet engines took over, and dust and sand was lifted in a cloud behind it. Once the pilot let the brakes off they thundered away past me like shit off a shovel. The aircraft lifted from the runway, catching the light a couple of times with a couple of brilliant dazzling flashes, then banked, turned to starboard and disappeared – still low – out into the northwest.

Nancy had raised his hand once more, as they passed me. I never saw him alive again.

They were overdue after three hours, and an hour later Control started the process of phoning around all the other RAF stations with runways on the Canal Zone – seven or eight in all – as well as a couple of emergency strips. I walked out to the end of our strip in the twilight, sat in the dirt, and watched out to the north and west. After an hour I saw a shooting star: a meteor perhaps.

For a while the lion sat opposite me on the other side of the runway, maybe twenty yards away. In profile she was like a miniature sphinx. Her tongue lolled out, and she was also looking out to the northwest. When she thought it was no longer worth waiting, she got stiffly up, and slid away into the shadows. Minutes later I heard a jeep's engine. It was dark, and Pat Tobin had come out looking for me. We drove to the stores shed, and had a bit of a party with the lads.

I was hung-over when I drove the radio truck out of the compound at Deversoir, and clipped one of the concrete-filled oil-drum barriers that did little to protect us from homicidal natives on camels. The drum burst, rolled some distance and ended up alongside the shack everyone used as a bus shelter. Small pieces of shattered concrete now littered the gate. An RAF Regiment corporal tumbled out of the guardhouse, followed by a couple of his gunners who wanted to know what the fuss was about. I stopped the Austin and climbed down.

Anyone can make a mistake I suppose. I'd just made mine, but next that same morning it was the corporal's turn, for he screamed that immortal military phrase at me, 'You *dozy* little man, what the fuck do you think you're up to?'

Like most corporals, he had been promoted on account of the distance he could get his voice to carry, and as usual it was the word *little* that actually did it for me. They had probably heard him in Cairo. I had my back to him as I climbed down, so all he could see was a slightly undersized driver, dressed in clean but rumpled KDs. I reached into the cab for my old RAF peaked cap as I turned to him, and pulled it on, not with a flourish, but with that tug which says *You're stuffed, sonny*. You should have seen his mug when his instincts kicked in. *Bollocks, an officer!* One of the Gunners went white and froze, and the other disappeared back inside again as fast as a ferret down a rabbit hole. I spoke quietly; that always sticks the knife in further. 'If you ever speak to an officer like that again, Corporal, I'll take your stripes and push them so far up your arse they'll come down your bloody nostrils. Savvy?'

'Yessir.'

'And clear this fucking mess up.'

'Yessir.'

The Austin was scraped but not bent, so I remounted. The corporal remained rooted to the spot until I beckoned him over and said, 'One of your men made himself scarce as soon as he saw I was going to be awkward . . .'

'Yessir.'

'Get rid of him. You want someone who'll back you up in a spot; not someone who scrams at the first sign of trouble.'

He blinked, said, 'Yessir,' again, and saluted. I touched the peak of my cap to him, and put the rusty old box into gear.

When I was out of sight of the camp, I stashed the RAF cap behind the passenger seat, and pulled on the Jerry job. I thought

I looked quite dashing, but it didn't make me feel any better. I had to sit at the end of our junction with the Ismailia–Suez road, and wait there for the rest of the convoy, which was late. They were running on Army time, which is not quite the same as yours.

When they turned up Sergeant Clare was in the lead jeep, which was a relief . . . and a fresh-faced second lieutenant sat alongside him, which wasn't. Clare brought the convoy to a halt, but it was the officer who walked over to me. He was a lanky, bony specimen with a gangly walk. I imagined his joints spontaneously disarticulating, and him collapsing in an India-rubber heap on the road. I didn't get down, so for once my conversation was conducted from the position of power: I began to understand how all those six-footers felt when they were dressing me down. His KDs looked new. They were immaculate.

He touched his immaculate cap with his immaculate leatherclad stick, and smiled an immaculate smile. 'Smart-Watkins. Edward . . .' Obviously he'd had problems with his English language lessons at school, since his sentences came out back to front.

'Bonaparte-Bassett. Charles . . . you can call me Charlie.' It did not raise a smile, except from the guy with the gun in the back of Clare's jeep.

'One of the French Bonapartes?'

'No. One of the Belgian ones. We danced at the ball in Brussels on the eve of the battle of Waterloo, and then we left the French ones to fight it. They lost.'

'I see. Jolly good.'

'That's what we thought, too.'

He had a curious little smile, which sat under a curious little moustache. Fussy. If I had been his CO I wouldn't have let him get away with anything as daft-looking as that.

'I'll send over a driver . . .'

'It's OK, Edward . . . I can manage. Sergeant Clare taught me last month.'

He twitched. He definitely twitched, and lowered his voice so that we were the only two who could hear him, 'I'd prefer it if you didn't use my Christian name in front of the men, Charles . . . technically I outrank you: it's a matter of courtesy.'

'I'm in a completely different service, but *technically* you could be right. What *do* you want me to call you then?'

'I thought about that problem on the drive here. Perhaps we could call each other nothing: honours even.'

'I still don't need a driver.'

'But I need you to need one. Officers don't drive in our mob . . .'

'Matter of courtesy again, I suppose?'

'Precisely.'

He touched his cap peak with his stick again as he walked back to the jeep. I suppose that he'd won the first round. Roy Rogers had been climbing down from the back of one of the wagons anyway. I didn't mind that. I shifted over to make room for him. He was wearing a regulation forage cap which looked old, but almost unused, and balanced precariously on his thatch. What had happened to the Afrika Korps?

'Hello, Roy.'

'Hello, sir. Ready to roll?'

'Yes. Who *is* that guy?'

'New officer sir. The Sergeant was asked to take him out and familiarize him with the terrain.'

'He's an idiot.'

'I can't argue with an officer, sir, an' you're an officer. The lads are saying he's from that strange county in the middle of England, sir.'

'Where's that?'

'Cuntshire, sir.' He made me laugh, and the laughter made my head ache, so I leaned back in my seat, and pulled my hat over my eyes. Trigger placed us in the middle of the small convoy. There was something deliberate about the way he lunged for a gap in the line which I was sure the following vehicle had not intended to leave for us.

Before I closed my eyes I asked him, 'What was that about? We could have waited until the others were past.'

'No we couldn't, sir. If the Gyppo 'as a go at us, he'll either go for the lead lorry, to stop the convoy, and make us all a target . . . or for Tail End Charlie, 'oping we'll be too far down the road to fight back properly. You and I will quite happily bowl along in the middle, sir, where the wise men are.'

'You've done this before, haven't you?'

'With respect, sir; you may have sand in your shoes, but you still have a lot to learn.'

'*Ave Cæsar,*' I replied, but the words made me think about Nansen, and I didn't speak a lot for the next hour.

We stopped at the roadside beyond Mile Twelve, and had a brew-up . . . obviously waiting for something because Smart-Whatsit was clearly in no hurry to get going again. After twenty minutes 4 RTR, in three tired-looking Centurion tanks, lurched out of the seaside, crossed the road in front of us, and set off into the blue. They made good time in the rough hard ground, and were soon out of sight, although for a while you could track their progress on the near horizon from the dust clouds. Get-Smart called us all together.

'We're running into the desert now, lads.' He made it sound as if we were trying to round Cape Horn in the dead of winter. 'Therefore I want maximum vigilance from everyone. Who knows what may lie beyond the next ridge.'

Trigger played dumb, and treated that like a question. He held up his hand and said, 'I do, sir.'

Clare, standing behind his officer's line of sight, shook his head in warning, but Trigger ignored him.

The officer asked, 'What would that be, Rogers?'

'Another bleeding ridge, sir – beggin' your pardon. There's thousands of the buggers out there.' . . . *and at least three tanks*, I thought, but I kept my mouth shut.

'Thank you, Rogers.' Was he brighter than he sounded? Did he know when the piss was being taken of him? 'See me tonight. I might have a small task for you.' *Yes*, he did.

Before we mounted up he pulled me to one side, and asked, 'Mind if we lose the Jerry titfer, Charles? Not good for discipline if an officer gets away with something the oiks have been hauled over the coals for.' I didn't answer. I just flung my cap over my shoulder, and in through the radio wagon's open cab window, and turned away. This man could seriously get on my wick if I let him.

Up alongside Roy Rogers I asked, 'Why didn't you say something about the cap?'

'Testing yer powers of observation, sir. I wondered when you were going to ask me why I was wearing this regulation apology for a piece of headwear, issued by the British Army.'

'I noticed, but decided not to embarrass you by asking. It looks like a khaki banana skin balanced on top of your head. Why are you wearing it, then?'

'Because the officer insisted, Mr Bassett . . . and put me on report for questioning his decision.'

Smart stood up on the seat of his jeep, and waved us forward, like wagon master Ward Bond in those *Wagon Train* television programmes, or Lash Larue at the Saturday morning pictures.

Trigger must have agreed with me because he muttered, 'Wagons-ho!' I wondered if anyone had ever said that sort of thing in real life.

I looked out of the window and muttered to myself. I didn't

intend anyone to hear me, but Roy must have picked it up. What I said was, 'We're going to have to do something about this mad bastard.'

To which Roy responded, 'I'm going to pretend I didn't hear that, sir . . . and I'm going to pretend even harder that there isn't a man out on this scheme who won't agree with you.'

It looked as if I was in for a fun few days.

We turned into the blue, following the tracks left by the tanks. You can't mistake a place a tank has been because it knocks flat everything it can't merely pulverize with its weight. My old major used to call it *tank spoor* . . . and had taught me how to track them across Europe. Anyone with an educated eye could do the same out here. To begin with, we made three times the speed that Clare had managed on my previous scheme, but there were two prices to be paid for that. First it ripped the tyres of the bigger wagons to shreds. We had to change three of them, and at that wastage rate we wouldn't get through the first day . . . and, second, we lost so much time hanging about changing wheels, that overall we travelled less distance than going at the slower pace.

During one of these unscheduled stops – the stricken truck needed to be partially unloaded before it could be lifted – Trigger wandered over to a couple of the others who were grabbing a swift fag, talked for ten minutes and sauntered back.

He must have decided I was an ally because he said, 'Apparently Smart Alec has told the Sergeant that we're getting these blow-outs deliberately because we don't like him forcing the pace. He says we've got to *quote*, be kicked out of our customary complacency, and turned into proper soldiers, *unquote*.'

'Don't look at me: I'm in the RAF.'

'I'll let that pass, sir, seeing as some of us is not so sure about that . . . but I will say that for the first time I might be seriously envious of you.'

'Don't be. You lot are occasionally killed by the wogs. My lot are occasionally killed by the wogs as well, but then more frequently killed by our own mistakes. When you fuck up at twelve thousand feet the only place left to go is *down*.'

'Might I 'ave 'eard that you lost one of your fighter planes yesterday, sir?'

'You might have.'

'Anyone you knew?'

'I share a tent with him.'

'Bad luck, sir. I'm sorry to 'ear that.'

Bad luck, sir. Last words on Oliver Nansen, photographer. I can still picture him today, and wonder what he would have made of his life if it had got any further.

We got going again soon after that, lurching more slowly this time – maybe Sergeant Clare had been able to talk sense into our bold leader. The cab got hotter. I spread a handkerchief over my head, under my old RAF peaked cap, and let it cover my neck. Trigger did the same, but his small forage cap couldn't hold it in place. We both stripped to the waist, and still sweated. I don't know of any proper serviceman who gained weight in the Canal Zone: the only fat people you met were senior officers and wealthy Arabs. By the time we stopped for a breather, we were both all in.

Smart Alec called us all together after we had fed and watered. He was good at calling people together: they get taught that in Brown Jobs officer school. He'd placed a small table top of wood over the desert stove I've told you about before – a small Castrol oil drum full of sand, topped off with petrol and set alight. The hot sand retained the heat, and you could brew up on it in minutes. It could also burn things, but no one had told him that. He opened a map on the impromptu table.

'Gather round, lads, I want to show you where we are, and what we're doing.'

He placed the point of a silver propelling pencil at a position on the map. Even with my rudimentary navigational skills I could see he was about an inch out. The point rested on a ridge point: we were actually in a wadi at least three miles away.

He said, 'We're here . . .'

I sensed Trigger's arm being raised. He was alongside me, and we were behind the Lieutenant, so I firmly pulled it down again. He'd done himself enough damage for one day; let someone else try. No one did immediately.

'We're going *into the blue* up here . . .' Somehow the words didn't work the way he used them. Maybe he hadn't earned them yet; it was as simple as that. '. . . following the three tanks which preceded us. This is an exercise – a *proper* military exercise – and I intend that we shall win.'

'Win what?' one of the squaddies muttered. Smart Alec picked him up.

'Win over the other side – another patrol that's coming into the desert from the Suez – Cairo road. They are supposed to ambush us, and we are not going to allow ourselves to be ambushed. Anyone from my patrol who ends up 'killed' or 'captured' in this exercise will be up on a charge. We need to know that we can fight and win in the desert – and therefore this area of desert has been certified available for exercises for the first four months of the year.'

One of the unwary asked, 'Do the Gyppoes know that, sir?'

'Don't call them *Gyppoes*, Green. Try *Egyptians*. In answer to your question the Egyptians do know that. They won't interfere because this area is under British protection.' We were protecting several thousand square miles of absolutely fuck-all with a canal running through it. 'And because this is an *exercise*, most of you will be issued with blank ammunition before we move on. Keep your live rounds in your ammo pouches, and your weapons loaded with blanks.'

Green, God bless him, was a Geordie, and a persistent bugger. '. . . and if the Egyptians start shooting at us with *real* bullets, sir?'

'Reload with live ammunition, Mr Green, and let the buggers have it! Do I really have to tell you that?'

As far as I could see there was a flaw in this operation, which the planners back at base hadn't spotted. In my experience, it was the guy who got the first shot in who usually survived a homicidal encounter. If we met a band of renegade Gyppoes intent on murder, we were likely to be at an initial disadvantage. The mad sod was going to get someone killed.

The wooden table top on the desert stove was beginning to smell very warm, and if I wasn't mistaken Smart's map was beginning to char at the edges. He whipped it away, and began to beat at it with the other hand, dancing around and shouting, 'Bugger, bugger, bugger!' and then it was, 'Mount up; mount up . . .' as if we were a troop of Household Cavalry.

As Trigger and I trudged to the radio van I whispered, 'Find out what the Sergeant thinks about all this, because I don't know about you, but it's making me windy.'

'Mutiny's a capital offence in the Army, sir.'

'Only if you're found out.'

'Sergeant Clare wouldn't approve.'

'Who would be asking him to?'

In the Austin's oven of a cab, I had left my jacket draped over the back of the driver's seat; I felt into its pockets to make sure my own small pistol was still there. Don't worry; I wasn't planning to murder the sod.

Before we moved off the Army signaller sent off a positioning call – he was niftier than I would have thought, but also had that look in his eyes: the one that said his hands moved faster than his brain. He also signalled to the Centurion tanks somewhere up ahead. I thought I'd have to keep an eye on him.

Then I took over for fifteen minutes, and searched the ether for the sounds of unfriendly aircraft. They must have been having a canny afternoon, because they weren't talking to each other.

When I came out of the back of the van, Smart glanced across at me from his jeep. He looked angry, and tapped his watch. Then he raised his arm, and hooked it forward. *Wagons ho!* He probably didn't want to be late for his tea.

That evening we stopped later than Clare would have done, and scrabbled around for a decent, defensible camp site and solid ground. We ended up in a wadi with a stone ridge on one side and a softer ridge of coarse stuff on the other . . . it petered out into blown sand if you walked far enough in that direction. The Sergeant suggested a lookout on one of the ridges, but was quickly vetoed by our bold officer.

'There's no one out here, Sergeant, except the Red team, and they're days away.'

'This is technically a high-alert zone, sir. Terrorists have attacked our schemes before.'

'Don't be such an old woman, Sergeant. I've told you we are alone, and safe; take my word for it.'

'Yessir.'

We were setting up the circle for the night, and stringing the barbed wire between the trucks. It was the same bloody simile again, wasn't it? – covered wagons. Some of the men were digging out scrapes under the trucks to sleep in, or to jump into if we came under fire. Not even Smart could complain about that; it was SOP – that's *standard operating procedure* to you. Just after he stopped speaking the inevitable Arab on the inevitable donkey rode into camp, bleating about his eggs. I was sure it was the same one I'd seen last month, even if we were eight hundred miles from there.

Smart drew his pistol. I hoped it was loaded with blanks.

'Where the devil did he spring from?'

The Arab just grinned hopefully. He had an egg in each hand. Allah be praised they weren't large enough to be mistaken for grenades.

Clare said, 'Nobody knows, sir. It happens all the time. It's a mystery.'

'He must have followed us. Tell him to go away.'

'If I just bought his eggs he would go away faster, sir.'

'Bugger that, Sergeant. Just tell him to push off.'

Clare turned, and spoke to the Arab in Arabic. That surprised and gratified me: it meant that at least one person hadn't wasted his time out here. There seemed to be a lot of shrugging at one another involved. Eventually the Arab snarled something and turned his mule back, pausing to hawk as he did so. His gob fell close to Smart Alec.

Trigger said, 'I wonder what he did with his bint. I wouldn't have minded a look at her.'

I didn't snap at him, but I wanted to. That was interesting. It was a different Charlie, wasn't it? Ten minutes later Smart ordered Roy to double out into the sand, and dig a latrine. That was unusual.

What they'd taught me on the last scheme was that when your time came you wandered off into the blue with an entrenching tool, dug a hole and dropped your trousers. Then you covered it up when you were finished. If the security situation was truly dodgy you took a mate with you, and he turned his back as you dropped your kegs, but covered you with his gun. Smart Alec, however, thought that arrangement unsoldierly. Where soldiers stopped for the night a latrine hole was to be dug, all ranks for the use of. What's more the latrine had to be at least twenty yards away. And what's more than that, two small slit trenches had to be dug between the latrine and the camp, so you had somewhere to drop into if you came under fire on the way. Smart Alec assured us we were unobserved by hostiles, but he still wanted his latrine and two trenches. All evenly spaced. Even although it was in the softer stuff, it took Roy an hour and a quarter, and he was knackered when he came back. He sat with his back against the Austin's big front wheel and panted. It was cooling down and there was a light breeze. It probably came all the way from the Med, because there was now damn-all between it and us, and it dried the sweat on Trigger's body.

He said, 'Fucking bastard!'

'Making a fucking point,' I observed, and handed him a mug of char.

'Thanks. He's got it in for me.'

'. . . only because you took the rise out of him.'

He grinned ruefully. 'Yeah. There was that. I'll have to watch my lip.'

'Because mutiny is a capital offence in the British Army,' I reminded him.

'Only when you get caught, sir. I seem to remember some officer telling me that.'

After he finished his char and poured the dregs on the earth between his feet, he stood up and wandered over to the cookie for some grub. The rest of us had already eaten.

The fun started later in the evening. Most of us were gathered around the stove, wearing either jackets or blankets around our shoulders. The stove gave out no light, but a bit of residual heat, and it was cool for the time of year. There was a card school going around a hurricane lamp, and despite his committed view Smart had put two men up in the trucks as lookouts. Maybe the silly bastard was educable after all. When my bowel performed a serious ritual of summoning, I stood up, picked up the entrenching tool and a small torch, and started to move out of the light.

Smart Alec glanced up.

'Where are *you* going?'

'To christen your new bog.' Factually inaccurate, Charlie. It was no longer a virgin.

'Bit late.'

I was almost at the legs-crossed stage, so I wasn't as patient as I might have been.

'The way I see it is that you're going to get my shit here, or in your latrine, but either way you *are* going to get my shit.'

Somebody laughed wheezily from the shadow. At least it wasn't Trigger. I didn't want him in more trouble than he was.

Smart Whatsit frowned, and said, 'I'll come with you. Wouldn't want anyone wandering off into the dark, and getting lost.' He sighed as he got up, as if my bodily functions should have a more considerate sense of timing.

As we stepped out of the cover of the lorries I said, 'It didn't have to be you. One of the others could have come.'

'And have an oik sniggering over the sight of an officer's bare backside? I don't think so, Charles.'

'Not good for morale?'

'Absolutely.'

We were halfway between his two fire trenches when some bastard opened up on us from a half-mile away. At first I thought that the patrol he said wouldn't reach us for days had worked around our flank, and ambushed us. Two officers heading out into the blue for a dump must have seemed like a godsend to them.

I said, '*Bastards*!' Then I heard the bullets zipping past. They make a peculiarly personal sound when they're close to you. I turned on Smart and pushed him backwards away from me. He ran until he found the first trench, and dropped in it. I followed this from his bobbing torchlight. I ran about seven paces in the other direction until I literally fell into the outer trench. The initial shouts and clattering around coming from our small circle of trucks descended into order. I heard Clare conducting some sort of a roll call, and getting a satisfactory answer.

Smart Alec shouted out, 'Who is it, Sergeant Clare?'

There was an immediate fusillade of incoming rifle fire. I heard the bullets pattering around me, and made myself as small as I could.

'Gyppoes, sir . . . and for God's sake keep quiet. They're firing at your voices now.'

'Give us covering fire' . . . another half-dozen shots.

'No point, sir. I wouldn't know where to fire. I can't see any muzzle flashes. The lads are reloading with live ammo now. You OK, Mr Bassett?'

'Yes.' I kept it low, but there was a single shot, and it came too bloody close.

'Keep your heads down, sirs, and I'll try to work out how to get you back. You may have to stay there until they withdraw . . . there's another load of fireworks over to the west; they must be having a go at the tanks.'

The hole I was in was just big enough if I drew my knees up and lay three quarters on my side, with my head below the parapet. Once I'd sorted out the noises, and fitted them to what Clare had said to us, I could work out what was happening. It looked as if a number of wogs were having a go at the three tanks which were ahead of us. They must have seen our lights and left a few friendly natives the task of keeping us out of it. I just hoped someone had been able to get to the radio.

I was there for hours, and staving off the cramp became the second worst problem. My worst problem was the reason I'd landed up out there in the first place. Whether I liked it or not, my body was about to evacuate on a grand scale, and there was nothing I could do about it . . . but, wogs or no wogs, I was damned if I was going to lie in my own excrement all night. So I pulled down my trousers, shat on my own hand, and flung it over my shoulder and out of the trench. Then I wiped my backside with that bloody horrible great services handkerchief – I always knew it would come in handy for something – and rubbed my hand in the sand until it was clean. That occurred four or five times before my belly stopped aching. The trots I'd been warned to look out for on the trip to Istanbul had finally caught up with me in the desert triangle between Suez, Ismailia and Cairo. Believe it or not I eventually went to sleep. There was nothing else to do.

When I awoke it was light, and the ground was shaking like the aftershock of a small earthquake. After a session of *overtures and beginners, gentlemen please*, my brain told me the tanks were coming back down their original track.

Clare's voice carried to us . . . 'I think you're OK now, sirs, the Seventh Cavalry's arriving . . . you can get back here in a couple of ticks.'

Then I heard a howl of rage that might have been the scream of a demented tiger, or a second lieutenant tried beyond endurance, as Smart Alec shouted, 'Mr Bassett . . . Mr *Bastard* Bassett, *sir* . . .'

It was only old habits that made me stand stiffly to, swing round to face him and answer, 'Yes, sir?'

'You're on a fucking *charge*, sir!'

He was standing in his slit trench literally shaking with rage. Spitting with it . . . *covered* in it, actually. Covered in diarrhoea. The brown stains and streaks, all over his beautiful KDs, told their own story. Ah well, Charlie. You can't win 'em all. Bloody good shots all the same, even if the thought of deliberately taking aim had never entered my head.

*

He glowered at me throughout breakfast, but never said another word. Perhaps he didn't trust himself. On the other hand several of the blokes contrived to touch me on the shoulder or the head as they passed me. A curious show of solidarity. It was as if I had passed the initiation ceremony, and had been admitted into the Lodge. Even Sergeant Clare brought me another mug of char, and winked before he turned away.

I thought that Smart Alec would want to have it out, but he wasn't the type. When I faced him off all he said was, 'Don't say a word, Charles. I shall report you to your senior officer as soon as we're back in base. Just consider yourself on a charge . . . because you bloody well will be if I have anything to do with it.' Something like *conduct prejudicial*, I presumed. I leaned forward until my mouth was close to his ear.

Perhaps he thought I was going to plead or apologize, but I whispered, 'Go fuck yourself, idiot.' In for a penny in for a pound: my dad used to say it all of the time. Smart flushed like a girl being asked to dance by a bloke she didn't fancy. I looked up as I turned away from him. Five geese flew high over us in a nice tight V formation. Where the hell had they come from? Maybe Nancy would be up there one day.

The tanks soon split. They'd taken a few hits the night before, and their sandy-coloured armour was marked by bright streaks of bare metal where the wog bullets had bounced off, but the tankies were made of sterner stuff than us, and lurched off into the sand again. They were friendly guys, but quite mad.

We got a recall. Roy and I were sweating in the radio wagon when a string of signals came through for the Brown Jobs. They were in code, but he recognized the form, without summoning his own signaller.

'Come home, sir; all is forgiven.'

'Not in my case.'

'What did you expect, sir . . . throwing shite all over the Patrol Leader like that?' It was a phrase someone had used to describe the Lieutenant which everyone had quickly adopted. It wasn't insubordinate, because it described his role accurately. It also made him sound like a Boy Scout, so he bloody hated it.

'I didn't mean to. I just didn't think.'

'I'll bet *he* did: all bleedin' night! Can you imagine him lying there waiting for the next handful to arrive . . . and having to keep quiet and put up with it? Bloody wonderful, sir. I'll take him his messages now. It will take 'im an hour to decode them.'

I got a big signal on one of my sweeps. Its bearing was moving too fast across the terrain to be anything except an aircraft, and it wasn't that far away. Now what? I gave Watson a quick burst to let him know I was on to something, and then went back to it. Then there were two. The signals didn't seem to have that air of urgency which screamed operations, so I reckoned it was a Gyppo air force reconnaissance mission out over the Delta, or the salt marshes behind Port Said. Watson had wanted to know if the Gyppo air force Lancasters were airworthy – I reckoned he had his answer.

You have to wonder about the War Office and the RAF sometimes. What idiot had thought it was a good idea to sell the Egyptians half a dozen of our old war-surplus Lancasters, which might then be used to bomb our own boys? It's almost as if the people in the room trying to run the Army in the Canal Zone never spoke to the guys in the room next door, who were busily flogging off the RAF's spare kit. If a bunch of renegade Nazis had come back from Brazil and asked to buy a squadron of Spitfires, would the mad sods in Whitehall have set the cash registers ringing? – sadly the answer is, *probably, yes*. They never ever bloody learn.

Roy Rogers came back.

'What's up?' I demanded.

'The scheme's been scaled back, just as I thought. The patrol coming up from the south got lost, and ran out of water. Everyone is panicking, and the Air Corps is trying to get an Auster down to them. What a cock-up!' The Army Air Corps ran their own artillery-spotting and reconnaissance aircraft.

'Can't say I'm sorry. Are we going back then?'

'Not immediately. The covered wagons will remain here for the time being, whilst we set off through Indian country to find those bloody tanks.'

'Who do you mean by *we*?'

'You and me, *Kemo Sabe*. Our master has ordered it, and we must make it so. We have to take one of the jeeps.'

'Why don't we just signal them?'

'I asked him that, sir.'

'What did he say?'

'*Security, Mr Rogers. Walls have ears.*'

'He's off his fucking head! There *are* no walls out here – just miles and miles of fucking desert.'

'I take your point, sir . . . although I remember there's some sort of ruin out there somewhere. He thought the tanks might be making for it.'

'. . . and I'm one of his radio operators. What happens if he wants to signal the RAF?'

'Our man Baloo will have to sub for you until you get back sir. Mr Smart-Watkins has his punishment strategy for us well worked out. It's going to be as hot as a Dutch whore's fanny out there this afternoon.' It happened again. I was made slightly uncomfortable by Trigger's phrasing – that was interesting. But when in Rome, and all that.

Baloo was the army's own sparks – a big hulking bear of a man, hence his nickname. He was a bit of a slow thinker, as I've already indicated, but he came from Cardiff so what did you expect? Every one had nicknames then. Just *why* are modern men so reluctant to accept one these days?

'Will Baloo manage?'

'He will, if you preset your dials and switches for him, sir, and tape over the dials so he can't change things.'

'What a cock-up!'

'I said that before, sir.'

'I agreed with you then as well.'

We set off after we had fed and watered. We had a jeep, a map, an old field compass and a precious gallon of water. After we breasted the first ridge I pulled off my old cap and flung it in the back. I pulled the Afrika Korps job out of my small pack and stuck it on.

Roy had found a dirty black beret from somewhere. He was wrestling with the steering wheel when he said, 'Permission to change hats, sir?'

I just grinned at him, and his forage cap joined mine in the foot well behind us. I said, 'Of course, Roy, and we can give up the *sir* again out here, if you like. Most people call me Charlie.'

'That would be difficult, sir, but I could call you nothin' if you wanted.'

We agreed on that. It was the first of his conclusions which had matched Smart Alec's: maybe he had the makings of an officer after all.

I can find my way around a map because our navigator in *Tuesday*, our wartime Lanc, had shown me the rudiments. It might have been a morbid way to look at things, but on our crew you always learned to do someone else's job, in case he copped it. We were heading for a heap of stones left by the Romans, somewhere out ahead of us, but the navigation wasn't essential . . . we just followed the tracks that the Centurions had left. Hey, *Romans* . . . *Centurions*; that was quite good. Their tank trail was about fifteen feet wide, and stretched into the distance. You could easily see where they had broken through the crests of the ridges they had crossed. Maybe this wouldn't take so long after all.

And pigs might fly. This is Charlie's world, remember?

The going definitely got softer. We had to use the sand mats in places, and Trigger warned me that we might have to unship the metal sand boards if this got any worse. Then we found a Centurion tank. It was empty, and its metal hull was too bloody hot to stand on for long. It had thrown a track in a softish wadi, under a hill of blown sand. The digging all around it told us a tale.

We found its crew of four half a mile further on, taking a breather. A sergeant and three men, who all turned as they heard Roy gunning the jeep through some loose stuff.

The sergeant stood up with a weary grin on his face, and when we were up alongside I asked, 'Anyone fancy a lift?'

'Christ, it's a Jerry: don't you know the war's over, chum?' I'd forgotten my cap. Then he said, 'Thanks, chum; thought we'd have to walk the rest.'

Trigger coughed and said, 'Thanks, chum, *sir*, I'm afraid, Sergeant. I have the misfortune to be driving an RAF officer in disguise.'

It didn't faze the man. He asked me, 'Are you the one out with Peter Clare, and that new Lieutenant?'

'I'm afraid I am, but don't hold it against me. Do you lot want to hop on?'

They did and they did, if you see what I mean. With six of us now, we bogged that much quicker if we strayed into the soft stuff, but we had three times as many people to get out and push, so it evened itself out. We caught up with the two remaining

Centurion tanks an hour later. The Lieutenant in charge was just about to turn back to look for his lost charge, which, it just so happened was his only vehicle with a duff radio – he'd left them re-attaching a thrown track. Their radios were short-range jobs anyway – not good for much more than calling the next fag break.

'We'll look at the radio for you on the way back,' I offered.

'Tomorrow,' he told me firmly. 'It will be nightfall in an hour. With only the palsied lights on these things you won't want to be messing about out there in the dark.'

If I am honest – and this will earn me no credit among the tankies – I have to tell you that our friends in the Royal Tank Regiment don't make very good char. But their bully and bean sandwiches are desert food to die for. Their cookie had even baked a walloping great tray of bread pudding on top of a tank engine in the course of their travels, and we finished our meal off with a hefty chunk of it which set in my stomach like concrete. If only I'd had that the day before I wouldn't have been in so much bother, would I? We sat round a desert stove between the metal giants, and jawed by the light of a small roaring Tilley lamp, and a big low full moon. You could almost imagine reaching up and touching it: you never get moons that size in Blighty. We leaned our backs against the armour plates which reached down to cover the tops of the tanks' tracks – I never learned what they were called, but they retained the heat of the day and it was quite cosy.

At one point the Lieutenant leaned towards me and asked, 'Why did you come out here? Why didn't you just radio?'

'Our bold leader was worried it would give his position away to the wogs again, so he sent us to find you. Only one message: the exercise is off . . . we've got to go home.'

'I gathered that.'

'Are you disappointed?'

'Somewhat. I rather enjoy a bit of tanking.' He was the only one I ever met who used the word that way.

'I met some American tankies in the war in 1945 – in Europe.'

'What were they like?'

'As mad as monkeys. We liked them a lot.'

He didn't respond. He just looked across the light at one of his sergeants, and grinned. This mob seemed to have got it all together.

Later I commented, 'When I was getting a briefing I was shown a place on the map with some ruins. Is that far?'

'You could hoof it along this Bedouin track in twenty minutes if you watched where you put your feet. Do you want to see it?' He actually used the word as if it was spelt *Bedou* – Arab-style. I thought he was offering me company until he said, 'Someone will lend you a torch.'

The contrast between this lot and our nervy Smart Alec couldn't have been greater – they were telling me to wander off into the blue on my own. A couple of the guys looked amused: they wanted to know what I was going to do. What I decided was that I'd better see a bit of old Egypt to tell the kids about, while I could . . . I'd seen bugger all so far.

Before I set off the Sergeant we'd rescued from a walk on the wild side advised, 'Watch out for the snakes, sir. They like the big old stones, and they are all poisonous. Don't go stroking them like they were cats.'

'No, Sergeant. Didn't Cleopatra try that and come unstuck?'

'It's not far, but if you get lost, stay put, and shine your torch upwards now and again. I'll come out and find you.'

I took my small pack, in which were a water bottle, compass and my pipe and tobacco. Once I was away from the tankies the moon was so large that I didn't need the torch. It shone a cold white light on the old narrow track, and even the smallest of boulders threw a shadow. I made plenty of noise, whistled and kicked stones. Maybe if the snakes heard me coming, they'd get out of the way: there was nothing out here big enough to look on me as a snack anyway. It was cool, though, after the heat from the tanks, and I was glad of my jacket. After ten minutes I stopped, and lit up.

Apart from the occasional distant laugh or shout from the camp, it was absolutely silent out there, and I lost even those noises after the second ridge. That huge moon and a billion stars – you've never seen anything like it. I felt something like a huge sigh go out of me . . . and felt suddenly and oddly content to be myself, and who I was, and where I was, and when. It was as if life stopped just briefly, in order to give me a breather. I know that you'll laugh, but it was one of those moments after which you've never once ever been afraid of death again. *Dying*, yes – I know that's going to hurt – but *death*? No. I was in the most barren place on earth, where the animals and insects and even some of the humans wanted to kill me. Where there was no water, and nothing but stones and sand, and little Charlie was taking time to play the philosopher. My old dad was going to love this when I told him.

What they'd told me was that the ruins were on the far side of a rough scarp and, because they were precisely where the hard desert met the sand sea, they ducked and dived a bit. It all depended what the wind had been doing. Sometimes all you could see, they'd said, were a few stones poking above the sand . . . and sometimes the ruin was very exposed. Something built by the Romans they thought. Nobody had seen it on this trip. They didn't seem even vaguely curious.

The track angled over a ridge in the moonlight. There was a thick band of shadow before it: I'd have to watch myself. The Lieutenant had assured me that the Gyppoes were far away – *back in Cairo by now*, *old boy*, *bearing a couple of their wounded* – but that didn't stop me being reassured by the weight of my little pistol in my pocket.

When I thought of Romans, I tended to think of gladiators in the amphitheatre, traders in the forum, and Vivien Leigh in skimpy slave-girl outfits, but what I saw on the far side of that ridge was none of these. It was a theatre. Columns and walls, and semicircles of flat stone seats: everything was bigger than I had imagined, and deep, and still standing head-height to a tall man. I was at the top of the ridge, which was actually the top remaining level of maybe fifteen or twenty tiers of seats: sand was pushed up into their angles, so in a way they looked like a series of descending waves under the moon. And the moon. It was behind and above the stage; almost balancing on the wall of remaining masonry. It dazzled me.

The man standing low in the stage area didn't dazzle me at all. In fact he looked rather annoyed to see me. The feeling was mutual. As I turned away he spoke.

'Do not go, English soldier.' He spoke conversationally, and in a cultured deep voice. He hadn't raised his voice, since the theatre was still doing its acoustic magic. One of my problems was that I wasn't an 'English soldier', was I? – Not in the technical sense, that is – whereas he *was* a soldier, and dressed like one. His KD trousers were proper trousers, not shorts. I was also pretty certain that he wasn't English. What had that tankie said about the wogs? *Back in Cairo by now, old boy*. Yeah: ask me another! This man not only looked like a soldier, but the sort of soldier you didn't fuck about with.

And his suggestion was not a suggestion at all: it was a bloody order. What had I got myself into this time?

He beckoned me to come down to him. I thrust my hand into my jacket pocket for the reassurance of my pistol. He shook his head, and glanced to my right then to my left.

341

I also glanced to either side. To my left was a soldier I hadn't noticed as I climbed the brow. He was leaning against a jeep smoking a cigarette, and cradling a sub-machine gun under one arm. The jeep looked newer than ours; one of those French Hotchkiss things. He looked awfully smart, had crinkly black hair, and smiled encouragingly. He was obviously not going to shoot me immediately. There was another soldier sitting on the ground about twenty feet to my right. I had walked up between them. So I smiled back, took my hands ostentatiously from my pockets and climbed carefully down the tiers of seats. It felt like *take me to your leader* time. It was probably meant to.

The man I finished up facing was taller, broader and a bit older than me. He had a black lip-liner moustache, and black hair like his minders. He was handsome in a Clark Gable sort of way. I had hoped that these might have been French, but up close there's no mistaking an Egyptian.

He asked me, 'I know that you are alone, but are you armed?'

'I have a small pistol. Right jacket pocket.'

'But not in your hand.'

'Obviously. There's no point. I couldn't get all three of you.'

He smiled, nodded and asked me, 'Name?'

'Charles Bassett. You?'

He smiled again. I reckoned he was one of these guys who liked being talked back to.

'Gamal.' He said the word fast: I almost didn't hear the g.

'Pleased to meet you. What does that mean?'

'My mother said it meant *handsome*; but my father insisted it meant *camel*. As I watched my nose grow to dominate my face, I realized that my father was right.' He gave a short chuckle – two sounds – as if the memory amused him. 'Your name, Charles, means *manly*.'

'I didn't know that, sir. They should have called me something which meant *small* . . .' Why did I call him *sir*? I've told you I have had problems with that before. He wore absolutely no badges of rank, but I was certain he outranked me a thousand times over.

'I am very interested in names. You can tell much from names. I study the names of Englishmen. Your General Montgomery had a picture of his adversary general, Rommel, in his caravan. He stared at it every day in order to get inside Rommel's mind: he achieved that eventually, and beat him. I study *English* names. One day they will take me inside the minds of your generals and politicians.'

'I don't think you'll find much there, sir. They mess up almost everything they try to do.'

He smiled again, as if he had learned something useful. Maybe he had. 'Do most English soldiers think as ill of your leaders as you do?'

'I don't know about English soldiers, sir: English *airmen* do.'

'Ah. You are in the RAF.'

'Pilot officer.'

'I am a colonel.'

'I guessed you were paid more than me: you have a better uniform.'

This time he laughed aloud. I sensed his two men paying attention. He walked away from me, and sat on the stub of a column. There was another near it; he motioned me to it with a wave of his left hand. The moon threw our shadows on the flagstones beneath our feet. They bent like gargoyles on an English church.

He asked me, 'What are you doing here?'

Tell the truth, or make something up? Does *here* mean Egypt, or this bloody ruin?

'The truth is, Colonel, that I hate your bloody country and will leave it soon, but I have not seen any of your great antiquities. We are camped a couple of ridges back, and I walked here because I was informed that there was a Roman ruin. I wished to have something to tell my sons about when I returned home. Your turn.'

'My turn?'

'What are *you* doing here? I was under the impression that this particular empty piece of your country was out of bounds to all military units except the Brits.'

'Ah, yes. But my family used to come out here, and picnic, you see – before the World War. Our parents were teaching us that there was more to history than pyramids and temples . . . and this is not Roman, by the way. It is Greek, and it is a theatre – the Ptolemies built it. They were great pharaohs, a wonderful dynasty, but unfortunately they were also Greek. The Greeks are like your generals and politicians . . .'

'In what way?'

'Sooner or later they mess things up.' He smiled surprisingly gently as he delivered the punch line. I laughed, and he explained, 'I come out here sometimes – with a bodyguard alas. We can no longer move freely in our own country because of you. I come out here when I want to think. When I have difficult decisions to make.'

'It would be a good place for that,' I told him. 'Is one of your difficult decisions what to do with me, now that you've captured me?'

He didn't answer me directly; merely leaned one elbow on his knee, and his chin in the palm of his hand. He had unconsciously adopted the pose of Rodin's *Thinker*. He really had come out here to make a decision.

He glanced up at me, and asked, 'Will you tell anyone that we have met?'

'I don't think that would be a good idea, sir, do you? Anyway I don't know who you are, so what would be the point?'

'What if I became an important man in several years' time? Appeared on your cinema newsreels?'

'I should remind my boys of the Greek ruin in Egypt I had already described to them, and tell them I once met a man there who was making a difficult decision.'

'Even if you realized then that I was not a friend of Britain?'

'I wouldn't let that worry you, Colonel; neither is anyone else.'

He snorted again, and asked, 'Do you know what I think, Englishman?'

'No, sir.' But I was bloody well going to be told, wasn't I?

'I think that maybe your sons have just saved your life.' He paused, and we looked at each other. Just two men sizing each other up. 'When you get back to England say hello to them, from a man named Camel. That will make them laugh . . . but never come back to my country in uniform again . . .'

'Fine, Colonel.'

As I stood and turned away he said, 'Now: be Lot's wife. Walk away from me, up those steps, and never look back. Walk back to your comrades. Stay safe. Go home. Salute your children. Live long.'

I intended to. I stood and said, 'Thank you, Colonel,' and held out my hand.

He shook his head. 'No. I am sorry. Not while you occupy my country . . .' He made a quick crossways motion with his right hand, waving me away. Dismissed.

'In happier times then, maybe . . .' I told him.

I walked up the tiers of seats leaving my footprints in the sand. At the top the soldier with the Tommy gun shifted his weight against the jeep, and grinned again. He must have been used to looking after his eccentric boss. I walked away down the track, but a hundred yards on stopped, turned and looked back. Neither of the soldiers nor the jeep was there. I had heard nothing. Don't ask me how they did that. It's a mystery. I'd seen a bit of old Egypt and got away with it. I'd seen a bit of new Egypt as well, but I didn't know it at the time. What goes around comes around.

When I got back to the tank laager two Arabs had joined them around the desert stove. One was performing magic sleight-of-hand tricks: a gully-gully man . . . and the other was selling fruit. I don't know why we even bothered. They disappeared during the night, and didn't steal a thing despite what people tell you about the wogs.

We turned back in the morning after sleeping in and on the vehicles, and being shaken out at dawn for the best part of the day. The tankies topped up their fuel tanks from spare petrol in jerrycans lashed to the hulls. It did cross my mind to wonder how close to its flashpoint the petrol in them became in the heat of the sun. Then they ran the engines to warm them up before they set off behind Trigger and me, and the lost crew. When I drove over the edge of the wadi in which I remembered we'd left the crocked Centurion I realized I'd cocked my navigation up.

'Let me see the chart, sir,' Roy Rogers asked me. After he'd spun it round and looked at it from different angles he offered, 'I'm pretty certain that this is the right place.'

'That's what I thought.' That was odd because there was a problem. The tank sergeant perched behind me expressed it for all of us.

'Then where's my fucking tank?'

Part of me thought *this can't be happening again*, and that whipping two tanks inside a couple of weeks was gilding the lily a bit, so I kept my mouth shut. One of the Centurions we hadn't lost was perched on the ridge behind us.

The tank commander hopped out, and strolled down. 'Why've we stopped, lads? Trouble?'

'Could be,' I told him. 'The last time we saw your third tank it was about four yards away from here without a track. It was going nowhere.'

'Someone's stolen it?'

'Looks like it.'

'Bugger! How can you steal something that size?'

'They stole a Comet a couple of weeks ago.' I pointed out. 'In Suez.'

'That's just a fairy tale, Charlie. The British Army doesn't lose its tanks; not until now, anyway.' Ah. So that was it: least said, soonest mended.

There was also a story I'd heard about two British drivers stealing a couple of Comet tanks from a tank park in 1948, and handing them over to the Israelis, but this wasn't the time to bring that up either.

He looked pensive. 'I could get cashiered for this; and Mr Owen could lose his stripes.' He said it again, 'Bugger it!'

I asked him, 'What would you need to move a tank that won't work?'

'These buggers weigh more than fifty tons, sir.' That was the Sergeant, Owen. 'If you can't get the track back on her you'd need a tank transporter. But you'd never get one of those big bastards out here on this stuff.'

'So somebody got the track back on it.'

'Not possible, sir. It couldn't be done.'

His Lieutenant kicked at the dirt and stone a bit before telling us, 'That only leaves one possibility.'

Trigger finished his thought off for him, 'That it hasn't moved at all. Some bugger came up during the night and buried it.' He was obviously brighter than the boys who'd lost the tank at Suez.

347

If *they* had come to a similar conclusion, they could have saved me the drive.

In my memory there are only minutes between what was just said, and one of the tank crew saying *Oi*, in a loud and startled voice. He'd wandered a few yards away from us, and had felt the earth move beneath his feet. Literally, that is . . . and it was nothing to do with a woman.

A few minutes later my jeep's spade cleared a few inches of loose soil where he had been standing, and we found ourselves on the flat top of the Centurion's turret. It settled another inch while I was on it, and seemed canted slightly to one side. I jumped off, and scrambled back.

'Bollocks. This stuff must be like quicksand if you weigh fifty ton. Can you pull her out?'

The Lieutenant answered, 'Not a chance. I'd better radio a report in. Will your people relay it on to mine for us? All of a sudden I've gone off the wilderness. Bugger knows how we're going to explain this.' Then the technician in him took over, and mused, 'I wonder how far down she will go?' At least he seemed quite cheerful about it; although it was inevitable he'd face an inquiry when we got back.

'Do you want me to mark it for you?' I asked him. 'I could use one of your remaining radios to get an exact position for you if you liked.' The tank gave another lurch. Soil trickled onto its turret top again.

'Could you?'

'Not a problem, sir.' Although I had my doubts.

I used his own tank, Watson's wavelength, and my *Morecambe* call sign . . . and was pleasantly surprised to get a good signal. M'smith wanted to know what I was doing. I asked him to set up a triangulation on me. He wanted to know why.

'Don't bloody argue, Hector. Just bloody do it.'

'Do you want me to tell the boss?'

'Might as well: he'll probably use it as evidence at my trial.'

'Are you in the shit again, Charlie?'

'That is an exceptionally good guess; now do your job, and lose yourself. The man I'm with has other signals to make.' It was as hot as hell inside a bloody tank, despite the blowers, and even with it just ticking over, it was difficult to hear yourself speak over the engine noise. I was damned glad to climb out into the air again.

'Why don't we stay with you until you reach the road?' I asked the Lieutenant.

'Won't that annoy your temporary guv'nor with Sergeant Clare's patrol?'

'I'll radio him. Considering the state of our relationship at present, one more bit of disobedience won't make any difference. I'll tell him you need my radio skills. If you put a rope around my waist I'll get inside your sinking giant, and pull the radio out. You won't want to leave that for the wogs.'

'Don't worry about that, we'll just blow her up where she is.' I suppose sharp decision making is what we pay young Army officers for, and should be grateful when we find one capable of it.

That's exactly what he did, and the leviathan settled another couple of feet as he prepared her. It was like watching the end of *The Flying Enterprise* on a cinema newsreel, except that no one put *her* out of her misery, did they? The Army is exceptionally good at blowing things up: from a quarter of a mile away they made a very satisfying bang . . . which was followed by a number of others as the blank ammo went up in sympathy, and a black cloud of oily smoke. Everyone looked happy except Sergeant Owen, his driver and two men. They looked as if they'd lost a friend. Then we went back, and filled the hole in with spades. That took a couple of hours, and everyone took a shot. I needn't have worried about an excuse for Smart Alec, since the tankies needed me and my jeep to get their tankless crew back to civilization anyway – they would have fried riding on the tank hulls.

We drove out of the blue, and back onto the black stuff two days later, and an hour down the road came across Smart Alec's little convoy waiting for us. I swapped the jeep for the old Austin again. Trigger hopped down at the Deversoir turn-off; we stood in the road and shook hands. Peter Clare also came back to shake hands with me. We didn't say much as an insistent bleating horn from Smart's jeep contracted the goodbyes.

Clare said, 'This was an interesting trip, sir, but don't take it to heart. We get them right sometimes.'

'I know you do, Sergeant. A lot of that crap was out of your control.' I regretted the phrase as soon as it came out. He grinned.

Trigger said, 'So long, sir. See you in Ish sometime.' I'll swear that the word *Charlie* was on the end of his tongue.

I had to queue at the Deversoir gate behind a line of Water Carriers – Commers, I think – and as I drove the old Austin up to its slot behind the stores shed I felt kinda blue.

I needed a bath and a beer. Let's run that again, and put the words the other way round: first things first.

PART THREE

Snap, Crackle and Pop

Chapter Seventeen

Love me or leave me

When I awoke the tent was beginning to light up with the morning. A shadow passed the tent wall silhouetted by the early sun. It was low, slinky and lion-shaped.

Nancy lay on one side on his camp bed, his head propped up by hand and elbow. He was watching me.

He said, 'Hello, Charlie.'

He was wearing exactly the same clothes I had last seen him in. They looked OK, except maybe a little charred around the edges. He smelt of gasoline and cooked pork, which was a smell I was familiar with – a very pink smell.

I was so tired that I literally couldn't lift a limb. I managed, 'I'm still asleep, aren't I?'

'If you say so, old boy. I wish I was.'

'Go away. I've seen things like you before. You're dead.'

'Got it in one. Dead and gone to Heaven.'

'What's Heaven like?'

'Just like the Muslims tell us; all wine and willing women – they have a much better Heaven than us, so I chose theirs.'

'What happened to you?'

'I don't quite know. I was looking down, fiddling with a camera, when it happened.'

'When what happened?'

'When I died; just like that – I never felt a thing.'

'Where's your aircraft?'

'Where do aircraft usually go when they die? Buggered if I know.'

'You know what I mean, Oliver.'

'Yes, but I'm trying hard not to think about it. Somewhere out in the Sinai, I suppose.'

'What do you want?'

'Apart from your company? Nothing much . . . nice to say à bientôt, though, don't you think?'

'Nothing else?'

'I'd prefer you to get your hands on my photographs before anyone else does . . .'

'Where are they?'

But I was losing him. He shimmered as if a series of invisible waves ran through his image. I yawned. It was the first movement I had been capable of.

Nansen whispered, 'Bye, Charlie. Until the next time. À la prochaine.' I didn't want there to be a bloody next time. I blinked slowly, and he vanished. The bed was empty. Two blankets neatly folded at its foot. *Who did that?* I thought, and was helpless to prevent myself drifting into deeper sleep. The smell was still there, and my mind turned back in upon itself.

A few hours later I *did* wake up. I still had the taste of beer in my mouth. Someone was outside the tent calling my name.

'Charlie. Are you in there, Charlie?' Daisy.

'Yes. Give me a minute.'

'Are you decent?'

'I said, give me a minute.'

I pulled on the spare shorts and shirt I kept in the small locker, and then opened the tent flap. The daylight dazzled me: I would never get used to it.

Daisy asked, 'Ugh. What's that horrid smell? Have you been cooking in there?' I didn't answer so she added, 'Mr Watson is in wing commander form again this morning, and is asking for you. I think that you're in trouble again.'

'Make an excuse for me — say twenty minutes? I haven't washed yet. Any news about what happened to Oliver?'

'No. I wonder what's happened to his photos.'

I remembered what he'd said in my dream. 'What photos?'

She didn't reply immediately, then, 'I think he was planning to set up an exhibition of photographs from the Canal Zone when he got back. He thought it might get him a job with a news or photo agency.'

'He never told me that.'

'. . . maybe I was mistaken.' She looked away, and rubbed an eye. 'Speck of sand; there's a bit of a breeze this morning.' It was kinder to leave it at that. 'Anyway, I brought you this. It arrived the day before yesterday.'

She handed me a postcard of a pretty girl in a spotted bathing suit. In one corner of the picture were the masthead words from the magazine *Tit-Bits* . . . it must have been given out free with the mag. It was addressed to me, but all the message area bore was the imprint of two lipsticked lips. The UK postmark was too obscured to make out a place name. Silly really, but my heart lifted immediately. I didn't know who it was from, but somebody out there liked me. When I ducked my head back inside the tent Nancy's smell had gone.

'I suppose you're expecting some leave after that shambles?' Watson said. So far there had been no complaints, and he'd offered me a mug of char. I was worried about that.

'I wouldn't mind, sir. What I *would* like is to get on with whatever job you've brought us out here to do, and then go home.'

'Wouldn't we all; but be patient. It's coming. Just wait for us to get the hardware and bodies together.'

'I thought it was urgent.'

'It is, but that aeroplane has been out there nearly eight years now. Another month won't make any difference.'

'What's my role in the operation, sir?'

'Identify the bally thing to begin with, and after that make yourself as useful as possible until we fetch you out. I'll make sure you have a usable radio.'

'Who's in charge?'

'You can be, if you like, but I'd leave it to Hudd if I was you: he's good at this sort of thing.'

'Just what sort of thing is it, sir?'

'An irregular sort of thing.'

'I don't think I like Hudd.'

'Hudd doesn't like you either. Thinks you're a bit of a girl.'

We slurped tea at each other: a period of relative calm.

Then he asked, 'You didn't really hurl shite all over your patrol commander last week, did you?' I heard Daisy giggle from her den in the side room. 'Shut up, Daisy; it's not funny.' Then he added for my benefit, 'I have a suggestion from a Major Manners that you should face charges.'

'What is it, sir, *conduct prejudicial*?'

'No, not quite as bad as that – *conduct unbecoming*. You could end up back in the ranks again.'

'Frankly, sir, that could come as a relief. Guilty as charged.'

'But then it would be difficult to send you home. As an Other Ranks reservist you'd probably have to do the three full years out here.'

Bollocks! 'I'm innocent I tell you!' I tried to sound like Eccles, from *The Goon Show*. I heard Daisy giggle again. This time he didn't correct her. His grin cracked his face.

'Why don't you tell me what happened, my boy? I've been looking forward to this since the signal came in.'

I told him. He giggled a lot, just like Daisy. Despite what Hudd thought, it was Watson who sounded like a girl, not me. Then he went to his cupboard, and poured us a couple of drinks. The sun wasn't over the yardarm yet, but it was readying itself for a bit of a jump.

'I'd like to propose a toast,' he said. 'To the RAF dropping the Brown Jobs in the shite for once.'

'What about me, sir?'

'Promoted. Flying Officer at least, I should think, once they hear about this back at Command. The story's all over the Canal Zone, after all. I heard it before you got back. You'll probably get a medal.'

'You mean it's OK?'

'I mean that I shall have to teach Major Manners some manners. Something to do with his man leading a patrol into jeopardy, and unnecessarily exposing them to enemy fire. It won't come to anything of course. They want the problem with that tank hushed up.'

'You heard about that, too?'

'My job: hearing things. Take a couple of days, if you like.'

'Can I have my fifty quid back yet?'

'No. I might keep it to pay for all my drink you swallow, and to take Daisy out on the skite one night.' I suppose that I should have been grateful that God was back in His heaven.

When I went to see Pat he did the usual thing of walking me down the stores shed away from his leader. The latter scowled but didn't complain. I guessed that Tobin had his hooks into him as well. Before I could ask him anything he asked for my bank book, and credited me another thirty-two quid which he signed off with a flourish.

'What was that for? I didn't think I had anything left to sell,' I asked him.

'Several KD uniforms, four pairs of working boots and another set of blankets. The Gyppo tailors love 'em.'

'I don't have them.'

'That's the point, Mr Bassett. We indent for the stuff you don't have, and flog them.'

'Won't Daisy figure out how much I'm using, and get worried?'

'Do you know how much knickers and ladies' pyjamas go for on the open market, sir?'

So Daisy was in on it as well.

'Can you give me some wog money? Thirty quid should do. I've got a bit of leave coming.'

'By this afternoon, sir, don't worry. But that's not what you came for . . . I can guess.'

'No. I want a gander in Mr Nansen's private locker. I'm sure you have a spare key.'

' 'ow could you ever be sure I'll keep *your* private things private, if I shows you his? It wouldn't be ethical . . . he's only been gone a few days.'

'I won't care when I'm dead, Pat, and Nancy's *dead*. Gone to heaven. I met him in a dream last night, and he told me so.'

RAF guys are a superstitious lot. He said, 'You don't mean that, sir.'

'Yes, I do. He's bloody dead – cooked to a turn . . . and he told me to look in his locker,' I lied. 'I want to lift anything embarrassing out of there before the CO gets his mitts on it. I'll order you to, if you like.'

He gave up. 'That won't be necessary, sir. We're all in this together, aren't we?'

I left him all of Nansen's clothes, and there were a bloody sight more than you might imagine – interesting knick-knacks –

souvenirs he had picked up. A dozen unexposed rolls of film. Some bazaar leather suitcases and four rare bottles of Whyte and MacKay's. In the bottom of the capacious locker – which was the size of a small cupboard – I found a carved rosewood box with a barrel-shaped lid. It was about a foot deep, and a foot and a half long. It was full of long, flat cardboard boxes of photographs and negatives, and a couple of notebooks. I left him the chest, and took the contents away stuffed into a nice leather music case. Honours even. I even had that warm *mission accomplished* feeling when I walked back into the tent. When I sat down on my bed with them, I thought I heard Oliver say *Thanks*, but when I looked up I was alone. I wish dead people wouldn't do that.

I had looked in on Daisy as I passed back, and told her, 'I found Oliver's photographs; so no sweat,' but was unprepared for her reaction. She played an absolutely straight bat. These days a youngster wouldn't understand a cricketing metaphor, and would say she blanked me. In fact a youngster wouldn't understand the word *metaphor*, would they? Our language has become peculiarly uncomplicated over these last few years.

'What photographs?'

'The ones you were wondering about.'

'I don't remember that, Charlie.'

There was one of those pauses I play the music in. This time it was one of those wog songs 'Ah yaa zain', which means *Beautiful one*.

Daisy dropped her eyes first, so I said, 'Sorry. My mistake.' I could have said *I wasn't born yesterday*, *either* . . . but I was never that cruel. It did make me curious to see what I had.

I understood the problem as soon as I began to spread the pictures out on my bed. Nancy had a wonderful eye for his subject, no doubt about that. Very talented. Tired and ill-equipped British soldiers had never looked nobler, nor so tired or ill-equipped. Drunken matelots smashing up a bar in Port Said

looked just as unpleasant as we truly know them to be. A Red
Cap clubbing an Arab child looked just like a copper clubbing a
child. Nansen had created an invaluable historical record of Brits
at large in the Canal Zone, but not one the British War Office
would ever want to come to light. But that wasn't really a
problem, because I knew I would eventually figure out what to
do with them.

The real problem was that he'd photographed half the British
women in the Canal Zone, as well – and most of them had taken
their clothes off. Even a good number of Egyptian girls had fallen
under the spell of his fancy Leica camera. In ten minutes I saw
seven people I thought I'd met. Haye with an e was one of them,
and so was the corvette skipper's wife. I guessed that, if I
persevered, I'd find Daisy in there somewhere. I shoved them
quickly back into the case, and stuck it under my pillow. Christ!

I walked around with it for half a day, not daring to let it out
of my sight. Who else knew they existed? What I had on the end
of my arm was nothing less than a case full of dynamite, and Mrs
Bassett's son was bright enough to realize it. If I had been
Nansen, I might have come back from the dead myself; just to
find out what happened next.

I could have destroyed them all immediately, which might have
been the clever thing to do . . . or I could think before I acted,
for once. I needed to buy time, and that meant stashing them
where no other bugger could get their hands on them. And I had
nowhere safe to hide them. Pat would have a key to my allegedly
safe locker. If I asked Daisy to lock them away, she'd quickly
cotton on to what they were. I went to see my friendly SWO. I
reckoned he owed me one. He looked tired.

'Out last night, SWO?'

'A couple of wogs came through the wire, sir, and broke into
the pharmacy. We still don't know all that they got away with.

What can I do for you, Mr Bassett? Come to volunteer again? Almost nobody does, you know.'

'I've a couple of days' leave coming; I'll give you a night after that, if you like. No, I came to see if you could think of a solution to a little problem I have. I've got a pile of personal documents I don't want to fall into anyone else's hands when I'm away. I need to leave them safe and secure. I'm afraid they'd be nicked from my tent or my locker.'

'What about your CO?'

'I've thought about that. People are going in and out of his safe all of the time. I wouldn't rest happy . . .'

'Would they fit in a large dispatch envelope?'

'Yes, they would.'

'Put them inside a sealed envelope, inside a sealed dispatch envelope, and mail them to yourself "*addressee only*". They'll be kept at Base PO until you collect them.'

Now why didn't I think of that?

I sifted through the shots, and took out a few. Then I did as he'd said.

I trundled north on the RAF bus. The Regiment corporal was on the gate again, and recognized me through the window. He started what began as a salute, so I quickly grinned and waved back, and his salute turned into a waved hand. No hard feelings then.

I got off in the square at Ismailia and hoofed it to the Kettle. It was closed again, so I would have to use the back way in. A hurdy-gurdy man was grinding out Arabic tunes on a wind-up box in the street outside, and an ice-cream seller stood alongside him. I ate an ice cream, and listened to the monotonous musical howls before I nipped down the side alley. They watched me go with expressionless faces.

Yassine was seated at one of the round tables. One of the small bands was practising, and one of the girls danced sinuously around them for fun. The laughter was infectious – nothing like when they were doing it for clients. The noise was overwhelming, so David and I had to shout over it. The dust the dancer raised sparkled in the shafts of light pouring in from small high windows.

I slid into the seat opposite him. 'They are tremendous.'

'When they perform for themselves, yes. They used to be the old King's favourites.'

'Can you put me up for a couple of days?'

'Of course, but we'll have to be careful: the British authorities won't like it if they find out. Times are tense again, and I am closed down. Maybe for good this time.'

'I'm sorry about that. I didn't check the alert before I left. That's going to kill me one day.'

'You should have noticed all the brave British soldiers carrying their wooden clubs . . . but, God willing, you will have a long life, Charlie Bassett.'

One of his boys had brought us beers. I lifted mine and said, '. . . and you, David. Long life.' We toasted each other. The music, singing and dance built in a noisy crescendo, then stopped abruptly. The girl collapsed in front of the band, like a puppet whose strings had been cut. 'Will my things be safe here?'

'Of course not, but they will be safer than on any of your British bases.' It was the third time in minutes he had used the word *British* with a curled lip.

'You're not all that keen on the Brits at the moment?'

'You keep closing me down. Soon it will be impossible to trade.'

'I am sorry about that.'

He shrugged and muttered, 'Inshallah.' He was becoming an Arab again. Arabs were becoming Arabs again all over the Middle

East, and that was going to be a problem for us one day. I know I've said it before, but Lawrence of sodding Arabia has a lot to answer for.

Yassine gave me an airy room along the top corridor. The door looked a hundred years old, and closed with a sliding wooden bar on the inside. There was an old, upright fretted cupboard and a bed large enough for six, covered by carpets. A creaky fan revolved overhead. It would do.

The music filtered up, a slower number with a lot of hand clapping. I asked him, 'What's that called?'

'"*Mnishebak*" – it means *The view from my window*; it's very romantic. You like it?'

A male tenor voice suddenly weaved through it, sounding like the muezzin calling his people to prayer.

'Very much. If we listened to each other's music more often, we wouldn't fight as much, would we?'

He put his arm around my shoulders. It was like being hugged by a gorilla.

'Maybe we make a good Arab of you yet, Charlie Bassett.' Why did so many people want to turn me into something else?

'No fear, my foreskin's staying exactly where it's supposed to be.'

We could both laugh at that. Next he called me a cab to get me out to the compound at El Kirsh, but warned me not to get into any cab not arranged by him.

'But this guy's safe?'

'Anything happens to you, I cut his throat. He understands.'

'Thank you, David. I owe you a lot.'

'You will pay me back a lot as well, never fear.'

Haye with an e was on duty, so I said I'd see her later, and walked up to see if Mrs Holroyd was in. She was in, and in a fine bleached cotton frock. Her fine gold ankle chain glinted in the sunlight when she stepped out onto the veranda. I suddenly wanted her. Why hadn't that happened before?

She said, 'Oh, it's you!'

'I'm afraid so. I can go away if you're expecting anyone else.'

She laughed, '*Here*? Come on in.' She had been listening to soft, steady jazz on the radio, and had left it on. Not long after that we began to call it 'modern jazz', which seems incongruous nearly sixty years later. She had been drinking something like a Martini from one of those parasol-shaped Martini glasses, and offered me one.

When I was sitting opposite her, glass in hand, she asked me, 'Passing visit, or deliberate?'

'Deliberate.' I sipped the drink. The gin and vermouth mix seemed the authentic thing.

'To what end?'

'I wanted you.'

She crossed her legs, and tugged the dress over her knees. Her skin was a kind of golden-brown colour.

'Didn't we try that a few weeks ago and decide it wouldn't work? What's changed?'

'When I saw the hair on your belly look so fine and soft I knew I had to touch it.' I didn't actually mean *belly*, but it seemed the politer option. Not bad for a conversation stopper, Charlie, but make sure you're not close enough to cop a slap in the moosh. Her mouth popped open. A nice little round *o* with just a trace of pastel-pink lipstick.

'But you've *never* seen me . . . !'

'Not until a day ago. Now I want to see you again.'

I fumbled in my small pack until I found the envelope I was looking for. Prints and negs. I handed it to her, and she studied the three photographs for a long while before saying anything.

Then, quietly: 'Where did you get these?'

'I rescued them. Nancy copped it in that Meteor crash last week. I recovered his photographs because someone suggested that it would be a kind thing to do.' It wasn't quite a lie, but I wasn't sure she would believe the truth.

'I wondered if that had been him.'

'I'm sorry.'

She didn't say any more for a few minutes. She turned the photographs around and looked at them from different angles, but I don't think she was seeing anything. Maybe memories.

Then she asked me, 'Are there any more prints or negatives?'

'Of course not. Not as far as I know, anyway. It's up to you what you do with them.'

'. . . and you wanted to see me like that?'

'I've thought of precious little else since I saw them. You can slap me if you like.'

She looked down with a small smile, and shook her head. The gesture was so slight I almost missed it, and I went on, 'Look, seeing you in those photos was an accident, but one that I'll never regret as long as I live.'

I followed her out of the room, along a short corridor and into a shady bedroom.

What she said as we began to undress was, 'Only once.'

We stayed there for the rest of the afternoon. Eventually we lay smoking a cigarette between us, and allowing the sweat to dry on our bodies. From the radio a pianist was steering out 'On Green Dolphin Street' – I've probably already told you it is one of my favourites.

Jill asked me again, 'Do you have any more photos?'

'Of you? No, I told you.'

'I meant of anyone else.'

'Yes.'

'Will you give theirs back, too?'

'If I can.'

'. . . and use the same line on them, as you've used on me? Carry on where Oliver left off?' That was interesting.

'I hope not. But if I do, it won't mean the same as it did with you.'

'I didn't disappoint you then? Sometimes the reality doesn't match up to the dream.'

I bent to tickle the point of one of her breasts with my tongue . . .

'. . . and sometimes it exceeds all expectations. You are the most beautiful woman I have ever seen.'

'Oliver never said that.'

I did it again. 'Then let me say it for him.'

Later we spoke again. I started with, 'Can I ask you why you did it? Let Oliver photograph you like that, I mean?'

'I've been asking myself that ever since you produced them. It seemed very natural at the time. Oliver had a way of looking at you that made you want to take your clothes off.'

'X-ray eyes? Is that what you mean?'

'No, almost exactly the opposite. Some men strip you naked with their eyes as they look at you. That's mostly pretty horrid. Oliver just looked at you, and you knew he loved what he saw: it made you want to take your clothes off, and show him the rest. Afterwards he would get his cameras out. I wonder how he did that.'

'I wonder if he *did* know he was doing it?'

She snuggled into my shoulder and said, 'You know? That was a very perceptive thing to say, Charlie.' Minutes later her breathing became deep and even, just like the snow on the Feast of Stephen . . . and she went to sleep. All men value different characteristics in women, but, if you think about it, a woman can pay you no greater compliment than the simple act of being willing to go to sleep alongside you. Whatever you do, in whatever walk of life, no one ever shows more confidence in you than that. I slept too, and it was later in the evening I left her, and slipped up the road.

Haye with an e laughed when I gave her her photographs.

'Oh God: that was such a lovely night. Oliver was a very bony man, you know. After you'd made love with him, you were somehow bruised all over.'

'You don't mind me having seen them, then?'

'Of course not.'

'. . . and it won't ever help you decide to sleep with me?'

'Of course not, again. Why should I want to do that? You're much more fun at arm's length. Some men are, you know.'

'Every time I look at you, it will be difficult to see you other than as naked as in those photographs.'

'Wizard! I know. I'll sit there, and watch you squirming. I told you you're much more fun at arm's length. Coffee or tea?'

We drank tea and toasted hot cross buns that somebody's maid had made too many of. Then we drank gin with limes. It wasn't the make-believe rough stuff, so maybe a stock had come in from somewhere. When it was late she lit the fire in their small sitting room. Not because it was cold, but to make us cosy. I said, 'Another woman told me that Oliver only had to look at you for you to want to take your clothes off for him.'

'Mmm, she was probably right. It didn't seem to take long before I was in the buff.'

'What can I do to achieve the same effect? It would make life much easier for me.'

'I don't think you can, Charlie. Anyway, you have a very different effect on women; hasn't anyone told you?'

'No, and if it's nasty, don't you tell me either.'

'It's not. It's rather sweet.'

'Well, then?'

'The way you look at me sometimes makes me want to make love: desperately, violently and quickly; sometimes you actually make my stomach churn – funny isn't it? If I was married to someone else, I suspect I'd want you even more.'

'So why *don't* we for heaven's sake? I'm here, aren't I?'

'I don't know, but speaking for my sex as it were, our response to you *scares* us; so we back off. Then, having escaped your evil clutches we inevitably jump straight into the arms of the next man who asks. Maybe for a kind of emotional safety.'

'Are you saying that not long ago you wanted me so badly you went to bed with someone else?'

'Precisely.'

I stood up, and probably pouted like Brigitte Bardot.

'I'm bloody well going home,' I told her.

'Don't be silly. You've missed the last bus, so there's no safe way of getting back to AS. Anyway, you've already made love today . . . so don't be greedy.'

'How can you possibly tell that?' I asked grumpily.

'Because your eyelids are still blue. Everyone's eyelids are blue afterwards, haven't you noticed? It makes me want to kiss them.'

That's what she did. I loved the soft pressure of her lips against my eyes, but it didn't make much difference: I slept on the settee. Her Aussie pal came off duty at three, and woke me up coming in. I got up and wrapped a sheet around my body.

She said, 'Sorry. I didn't know anyone was here.'

'That's all right. I wasn't sleeping deeply. Are you going to have a cuppa before you go to bed?'

'Yes. Do you fancy sitting up for half an hour and letting me natter? I've had a terrible day.'

I'd had rather a good one, so a bit of payback wouldn't be all that out of order,

'OK,' I said.

*

Susan did something I hadn't seen before. She heated milk in a pan on the stove and poured it over our breakfast cornflakes. They immediately went soggy, but the creamy yellow smell that lifted from them was sublime.

'Good?' she asked: mouth full.

'Very good.' Mouth even fuller.

'Did I rather brutally turn down a request to sleep with you last night? Sorry; those words came out mixed up a bit, but you know what I mean.'

'Yeah. You didn't give the suggestion much thought.'

'Never say die, Charlie. There's always a next time!'

'You're a cow.'

'God, and don't I know it; but I enjoy it so much.' Big, big wicked smile. I believed her. Maybe she was a mornings person after all.

'Can we talk about something serious?' I still had something on my mind.

'If you must . . .'

'Do you remember us once talking about the things you could do, and couldn't do to get someone into bed? If you were staying honest, that is.'

'I remember *you* wanting to talk about it. What of it?'

'If one of the women who I returned Oliver's photographs to took me to bed as a finder's reward, which side of the moral border would that lie on?'

'I should say . . .' She paused, and gave it a thought. 'I should say that it sat exactly *on* the border, Charlie. Could be OK; could be pretty bad. It would all depend what you thought of each other afterwards. Any good?'

'It will have to be, won't it?'

'Is that what happened?'

'I'm not going to tell you.'

*

I turned down her offer of lazing around for the morning, and walked back down to the main gate for a secure bus. Outside the Holroyds' bungalow I dropped a step, and Jill stepped out on to the veranda. She was dressed the same as the day before, and smiled. That was a relief.

She said, 'No point you coming in: this is the maid's day.'

I grinned, 'You warned me "only once", anyway.'

'Would it be OK to change our minds occasionally?' Of course it bloody would.

'It would make me the happiest guy out here. I'd sign on again!'

'Good, that's settled. Wait here a minute. I have something for you.' When she came back, she handed me one of the photographs. When I turned it over there was a lipstick imprint on the back: perhaps that was fashionable all of a sudden. 'Make sure that no one else sees it. I don't know why I'm taking such a silly risk.'

'No risk at all. It'll be in my shirt pocket every minute of the day.'

'You don't love me, or anything messy like that, do you?'

'No, not yet. If it becomes inevitable, do you want me to run away?'

'Yes, Charlie. As quickly as you can.'

There's nothing quite like being told, is there?

I did some shopping on Main Street: ordered a couple of linen suits made up. They would be delivered to the Kettle before I left the next day. An MP spotted me in the street, called me over and demanded to see my leave chit. After he handed it back to me he reached into the back of his Land-Rover and gave me a pickaxe handle.

'Don't go out without one of these again, sir. If you gets into trouble, some poor bugger like me has to risk his life getting you out again.'

I hadn't looked at the problem that way. 'I won't, Sergeant. I don't know why I overlooked it this time.'

'You're not the first, sir. Hand it back in at your gate; then someone else gets the use of it.' It was a battered old thing with a sweat-marked grip. I didn't like the look of the stains around its head, and felt awkward carrying it into the back of the Kettle.

Yassine grimaced when he saw it. 'You must have joined the British Army, Charlie.'

'Take the fucking thing away, David, and burn it. I can't stand the sight of it.'

'Good, we are still agreeing on some things.'

'We have business interests in common, and agree on *most* things. Have you fixed up your business ties to Bozey yet?'

'Your Mr Borland? Yes. He drives a good bargain.'

'You mean a hard bargain.'

'No, I mean a good bargain. The sort that leaves both sides feeling satisfied.'

'I trust him.'

'So do I; and *we* trust each other, despite the politics all around us.'

'If your boy could oblige with a couple of beers, I shall drink to that, David.'

He did, and we did. Yassine asked me, 'Are you going out again?'

'Not tonight. I thought I'd stop in, and watch the floor show . . . I presume that the back door will stay open, and the show will go on?'

'In the best Hollywood tradition? Of course.'

'So I shall eat and drink here tonight if that's OK? And also pay my whack. That would make me feel good – a part of the place.'

'As you wish, Charlie. Tonight will be a good night to stay in.' I thought he was talking about the floor show.

He bloody wasn't.

The riot started at about nine in the evening, and rocked its way around Ismailia for the next few hours. They stayed clear of the main administration areas of the town, and the wealthier suburbs. That was interesting. Yassine and I stood at one of the Kettle's third-floor windows and watched the houses in the poor Arab quarter burning.

'I don't understand,' I told him. 'They're burning the wrong houses.'

'The poor always do. They riot in their own streets because they feel safer there, and when they lose control they end up burning their own houses. With their enemies – the rich and the foreigners – living all around them, they destroy, instead, what little they have themselves. It happens in poor communities all over the world. It must be a form of madness.'

'Like a scorpion stinging itself to death if you put it in a ring of fire?'

'Have you seen that?'

'Some of the airmen at the base do it when they are bored. It's cruel and stupid.'

'The poor *are* cruel and stupid. It's all we allow them to be.'

'There's a new government since you tossed King Farouk out. Won't things be any different for them now?'

'Marginally. But the wealthy will restrict what the government can do of course. The differential must be maintained. When the poor become less poor, the rich will want to become

even richer. Within a year the newspapers will be calling for
Farouk's return.'

'What was he like, this King Farouk?'

'Fat and greedy, like me.'

'You're depressing me, David. Let's go and have another
drink.'

When I went to bed at one I found Mariam there, and because I
am weak-willed, I let her stay. But after Jill, her body seemed so
spare, so juvenile, that all we did was sleep. Until two hours
later when Yassine rushed into my room with two other women,
and some Arab clothes over his arm.

'Get up, Charlie, get up; the English are here. They are
searching us . . .'

'Uh . . . I'll use the back door.'

'Too late: they have it covered. Here, put these on.' He threw
me the clothes. 'Quick, quick.'

The main garment was like a djellaba, but more voluminous,
and there was a headdress that went over my head like a sack,
leaving only a slit for my eyes. Then he ushered me into a corner,
pushed me down, and pushed the three women around me. That
included Mariam, who was still naked.

'You are terrified of the soldiers, understand? All of you . . .
terrified,' he hissed, and made himself scarce. The women murmured. The noise of the search – doors banging, voices raised
– drew closer. Then there was the voice of a squaddie loud
inside the room.

'Jackpot, boys – I've found the bints!'

I risked a glance. He was a redcap and a private: a big florid
fellow. In some places he would have been called a constable. I
saw the way he was eyeing Mariam, and found that I was gripping
my small pistol under the rags I wore. How had that got there?

The women made a great show of whimpering and wailing, and one of them drew her clothes around Mariam's nakedness. Then there was another voice in the room, and I risked another look. A young corporal.

He looked harassed, and snarled, 'Trust you, Nesbit. I told you to stay away from the women. Bugger off and search the next room.'

'Search the women first, sir?'

'Of course not. You heard me; bugger off.' Nesbit, bless him, left at the second telling. The corporal had to raise his voice to make himself heard to the women.

'Don't be scared; you won't be harmed. We are looking for terrorists and Europeans. Have you seen any tonight?' I felt, rather than saw, Mariam vigorously shaking her head. He glanced around; there was nowhere obvious for anyone to hide . . . so he tried a reassuring smile, which came out as a bit of a death's-head grimace. 'I'm sorry you were frightened, ladies. Fasten the door behind me – I will leave a mark on it, and my men will not return. Do you understand?'

Mariam nodded, and stood up. The corporal copped an eyeful, as was intended, and backed out. Mariam closed the door and slid the big wooden draw-bolt across, then crossed the room and got back into the bed. The women sat on its edge, and all three chatted quietly away as if nothing out of the ordinary had happened. Who knows, maybe it hadn't?

I squeezed into the space on the floor between the bed and the cupboard, as if I was still scared – if I kept my head down it would afford me some cover if the bastards came back. Once in the next twenty minutes the door was rattled from the outside, followed by a raw guffaw. It sounded like the man Nesbit again, and I promised myself to do something about him if I ever came across him on the outside. After twenty minutes the noise of the search began to retreat. Car doors slammed. Engines revved outside in the street. And then there was silence.

A few minutes later Yassine was back in the room. His grin split his face from side to side. 'You make a good woman, Charlie – you know that? It wouldn't take much for me to find you attractive!' He pulled the two other women up from the bed, and put his arms around them. One giggled.

I pulled off the women's clothes over my head, and asked him, 'Can we carry on this conversation tomorrow? I'm shagged out.'

He grinned again and wheeled his charges about. With one hand on the bum of one of them, he managed to wave to me with the other. As they threaded through the door one of the women laughed, and then the other. This time I made sure I bolted the door.

Mariam sat up, smiling, and asked me, 'What was it like; being a woman for a change?'

'I don't know. I wouldn't know until I was flat on my back with someone bouncing up and down on my belly, would I?'

'We can find out, Charlie.'

I've told you before: I'm weak-willed as far as women are concerned. When I remember Mariam now, I remember a lithe girl who always put her heart and soul into it. Several other bits as well. The problem with trying to turn over a new leaf is that it's often worse than the one you hid under before.

'You knew the riot was going to happen, didn't you?' Black coffee and brioches – very French. There are a lot of very French things along the Canal Zone. That's because the bloody Frogs actually dug the thing in the first place. It would also explain some of the unnatural tricks the local girls could turn.

'One hears things,' Yassine told me. 'One can hardly help it. Mainly pillow talk. The men talk to my girls . . .'

'. . . and your girls talk to you, and you sell what they tell you to whoever wants to buy it. I get the picture. It sounds just like Berlin. I could learn to like it here if it wasn't so full of soldiers.'

'I knew we'd get on.'

'Thank you for saving me from that British police patrol last night, but I still don't know why you did it.'

'Because when the authorities close me down this club becomes out of bounds. Any British serviceman caught here is arrested, and the closure of the club is extended . . . and the girls are dragged away for medical tests, which is humiliating for them. The British harass me. They will not be satisfied until they have closed me down.'

'What will you do then?'

'I have other clubs, but it will be a pity. I have good memories of this place.'

'Has someone got it in for you? Something personal?'

'Mr Watson told me that "prevailed has *prevailed*", then he laughed at me and said I should work it out for myself. Perhaps you can tell me: you know how Englishmen think.'

'We try *never* to, David – that's the key to understanding us. Tell me something about Mariam before I go. Has she any . . . well, *expectations* of me?'

He laughed as if I'd asked a stupid question. You should know by now that it wouldn't have been the first time.

'Did you give her a present?'

'I left her money: it's the only thing I had.'

'Send her a proper present – something made of gold to remember you by when she is an old lady. That will please her . . . but she has no romantic aspirations, if that is what you mean. She is saving up to get married to a nice Christian Lebanese boy, who happens to think that she is a maid in a very correct household.'

'Will he be disappointed?'

'On his wedding night, after his first surprise at the range of her abilities, I should imagine he will be delighted . . . and after that, in thrall to her as much as the rest of her friends are. What you must understand is that she knows she is getting more out of her relationship with you than you are. She is in charge; not you.' He was actually stifling a laugh.

I asked him, 'What?'

'I probably shouldn't tell you, but before you returned yesterday afternoon she asked me a question about you.'

'What?'

'She asked *Do you think Charlie has any expectations of me? It would be sad to disappoint him.* See: almost the same words, and the same concerns. You really are two very honourable young persons. Maybe you should develop expectations, after all.'

I knew that in the street outside they would be clearing up after the night before: and, in the Arab quarter, houses damaged beyond repair would be being pulled down and rebuilt.

'What was the riot about?'

'It was a protest: but not serious. Only two killed. Partly to tell the Brits to get off the Canal, and partly to celebrate a pocket rebellion that happened here last year. Many policemen who belonged to the Muslim Brotherhood were killed.'

'I heard about that. Didn't a mob kill some Britons, and then take cover in a clinic of some kind, and a police station? We had to bring the tanks up to stop the fighting.'

He sighed and said, 'If you say so, Charlie.'

'Wasn't that the way it happened?'

'No. Not exactly. That's not the story they tell on the streets.'

'What then?'

'Some Europeans were killed, and the killers should have been arrested and tried for murder. Your authorities failed to do that: they reacted far too slowly. The mob got out of hand, and the authorities found they had a small-scale insurrection on their hands. When the tanks eventually arrived, your commander found that they had been issued with the wrong ammunition. If he had assaulted the buildings with normal high-explosive shells, the casualties would still have been high, but maybe less than half of the eventual number.'

'What did he use?'

'Armour-piercing shells: I believe you call them APs. They smashed the buildings and the people inside them to pieces. What is more, it is suggested that he ordered his crews to fire off *all* their ammunition, and take none back to barracks, in order to cover the mistake that he had made. Egypt will never forgive you for that day's work, Charlie. It will become the first day of the end of the British presence in the Canal Zone.'

'Do you really believe that?' It seemed such an incongruous thing to say. After all, we had a hundred and fifty thousand representatives of the most highly mechanized army in history, parked on his lawn.

'Yes, I do, Charlie. If I was a good chess player I would tell you the endgame is coming on. From now on it will be impossible for any individual in the Middle East not to take sides, and one day one of those sides will be bigger than yours, and will shove you out.'

One of his boys poured us more coffee. I asked him, 'What you just told me about the tank action. Do you know that to be true for a fact, or is it one of those political myths that are repeated so often they become history?'

'Truly, Charlie, I don't know and I don't care. It doesn't matter any more. Martyrs win wars for you even before battle is joined. If ordinary Egyptians are repeating and retelling the story already, you will *lose*, eventually, and they will win. They will rise, and you will have to decide to leave, or create a bloodbath.

I think you will leave, and if I want to stay, I shall have to cut my cloth accordingly. I like that turn of phrase, don't you?'

'Will we still be partners?'

'Of course; and friends.'

'Then, as a friend, are you able to give me the names and addresses of a person I could trust in either Istanbul or Kurdistan, if I was to find myself there alone and without friends?'

He frowned before he replied, 'Yes, I can do that. They would be businessmen, like us. They would want favours in return for helping you.'

'I assumed that. More importantly, would you do that for me without asking me why I am making this request?'

'Naturally, Charlie . . . but you must take care of yourself. Mariam would probably stick a knife in me if I allowed you to come to harm.'

'I'll tell her not to.'

'OK, deal.'

We shook hands over the breakfast table. I told him one more thing, which was: 'When that MP burst into the room last night, I found that under that delightful costume you provided I was clutching my pistol. It wasn't until afterwards that I realized that if he had taken one step towards the girls, I would have shot him down without a thought.'

'Then you came close to choosing sides, Charlie – always dangerous. But I'm glad you didn't shoot. If you had, we would have had to kill all of them. Sad to think of the families without fathers, yes?' He was probably telling me to grow up.

I mooched around the club all morning, keeping out of sight of the Egyptian policemen barring entry. Mariam came down and played draughts with me while the club staff cleaned around us.

I said, 'Your eyelids are blue.'

'I colour them.'

'No: it means that you made love last night. Our eyelids become blue after we have made love.'

'How do you know that?'

'A lady told me.'

'She must love you very much to tell you secrets like that.'

'No . . . I don't think so.'

She turned her head away and smiled.

I also solved a problem for David Yassine. I found myself doodling the word *prevailed* again and again on a beer mat. Parts of it began to look familiar.

When I worked it out, I waved him over and said, 'Are you familiar with the English word *anagram*?'

'Of course I am. Besides, it's not an English word; it's Greek.'

'Doesn't matter – look at this.' I wrote the word out afresh, *prevailed* – and then wrote the words *evil padre*, after it.

'What does that mean?'

'If it means that the local Church is after you, old son, then you've had it. Fucked. Pack up your tent and scoot back to Beirut.'

'No,' he told me, 'I think I'll stick around, now I know what the problem is.'

Chapter Eighteen

Jazz me blues

'Did the tanks really use APs to winkle out the terrorists in Ismailia last year?'

'I told you not to ask questions, Charlie. It's the sort of thing that gets you noticed.' Watson looked cross.

'That's not an answer, sir.'

'It's the nearest bloody thing you're going to get. I warned you, *drop* it.'

'Have they found Oliver Nansen yet?'

'No, and nobody's looking any more. The wreck will turn up somewhere sooner or later.'

I realized that he'd just spoken my own epitaph as well. If I didn't come back from one of his little jaunts, they would forget me too, until my body turned up somewhere sooner or later. Under his avuncular exterior he was as cold as a shark.

He continued. 'There's a band over from the UK on at the cinema tonight: I got you a couple of tickets so you could take Daisy. Not my kind of thing.' He handed me a flyer for the Ivy Benson All Girls Orchestra. I didn't know how well orchestral music would go down with the troops, but the all-women element would guarantee a decent crowd. Maybe I'd misjudged him. Maybe not.

As I left he said, 'Get your things together; you'll be off in a few days.'

'I thought you said it wasn't urgent, sir.'

'It is now. There are some other sods out there looking for it. You'll be off as soon as Hudd gets here.'

'Where is he at present, or aren't I supposed to ask?'

'Where the hell do you think Australians are most of the time? Bloody Australia of course! Best place for 'em! Sometimes I think you're a bit thick, Charlie.'

I looked in on Daisy as I left him, handed her an envelope on which I had printed her name, but said aloud, in case Watson was looking, 'Could you post that for me?' and, 'See you tonight if you want to hear this band.'

'Love to, Charlie. I've run out of books and magazines.' I wondered if she'd realized what she now had in her hand: she hadn't run out of pictures to look at, anyway.

She played 'Jazz me blues', and the notes from her silver cornet fell around the open-air camp cinema like silver raindrops. There wasn't an empty seat in the house.

This was the new cinema, built closer to the centre of Deversoir, and its periphery was patrolled by cops during the shows. The old one had been built too close to the fence line, and too low apparently, so the wogs kept lobbing hand grenades into it, and spoiling the films. The WD never likes to admit a mistake, so the first counter to that had been to put a wire fence around the top of it, but the Gyppoes responded by using old-fashioned slings to get the grenades over the top. It's a nice picture: a people's army taking on a mechanized military monster with the same sort of sling David used against Goliath, and forcing a retreat. The Gaza Palestinians are using exactly the same slings against Israeli tanks today.

Watson had done us proud, of course; we had a seat in the

front row on the end of a line of staff officers, and what goes around comes around, because Dr Jazz spotted me as soon as she came on stage. She winked very obviously at me as she sat down, and from behind me a great roar went up. Someone behind dug me in the back, and someone else patted me on the shoulder.

Daisy whispered, 'Does she *know* you?'

'I met her once, in Croydon of all places. She became intimately acquainted with my bum. People usually go to Croydon to die of boredom.'

'*I* come from Croydon. I went to grammar school there.'

'In which case I take that back. With you and Dr Jazz both recommending it, it must be the most interesting place in Blighty.'

'Is that her real name?'

'No: I never learned that. She was a doctor at my medical. Later that night I caught her playing jazz in an old pub named the Dog and Bull – it's wonderful how pub names stick in your mind.'

That was all we had time for. They kicked off with 'I cover the waterfront', and the boys went totally mad. I suppose that I'd earlier associated the word *orchestra* with classical music. I couldn't have got further from the truth. These girls played jazz and swing so hard that Major Glenn Miller himself would have snapped up any of them for his USAAF band. I can recall now looking up at the soft night sky, and those billions of stars, and letting the jazz wash over us, and making a mental note to create some memories of the night. They played 'Ladybird' and 'Jealousy'. Thousands and thousands of honeyed notes surrendered to the night sky. I wondered what it sounded like from beyond the camp's boundaries – out in the blue.

The doctor herself actually sought me out in the beer queue at the interval.

She said, 'Sarah Drake,' as she held out her hand. 'We were

never introduced before. The girls call me *Ducky.*' She knew my name, of course, and I introduced Daisy, who looked a bit overawed.

I asked Sarah, 'What happened to doctoring?'

'It can wait. If you had to choose between this, and sticking needles in hairy bums all day long, what would *you* do?'

'I see your point. Depends how clean the bums were, I suppose, and whether I liked inflicting pain. I even thought you were a bit of an Irma when I met you. You're a very good musician, you know.'

'I know darling; you don't have to tell me. How do you think I got the job? What do you do over here anyway? I remember you were a radio operator, but I haven't seen any aeroplanes since I've been here.'

'I skive mainly, but we do have a few kites if you know where to look for them.'

We'd arrived at the counter, and I paid for six beers. They could have been larger, but at least they were cold.

I asked Ducky, 'How many shows are you doing?'

'Three in the camps, one in a Kiwi transit camp up in Port Said, and a few of us are playing at an embassy reception in Cairo next week. We'll catch up with the main band in Cyprus, and do a couple of shows there.'

'Busy schedule.'

'Not busy enough: most of the girls in the band will be pregnant by the end of this tour, if they're not careful.'

'But not you?' I chanced it.

'Trust me, darling, I'm a doctor.' And I'm Charlie's Aunt!

'You fancy joining us for a drink afterwards?'

'Sorry, Charlie; some old wing commander's already booked me. Nice meeting you again, though. Nice to know the jabs I gave you kept you alive.'

The stage bell was ringing for round two. I said, 'The one you didn't nearly killed me.'

She frowned and said, 'Say again . . . ?'

'Never mind. I'll tell you next time.' We split. Crowds of KDs swirled between us, and Daisy and I concentrated on getting our seats back without spilling the beer.

I said, 'You were a bit quiet, Daisy.'

'She's very glamorous: I didn't know what to say.'

'She sits down to pee, Daisy: just like you. I shouldn't let any of the rest of it bother you.' I was reverting, wasn't I? The magic dust must have been wearing off.

Daisy was quiet, but as the beautiful band filed back on stage she whispered, 'Sometimes, Charlie, you can be absolutely *foul*.' Me and my big mouth, I hoped I hadn't lost my only ally in Watson's camp.

It didn't stop her giving me a goodnight peck on the cheek after I'd walked her back to her quarter.

'Thank you for a lovely night, Charlie. Just for a few hours it was like being back at home.'

'You're not still mad at what I said?'

'Of course not . . . and thank you for giving me my photographs back.'

'What photographs?' I asked, and stole a real kiss before I left her there. It seemed to me that the taste of her kiss was still on my lips when I climbed into Hudd's bloody aircraft the next morning.

It was another Varsity, with an especially modified passenger door to enable the passengers to jump out. To jump out three thousand feet above the ground, that is. It was a very pretty aeroplane, but you won't be surprised to learn that it was hate at first sight as far as I was concerned. It was painted a washed-out tawny colour on top, and a washed-out bluey colour underneath, and the two colours sort of washed into each other: I'm sure you get the picture. It had Australian national markings, in order to comply with international law, but they were so small that you had to look for them. I thought it was a serious sort of aircraft.

Hudd's man hawked like an Arab and said, 'Triffic camouflage, mate: no one can see us up there.'

'They won't have to, will they? There will be just us and the mountains and a few thousand goats. But they'll hear us coming for miles.'

'You Poms always find something to whinge about; you know that?'

I was still digesting Hudd's briefing. The Varsity door slid open instead of being hinged, and it had been enlarged. All I had to do was sit on the ledge, and roll forward when they told me to. And I didn't have a plonker to pull. I was hitched up to the aircraft on a static line which deployed my parachute after I was in clean air. That was the theory of it, anyway. If the main chute didn't deploy, I had a small emergency job on my chest, and I could pop that by hand. If I could find a hand. The really silly bit was a package the size of a kitbag tethered around my ankle. It was supposed to hang six feet under me as I fell, and hit the ground before I did. Hudd cautioned me about getting tangled up in it as I rolled . . . and, because of the extra weight of course, I was going to fall a lot faster than I had before.

'Piece of piss,' Hudd said after he had finished explaining.

'No, Hudd, pissing myself is what I will be doing on the way down.'

'I'll make sure I'm not underneath you then, mate; so you can jump first. You'll be all right, Charlie. I had you investigated when your name came up.'

'What do you mean *investigated*?'

'I got some pals to ask some of *their* pals a few questions. They said you were all right. One RAF copper called you *a homicidal Englishman*. You really shoot one of your officers a few years back?'

'Nobody's supposed to know that. The bastard went mad, and tried to kill me. What was I supposed to do, lie back and think of England?'

'Keep your hair on, mate. You can shoot as many of the bastards as you want as far as *we're* concerned.'

'But you're an officer yourself, aren't you?'

'Yeah; but I didn't start out that way, did I? And it still don't feel right.'

That did it. It broke the tension in me. I stuck out my paw and shook his hand.

'Then I'm your man, Mr Hudd. I thought I was the only one in uniform who felt like that.'

'Christ no, Charlie. There's bloody thousands of us. Mount up now, before you make me cry.'

What was that song from the 1930s? 'Here we go into the wide blue yonder'. The bastard composer must have written it for me.

Daisy was standing at the end of the airstrip waving to us with a coloured scarf. The Varsity's twin Hercules radials blew sand all over her, and for a moment I lost sight of her. When I picked her up again, I could swear that bloody lion was sitting meekly alongside her.

The Varsity bounced a couple of times on its short nose-wheel as the pilot ran her up against her brakes, and then he let her go. She was a smooth old bitch, even if I say so myself. When was that? About 10 o'clock on an April morning in 1953. What I was thinking about as we became airborne was my old man, and his *Redcoats go home!* and I smiled. He would be having his breakfast just about now . . . if he wasn't in jail again.

*

'Ya gotta remember, Charlie,' Hudd's man yelled in my ear. 'Sit with ya feet over the sill, hold ya sack in ya lap, duck down an' roll forward. Once yer outa the ship let go of the sack an' its weight will pull ya upright. Then the 'chute will open with a bang. You jumped before ain't you?' I nodded. He added, 'Piece a piss.'

Second bastard to tell me that in a few hours. We were droning over brown mountains. We had been droning over brown mountains for hours. Some of them still had snow on their boots.

I yelled back, 'What if we get split up?'

'We won't. You'll jump first, an' we'll steer our 'chutes to land near you. Piece a piss.' We'd have to do something about expanding his vocabulary if we got away with this.

Ten minutes later I was sitting on the sill, clutching that bloody kitbag to my chest. My feet were out of the aircraft, and were being swept sideways by the slipstream. Someone who called himself 'the jump master' was crouching behind me, and I was literally shaking with fear this time. The only concession to safety was the silly thing like a racing cyclist's helmet I had on my bonce. A small red light came on above my head; I tucked my chin into my chest, and waited for the tap on my shoulder. It never came. The bastard behind me pushed my head down further, and rolled me out. Cold air on my cheeks. Tears dragged out. I let go of the sack. Jerked upright . . . and then that other bloody jerk as the parachute snapped open with a pop, and the canopy crackled above me as it sorted itself out. Three jumps so far, and the parachute had opened properly each time. I tried to calculate the odds of the next one going wrong, and couldn't.

Peace. Cold right hand because I had lost my glove. Brilliant blue sky. A few puffy white clouds sailing like yachts above me. I looked around: Hudd's man was literally only twenty yards away. He grinned, and actually took one hand off his shroud lines to wave. That spun him away from me, and I watched as he straightened his shrouds, and used his deadweight as a pendulum, to bring himself back. By twisting my head to look over my other shoulder, I could see Hudd above me, and over to the left – not much further away. He had his knees and feet together, just like in the book. I tried to copy him.

Only minutes later, it seemed, the sack attached to my right ankle hit the deck, followed by me. I rolled once before it dragged me into a shallow gully and wrapped me up in my shroud lines. The parachute continued to billow above me like a captive balloon. If you've jumped you'll know what I mean: we've all been there at least once.

As I landed, I distinctly saw a small snake wriggling to get away from me: my shadow passing overhead must have spooked it. It must have mistaken me for an enormous bird of prey. It looked like one of those small desert vipers. As I sat up, I saw similar flashy movements in the clumps of scrubby hard grass around me. So I shouted,

'Snakes!'

Hudd's head poked over the edge of the gully. He said, 'Shut up, Charlie. You'll scare them. Just watch where you put your hands and feet an' you'll be OK. Stand up now.' I stood, feeling a little foolish. 'Now bend, pop your sack, and hand its strap up to me.' The sack had a snap release from the leather strap that had secured it to my ankle. I bent down and did as he said. Looking for those tell-tale shapes in the grass, I saw one. It was a yard from me, and watching me with beady yellow eyes.

I knew a rattlesnake named Alice once, and rather admired her uncompromisingly vile temper, but we always outnumbered her so that was OK. Now the boot was on the other foot, and I didn't like it. The bloody things were all around me. I handed

Hudd the line attached to the sack, and he hauled it up to where he was standing. Then he reached a hand down and pulled me out.

Hudd's man was sitting in the scrub a few yards away. He had pulled his arm out of his jacket sleeve, and had split his shirt sleeve up to the biceps. He was injecting himself. He was giving himself an injection in the back of his hand, and then another high up on his arm.

'Antivenom,' he said cheerfully. 'Snake bit.' He showed me two small puncture marks on the back of his hand. The skin around them was reddened to the size of a sixpence. 'Bit right through me glove. Feisty little beggars ain't they?'

'Are you going to be all right?'

'We'll soon know if I'm not, won't we? Wonder what they taste like.'

'What do you mean?'

'If we run out of food, we can eat them,' Hudd said. 'I ate a Brown Snake once. It tasted like a gamey old chuck. Can you two get yourselves sorted out? I want to get moving.'

We each had a pack in the sacks that had come down with us. Theirs looked bigger than mine, but I had two. I had a second small canvas pack into which was built a small radio and a Morse key. It weighed just over a pound and had a range like an albatross. I liked it so much that I'd already decided to keep it once the show was over. My other pack looked much smaller than theirs. It contained food and water for a few days, a first-aid kit I hadn't been briefed on, and changes of socks and smalls; Hudd had been insistent on the socks. It also contained my small pistol and fifteen spare rounds – but I hadn't told them about that.

We each wore long KDs, rubberized lace-up ankle boots and an old US-style leather flying jacket – Hudd said no one had ever made anything better for the field. Quite like old times for me:

I'd owned one once, but I didn't tell them that either. Each of the jackets had a goolie chit stitched into it, and for the nervous among you I'd better explain what a goolie chit was. A goolie chit was (and maybe still is for all I know) a notice in a local language addressed to anyone who might find or capture a distressed airman, telling him that a reward was offered for said airman's safe return – with his balls still hanging where they should be. *Goolies* was said to be the Hindustani word for testicles: hence 'goolie chit'. The RAF is nothing but thorough, so they gave me another on printed paper, headed up with a jolly-looking Union Jack and translated into Arabic, Kurdish, French and Greek. I'd rather have taken my chances with the Arabs and Kurds than the Frogs, but this isn't the place to go into that.

There was one other thing. If the goolie chits didn't prove all that persuasive, we each had a big .45 in a canvas holster around our waist, and Hudd and his man had Stirlings. I felt as if we should be asking directions for the OK Corral.

Hudd took a bearing with an old marching compass, and we set off on a goat track, up a slope of stony ochre-coloured ground overlaid with that same rough sawgrass. All around us were mountain tops, and they seemed steeper and more oppressive the higher we climbed. That was interesting: my logic told me it should have been the other way round.

I reckoned the snake venom and antivenom were taking their toll of Hudd's man. He didn't complain, but I could see he was sweating pints, so after half an hour I called, 'Drink, anyone?' to give him a breather.

Hudd, who had been leading, swung round with an angry look on his face.

But he took in the situation immediately, wiped his forehead on his sleeve and said, 'Yeah. I'm parched. Five-minute bums down.'

We had dumped the jump helmets; the snakes were welcome

to them. Both the Aussies favoured wide-brimmed bush hats, but I'd brought my Jerry canvas desert cap. It was just the job. Hudd looked a bit askance at it, but didn't say anything. Sitting down wasn't all that dangerous: most of the snakes were in the gullies, and there were fewer the higher we climbed.

'Why are there so many bloody snakes up here?' I asked Hudd. 'I hate the damned things.'

'Plenty o' food, and damn few predators I'd guess . . . and I'd also guess we arrived the weekend they came out of hibernation, cold and cranky. Come back in a fortnight's time and you might not see one.'

'Can we go away, and come back in a fortnight's time then?' I asked. That raised a weak smile from Hudd's man. I guessed he was suffering.

Hudd replied, 'Don' be so squeamish, Charlie; you sound like a drama queen.' That raised another smile. We drank a few mouthfuls of water, and ate a couple of squares of something hard that tasted like third-rate chocolate. It was so tough you had to suck it.

I asked, 'How much do your packs weigh?'

' 'bout sixty pounds,' Hudd told me.

'. . . and mine?'

'Half that.'

'Why don't we even out the load?' I was thinking of Hudd's man, who glanced up quickly, and shook his head.

Hudd said, ' 'cos I need you to keep up with us, Charlie. You wouldn't get a mile with fifty pound on yer back.' At least he'd told me straight. His man grinned up, but didn't say anything. He might have just appreciated the thought.

'How far are we from the aircraft?'

'Two mile, say; less than three. Get there in time for tea.'

'I didn't realize we were that close. I didn't see it at all on the way down.'

Hudd grunted.

'Good. That means you were doin' what you were told.' He stood up and stretched. 'C'mon, time to move on.' He reached out a hand to haul his man to his feet, taking care to choose his good arm, but even so Hudd's man winced as he stood. After six paces he stopped, bent over and vomited.

'Teach you not to drink so much before a job,' Hudd told him. 'You had a skinful o' beer last night.' It was a light enough comment, but as he turned away from us I could see that our glorious leader was worried.

We came out upon the plateau suddenly, an hour later. Both Hudd and I had matched ourselves to his man between us, and our pace had slowed. This was one of the strangest places in the world: it could have been invented by Conan Doyle or Mr Rider Haggard. We were surrounded by horrible brown mountains on all sides, with only one pass to the north. Great crumbling crags of brown rubble. The pass looked narrow, but it was obviously wide enough for a fairly big aircraft, because Tony Frohlich had brought his Stirling bomber through there. It was as far as you'd get, though: for anything other than a V2 rocket or a modern helicopter, the mountains around us were a ring of death.

The floor of what was now obviously an old volcanic basin rose up a few hundred feet from the mountain roots, until it levelled out to form a large flat plateau of stony red and ochre earth, covered in terrible sawgrass that tried to cut through your trousers as you passed. If I had seen lost dinosaurs grazing in the distance, I wouldn't have been all that surprised.

. . . and a mile away sat a black aircraft, glinting in the sun where the frosts and the winds had stripped its paintwork. I examined it through a small pair of bins that Hudd's man handed me. Even at that distance, I knew that a part of my job had been completed: I'd seen this patched and cranky old cow before. So, there was Watson's pot of gold, but where was the bleeding rainbow?

An hour later I sat in her shadow, and whistled 'Jazz me blues'. The only other sounds were the wind sighing through the grass, and the cries overhead from a few high-circling birds of prey. Hudd called them *eagles*, but I could see their long necks. They looked like bloody vultures to me, and I reckoned they were sizing us up.

I tell a lie. Frohlich's old bus was also singing her own sad song; but very quietly. She was probably pleased to see some Anglos again. I picked up on it as we walked towards her from perhaps half a mile away, and oddly it became no louder or clearer as we approached. It was her death song, and its noise level *remained* level once you were in range: a gentle keening sound of the wind flowing over her surfaces, punctuated by an occasional creak from her flying planes, or her aluminium skin expanding in the heat. After all of this time there was no pressure in her hydraulics, and all of her lines had slackened off, so her elevators and ailerons moved fitfully in the breeze, without proper restraint – just as if she was airborne. I'll bet the old lady still wanted to fly. She made me want to weep.

Even from a mile away, I could see that Frohlich's mob had achieved a perfect landing. In places you could still see the fat grooves in the earth made by her huge landing wheels, and smaller doubled tail-wheels. I took Hudd's man's pack from him around then, and Hudd took mine. I still don't know how he dragged a hundred-pound burden and helped me steer his man at the same time. We propped his man up in the shade – against one of those main wheels. It was flat, and the rubber was cracked and perished. It was beginning to settle into the ground, pressed down by its own thirty-ton deadweight.

Hudd gave his man one of the water bottles, then bent down and ruffled his hair.

'You gonna be OK, mate?'

'Sure. Give me an hour. Quick recovery times my speciality.' He actually looked grey, and was still sweating.

'Charlie 'n me's gonna walk around an' have a shufti – see what's left. You stay here.'

'Sure. I'll see it later.'

Hudd began to walk in shadow towards the nose of the great beast, but I knew there was no way in for us there, so I stopped him and turned him round. We walked aft.

As we did I told him, 'There's something in the rear turret. I think it's a body.'

'I know. I saw it as we marched up. The guns are gone as well. Would they have flown without them?'

'No. That would have given the game away that they were up to something. We'll have to check the front turret as well. I think the local tribesmen have probably stripped out the guns and ammunition, so we'll have to go canny if we meet them. They could now have some decent fire power.'

'Ye're starting to think like an Aussie soldier, Charlie boy. I'm proud of you.' We were at the small rear hatch by now. It was set into the side of the body near the tail, and had rounded corners. If my memory of the type served me well, there should be a short metal ladder we could pull down. Up close, the old girl had lost more of her paint than it first looked – the winter storms had flailed her for eight years after all – and under the relentless sun her flanks were warm; you'd think she was still alive. But appearances, they say, can be deceiving. Like Hudd's man, for instance; he still looked alive as well. The door wasn't dogged shut: it was open about an inch. I paused.

Hudd asked, 'What's the matter?'

'I wanted a look at what's in the tail turret first; and then I was thinking about snakes. This old bugger could be full of them.'

'OK . . . but don't worry about the snakes. I haven't seen one since we got up here on the flat. Less cover for them, I guess. Anyway, if you think about the effort they'd have to make, climbing up the undercarriage before they could get inside, I don't think it would be worth it. It's not as if there's anything here for them.'

By then we'd walked around the tailplane and were peering into the rear gun turret. What was in there had once indeed been a man. He'd also been dead some while. The Plexiglas of the gun turret had clouded over the years, but I could look into his eye sockets through the spaces that his machine guns would have once occupied. He didn't look back at me.

'Well?' Hudd asked.

'He's not in flying clothing. I don't know what the locals wear, but he could be one of them, or someone who came looking for her.'

'Snakes?' This was the part of the aircraft closest to the ground.

I scrutinized the floor of the turret. 'No.'

'Told yer! They got more sense. Let's get inside.'

The door creaked as I pushed it open, and we had to wrestle with the ladder. This old bitch did what all large empty aircraft do when you get up inside them. She moaned and groaned a bit, and occasionally you could feel her shift as our weight transferred from rib to rib. I was pleased that Hudd ignored the body in the library at first. Instead we moved forward, through shafts of light from her fuselage windows. They were surprisingly large for someone brought up on Lancs, like me. There were animals inside, but they weren't snakes. They were small lizards that darted into the dark as soon as our shadows fell on them. The inside of the aircraft was fairly gutted: I told you appearances can be deceptive. The radios were gone – that was the first shack forward that we came to, and someone had ripped out the navigator's table and all of the crew seats. It meant that somewhere in a Kurdish house Papa was proudly sitting in the pilot's seat. Most of the internal wiring had been hacked out and carried away.

Hudd was impressed by the space inside. 'You could make a fair-sized airliner out of this.'

'They did that with a few after the war: a row of seats on either side and a corridor between them. I don't think they caught on.'

'Where did the bombs go?'

'Downwards most of the time: mainly over Germany or France.'

'Ha. Ha. Bloody ha. You know what I mean.'

'In the bomb bay under us, and in four separate bomb cells in the wings between the inner engines and the fuselage: the main spar took their weight.'

'I haven't a clue what that means.'

'Good: it probably means you were paying attention to all of your other lectures. I thought you were a qualified pilot?' It was good to get one back.

'I am, after a fashion – I jest passed up on the lessons in airframe construction. You don't need to be a vet to ride a horse.'

There was something wrong with that, and I hadn't liked the way he eyed me up. I asked him, 'Why are you interested in the bombs anyway? She wasn't carrying any, as far as I know.'

'I'm interested in the bomb *spaces*, sport, because I can't see no boxes of dosh. Wasn't that what we came for? Can we get into the bomb bay from here?'

'I don't know the Stirling, but there's bound to be access; probably from those plates on the floor – because the engineer had to release the bombs by hand if they hung up in the racks.'

'But there are not likely to be any there at present?'

'If there are, then I'm off. A fused bomb sitting in the heat and cold up here for years is likely to be pretty unstable: not a nice bedfellow. Why don't we finish our walk around the outside, and see what we can see?'

Hudd's man was where we'd left him, now sleeping like a baby. He was breathing slowly and regularly and had a quiet smile on his face, which was good. He was also perspiring profusely, which was bad.

Hudd said, 'Leave him be. He probably needs it.'

We walked around the black bomber on the ground. They say that when an aircraft *looked* right, it *was* right. You wouldn't say that about Frohlich's Mk III Stirling. She had long spindly legs like a heron, a snub nose like a bulldog, a long thin fuselage and short, fat wide wings. It was as if her four main design components had been borrowed from different airframes and bolted together in somebody's backyard . . . but before the Lanc and the dear old Hallibag came along, she was considered state-of-the-art. Maybe that's the right phrase. Maybe Picasso or Roland Penrose had a hand in her somewhere.

'What an ugly bastard!' Hudd remarked.

'Beauty, Hudd, is in the eye of the beholder and not skin-deep.' Two clichés in one sentence; not bad, Charlie. 'She could leave more bits in Germany, and still get home, than any other aircraft in the 1940s or since. She is one tough old bag, believe me.'

'But she had her bad points as well?'

'She had to fly around mountains, couldn't carry all that much, and was slow.'

'But she got *here* . . .'

'Yeah she did, didn't she?'

By that time we'd completed our walk round. The only interesting thing I'd noticed was that the starboard tyre was not only deflated, but there were huge pieces of it missing – cut out and half-inched by whoever had robbed her out in the first place. I wondered what they could possibly make from bits of aircraft tyre.

Hudd asked me, 'Well?' He was good at saying *well*.

'The bomb doors haven't been opened.'

I'd tried to slide a knife blade between them and failed. I've still got the knife; it sleeps between my mattress and the bed frame. The dirt that I scraped from the junction of the bomb doors was bonded with grease; nothing had been there for a long time.

'Why do you say that?'

'They don't look it. Another part of my brain is saying that if anyone *had* opened them, what would be the point of closing them again . . . and would they have had the means anyway?'

'So the stuff could still be here?'

'I didn't say that.'

'. . . but you thought it, just like me.'

Hudd must have been an optimist. I actually was thinking it unlikely that anyone had left that amount of dough hanging about, so it must have been in boxes in the cabin.

'If you say so, Hudd.'

'We got homework to do. Let's have some grub, get sorted and work out where we're going to spend the night. Then we can start in at it.'

'We can sleep inside her if you're sure there are no snakes . . .'

'There you go: halfway there already . . .'

Hudd cooked up a stew and brewed a pan of char on a stove no larger than a can of baked beans; it was a remarkable little thing. I decided not to ask him what the meat in the stew was . . . I found I was ravenously hungry anyway. He only made enough for two. I nodded at Rip Van Winkle and said, 'What about him?'

'He couldn't keep the last lot down, could he? No point wasting it, so let him sleep instead – it will do him good.' *Will it?* I thought. As if he could read my mind, Hudd looked up and added, 'He's had as much antivenom as he can take. Any more than that will kill him. All we can do is wait.' Cheerful bastard, wasn't he?

As the sun sank beneath the mountain tops, the air cooled quickly. We wrapped Hudd's man up, and then climbed back in the bus.

Hudd said, 'The way I see it is that we've got to lift all these plates one by one, and look underneath them.'

'I can't see how they lift. It might take ages.'

'You got a better idea, mate?'

'Up in the office; I might be able to work out how the bomb door release works: it might *still* work.'

'I doubt it; it's not a bloody Volkswagen.' The evil little Jerry cars were already earning a reputation for reliability and longevity. 'Look: you go try that, and I'll get to work down here, but before you do anything get a signal off to Mr Watson. Tell him we found a black bird, but no golden eagles, and keep it short.'

'Golden eagles?'

'The Yanks used to put eagles on all their golden dollars.'

'We're not looking for golden dollars, Hudd, we're looking for paper ones . . . and the gold coins were sovereigns, weren't they, not dollars?'

'So it's a mixed metaphor, Charlie: stop being so literal. He give you a code pad?'

'Yeah.'

'Then get on with it: we got an hour o' daylight at least, if we're lucky.'

I set my dinky radio up not far from Hudd's man, and ran the copper aerial up to one of the massive propeller blades. That way the whole of Frohlich's monster would become my aerial – the resulting signal would probably burst Watson's eardrums. Hudd's man stirred just as I was packing it down again.

I walked across to him, and squatted down. 'How you feeling?'

'Better, but crook. Those little bastards pack quite a punch.' He showed me his bitten hand. It was swollen and mottled dark-red in places. 'I'm thirsty.' I gave him a drink before I climbed back inside the aircraft. The last thing he said before he closed his eyes again, was, 'This is silly.'

Hudd still hadn't got into the bomb bay by the time we quit at dark. I had identified the bomb-door release handle, and a heavy-duty cable leading from it. There was also a hydraulic line, but in the half-light I couldn't see if that was associated with the gear for the bomb doors. I skinned my knuckles half a dozen times before it became too dark, swore, and gave up. If I'd expected Hudd to be sullen or downcast at our failures I was wrong. We made a fire with dried thick grass, and wood from scrubby bushes no higher than it. The tree wood popped and sparked in the flames. Hudd said it was juniper. He sat across the fire and told tales of his service in Malaya and Indo-China. Most of the tales were funny and ribald, almost as if he thought soldiering was a way of extracting as much fun out of life as possible.

The stew tasted the same, though, and his man managed a couple of mouthfuls. His temperature had dropped, but he shivered for Australia, no matter how much we swaddled him in all the stuff we had. Late on we scuffed the fire out, and loaded our gear into Frohlich's Stirling. We had a sleeping sack each: thin canvas cotton treated on the inside with a rubber solution: once you were inside and buttoned up none of your body heat escaped.

401

Hudd's man groaned as we loaded him into his. We played that kids' game, Sardines, sleeping side by side and touching, with Hudd's man in the middle . . . stretched out on the plates which had so far defeated us. The wind got up a bit; the airframe creaked and groaned, and but for the roar of four engines, and the fingers of searchlights probing the night skies, I could have been back over Germany.

Chapter Nineteen

Just a closer walk with thee

I woke in a cold dawn, put a hand out of my sack but pulled it back quickly after contact with the aircraft's cold, damp flank. Hudd was snoring. I thought his man was breathing more peacefully. He stirred as I pulled away from them to get up, and gave me a quiet smile. For a moment he looked as innocent as a schoolboy.

I took a leak over the twin tail-wheels for luck, just as we used to on the squadron. It's one of those memories that make you smile. Then I walked round the old bitch a couple of times, flinging my arms around my body to warm myself up and get rid of the stiffness from sleeping on a hard surface. I wouldn't have noticed that when I was sixteen. Then I stood underneath her crew compartment in the nose, and imagined the cables and lines running down from the bomb-door release, and how they crawled through the airframe to the hydraulic rams against the doors. Then I collected scraps of old wood and dried grasses, and started a fire under the high port wing, and climbed back inside to search for breakfast makings in the pouches.

Hudd, squatting a couple of feet from his man, turned and said, 'You should have told me. Given me a shake.'

'Told you what?'

'That Freddy was gone.'

I knelt by Hudd's man, who was indeed quite dead. He looked peaceful, but when I touched his good hand, which was outside the sleeping sack, it was icy cold, and stiff – he'd been dead for hours.

'But that's not possible. I saw him a few minutes ago when I got up. He looked better. He even smiled at me.'

Hudd just stared at me. There was nothing either malevolent or friendly in his stare. Eventually he said, 'Maybe you've been outside longer than you think.'

'No.'

'Well, maybe you were still asleep, and dreamed it. That happens. '

There was no point in arguing. 'Yes, Hudd: I'm sorry. He was a friend of yours. I didn't even know his name until you just said it.'

'He didn't use it all that often,' was all Hudd said. 'He was secretive.'

We buried Hudd's man under the shadow of the other wing, using our small entrenching tools to dig and scrape him a decent grave. The soil was stony, but very loose, so we managed a decent depth: probably four feet. Hudd made us dig another then, because it had always been his intention to get the guy out of the rear turret before we left . . . and the two graves took us the best part of half a day.

Hudd didn't seem in any hurry now. I figured out why: we probably had plenty of stores – by his definition – now that there were only two of us. We examined Hudd's man's bad arm before we tied him into his sleeping sack. From the fingertips to the shoulder it was twice the normal size, and a mottled deep red and black. At his shoulder, major veins stood out a steely blue. He must have been in agony, and kept his trap shut all that time.

'Lesson learned,' Hudd said.

'What?'

'First one of us that gets snake-bit, the other one shoots him.'

I've never been a brave man, but looking at that terrible arm convinced me for the time being. 'Agreed. Do you want a marker on the grave?'

'No, we never do that sort o' thing in my mob. I'd say a prayer if I could. I've seen Fred pray for others: he always had the words. I can't seem to remember any.'

'I know the words of a slow jazz number they used to do at funerals in New Orleans. I think it was a hymn. I can speak them if you like?'

'Yes, please, Charlie. That would do.'

I started to give Hudd's man the words of 'Just a closer walk with thee', but somehow they didn't seem to come out right, so I ended up singing them for him. I've never had much of a voice – kind of harsh and tuneless – but maybe hearing a human voice at all up on that awful plateau was something, though. The noise was lost in the vast basin.

Hudd said, 'That was good, Charlie; let's find a coupla big stones to put on him, an' make a cuppa char.'

The Aussies are as bad as us: the only other race in the world which attacks overwhelming sadness with cups of tea.

There was a big cotter pin behind the bomb-door release up in the Stirling's office. Hudd walked forward to join me after he had become bored with the floor plates, and pointed at it. 'What's that do?'

'Don't know. Could be something to do with the bomb-door locks. I haven't looked at it yet.'

He reached over my shoulder with a pair of pliers, and yanked it out. The result was immediate: a rumbling sound somewhere beneath us, and several dull thuds one after the other.

'Let's go outside and look,' he ordered.

The bloody doors under the fuselage were gaping open of course. Long, narrow parallel doors which had covered the cells in the narrow bomb bays. Dust was still filtering down in the sunlight. A number of gold coins, which hadn't been there the day before, glinted at our feet close to the remains of a wooden box.

'About a dozen each,' Hudd said. 'That should get us a few beers.'

'It's not ours, Hudd. The Treasury will get very humpy if we nick it.'

'No they won't: Watson said we could keep the coin. It was the paper money he was after, and that's not bloody here, is it?'

'Apparently not; so what do we do next?'

'Tell Watson, and find out what his plan B is. He always has a plan B. Then set off north, I guess. The first village is over the foothills; it will take us all day.'

'What about the thing in the back turret?'

'Oh yeah. Forgot about him. Eat first, then stick 'im in the ground.'

'I don't want to be walking in the dark with all those snakes around.'

'If it's cold they'll be coiled up; they won't move.'

'That's what I mean. They'll get our big feet all over them, and start getting mad.'

Hudd sucked on a piece of grass he had cut. 'See what you mean; let me think about it.'

When we were sitting and eating I asked him what was in the stew: it was growing on me.

'Roo meat. Kangaroo. Pound for pound, the most nutritious meat in the world. We carry it dried in strips like jerky. It worry you, mate?'

'Meat's meat, Hudd. We ate whales in the war.'

'Never did that. What's it taste like?'

'Whale.' I remembered the flavour of that fishy meat. 'Disgusting. Only morons or Japs would eat it unless they had to.'

When I lit my pipe he said, 'Wish you wouldn't do that, Charlie. It's not good for you.'

'How?'

'Gives you lung diseases. Smokers die early.'

'That so, Hudd? I suppose drinking's not good for you either.'

'That's right. Drinkers die early, too. Look what happened to Fred.'

'That was nothing to do with drinking. It was because a snake bit him.'

'How do we know that?' Hudd asked me. 'All I know is that Fred drank too much all his life, an' he died early. The statistics speak for themselves.'

I got my pipe stoked up and going well, before I asked him, 'Who doesn't die early, Hudd?'

He considered the question for so long that I thought he wasn't going to answer. Then he shrugged and said, 'Old folks, I guess.'

It was time for us to get that bag of bones out of the rear turret.

I showed Hudd how the door in the back of the turret opened. It didn't, so we had to take a hammer to it. When it eventually moved aside the thing in there fell back towards us. I instinctively jumped back. Hudd didn't. It had desiccated in the sun for so long, and the turret was ventilated of course, that it didn't smell too bad. Just that dusty putrefactive smell that grabs at the back of your throat. He was curled up like a homunculus: there hadn't been much room for him. He had no shoes on, and one copper-brown foot was three times the size of the other. Snakes *two*, humans *nil*. Hudd must have thought the same.

'Snake-bit; but he's been up here a year at least. Recognize the uniform?' He was dressed in plain KDs without any markings, and hadn't been too old. His shrunken face had been younger than mine when he died. Dark crinkly hair, which was falling out in clumps – it looked as if something was getting at it – and bad teeth. I shook my head.

'No. What do you want to do with him?'

'Find out who he was, mate; then bury the bugger. Maybe he can tell us where the dosh has gone.'

We found an ID bracelet on his wrist. The metal had discoloured, but it was possible to make out the writing on it, which wasn't in a Western script.

'Arabic?' Hudd asked.

'Dunno. It's quite like the Egyptian Arabic, but not quite right. Keep it; we'll check it later.'

Watson did not take the news well. I'd forgotten he used to be an operator himself in the cat's-whisker days. The Morse came back from him like machine-gun fire. I told Hudd, 'He thinks it's our fault.'

'No, he doesn't . . . but he's got to take it out on someone. We've lost one man already, and we haven't found the money. That's not going to look very good in his memoirs, is it?' I re-examined this statement in my head and came to the conclusion that I didn't like the word *already*. Nor would you.

I sent back, '*If you can't be civil, be quiet*,' and pulled the aerial out. That would give Watson apoplexy. 'I'll try him again in an hour,' I told Hudd, '. . . after he's calmed down. He's bound to think of something for us to do: he hates idle staff.'

He looked at me quizzically.

'Aren't you taking a bit of a chance talking to your SO like that?'

'Not really. He got me out here under false pretences – I was already time-expired, but didn't know it – and, despite the bluster, I think the only thing he can do with me is send me home in disgrace.'

'What if you're wrong?'

'I'll end up in the nick again. My old man's probably inside even as we speak: it goes in the family.'

I may have been wrong, but after that I think Hudd looked at me with a new respect. Well done, Dad! We buried the dead soldier alongside Hudd's man. Hudd wanted me to sing the same words over him, but I turned him down.

'He wasn't one of us: besides he probably had some dago religion and wouldn't have appreciated it.'

'You're all heart, Charlie: as sensitive as a fucking brick.'

I thought that was a bit rich coming from him. So I flung back, 'That's what all the girls say,' and showed him my pearlies.

While we were brewing up he asked me, 'Show me that bracelet again: I'm sure I've seen writing like that somewhere.'

I looked from where we were sitting in the shade of the black bomber towards the two graves, and for the first time took in that it was just me and him now . . . and this fucking wilderness. I asked myself what my dead pal Tommo would have done in this situation, but the answer that came back was that he didn't know, either. All he could come up with was that I'd better watch out for myself. Thanks, Tommo; I could have worked that out for myself.

Hudd threw the lees of his tea on the fire, stood up and stretched. While I had brewed up he had been sorting his man's effects. He gave me a small pair of binoculars and a Fairbairn-Sykes dagger. I still have them: throwing your history away isn't that easy. I'm looking at the knife as I write, right now.

He said to me, 'I want you to go around the other side,' he gestured at the Stirling, '. . . and examine the countryside carefully, from the foothills of the mountains right up to where we're standing.'

'What will you be doing?'

'This side: I'll take the south and east, you take the north and west.'

'What am I looking for?'

'Horses: small horses. Wild ponies maybe, or wild asses.'

'Why? We haven't seen any so far.'

'Nah, but we seen their tracks; all over the shop. Some small hoofs have been chopping up the ground: didn't you notice?'

'No. Show me.'

He did. In places the signs were clear. I was angry with myself that I hadn't noticed, and he must have picked up on that.

'Don't fret, Charlie: it's *my* job – just like the radio's yours.' It didn't help. I was determined to do a decent job now, so I scanned the brush and the mountains for at least twenty minutes. When I walked back, he was waiting for me. 'Anything?'

'No.'

'Me neither. You know what that means?'

'No.' Again.

'That maybe they weren't wild. Maybe somone rode them up here, or maybe they were pack animals?'

'And they were used to carry the money away on.'

'Right. Getting a vehicle up here would be bloody nigh impossible.'

'How old are the tracks?'

'Fuck knows, Charlie. I'm not Geronimo.'

'What next?'

'Phone God; ask him what he wants us to do . . .'

We didn't have a telephone. I tapped out a placatory message to Watson with my key: his hour was almost up anyway. He still had an immaculate hand in terms of his Morse sending, and his first return was to ask if we were OK, which meant that he had it back together again. I replied *so far so good*, and told him the rest. He asked me to wait five, which meant that he and M'smith would be scrutinizing the charts. When he came back he asked us to look out for animal tracks out between north and NNW . . . on a heading of say, 330 or 340 – and if we found them to follow them out. The afternoon was drawing in, so I sent, *tomorrow*. He replied, *OK*. No dissent from Watson was unusual: he probably realized that another day wasn't going to make any difference.

When we looked carefully where Watson had told us to look, we could see the scrub and the grass had been trampled or broken more frequently than any of the stuff around it . . . not that the breaks looked all that recent.

I muttered, 'I hate it when he's bloody right all the time.'

'We'll be heading in the right direction anyway, Charlie,' Hudd pointed out. 'We have to head north to Van or Tatvan before they can get us out.'

'Tatvan and Van? I take it that they are towns rather than ruined trucks parked in the desert somewhere.'

'I don't know as you'd quite say *towns*, Charlie. Depends on yer definition.'

At least Hudd had spoken about getting us out. That was a start. I don't know why I hadn't worried about it before. We sorted ourselves out in preparation for our second night on the plateau. Hudd showed me how to set snares in the brush.

'What for?' I asked him.

'Rabbits maybe; the snakes have to live off something. Rabbit for breakfast is brilliant.' I thought that the vipers were more likely to catch lizards and mice, and I wasn't going to start chewing on those: you could take the Special Forces thing too far in those days. But I kept my mouth shut.

We had to range a bit further this time for scraps of dead wood and clumps of grass, and we made a bigger fire that

411

evening, further away from the aircraft. Hudd cooked us another pan of Roo Stew which we washed down with warm tea.

'Last tea,' he warned me, 'until we find water. There are melt streams down in the foothills, but I won't take any chances.'

'I was trying to remember what beer tasted like.'

'And did you?'

'No.'

'Don't put any more stuff on the fire. When it burns down, we'll turn in.'

He climbed up into the black bomber before me. I sat by the embers of the fire and smoked a last pipe. I thought about the boys. They would have been asleep for a couple of hours already. The bar in Maggs and the Major's pub would be smoky and noisy. Maybe someone was playing the out-of-tune piano in the corner. I wondered if Flaming June had made up with her lost soldier, and if Captain Holroyd and his lovely wife were propping up the bar at Abu Suier. When I crawled into my sack up in the black bitch's belly, I was thoroughly dissatisfied, and it was all my own fault.

When I was in my fifties, and living in a decent-sized city for the first time in my life, I found myself drawn to the art galleries. I had an immediate affinity with the surrealists, because, as far as I was concerned, they were actually *realists* in a deeper sense. Surreality is all around you; all you have to do is look . . . and if you're already wondering where this is going, it's all because of the guy who knocked on the door the next morning.

The knocking on the aircraft's door wasn't assertive; it was just a polite knock. The sort a neighbour uses when he comes to call. Neither Hudd nor I had heard him approach, but we managed to scramble up to the door together. I opened it. Hudd poked his Stirling out, and when nothing happened, his head. Nobody shot at it. My head was there after a decent interval, but then I always was a nosy bastard. A small man, in an immaculate grey lounge suit with a pinstripe, was sitting astride a donkey. He had a parasol to ward off the sun, and a beaming smile on what looked almost like an Asian face. About thirty, narrow-featured and exceptionally handsome. I'd bet he never had a problem with the girls.

'Good morning,' he said in an exquisite English accent, '. . . *beautiful* morning.'

Hudd was momentarily speechless, so I took over. 'Good morning.'

'I saw your fire last night, and thought I'd ride over to say hello.' Then he laughed and said, 'Hello.'

Hudd said, 'Wotcha.'

'We brought you some breakfast.'

'Nice of you.'

Then our visitor enquired, 'I suppose you've come for the money?'

I started to laugh; couldn't help myself. Hudd snarled, 'Shut it, Charlie.'

But the Asian, Indian or whatever he was, said, 'He's English, sir . . . let him laugh. English passengers told jokes as the *Titanic* sank; quite admirable actually.' He'd expressed our dilemma quite neatly, I thought, because my problem was with one of the words he'd used. He'd said, '*We* brought you some breakfast.' The *we* in question were a dozen tribesmen sitting around us in a half-circle on small ponies and donkeys, and they were armed to the teeth. One even had what looked like one of the .303 machine guns from the Stirling slung across his back.

I said, 'I don't suppose our goolie chits are any use?'

Smiler replied, 'None of them can read. I could read it to them if you liked, but you'd have no way of knowing that I did so faithfully. You'd have to take me on trust. They say it's difficult to trust a Kurd.'

Hudd sniffed, and wiped his nose on the back of his hand. Only real men do that. It's probably a dominance gesture they teach them at Special Forces school. Smiler didn't seem to notice.

Hudd asked, 'What did you bring?'

'Eggs and slices of lamb salted and smoked. Not unlike your bacon. I miss bacon. I was at Cambridge University. We had bacon for breakfast every morning. Here it is mainly grains.'

'Why don't you get down,' I asked him. 'We can talk.'

'We brought fresh water as well,' he said. 'They make wonderful tea.'

'My name is Charlie Bassett,' I told him. 'Pleased to meet you.'

'Şivan Mohamed Van,' he came back. 'I'll explain that later.' I realized that I actually didn't know Hudd's Christian name, so I left it to him.

Hudd just said, 'Hiya,' and ostentatiously put the gun down. It was funny how you felt the tension go out of the scene immediately.

Van's men made two decent fires, and gathered around one of them scoffing something that looked like blue porridge and quarrelling good-naturedly. They were young and a boisterous bunch, who laughed a lot. Most of the jokes were on us, I guessed. They were small men – I would have fitted in here – but the guns, swords and lances they were carrying definitely made them look bigger. I didn't look too closely, but I reckoned that a couple of the lances were adorned with hanks of human hair. Bloody scalp hunters!

One of them fussed around Van, and also made our breakfast. It started with the tea, and Van had been right; it was exquisite.

'When were you at Cambridge?' I asked him.

'Immediately after the war. Your university needed the money, and Pater was ready to pay.'

'What did you study?'

'Absolutely nothing, old boy. I sowed my wild oats: girls, alcohol and as many other un-Islamic things as I could find. Three years later I came back to take my place in the family. Here I am a pious and responsible man – with three wives.'

I reckoned he'd done all right for himself, and asked, 'You didn't get a degree then?'

'Of course I did, old boy: Classics and Mid-Eastern Studies: First-Class Honours. My father always gets what he pays for – it is a matter of principle.'

'I suppose it is, really. Nice tea.'

'Thank you. Did you go to university also?'

'No, my family could never have afforded it.'

'Don't forget to tell him you were too thick, as well,' Hudd offered.

'That too,' I said. 'Life's unfair.' But I was grinning.

'That's exactly what I thought when I saw your fire. After all this time I had hoped that we might keep it.' He was talking about the money again.

I said, 'We've come to negotiate about that.'

Van shook his head. 'When you're British and you own some thing, you don't negotiate over it. You reach out your hand and take it back.'

Hudd nodded gravely, and observed, 'It's a matter of principle,' as if he had just invented the phrase. I glanced over at Van's army whooping it up at the other fire. *Easier said than done*, I thought.

The eggs were small and gamy-tasting, but to me they tasted wonderful. Van's man had scrambled them in a kind of curd. Terrific. Kurds with curds; that's not bad, Charlie. We finished off with another cup of scented tea.

'It's from Iraq,' he told us. 'That part of Iraq was once part of Kurdistan. One day it will be again.'

415

'Who took it away from you?' I asked. I get all the dumb questions – that's my role in life.

'The British did. You aren't all that popular around here.'

'I heard that your people never surrendered.'

'That's not surprising, Charlie. There is no word for it in our language; we can't surrender because we do not know what a surrender is.'

'Which could make you a difficult neighbour to get on with?'

'. . . or the very best of allies. Your choice.'

I didn't even give Hudd a chance. I said, 'We want to be your friends.'

'Good choice,' Van said. He muttered something to his man who was cleaning the utensils with dirt – interesting, but just work it out. He went across to speak with the others. Seconds later they surprised me by beginning to shout and jig about, and fire their guns in the air.

'Well done, Charlie,' Hudd groused. 'I think you just started an uprising.'

Van touched me on the shoulder, 'Don't worry . . . but before you pack you must tell me why you buried the Jew.'

The man in the turret had been one of an Israeli party sent out to recover Frohlich's cargo several years earlier. The implication of that was that at least one of Frohlich's crew had made it all the way to the Promised Land. The Israeli in the turret had been bitten by a snake, and abandoned by his mates. At the time I thought that was a very Israeli way of looking at things: they've changed since then. He'd shut himself in the turret when Van and his people had turned up, and threatened them all with a pistol.

'It was very sad,' Van told us. 'We could probably have saved him. There are several useful antidotes. All you have to do is chew one of the grasses, and spit it inside the wounds.'

'How did you finish him?' Hudd: being awkward again.

'We didn't. The snake already had. We watched him until he was dead, and then left him there. He seemed to be where he wanted to be.'

'How many were there in his party?'

'Fifteen. They were heavily armed.'

'Did you finish them too?'

'No: who wants to make an enemy of Israel? Any people unafraid of blowing up a hotel full of British soldiers are not going to stop for a few Kurds. My father knew what to do. He believed that Israel will dig its own grave if we give it a big enough shovel.'

'So? What happened?'

'They claimed that the money was rightfully theirs, and they had come to get it back. But it wasn't theirs.'

'How did you know that?'

'Is it a Jewish head on the coins?'

Even Hudd smiled hearing this. He asked, 'So you never helped them: anyone else been up here?'

'They returned empty-handed, and hungry. My father said some Frenchmen climbed up here while I was in England. They claimed a cargo of money had been intended for brave French soldiers fighting the Germans in France. They wanted it back, but they were thieves. My father knew that it wasn't theirs.'

'How?'

'He was a man of the world, and so doubted the existence of any such thing as a brave French soldier, besides . . .'

'. . . it wasn't a French head on the coins either, was it?' I couldn't resist finishing the sentence for him.

'Precisely. George the Third. I always forget whether he was the mad one or not.'

'What happened to them?'

He made an odd fluttering gesture with the fingers of one

hand, and a grimace. It was as if he was saying, *They went*, and *Don't ask*, but he said, 'I wasn't here then.'

After a pause the size of Mount Ararat he added, 'Sadly some of them are still around. My women have one; he is a eunuch, of course.'

Inside myself I shuddered. I hope that I didn't show it.

They stood around and watched as we packed. Now that he knew that the writing on it was Jewish Hudd had no more interest in the ID bracelet. He planted a stick deep in the Israeli's grave, and hung the bracelet on it. The contrast to the lack of a marker on his man's grave – or his own when his time came I presumed – could not have been stronger. We rode away on two placid ponies, with our gear tied behind us. Each of our ponies was attached to the saddle of Van's donkey by a long halter, and followed it dutifully. All we had to do was hang on, and not get in each other's way.

As we started out Van looked back at us from under his parasol and said, 'The Jews came back. About two weeks ago . . .' He turned away before he finished the sentence.

That Egyptian colonel had asked me to do as Lot's wife, and not look back, and I had failed him. I didn't fail this time. I didn't glance back once at the black bomber. It took me all my concentration not to fall off the pony.

There's no getting away from it, even a large and sumptuous mud house is still a house made out of mud. Van's house was made of mud. You could see the hand prints on the wall where it had been patted into place. He proudly showed me some small hands a couple of feet from the ground.

'Mine. I was only five years old and already building my own house.'

His was the largest of about twenty built against the inner wall of a mudbrick compound. From the outside the complex looked like a fort. More remarkably, large as it was, you couldn't even see it until you were two hundred and fifty yards away, because it was the same colour as the ground all around it, and nestled in the shadow of one of those crumbling mountains.

'Your RAF taught us how to do this,' Van had said as we rode up to the gate. Its warped wood was bleached almost silver by the sun, and looked as hard as metal. His men were doing the hollering and shooting in the air thing again.

'*I'm* in the RAF,' I told him.

'Don't tell anyone that; they'll kill you! The RAF bombed us out of our traditional tents and winter houses in the 1920s. We learned to build homes you couldn't spot from the air, or from a distance. I'm educated enough to say *thank you* – with some irony – but my wives will have your balls if they find out.'

Hudd guffawed, and muttered, 'Hard luck, Charlie. You'll make a good soprano.'

I hate these bloody comedians; they've been around me all my life.

Van and I sat cross-legged on carpets in a small warm room, and shared a hookah. The smoke was cool and scented. I actually preferred a good old Navy Cut, but a guest has duties as well as a host. One of them is to keep his trap shut. Not always my strong point.

'Tell me about your name,' I asked him. 'Last month I met an Egyptian colonel who believed that you could learn things about a man from his name.'

'Şiwan Mohamed Van. It's very straightforward, old boy. I was my father's eldest son. He was the leader of our small family, a role I was bound to inherit. So he named me *Şiwan*, which means shepherd. That's my job now, just like Jesus – I am the shepherd to my flock. My second name is *Mohamed*, the prophet's

419

name, which was also my father's first name, and *Van* is the place from which our family originally came – Lake Van. There are several ways that Kurds construct their names, but ours is gaining in popularity: personal name, father's name and then place name. Your Egyptian friend was therefore right. As soon as I told you my name, you also knew my father's name, and where we were from.'

'I'm just plain old Charles Aidan Bassett. I don't know where the Aidan came from – some Irish saint, I believe. My father's name is Albert. On my birth certificate it says I was born in Stoke-on-Trent, although I don't know what my family was doing there.'

'How large is your family, Charlie?'

'I had a mother and a sister, but they are both dead.'

'Does that make you sad?'

'So sad that I try not to remember it. My father is still alive, but recently he has begun to oppose our government in the matter of foreign wars, and has been arrested several times. He might even be in prison now.' I paused to wonder why I had told this stranger so much about myself already.

He smiled, and passed the hookah back to me.

'. . . it is because you look at me, and think *This man is like me.*'

'How did you know what I was thinking?'

'Because I *am* like you. It might also be something to do with the native tobacco we are sharing: it has beneficial effects, it is said.' I should have paid more attention to that.

He then asked, 'Are you married?'

'I have two children, boys, but I haven't married yet.'

Şiwan laughed. He had a wealthy laugh; one that said that life amused him. 'Isn't that rather putting the cart before the horse, old boy?' I now found that rather funny as well, and also laughed aloud. I couldn't remember the last time I had laughed like that.

I know that by now you're worrying about Hudd. Well, don't. He was in a small windowless room off the one I was sitting in: counting the money, of course.

I found him later in the small room we had been allocated to sleep in. There were two small horsehair mattresses on pallet beds, and heaps of heavy blankets. Homely and clean. I knew that I wouldn't wake up scratching.

Hudd sniffed as soon as he looked at me, and said, 'Christ, Charlie; you haven't been smoking that stuff, have you? It will rot your brain, and make you sterile.'

'What stuff?' Then I understood. 'Oh, is that what it was? *I've* seen those Air Ministry films as well, and don't believe a word of them. I just feel a bit light-headed, that's all . . . and very relaxed. I'm sure I haven't gone sterile yet.' I was just justifying myself, of course, which was stupid. I should have realized what I was doing.

'What did you tell him?'

'Apart from name, rank and serial number? We talked about our fathers. His died last year, and he's still upset about it. Have we found Watson's money?'

Hudd sighed, 'Yes and no. The three boxes they keep in the small room have the gold coin. There's fifty or sixty coins missing, but that doesn't amount to much.'

'So we've found the money Watson said we could keep. I like you, Hudd; you never take your eye off the ball.'

'Stop messing about. We still don't know where the paper stuff is, and that's what's important.'

'Do you think Şiwan knows where it is?'

'I don't know. He acts as if he's given me *all* of the money, apart from the odd coin . . . and do you know what they've done with them by the way?'

'No.' I yawned; '. . . and you'd better hurry up and tell me; I'm just about out on my feet.'

'That's the dope you smoked, you dope. I think all of the missing coins have been handed out, and made into decorations. Each of his wives has two around her neck on pieces of electrical wire. He wanted to collect them all back for us, but I told him no. They should keep them. Do you know why he's helping us, when he's already run rings around the Frogs and the Israelis?'

'Something to do with a sense of honour I think. His father told him that the rightful owner would come looking for it one day, and it would cause problems for the family if they didn't hand it over. Apparently the old man said they'd had enough trouble with the British Empire already, without taking it on again. You'll find the words *rightful* and *owner* are very big out here. The Vans own about a thousand square miles of mountain, and would fight to retain every stone of it. It also helps that he was educated in Cambridge, and has fond memories of its women.'

'I've never been to Cambridge.'

'I have. I'll lie down now, and tell you about it. When I stop speaking you'll know I'm asleep.'

The next morning Hudd told me those were the last words I spoke that night.

After breakfast of yoghurt, cheeses and flat bread, I explained to Van, 'I need to radio my boss, and tell him our situation . . . but I don't want to do it behind your back, and make you suspicious. You can listen in if you like.'

I had waited for Hudd to go out for his morning stroll. He did that after his morning meal; usually with a small spade in his hand – and by the way, *spade* means shovel, not a suit in a card game.

Şiwan said, 'He can hear you from here?'

'Morse code only. We can throw a signal hundreds of miles these days with the right equipment.'

'I can't read Morse.'

'You'll have to take me on trust then. Though some say it's difficult to trust someone from Stoke-on-Trent.' I enjoyed that. Touché.

I sent, *Recovered coin with local help. Still trying.*

You're always trying, was what came back at me. *Don't know why we put up with you.* I didn't recognize the hand, but the opening challenge and responses had been OK so I guessed it was M'smith. Wrong again. If my head felt muzzy that morning I had only myself to blame.

Hector?

Daisy.

You take a great photograph. Tell the boss we'll check in again later.

Why did you do that? I asked myself as I stowed the aerial. Why do you always have to be a smart arse?

Van asked, 'What's the matter? Bad news?' There must have been something in my face.

'No. I just made a Smart-Alec comment which will probably hurt someone, and get me into trouble. Why do we do that sort of thing?'

'Usually because we can't resist it. I can't speak for you, old boy, but when *I* do it I suspect that it's at times when I lack confidence. My old tutor used to talk about the Spartans *getting their retaliation in first*. It's one of those phrases that make no sense, but actually make perfect sense. What do you think?'

I thought for a moment, and then said, 'I think your father left his family in very safe hands.' That seemed to please him. So I took a chance, and asked, 'What else did you find in the plane?'

His face fell. 'Ah; so you want that as well. I'm sorry, I should have mentioned it. They are up on the roof. Why don't you come with me?'

I followed him up an outside staircase. Hudd was just coming back; I risked a quick thumbs up to him as I passed. There were a couple of small servants' rooms on the flat roof. I wondered if the eunuch lived there. Alongside them a brown skin awning had been rigged, beneath which were two seats from the Stirling each fitted into a wooden frame . . . and its radios and batteries.

'Just my little vanity,' he explained. 'Sometimes I listen to music with one of the wives. I heard some of the London Olympics, relayed from Cyprus, and, last year, a Test match. I get a signal when the weather is clear. I will have them brought down.'

I laughed. When I stopped I said, 'No. They're yours. Consider them part payment from my government in recompense for the mayhem we've caused here.'

'Thank you, Charlie, but that is also interesting.'

'Why?'

'Because it means, I think, that you are looking for something else which has been taken.'

I hadn't handled that terribly well, had I? Hudd would kill me when he found out.

'Maybe I am. But if I told you what it was, I'd have to kill you.' I smiled to take the sting from it.

'My women would literally skin you alive.' He wasn't fazed. 'You must never cross a Kurdish woman, Charlie: devils incarnate.'

'I'll remember that.'

'We removed nothing else, Charlie. Maybe the Jews or the French did. I will ask. Our family Frenchman may tell us, if the women ask him.' There it was again; that little shudder inside.

When I told Hudd, I asked him, 'Do you want the good news or the bad news?'

'The good news: it's too nice a morning for the other.'

'He's going to lend us a couple of pack mules and a couple of tribesmen to get the coins out of here . . .'

'. . . and the bad news?'

'He knows we're looking for something else, but not what.'

That stopped him for a minute. I tried a Josephine Baker number in my head. It was 'After I say I'm sorry'.

Hudd eventually sighed, 'How'd that happen?'

'I was asking him questions: I was clumsy. Sorry.' Another pause. I finished the song.

Hudd shrugged. 'It happens. I've made mistakes like that. What else did they get from the plane?'

'Radios, batteries, the seats . . . miles of electrical cabling, *and* the bloody machine guns of course. I didn't ask about the other, but I think he's truly intrigued. He thinks that the Israelis or the French must have had something away.'

'What did you say about the other stuff?'

'I told him to keep them. That's when he offered me transport and free passage out of here.'

'What goes around comes around,' Hudd grinned. 'Well done, Charlie.' He'd stolen my bloody line, hadn't he?

We left the next day. The three wooden boxes were loaded on two donkeys, with enough blankets and supplies to get us across near a hundred miles of hill and dale. Not your friendly English hill and dale, but the unforgiving Kurdish variety. Mountain passes, dried-up river beds, and vegetation that wanted to rip your legs off. Van and his people turned out to see us go. Hudd had taken another forty coins from the boxes and handed them round, shaking hands with each person who received one. It was like he was handing out medals. I gave them Hudd's man's small pack and first-aid kit. They responded by whooping it up again, and shooting holes in the sky. Van gave me a hug, and called me brother . . . I think they were just glad of some company for a couple of days. The tribesmen he had picked to accompany us stood by the animals.

Van told me, 'These are my cousins; good men. They cannot betray you.'

'I know. I wouldn't expect any friend of yours to betray us.'

'You don't understand, Charlie . . . they *cannot* betray you.' He muttered something to our two companions, who both grinned at me and opened their mouths. They had no teeth. And no tongues. Someone had been a bit too handy with a knife. Just the same as Levy's man, Chig – what had these people got against tongues? At least we wouldn't be plagued by their whistling on the trip. Van said goodbye, and led his people back inside their fortress. The hard silver wooden door was closed. They weren't the types to watch us out of sight. I liked that.

Chapter Twenty

Over the hills and far away

It was me that did the whistling. I couldn't get that old school tune 'Over the hills and far away' out of my head. Hudd told me to shut up a couple of times. I didn't pay much attention to him, but when our guides looked nervous and signed me to pipe down I complied. I worked out then that we'd moved onto some other bugger's patch. These tribal leaders were like little local warlords, and we had to avoid them for three days. That meant no fires and cold porridge, until we came down the valleys and into the town.

It was called Van, of course. Everything around here was called Van. There was Van and Tatvan and all the other little Vans clustered around one of the biggest inland stretches of water I'd ever seen: that was Lake Van, of course. The first time I saw it, it sparkled a deep blue green in the sun, and a deep green aromatic smell came off the bushes we pushed through. Like juniper.

Our two guides were supposed to leave us and our boxes at a building known as the English House.

The small plump man with specs who bustled out of the clapboard wooden house alongside the small church shook hands with all four of us.

'Alan Weir. Been expecting you. Not really English: South

African, but every time I said *South African* these beggars said *English*, and eventually they won. Wanted me to be English, you see. Now I'm sub-Consul for these parts. Trade mainly.' He made you breathless just listening to him.

'Charlie Bassett,' I told him. 'You're the South African Consul?'

'No, British. Don't worry, you'll understand eventually.' He wore a dodgy dog collar on top of a grubby shirt. He was about fifty.

'And you're a priest?'

'Minister. Methodist. Don't let it worry you though.' He seemed determined that nothing was going to worry me. That was interesting.

Hudd gave the guides another gold coin each. They were delighted. One opened his shirt to show me that he already had two strung on a horsehair lanyard around his neck.

'Made him rich,' Weir told us.

'What will he do with it?'

'Buy another wife. He already has one; you can tell that from the tattoo on the back of his hand.' I'd travelled with the guy for nearly four days, and hadn't noticed the blue star just above a knuckle.

They helped us carry the boxes into Weir's house. Two boxes took two men each to lift. The third was lighter. They left that for me. I was sweating before I put it down. After Şiwan's people had left, laden now with panniers of flat breads, yoghurt, fresh water – and big toothless smiles – the minister told us, 'Some people might think your boxes safer in the church, but they'd be wrong. There is more than one Islamic sect, you see, and whenever they fall out with each other they burn our church down.'

I thought about it. 'That doesn't make much sense.'

'Does, you know. It's the only thing they can agree upon. Come and have some tea: you've missed lunch.'

I don't know what I'd expected, but cheese and watercress sandwiches, in proper white bread, weren't all that high up on the list. Earl Grey tea, too. I recognized it as such because it was what Grace's mother once served me in the orangery of her huge house, when I was still getting on with them. There we were, sitting beside a small fortune in gold coins, at the end of the fucking world, enjoying an English afternoon tea. I told you: surrealism is all around you – all you have to do is look.

Weir's guest room looked exactly the same as Şiwan Van's. Even the furniture, carpets and beds had come out of the same shop. Maybe they had used the same interior decorator. We shoved the boxes under the beds. Then I had a bath – the first hot water in nearly two weeks – and went for a snooze. Hudd was already on his back and snoring. Even from across the room, he smelled worse than our donkeys. When I awoke it was dark through the small window, and I was alone. I had a hard-on. That happens to men, you know, but we don't often talk about it. I was also thinking about Haye with an e. That was interesting.

When Hudd came down to the dining room he had spruced himself up. We dined local style, cross-legged on carpets around a low table. There was a mudbrick stove in the corner, throwing out a decent heat, and finer carpets between the niches in the wall. These small hollows contained candles, highly polished brass pots and small religious paintings . . . and a large wooden crucifix propped up in a corner reminded us where we were. The food had been served by a rather beautiful girl of about eighteen in native clothes; bright silks. She laughed a lot, and surprised me by joining us once the food was on the table. Her eyes and hair were as black as crows' feathers.

'My wife, Arzu,' Weir offered. 'Turkish. She was a server in our church in Ankara when we met. So we had to come out here.'

I smiled at her, pointed to myself and said, 'Charlie,' and to Hudd, and said, 'Hudd.' Then, 'Thank you for putting up with us.' I spoke laboriously, hoping that she could follow it. She smiled back prettily. I bet she did everything prettily.

'You are welcome; Alan likes entertaining, but doesn't often get the opportunity.' The only sign that English wasn't her first language was the way she strung out the five-syllable word.

Hudd nodded, and said, 'You speak wonderful English.'

'I learned at the English School. Alan taught me.'

'Minister,' I said to him. 'Consul, and teacher too . . .'

'*Head* teacher . . .' she corrected me.

'Keeps me off the streets,' he said, and laughed.

'. . . and he sells the bus tickets,' she added. I liked the way that smiles moved between them as if they were speaking a private language.

Ah, I thought, and asked him, 'Where does your bus go?'

'Istanbul; if your backsides can bear it. Takes three days on wooden seats . . . now, where do you want to start; lamb or goat?' He lifted the lid on two steaming dishes of meat and vegetables. The smells rose orange and yellowy from them, and thick, like London fogs. My mouth literally watered. I almost missed the blue star on the back of his hand as I handed my plate to him.

'So that's your plan. It's prosaic but very simple: I like that. We are going to escape on a bus. Why do buses always make me think of Piccadilly Circus?'

I was lying back on my bed talking to the dark. The room was warm – the stove chimney climbed up one corner – I was full, and I'd even had a bottle of beer to round the meal off: Weir made his own, and had told us earlier:

'Not strictly supposed to – but the Muslim administration turns a blind eye to Europeans as long as we are still useful to them. Owner of the flour mill, for example, is a very devout man, but about twice a week he will call in and ask me for a glass or two of "medicine" for his bad chest, and I send him reeling home a few hours later. He always leaves a sack of best flour. He's also the chairman of the local tribal council, so I never have a problem with labour for rebuilding the church after it has been burned down.'

I'd smiled. 'That sounds like an interesting arrangement.'

'It is: you can always come to interesting arrangements with God.'

Now Hudd replied to me, 'You couldn't be more wrong if you tried.'

'I'm not riding four hundred miles on a donkey, Hudd.'

'You'll do whatever I tell you to do. I do the logistics; you're only the brains of the outfit.' That made me laugh. Somehow I was laughing more frequently and more easily these days. I wondered if it was anything to do with Şiwan's tobacco.

'How old do you think Alan is?' I asked.

'Fifty. Fifty-five maybe?'

'Bit of an old goat, isn't he? Arzu can't be twenty yet.'

'Ask me again when you're fifty yourself, Charlie. You may see things differently then.'

I'd got my pipe going and a nice fug up. Hudd didn't complain this time. It wouldn't have occurred to me back in the Fifties to have asked anyone if they objected.

'When are we leaving here, Hudd?'

'As soon as I find out what those Israelis are up to, and if they got the paper money; I haven't forgotten it ya' know. If they were up on that plateau a coupla weeks ago they could still be about. I don't know if they got the dosh, but I want to be able to tell your Mr Watson one way or the other. Can you send him a signal from here?'

'I can try. There may not be anyone listening now he knows it's a cock-up.'

'OK. Try: tell him where we are, and that we're still looking for the dollars . . . and use your bloody code book.'

'Yes, master.'

'. . . and cut out the sarcasm.'

'Yes, master.' He threw a carpet-covered cushion at me.

Watson responded immediately. After that there were gaps in the transmission while we decoded between separate bursts. He surprised me by asking after our welfare first. *Warm, fed and safe as we've been in days* I sent him. He came back with *Take no chances: not worth another loss*. He couldn't bring himself to signal *Not worth another death* – we British can be oddly squeamish at times; I'm sure you've noticed. Or maybe Watson had a soft side after all. I told him where we were, and how we were fixed, and that I'd stick to my broadcasting schedule the next day. I signed off.

'He must be sleeping alongside the radio,' I told Hudd. 'He's worried about us.'

'Not as much as I am.'

'How are you going to find the Israelis?'

'How big is this town, Charlie? Two hundred houses? Three?'

'What does that mean?'

'All we have to do is stick around long enough, and I think they'll find *us*.'

'Oh.' I wasn't sure that I liked that.

The smell of the smoke from the stove lingered in the room. It wasn't unlike the smell of peats burning I'd come across in the west of Scotland a few years earlier.

I was sleepy when I asked, 'What do they burn in the stove, Hudd? It smells sweet . . . just like peat.'

'Camel and horse dung. They dry it out in long barns in the summer, an' it lasts all winter.'

Kurds with turds, I thought. That was even better.

In the morning we discussed our problem. The difficulty was that if either of us wandered around on his own we would be taking a big chance. On the other hand, both of us sallying forth together would leave our boxes unguarded, and that wasn't such a good idea either. We tossed for it. I got to stay at home while Hudd did our first recce. Neither of us was happy about it, but it was the best option. He could have gone out with Weir, but that would only draw attention to the minister, and ultimately us. Despite what he had said before, Hudd wanted to keep our presence at Weir's house as discreet as possible.

I waved him off like a wifey waving her husband off to work. I cleaned and checked my small pistol, and then read one of Weir's books. It was *Trouble Shooter* by an American named Louis L'Amour. Weir had an amazing collection of Westerns propped up between two massive Bibles. There's a message in there somewhere. Arzu flip-flopped in and out on bare feet from time to time: tidying, dusting, moving from room to room. Every time she passed near I got a whiff of her scent, stopped thinking about my book, and began thinking of other things; and she knew it. Maybe I should buy myself a camera, and try out Nancy's lines. Alan Weir walked through on one occasion speaking aloud – he was composing his next sermon in his head. He wore an amused smile. The day dragged on, and after our days up in the hills it was like being in prison. I even looked forward to Hudd's ugly old mug reappearing.

When it did we sat in the kitchen because it was warmer, and

Arzu prepared us Turkish coffee. Weir was out bothering his flock.

'There are a few Europeans around,' Hudd told me. 'Most of them are from the oil companies. BP has an office here, and so has Shell. They're exploring. So are the Americans and the French. It's a bit like a gold rush. The first one to find major deposits of oil will come up with an offer the government and locals can't resist – but the companies won't bid until they've actually found the stuff.'

'Is there much?'

'Loads and loads of it, apparently. It will just depend on whether it's cost-effective to get it out of the ground.'

'What about Şiwan's Jews?' Even as I said that I felt uncomfortable. 'I don't like saying that word anymore; isn't that odd?'

'The Nazis discredited it. Jews don't mind calling themselves Jews; it's only us. We think it makes us sound like Nazis. I know what you mean: the Israelis have murdered British soldiers and nurses, torn the Middle East in half, and still we can't call them what they call themselves. I usually say Israelis, but whenever I say it I feel like a coward.'

'What about Şiwan's *Israelis*, then?'

He made the effort and said, 'I met a drunken Welshman who said there's a bunch of Jews living in a villa down by the lakeside.' He grinned: like he didn't mean it.

'Well done. Was he one of your oilmen?'

'No. He works for the British Council.'

'What's he doing up here?'

'Looking for poets, he said.'

'*Are* there any?'

'Loads, apparently, and nobody knows what to do with them . . . they're nowhere near as useful as oil.'

I heard Weir come back and call a greeting. Arzu joined us at the table and helped Hudd draw a map on which he marked out the bars where men smoked, and drank coffee, and the small bazaars where people wandered. Weir came in after five minutes, and looked over her shoulder. They bickered amiably over whether the shops were marked in the right places. Their alterations had made the map almost unintelligible.

I asked Hudd, 'What's it for, anyway?'

'Your turn now: you can visit a few places tonight, and see what you can turn up. You'll need a map 'cos there ain't no street lights out there. Leicester Square it isn't.'

'What do I use for money?'

'Alan's changed a couple of sovereigns for me. You can buy a small family an' all their goats for that.'

'. . . and camels' teeth,' Arzu added. 'My father said that when he was a boy he could buy spices with camels' teeth.'

'What would people want camels' teeth for?'

'For good luck, of course!' There was no denying it. She had a delicious little giggle.

They dowsed the lights at the front of the house that night, so that no one would see me slip out if the place was being watched. Just before she opened the door for me, Arzu gave me a peck on the cheek, and I felt her hand in the pocket of my leather jacket. It paused when she touched my pistol, and then moved past it.

She wasn't being improper; she whispered, 'For good luck,' and her hand was gone.

When I put my own hand in the pocket I felt one of those big buck teeth a camel grins with. I turned back to say thank you, but the door was already closed. I heard the bolts go home. It was as black as in an outdoor privy out there.

I thought I saw a movement in the dark shadows across the road, and waited more than a minute before I shifted. No one stepped out to follow me. Things look different at night. Cats can even become lions. I walked down to the corner of the road between dull houses. The occasional window laid the occasional square of dull light on the ground. No pavements. Just as I reached the junction, a person stepped out in front of me, still in shadow. Someone in a nearby room lit a lamp, and our faces were suddenly illuminated by the light from its open window. My heart beat like a tom-tom.

She said, 'Hello, Charlie. I hoped it was you. I know somewhere they'll give us good coffee.'

Chapter Twenty-One

The Sheik of Araby

'Your parents gave you the wrong name, Grace,' I told her. 'They should have called you Tinkerbell . . . from *Peter Pan*.'

'Why?'

'Because you always turn up when I least expect you to, and then you make a mess of my life.'

'You didn't complain in Cyprus.'

'You never gave me a chance to. You sodded off again before I could blink my eyes.'

Grace bent over and extinguished the candle on the table between us with a moistened forefinger and thumb. It was the sort of thing she'd do; and she wouldn't change her expression even if it had hurt.

She said, 'I read a novel about Peter Pan once. It ended a year after the Darlings had returned to their family. Tinkerbell had died, and Peter couldn't even remember her name. Isn't that sad?' She always asked you questions that made you pause and think.

'I'll never forget you, Grace. Fat chance.'

'Good.' She put her hand over mine, on the table.

I asked her, 'What is this place?'

'It's an illegal drinking den. They had them in Ireland when I was delivering planes during the war. They called them shebeens there. They are places you can go and drink in whatever company you like – men, women or in-betweens – and no one asks you your religion, or for your identity card. Places made for folk like you and me.'

The place was dark, and smelled of hashish – now that I knew what the stuff smelt like. I'd followed Grace through the dark streets trying to memorize our route – twice I suspected she had deliberately diverted to confuse me. You entered this den through a wooden gate in what appeared to be a high garden wall, but found yourself instead in a darkened corridor like a tunnel. The dull light at the end of it was over something like a bar in a large circular room. You could get coffee, a hookah or smuggled beer. There were probably girls, or men or whoever you fancied on the menu, if you asked. It was busy: buzzing with low-pitched conversations.

We took a couple of bottles of beer each, and went into a small semicircular alcove. There were about twenty around the periphery of the room. Cushions and a curtain, low table, small oil lamp on the wall and a candle on the table. Grace seemed to know the form. She swapped a few sweet words with the owner – but they were in Turkish so I didn't understand what was said. The smell of the oil from the wall lamp hung around us like a crude scent. I didn't mind that.

Grace clinked bottles with me, and said, 'Cheers.'

'Did you know I was here?' I asked her.

'Partly. The leader of our little embassy has paid some of the street kids to let him know if any European strangers turn up. As soon as I heard the description of you walking out of the mountains, I think I knew. So I hung around the end of the street, and waited to see who came out of the English House. I saw the big man go in, and a few hours later you came out. Now, here we are.'

'Why didn't you just knock on the door?'

'I wanted to see you alone.'

'Why?'

Even in the half-light I could see how she dropped her eyes before she replied. Her voice dropped a register as well.

'I thought we could manage better on our own. The others would just have wanted their say, and have probably cocked things up: you know what men are like.'

I could have said something smart, but I just nodded, and asked, 'Cock what up, my pretty one?' I shocked myself. I don't think I'd ever used a pet phrase for Grace in my life. She allowed herself a brief smile, as if she'd won a point. She may have, for all I knew.

'The *deal* of course, darling.'

'What deal?'

'The deal for the money you brought down with you, of course. You have it, and I want it.'

'What's in it for me?'

'I will convince my people not to kill you – which is what they want to do at the moment. Shall we smoke one of those things together, for old time's sake?' She nodded at the bar, where a large man was preparing several water pipes.

'No. I never saw myself as a dope user. Booze and pipe tobacco will do me. I still smoke the pipe you gave me.' Grace ignored my last sentence.

She said, 'You can get opium here, you know. I always fancied doing that once; just to see what it did to me.'

'No, Grace.'

'You're an old square, Charlie. Not fun any more.'

'Does *square* mean . . . ?'

'Yes, old-fashioned and unadventurous. American teenagers are using it. You weren't like that when I first met you.'

'I'm older now.'

'And I'm not; is that what you mean?' Her bottom lip turned down.

We were back to Peter Pan again, weren't we? People who never grew up. Grace had started off by insulting me, and had turned that into a reason to feel insulted herself. It was something that couldn't have happened in a conversation between two men. Nothing to be done about it. And she was still the most enchanting woman I had met in my life. Nothing to be done about that either.

'We can get a room upstairs, if you like. It's quite private.'

In order to give myself thinking space I asked, 'How do you know about places like this, Grace?'

'Every town in Turkey and North Africa has a place like this, Charlie . . . you just have to know who to ask.'

Later we lay back on an old mattress covered in carpets. Where we touched, we stuck lightly together. Sweat. Grace always worked you hard I remembered.

She asked, 'Will your people worry about where you are?'

'Maybe, but I shouldn't think so. I was sent out to find where the Israelis were . . .'

'. . . and you found them.'

'I was going to ask you about that. What *were* you doing, there in Cyprus?'

'Exactly what I told you. There's a deal between your government and the state of Israel. Britain is going to support us when the Arab League girds its loins for another attack on Israel, but can't do so openly because that will offend NATO. I was tying up the last threads, that's all. They must have really been scraping the bottom of the barrel if I was the only person they could find who both sides would trust. When I ran off to Israel in 1947 I was called a traitor to my country: now I am a trusted intermediary. Isn't life odd?'

'So how does the deal work?'

'At the first sign of trouble, we storm through the Sinai and up to the Canal, gratefully capturing all of the arms and stores dumps the British have thoughtfully left behind for us. We could have reached the Canal in 1948 if our supply lines had stretched that far . . . as it is we've kitted out the Army with your war-surplus stores, and you are the best people to supply us with the spares.'

'You know where our secret supply dumps are . . . ?'

'Most of them.'

'Because we've told you?'

'Yes.'

'And the Egyptians *don't* know of course, but are desperate to find out.'

'Correct again, Charlie . . . and to think we once thought that Never-Never Land was only in a book!'

'What do we get out of it?'

'Your lovely bloody Canal, I should think. All of a sudden, Mr Churchill is scared the Egyptians are going to kick you out, and take it back. He talks about *the vital lifeline to our Empires in the East*. But he's mad: all of them are. You need someone to help you hang on to the Canal, and we need someone to help prevent the Arabs shovelling us into the sea the next time they have a go at us. A nice little self-preservation society of two.'

I lit a couple of fags from a packet of bootleg Players Navy Cut that came with the room, and handed her one. We lay on our backs smoking, an aluminium ashtray balanced on my belly.

'Grace?'

'Yes?'

'I knock along quite nicely in life, you know.'

441

'Do you?'

'Yes. I read the newspapers, talk to my boss, run a small airline. I think that I know the way the world works . . .'

'But?'

'Then I meet you again . . . and each time I do, after you've gone, I find that the world isn't like I thought it was after all. It's as if you change history every time I see you.'

She rolled over, and kissed me on the cheek. I felt warm tobacco smoke against my face before she spoke.

'Don't worry, Charlie. You're much better at it than most. You know nearly all the answers most of the time. I just fill in a few of the little gaps for you.' I felt a brief tickle on my belly, and knew that she'd flicked off her fag ash, and missed the ashtray. I hoped she'd look before she stubbed it out.

'Knowing what's in those gaps changes the way I see things.'

'Good. It's nice to know that someone's listening.' Hadn't Hudd said something like that to me? The flat pressure on my belly told me she *had* looked before extinguishing her smoke. She rolled away, and turned her back on me. 'I'm going to have a little nap now, darling, and when I wake up we can talk about the money.'

I looked at the ceiling. The room was completely black. It was like being suspended in space. Hudd had wanted to know if the Israelis had the money, before we split. It was clear now that they hadn't. All I had to do was get back to him in one piece, and tell him the news. And for the first time in my life, I needed to get away from Grace. That was interesting.

When I awoke, Grace was humming a tune. It was 'The Sheik of Araby'. Back in my prefab in Bosham I had a Tommy Dorsey recording of that. It was popular in the jazz clubs, where we roared out a vulgar version whose words we had learned in the war.

'How long have you been awake?' I yawned.

'Five minutes. I was bored so I started to sing. I wanted to find out how loud I would have to get before you sat up.'

'How loud were you?'

'Not very.'

'Shall we do what we usually do when you're bored?'

'No, Charlie. Let's talk about money.'

'You know your trouble, don't you?'

'No, what?'

'You're a square.' The words fitted nicely in my mouth. I'd thought since the war that the next adventures for the English language were being written in America. It was time the world started to pay attention to the American teenager. I bent over and kissed a big nipple on a small breast, but Grace pushed me away.

'*Money.*'

'You never used to be interested in money,' I told her cheerfully. 'It must be the people you're mixing with.'

'Shit!' Grace sat up. 'You don't think I'm serious, do you? We could all get killed over this!'

'You never used to be worried about that either, when we smuggled you on to *Tuesday's Child* and flew you over the Ruhr in 1944. You didn't worry about living and dying at all.'

'Maybe I'm older now,' she spat at me.

When I said, 'I've been trying to get you to admit that all night,' she flung herself at me in a fury, punching and scratching and sobbing. Very un-Grace.

It ended with making love again, of course. With Grace everything always ended with love making. But she quietly cried herself to sleep afterwards. That was new.

Before dawn, I woke her and asked, 'Would they really kill me for a couple of boxes of coins?'

'Don't be stupid, Charlie . . . not now you're beginning to do so well. You can do whatever you please with the bloody coins. I want the real money.'

'What for? It's fake isn't it? That's what I was told.'

'It's exceptionally good counterfeit dollars, Charlie. Billions of them. So good that you could pass it off anywhere in the world other than Washington. America has fully committed itself to rebuilding old Europe, and Japan, and its own peacetime industries. Its armed forces occupy parts of Korea, Germany and Japan. In order to counter the Reds it has a bigger Air Force establishment in Britain, Italy, Germany and Iceland than it had during the war. This is costing a colossal amount of money to keep going. America is fully stretched, she has no money to spare – absolutely none at all – and anyone dumping that amount of dud money on the market will simply bankrupt her.'

'But that won't do *you* any good.'

'The threat of it will do us good. If Israel has the cuckoo's egg and America knows it, she will have to support us through thick or thin. Israel will be able to sort out its neighbours, and any attempt to restrain us will be vetoed by the US within the UN. It's a get-out-of-jail-free card that will last for years.'

'And *we* want the money back to stop you blackmailing the Yanks with it?'

'Don't be so bloody naive, darling.' Grace yawned. 'You want it for the same reason as us. If you have it safely tucked away in the Bank of England you'll subtly indicate to our American cousins that you'd prefer them to support any British move to guarantee British control of the Suez Canal. The Americans wouldn't dare to interfere.'

'But I thought you said Britain and Israel are secretly cooperating over the Canal?'

'We are, darling, but we're like two wild cats tied up in a sack. Both of us would prefer to have the means to go it alone.'

I mulled this over for a couple of minutes then said, 'Poor old Yanks. Whichever way it turns out someone is going to have them over a barrel.'

'One thing is certain in the Middle East, Charlie. Either Israel is going to put her neighbours back in their place, and start building secure borders . . . or Britain will strengthen its hold on the Canal. But only one of those two things can happen, because it depends on who has control of your dud money. If Israel gets it the Americans will do as we tell them; if Britain gets its hands on it, America will support your illegally annexing the Canal.'

'What if the Yanks get it back themselves?'

'Then we're both stuffed, aren't we?'

'. . . and your people will kill me to get it?'

'They will kill you to get it, or to stop you getting it. Either or both.'

'You're beginning to move with a very unpleasant class of person, Grace. Do you know that?' At least she giggled when I said that.

'You're priceless, Charlie.'

'But I haven't got your money. All I brought down from the hills were boxes of coins: sovereigns and half-sovereigns . . . and funnily enough – which is why I believe you this time – my bosses said exactly the same as you: that we could keep the coin for all they'd care. All they wanted to see was banknotes.'

Grace was quiet for a long time, and then she said, 'Bugger.'

'There were two expeditions before ours – the local tribesmen told us that. One French and one Israeli. Maybe they got it.'

'No; I'd know that.'

'Maybe it was never there in the first place.'

'No. I'd know that too. Our best interrogators questioned the aircraft crew when they crossed over into Israel. The stuff was in the plane.'

'Where in the plane?'

'We don't know.'

'Didn't they tell you?'

'No. They held that detail back until we guaranteed them citizenship. Then some fool took it into his head that they were lying, were spies, and had them shot.'

Poor Frohlich, I knew him, Horatio. I didn't see that I needed to tell Grace that, but Grace was nothing if not sharp.

She asked, 'How come you're mixed up in all this anyway, Charlie?'

'They wanted someone to identify the aircraft: somebody they could control – I'd seen it at Tempsford a month before it got here, although I was in hospital by the time they ran.'

'That's where you burned your face and your shoulders?'

'That's right: what goes around comes around.'

It was an odd, peaceful moment. We had said all that needed to be said. Grace would tell her people what she'd learned from me. If I made it back, I'd tell Hudd.

If her pals didn't believe me, and genuinely thought I had the dollars, they would try to kill me for them. If they believed me, they *still* wouldn't be able to take a chance on my not being able to work out where the money was anyway . . . and if they wanted another shot at finding it they'd still have to kill me, to be on the safe side. Tails I lost; heads they won. I suppose we both knew that when Grace left the place she would be carrying my death warrant with her. I sat up and swung my feet over the edge of the old mattress. Yawned, and stretched.

Grace asked me, 'Do you still carry that silly little pistol of yours?'

'Yes.'

I pulled over my leather jacket, and took it out of the pocket. I handed it to her. What I was left with was a camel's tooth in my hand.

She asked, 'What's that?'

'A camel's tooth. Someone gave it to me for luck.'

She handed back the pistol, and I put it and the tooth in separate pockets. The pistol was shoved into the left one.

Grace said, 'Why don't you kill me: now? You'd get a head start. You and your pal could be away before they realized anything had gone wrong.'

'I couldn't do that, Grace. You know that.'

'Yes, Charlie, I do.' She said that very sadly. 'Bugger off. I'll give you an hour.'

I dressed silently; neither of us said goodbye. The place was in darkness still, and every direction I turned seemed to echo with the snores of contented sleepers. As I got to the street dawn was just beginning to show, so I slipped into the shadows, and tried to find my way back.

Alas, with Grace, things were rarely that easy. After I had been moving for twenty minutes, I became aware that I was being followed. I don't know how that happens: I didn't see or hear anything, I just knew. The streets seemed even darker than at night, because no windows shed light onto the roads. When I judged I was about three blocks from home I checked at a corner, and looked back to the one I'd rounded a minute before.

Grace should have been more careful. She stopped, but had already taken a step too many, and was out in the open. There was nowhere to hide.

She pulled an automatic pistol from her waistband, and fired it at me. Just like that. I hope that it was an instinctive reaction – something she didn't think about. In the split second before the first bullet hit me my brain was saying *Grace can't be doing this*. The bullet struck the wall a couple of feet off the ground, and ricocheted into my inside right knee. The leg was immediately numbed: it kept me upright, but I couldn't feel anything, not even the ground beneath my foot.

I must have thrown up my right arm in front of my face when she fired again. Stupid – how can you ward off bullets with an arm? It was a better shot this time, kissed my raised forearm in the fleshy part below my elbow, and spun me half round. Her pistol made heavy, deep booms as it fired: one of those horrible Russian things I think. As the bullet turned me, I suppose I reacted instinctively myself. I drew my small pistol with my left hand, aimed it and fired. Grace sort of twitched, lowered her pistol and nipped back out of sight. Maybe she staggered. How long had this taken? Five seconds? Ten? No more. How many ways did that American guy say there were to leave your lover?

I leaned back against the wall to keep myself upright, dropped my chin on my chest and breathed deeply. My sleeve was cut and wet. Grace didn't reappear. A light went on in a house across the road and, when I looked towards it, I saw a little girl of about six staring curiously at me. She waved. I gave her a weak smile, and pocketed my gun. Another light went on further down the road, and I heard a voice calling. Time to go, Charlie.

I got back to the English House after about ten more minutes of hobbling, using my good leg, and the walls of houses as a crutch . . . and taking several breathers. I pounded on Weir's door, and when he answered it, grumbling, fell into his arms.

'Tell Hudd we gotta get out of here,' I told him.

It wasn't yet light when I passed out, and it was dark again when I awoke twelve hours later.

'Keep your voice down,' Hudd said. 'We don't have to wait long.'

'What for?'

'Getting out of here, o' course. How d'ye feel?'

'Groggy, and my knee hurts.'

'It's got a bullet in it, that's why. But it's only just beneath the skin so it may not have done too much damage. Alan gave you a hefty jab, and knocked you out.'

'Where are we?'

'In a warehouse owned by your friendly smuggler. You gave me his name and address. How come you know people in this town that I don't?'

'Long story. Are we safe?'

'For the time being, I think. He won't take any money for helping us. He says he's doing it for a friend of yours . . . and that I owe him a favour. I've got a feeling I might regret this one day.' There was a smile in his voice. Hudd seemed to have kept things together in my absence, but I would have expected nothing less. I wondered when he would begin to mourn his man Freddy, or whether he was simply too professional for that. The place smelt of old fish, tar and ropes – that smell of tarred string I'll always associate with my childhood. Dad used to make me a bow with arrows every year: the tarred string lasted all summer.

'Have I been asleep all day?'

'Most of it. I had to gag you when you began to talk – it was a load of garbage by the way: something to do with the smell of fish being silver . . . what did that mean?'

'Don't worry about it – it was just an idea I'm trying out.' I moved my head from side to side, and could see, even in the gloom, that I was lying on the flatbed of a handcart with two big wheels. 'Can I sit up now? I'm thirsty.'

'Do it slowly, an' don't tip this thing over. Goat's milk or water?'

'I'd kill for a cold beer.'

'You may *have* to, buddy.'

It seemed to me that our whispers filled the vast shed with ghosts. I could almost see some of my old crew standing in the shadows. Toff, our mid-upper gunner, grinned at me and pointed at his right knee. He knew I was hurting. What was *he* doing there? He wasn't supposed to be dead yet. When I shook my head to clear my vision they faded back into the shadows.

Later I asked Hudd,

'What's that Israeli bunch doing?'

'Running about like blue-arsed flies. Apparently they've lost someone, and they're turning the town upside-down looking for her. You can tell me about that on the boat . . . it would probably scare me too much in here.' I couldn't actually imagine Hudd being scared of anything. 'They've already upset the local rozzers and the town council, which should slow them down quite a bit, but I'd still like to get out of here before they come looking for us.'

'I'm not good on boats, Hudd: I get seasick.'

'That could be the least of your worries.'

Just before midnight, Hudd and a great moustachioed Turk wheeled me down to a small harbour of fishing boats. Every jolt over every stone sent fire shooting from my knee to my brain. I bit my lip until I could taste blood in my mouth. My arm didn't feel that bad – just tight, so I knew they'd bandaged me. I felt helpless lying on my back on that bloody fish cart. Weir trundled behind us with another cart bearing the three boxes.

'What's the opposition doing?' I ground the words out from behind clenched teeth.

Weir consulted the Turk in rapid-fire Turkish. Then he told me, 'They shot someone, stole his lorry and have driven off to Tatvan in it because an inventive liar told them you'd be heading in that direction. That road is absolutely terrible. If they get back here before morning, all they'll get is a shoot-out with the local militia. Happy days.'

I thought that the inventive liar had better keep his head down for a few weeks, and next asked, 'What happened to the woman they lost?'

His exchange with the Turk took longer this time. In fact it was almost a conversation. Then Weir told me, 'Nobody knows. It's a mystery.' They'd taken a bloody long time to arrive at five words.

I smelt salt in the air, and heard the gentle tidal bumping of wooden vessels against a quay. I already felt queasy, but good old Hudd: he was getting us away by water – a man of many talents. We stopped. The last chill of the year was still there in the air. I looked at Hudd, Weir and the Turk and suddenly felt so grateful I wanted to weep. Their breaths steamed. Above them was the northern Middle East sky with its dancing stars. The cold air ringed each one with rainbow colours. Despite the pain I managed to log a memory of them – I had never seen anything as beautiful.

There is an island on Lake Van, not far off the shore from which we'd started. It is wooded, and cold, and it supports the ruins of a Coptic church or monastery. I know that because I've been there; you probably haven't. After twenty minutes we began to run in towards the island and my anxiety level climbed. Twenty minutes wasn't far enough away from the homicidal maniacs who wanted to kill me. I asked the time-honoured, 'Where are we?'

'Akhtamar Island. We'll be picked up from here.' That was Hudd.

Weir and David Yassine's Turk helped us ashore. I hopped on my good leg, leaning on Weir's shoulder. We lay up alongside the ruined church; its crumbling walls and the low scrubby trees around them hid us from the breezes off the lake, which lowered the seasonal temperature even more. After an hour or so I began to shiver. Weir and the Turk had already left; the chug-chug from the boat's engine couldn't be heard further than a few yards

451

– a good smuggling vessel, I guessed, but what would you want to smuggle across an inland saltwater lake?

'Now's as good a time as any,' Hudd decided. 'You can tell me where you got to last night, and exactly who shot you. It will help keep you alive.'

I don't know how it happened – partly it was my determination to stay awake, because I felt so desperately tired – but I found myself telling him Grace's entire story. About her ATA days, and coming to Germany with us in *Tuesday's Child*, riding the Lancaster's rear turret. About chasing her through western Europe and Italy at the end of the war, and her turning up in London in 1947 before escaping to Israel in a rusty tub of a tramp ship skippered by a Dutch pirate. About bringing up her son as mine. About Cyprus, and finally meeting her the night before. Did I tell him how irresistible she was? I don't know; I think so.

'But she tried to kill you?'

'I don't know, Hudd. I thought she would have been a better shot than that.'

'. . . and you hit her with your shot?'

'Again, I don't know. She didn't fall, if that's what you mean. She certainly twitched. Maybe I just startled her.'

'Maybe she wanted you to finish it. You said she'd suggested you kill her earlier.'

'She knew I couldn't do that.'

'Maybe you have.'

How can you bloody well respond to that? '. . . and maybe that's the last bloody thing in the world I wanted someone to say, Hudd.'

We'd reached a natural break. I was propped up against the church wall watching the stars. After a while Hudd watched them too. At some point he said, 'Sorry, buddy.'

I didn't reply immediately. Eventually I asked him, 'When do we get out of here?'

'First light.'

'What are you going to do with the sovereigns?'

'Give 'em back. I'll keep a handful for pocket money, but I wouldn't know what to do with the rest . . . and you don't need them, do you?'

'How do you work that out?'

'You got the look, Charlie. You're never going starve, are you? You know it and I know it.'

'I won't have time to starve, at this rate; some cow will probably shoot me again.'

'You don't think all women are cows, either. Do you?'

'No. You'll think I'm stupid, but I think that none of them are. The women in my life have been the best people who happened to me.'

'Which is how it should be. Freddy called them *comfort blankets*. I wonder if he's comfortable where he is now.'

'When I get to Heaven, Hudd, I know it's going to be a pub or a bar. Freddy will be there, and all my mates as well. You can come too if you like.'

'That would be fine, Charlie . . . as long as we can put it off for a few years. Why don't you shut your eyes for a couple of hours?'

I told him the truth. 'I don't feel well, Hudd. I'm scared I won't wake up again.'

'I'll wake you: trust me.'

He didn't need to. I dreamed about the black bomber. In my dream it was flying around inside that bowl of parched mountains, its four tired old radial engines screaming as it clawed for height. But there was no way out for her. She would fly until she dropped. Grace and the black bomber were all mixed up in my mind. The dream was so vivid that I could still hear those radials when I opened my eyes. And they didn't stop even then. There was an aircraft somewhere above the lake.

First light.

I could make out the shape of Hudd standing on a spit of shingle, with his arm outstretched, like someone hailing a bus at a request stop. Then his hand burst into flame and colour, lighting him up like a shabby angel. *Flare*, my mind said. When it died Hudd crunched back across the stones.

'Rise and shine, old son.'

'What is it?'

'A ruddy great Sunderland flying boat, come to take us home. It's on its finals now. Whatever you do, pretend you're pleased to see them. You never know when we'll want them again.' It was what my dad used to say about girls. I thought of Grace, and I began to cry.

I had always wanted to travel in a flying boat, and experience the drag of the water as you lifted off, but this wasn't to be my time. They tied me to a bunk, and wouldn't let me watch the take-off. Two blokes worked on me; one may have been the old man from the medical section at Port Said. He peeled my jacket off, and tut-tutted at the state of the bandage on my arm. It can't have been up to NATO standard. The other opened my pants from ankle to crotch with a pair of scissors, and observed, 'This knee's a bit of a mess.'

There was a prick in my upper arm – the good one – but I didn't mind that. Soon I was flying above the water beside the aircraft. The black bomber was somewhere out to port and a bit behind us, flying a nice parallel: we were taking her home, but only in my head of course.

*

Sleep. Perfect sleep.

Hudd came to see me in the small hospital at El Kirsh. It was almost a goodbye.

He asked, 'What's the matter with you?'

'Apart from being shot? I've woken up twice in a hospital on one trip. That's good going, even for me.'

'This place is full of nurses. I can't see what you're complaining about.'

'I'm bored.'

He flung my small pack onto the bed. I winced when it banged up against my leg. He didn't seem to notice.

'Your pipe's in there. I bunged in some fresh tobacco too, and a couple of books. OK?'

'Thank you. Don't mind me – I'll be laughing as soon as I'm on my feet again.'

'Mr Watson's sending the rest of your kit on . . . and your mail. Apparently a big envelope addressed to you burst open in the post office, and it was full of dirty pictures: the Provost's people might want to talk to you. How's the knee: permanent damage?'

'It'll hurt in wet weather, the Doc says. Apart from that I'd be playing football again in a few weeks, if ever I played the damned silly game in the first place.'

'Don't you like soccer?'

'No: it's an idiotic way to spend an afternoon.'

Hudd and I were never going to be a marriage made in heaven.

He said, 'I've got to ask you this . . . and this is for me, not for anyone else: it won't go any further, OK?'

'What?'

'Do you *know* where the rest of the money is?'

If, before you answer a question, you ask yourself *Can I trust this person?* then you can't. I thought that about Hudd, and then told him anyway. I reckoned I owed it to him.

'Maybe . . . can we say I have a good idea where it is, and leave it at that?'

'Thank God for that, I'd hate to think of Freddy going for nothing.'

'Don't you want to know where?'

'No, Charlie, an' *you* don't want to tell me.'

I filled and lit a pipe. I've told you that Grace had bought it for me years ago, so it reproached me as soon as I touched it. Someone had told me about a good pipe shop in a bazaar in Port Said, and I resolved to buy a new one there as soon as I was on my feet again.

Hudd said, 'I'm gonna come back with a coupla pals tomorrow, an' have a bit of a party, OK? The Doc says it's OK.'

'Then you're leaving?'

'Yeah. Few weeks' leave in Darwin. Blow my pay, an' get arrested breakin' up another bar.'

'After that?'

'We got some people up in Indonesia. I don't know fer certain – it was just a hint.'

'What's it like out there?'

'The women are hot, but their men are head-hunters. You pays your money and takes your choice.' Someone else I knew used to say that, but I couldn't remember who.

'I can't imagine you losing your head, Hudd.' You could take that two ways, couldn't you?

Daisy sat on the edge of my bed. I asked her, 'Why hasn't Watson come to see me? After all, he got me into this bloody mess.'

'He saw you last time, and once is enough for David: he doesn't like hospitals. He's actually very squeamish.'

'I'm going home after this, aren't I?'

'Of course you are. The rest of us'll be out here another few months and then so will we.'

She'd brought me two halves of Red Hackle in her shoulder bag. As she tucked them under my pillow she said, 'He wants to know if you know where the rest of the money is.' She said it lightly, but there was a catch in her voice. That was interesting. It was the first time I wondered who was really running the show. I'd had a few days to make up my mind what I was going to say.

'No, I think it was robbed out years ago, and split up into bits and pieces. That's the only thing I can think of. So now it's scattered – in small amounts probably – halfway around the world by now.'

'He wants to know if there's anything left undone; any t's left to cross.'

'That bloody aircraft is going to cause grief for as long as it's sitting out there. Why doesn't he get a Canberra in transit to pop a few thousand pounders into her by accident, and apologize to the Turks afterwards? Blow the blasted thing to Kingdom Come.'

'Is that what you want me to tell him?'

'Yes, I do, Daisy. Now, give me a nice peck on the cheek, and tell me what pictures you've seen recently.'

Haye with an e came to see me for half an hour each time she went off duty. The other guys in the ward were jealous. One night I asked her to marry me.

She replied, 'Don't be ridiculous. Why ever should I want to do that?'

'Because I love you.'

'I wouldn't worry about it. All men fall in love with their nurses. You go to bed with Florence Nightingale, but wake up with someone like me. It never lasts.'

'Didn't a film star say something like that?'

'Rita Hayworth. I suspect she knew what she was talking about.'

She was sitting on the edge of my bed where Daisy had sat. There was probably a regulation against that.

I said, 'You're the only girl I've proposed to, who I haven't first slept with.'

'So I'm the first girl you haven't slept with to say *no*. Let that be a lesson to you.'

I grabbed her hand, and laid it on my chest. 'Feel my heart beat: then you'll know I'm telling the truth.'

She laughed. 'Can't feel it. You don't have one.'

'Can I feel yours? It's underneath your left tit, isn't it? I'm sure I'd be able to find it there.'

Now she really laughed, but moved well out of reach. 'I thought we'd resolved to be a little more mature in our relationships with women, Charlie? Wasn't it something to do with showing a little more understanding, and respect?'

'. . . and look where it got me. A woman put two bullets in me!'

'Serves you right. I bet you deserved it.' That was me told, wasn't it?

Haye with an e was definitely not going to be the one.

Four weeks later I was at the school gates in Chichester waiting for the boys to come out. Randall, our Halton Air journeyman, had flown me the last leg from Beauvais to our airfield at Lympne. I phoned Flaming June from there.

'I know I should have called you earlier, but I was in hospital, and it was difficult.' She didn't ask why. Her voice came back flat, as if she was talking to the dead. 'You'll want your car back.'

'No. I wanted to hear you again. I've just landed, and want to see you.'

'You'll have to let me think about that . . . I've begun seeing someone else.' Bugger it! 'I'll call you; one way or the other.' She promised. I knew she'd keep her word, and I only had myself to blame, after all.

I had completed the rest of the trip on the rattler. I had last-minute presents from Egypt in my kitbag, and had filled in an hour with a couple of drinks at the station bar. The sun was shining, and it looked like a half-decent summer was on its way for a change. I was even home in time for the Coronation.

I met another father there: waiting for his children. He worked in the boat yard at Bosham.

He smiled and said, 'Long time no see: you caught the sun, Charlie. Where've you been?'

'Abroad. I was called up.'

'You missed the gales and the floods then?'

'When were they?'

'February.'

'Yes. I was in the Land of the Pharaohs . . .' I told him.

'Some people have all the luck.'

Yeah; my leg hurt, my arm hurt and I'd probably shot and killed the most wonderful person I was ever likely to meet. Like the man said, some people have all the bloody luck.

Last words

I saw David Watson not so long ago. He isn't one of those friendly spectres who increasingly inhabit my world. He's still real, but thin and bent these days – being at least ten years further along the line than me. It was at a squadron reunion dance in Edinburgh and, because I live so near, I couldn't find an excuse to get out of it.

After we'd swallowed too many drams he said, 'There's something I always wanted to ask you, Charlie.'

'OK.'

'What really happened to the money? Did you and that dreadful fellow Hudd make off with it?'

'No. Of course not.'

'But you knew where it was . . .'

'I think so. Probably.'

'Satisfy my curiosity. Tell me.'

'That's what Hudd said. But first I need another drink.'

He brought me a large single malt, and watched me top it off with water. 'Tell me.' His wife was at the table with us. So was mine, come to that.

Mrs Watson said, 'Yes, come on, Charlie. Tell us. David has dined off this story for forty years, and we've never known the end of it.'

I took a hefty swig of Glenmorangie.

'That bloody old Stirling had four extra bomb cells in her wings, didn't she? Two under each — and we never looked in them. I don't think anyone else did either. If you find out their dimensions, and work out the space needed for that amount of paper money in parachute containers, I think you'll find they just about fit.'

Watson went very red. When old men flush they *really* flush. I think it's something to do with the booze.

'But we bombed the bugger! Burned her out of existence.'

'Precisely. Bloody good job too!' I told him. It was nice to be one up at last.

I rounded off the night by copping a dance off his missus, which was more than I ever did before. We must have looked comical: me so small, and she's still tall and graceful. She wore a long, off-the-shoulder silver-grey silk dress, and could still turn heads. As the evening wound down she opened the massive handbag she invariably carries, pulled out her silver cornet, and strolled over to the small band.

Minutes later she was blowing her heart out — not bad for someone our age. It was 'Stardust'.

I danced with my old lady, and the ghosts started to move in. I saw Emily Rea, a Red Cross girl I'd once known, dancing with Glenn Miller. They looked absolutely perfect together. Funny; they'd bought it over fifty years ago. It won't be bad if this is what it's going to be like from now on.

Afterword

Dancing at the Blue Kettle, cures for hangovers, and other stories . . .

In 1948 or '49 two British Army drivers broke into a tank park in Palestine and attempted to steal two 30-ton Comet tanks which they intended to hand on to the embryonic Israeli Army. I don't know if they were successful – if they were, then there's a story in that – but, because the Army acknowledges the event, I suspect not. The loss of another Comet in the Canal Zone a couple of years later is less certain.

It is impossible to spend much time with the Suez veterans – many now in their seventies – without being told the story of how a group of Egyptian thieves, or klifty wallahs, stole and hid a Comet tank in battle order, by the simple deception of building a shack around it. This is not a loss that the Royal Tank or any other regiment owns up to . . . not that they would, perhaps. Red faces all round.

I recently asked for details of the theft from the Tank Museum at Bovingdon (probably the only place you will get to see a Comet these days), and was told by a historian that this was the *first* time he had heard the tale. He firmly dismissed it as a military myth. This is curious, because when you sit down with a Suez veteran it is inevitably one of the first tales told to illustrate the Alice in Wonderland world of the Canal Zone in the Forties and Fifties. Maybe the Tank Museum isn't listening hard enough.

I have heard three variations on the story so far, and two likely locations – off the Treaty Road close to Ismailia, and somewhere north of Suez. I borrowed the latter for Charlie's story. I enjoy hunting down unlikely tales, and I love proving experts wrong, so if there is anyone out there with the information to pin the tail on this particular donkey, *please* write to me. It would be marvellous to add another cock-up to our glorious military heritage.

Charlie's first voluntary parachute jump closely mimics my own, at Strathallan in Perthshire nearly twenty years ago. Having been told by the jump master that if I baulked at the command to *go* he would have no choice but to push me out of the aircraft I shuffled up to the exit with the thought '*No bugger's going to shove me out of an aeroplane!*' Thus I left the plane as soon as I was told, but before expected, cut a nice wide swathe in a field of oats a mile from the airfield, and had to walk in carrying my 'chute under my arm. If the farmer is reading this, please accept my belated apology. This was after a briefing which had concluded with a list of things most likely to go wrong with a parachute, so that big khaki nylon dome opening above my head was one of the most beautiful sights I will ever see.

The passing reference to a soldier hiding behind a tombstone in an English graveyard to avoid the attentions of a German fighter pilot is another family tale. My father, returning for a few days' wound leave after Dunkirk, was caught crossing a Carshalton or Beddington graveyard by a 'tip and run' raider in a Me.109. Having successfully hit the Carshalton gasometer with his single bomb – it went in one side and out the other without exploding – the pilot decided to take out his frustration on the lonely khaki figure in the graveyard. Dad hid behind the gravestone (allegedly) of a 'famous poet', but I've never been able to find out which one. This happened before I was conceived, so in a strange way I owe that poet my life, if you see what I mean. I haven't been to Carshalton for years, but even as late as the 1960s you could see the patches on the gas holder marking the bomb's impact . . . and I wonder if the German pilot is still alive?

Dungeness in Kent is nothing like as awful as I make it out to be . . . as long as you don't mind having nuclear power stations at the end of your garden. The Listening Ears – massive concrete dishes, designed and built between the wars to detect the approach of aircraft – can be found on an island in a flooded quarry at Denge . . . within walking distance of the Pilot Inn. Access to them is managed jointly by English Heritage and English Nature, who allow occasional guided tours in the summer months. The principle of detecting the acoustic signatures of approaching formations of aircraft is a redundant technology – it was kicked into touch by the development of radar in the 1930s . . . however, a Danish artist plans to build another one on the north coast of France, aligned with the Denge dishes . . . so in theory it may one day be possible to exchange words, unsupported by modern technology, with someone standing thirty miles away. It won't displace the mobile telephone, although why anyone would want to talk to someone in France beats me.

You can thank Errol Flynn for the aspirin and Coca-Cola recipe for a hangover cure. It appears in several biographies as both a cure and an amphetamine-like pick-me-up. I once made it up for the former reason, but the drink went the colour and consistency of an after-curry diarrhoea, and after the first sip I poured it down the sink. People come up with spurious cures for hangovers all the time, but G.P. Gibson VC relied on a pint of water and half a dozen lungfuls of pure oxygen . . . that sounds close to it for me. There's only one proper remedy, of course – moderation. I shall have to start acting my age, and drink less.

The Nigel Balchin novel Charlie found himself reading was *The Small Back Room* – one of the best novels about the condition of war (beginning with the finest opening sentence) ever written. There are plenty of copies around, so if you haven't read it yet, get down to your library or bookshop right away, because you have missed a rare treat.

I have always looked with suspicion on the uncritical support for the state of Israel offered by the United States, and cannot believe that it stems alone from the strength of a local Jewish lobby. There must be more to it than that . . . and that nagging suspicion informed part of this story. Contrast that unwavering support with the way the Americans turned on their old British ally when we attempted to annex the Suez Canal Zone in 1956. The British, French and Israeli conspiracy to seize the Canal was illegal and improper, of course – but if recent Iraqi history has taught us anything, it is that when the USA wants to illegally and improperly invade a Middle Eastern country it isn't slow to claim *our* support, and participation. Oh how I wish our prime minister had stuck out his chin this last time, asked, '*What about Suez in 1956 then?*' and left them to get on with it. Quid pro quo.

I have never met a man whose testicles were saved by his possession of a 'goolie chit', although goolie chits of various types were issued in different theatres of war, and you can still see them in museums today. *Goolie* is said to be the Hindustani word for testicle . . . although I can't find it in my *Hindustani Self-Instructor* (written by Abdul Hamid Khan – 'Army Language Teacher, Sialkot' – in 1936, and published for 3/8d: one of my favourite books). Goolie chits were multilingual notices issued to flyers after it was alleged that Afghani, Northern Indian . . . and maybe, later, Kurdistani . . . insurgents passed captured European men to their women, who would geld them, and turn them into house eunuchs. I'm tempted to speculate that the house eunuch was only a forerunner of the role of the young middle-class British male in the twenty-first century anyway. The chits promised a reward for the safe return of their carriers. What this has in common with the mislaid Comet tank is that I can't find anyone in print claiming to have had first-hand experience of involuntary gelding: not surprising, when you think about it.

The fact that Brits arriving in Egypt in the 1950s were still being terrorized by old sweats with tales of 'wogs with goolie knives' tells us more about ourselves than the Arabs in question. The goolie phrase definitely derived from the Northern Frontier provinces at the time of the Raj – and yet a hundred years later we were still not distinguishing between Afghanis, Indians and Pakistanis . . . and the many tribes of the Arab nations. Am I being unkind to remember that to the average Englishman abroad in the 1950s they were still all 'wogs'? No wonder it's now difficult to find a country in the old empire where a Briton is looked on with love, gratitude or admiration.

. . . but Charlie's past is, of course, an invented one. I have written before about how I stand before memories – my own, and other people's – like a child in front of a pick 'n' mix counter at what was once Woolworths, and take a few from here, and a few from there to mix into the world of Charlie Bassett. The Blue Kettle Club in Ismailia is an example of a memory that belongs to others. It did exist: but I've never been there. I have an old photograph of the art-decoish building, and the street on which it stood: a Fordson van stands outside the Blue Kettle's door . . . although it may have been permanently closed by 1953. It can be found in several of the Canal Zone memoirs. Some have written of it as *notorious*, or *dangerous* . . . one as *louche and friendly*. It was obviously one of those establishments that become mental landmarks – somewhere not to forget in a hurry. Although I have that photograph of the outside of the Blue Kettle, I have been unable to find anyone to tell me what it was actually like behind the front door — so the scenes I set there are necessarily a fiction. If I am so far wide of the mark that I offend anyone's actual recollections, they must write and put me right — readers do it all the time.

There is a Turkish restaurant the size of a large bus shelter on a small back street in the Old Town of Edinburgh. It is named Empires, sits opposite my local, The Waverley, and is one of Edinburgh's hidden treasures. I could commend it to my readers for its cuisine alone — artichoke hearts and meat balls to die for — but it is on Friday and Saturday nights that it comes into its own; when the belly dancer arrives. Liquid beauty made flesh. Dining out is easier these days: many eating houses offer a menu to remember . . . but Empires on a Saturday offers you a dining experience never to be forgotten. You have to take your own wine . . . I rather like that . . . but any Edinburgh reader who hasn't eaten there should take the opportunity while they can. The ladies from Empires danced effortlessly into this book: it is where the girls of the Blue Kettle crossed the boundary from the page and into life. If you have ever wanted to come face to face with someone from Charlie's world, pick up the telephone quick, and make a reservation.

One of the roles I share with Charlie is that of patron saint of lost causes. Show me a forlorn hope, and I'm your man: that's why Pan Macmillan and I have decided that we're going to Cyprus with him in '56 or '57, to stand alongside the British servicemen trying to keep the lid on that particular can of worms. It's going to be fun, so why don't you come along?

David Fiddimore
Edinburgh
May 2009

The Silent War:
Charlie Bassett's Play List

From time to time I have had letters from readers about the music that catches Charlie's attention in the course of his memoir. They teach me just how important popular music is for memory. For those of you who are interested, here is a selection of the music mentioned or alluded to in *The Silent War* and Charlie's preferred versions . . . in roughly the order they appear in the book. It was the music in the room as I wrote this story.

Sadly, as far as I know, no one has written 'The Blue Kettle rag': I live in hope that clarinet-meister Bernard Stanley (Acker) Bilk MBE, RE (Rtd) — a Suez veteran himself — may one day be persuaded to do so: he's the right man for the job!

'Beer barrel polka' — Josef Vejvoda & his brass band
'Blues for Jimmy Noone' — Kid Ory's Creole Jazz Band
'String of pearls' — The Glenn Miller Orchestra
'What is this thing called love?' — Tommy Dorsey (vocalist Connie Haines)
'Doctor Jazz' — Dutch Swing College Band (vocalist Neva Raphaello)
'One o'clock jump' — Duke Ellington
'Minnie the Moocher' — Cab Calloway
'Goodbye' — David Whitfield

'The Beguine' – Tommy Dorsey (vocalist Frank Sinatra)
'Big noise from Winnetka' – Bob Crosby and the Bob Cats
'Am I blue?' – Billie Holiday or Hoagy Carmichael
'Blue skies' – Josephine Baker or Tommy Dorsey/Frank Sinatra
'Blues my naughty sweetie gives to me' – Bob Scobey's Frisco
    Jazz Band
'Wild man blues' – Woody Allen
'So what?' (from *Kinda Blue*) – Miles Davis
'Singin' the blues' – Tommy Steele
'Ah yaa zain' Mohammed El-Bakkar and his Oriental Ensemble
'Mnishebak' – Mohammed El-Bakkar and his Oriental Ensemble
'Jealousy' – Ivy Benson and Her Girls Band
'Just a closer walk with thee' – Ken Colyer's Omega Brass Band
    or George Lewis
'Stardust' – Hoagy Carmichael or Her Ivy Benson Girls Band

Of the songs listed here, 'Blue skies', with its irrepressible optimism, has long been one of my lifetime soundtracks, but I would also commend to your attention the definitive recording of 'Doctor Jazz' – made by Neva Raphaello with the Dutch Swing College Band in the 1950s, and the remarkable Mohammed El-Bakkar, whose 1950s recordings are now sought after by modern belly dancers. Last, but far from least, I'll swing till I drop with the wonderful Ivy Benson, and her All Girls Band or Orchestra. I have some of their recordings, but I would love to hear from a reader who heard them at their dangerous best: what *were* they like in concert? The music never dies, does it?

Acknowledgement

This is the right place to acknowledge the responsibility that The Waverley Bar, St Mary's Street, Edinburgh, bears for Charlie Bassett's story. The Waverley and its jazz, Ean its owner, the captivating and mysterious bar staff, and my gang, The Waverley Writers, all contribute unconsciously to Charlie's voice. He is honoured to know them.